FIREBIRD

Also by Mark Powell

Prodigals
Blood Kin
The Dark Corner
The Sheltering
Small Treasons

FIREBIRD

a novel

Mark Powell

Haywire Books
Richmond
Virginia

HAYWIRE BOOKS

Note: The poem Susan Logan thinks of on page 223 is "The Last Hellos" by Les Murray. The author also wishes to acknowledge Martin Amis's Koba the Dread.

ISBN: 978-1-950182-02-2
Library of Congress Control Number: 2019940186

Cover Design: Baxton Baylor
Copy Editor: Nicole van Esselstyn
Author Photo: Pete Duval

First Printing

For Dennis Covington

In my country we have a saying — Mickey Mouse will see you dead.

— Robert Stone, *A Flag for Sunrise*

That there is money to be made in war is something we all understand abstractly. Fewer of us understand war itself as a specifically commercial enterprise...

— Joan Didion, *Democracy*

THE DOSSIER

July 4, 2013

THE PARTY WAS on the Greenwich manor of Erskine Logan, a plantation of wrought iron and American cheer. Logan was the CEO of Leviathan Global, and Hugh Eckhart went because it was expected of him. This was, after all, the day that the Lord hath made: the Fourth of fucking July.

But more than that: it was time.

Hugh had woken that morning with the sense that death was very near, and this nearness was a welcome thing. He'd been reading about the saints again, not the Christian martyrs flayed alive or speaking to wolves and birds, but the woman running the methadone clinic in coal country, the man planting trees in Haiti. The girl who kept doing her algebra even after the Taliban threw acid in her face. It was as pointless as it was shaming. He'd always known he hadn't done much with his life, though only lately had he realized the full extent of just how little. But it was clear now, and that morning he had felt, for the first time since his years in the Covenant, prepared to do something.

He'd also felt the knot in his right testicle.

A bundle of gathering cells that signaled finitude.

But lately everything seemed to signal finitude.

Lately, he seemed to find death all around him.

A ridiculously melodramatic thought, but what the hell was he supposed to do? Not think it?

A chartered bus shuttled the thirty-something associates and their pretty wives up the Henry Hudson Parkway, the mood festive, all backless dresses and the ice-cream optimism of the rich getting progressively richer. Someone popped a bottle of champagne. A man said, *no, no, it's still at anchor and Credit Suisse is about to lose their shit.* A little blond-headed princess ran the length of the aisle hugging her iPad.

Hugh sat alone, and though he was sweating alcohol, he appeared competent enough. There was something in his eyelashes not unlike dandruff, but at least he'd managed to scrub away the eyeliner from the night before. He'd misjudged someone, and that someone had spat in his face, this in a tourist bar off Times Square.

When the bus pulled to a stop, he waited for everyone to pile off before descending through a fog of perfume and Skin-so-soft, the photogenic children already veering toward the Shetland ponies, a band already working its way through the Isley Brothers.

It was just after noon, the day bright, the air light and moving off Long Island Sound in a way that conjured all things nautical, the summer regatta, the sails and flags, and he stood outside the ivied gates to take its measure: the bankers and breeders of Arabian horses, the financiers lounging on patio furniture. A vast lawn of pro-growth pro-Americans, their teeth gone soft with the years of plenty.

He touched the thumb drive marked COSY BEAR, and started down the veranda steps. The estate backed to the Wild Flower Sanctuary, an expanse of green grass edged by foxglove and baneberry. In the center sat a giant tent surrounded by an army of caterers and picnic tables, all of it hung with red, white, and blue bunting. The house itself dated to the Revolution and sheltered, as Hugh understood it, the living ghost of Susan Logan, Erskine's wife. The Logans' daughter had died the previous summer of an overdose, and since then, Susan Logan was said to be functioning on a cocktail of Vicodin and regret.

Hugh could sympathize.

He'd been awake for the better part of three days and shook with exhaustion, the eyes that wouldn't shut, the thoughts that wouldn't sit still. He'd lain in bed that morning, right hand cupping his balls, and watched the walls weep, great fat tears that came sliding down the painted brick, and though he had spent the night before drinking how many whiskey sours he couldn't say, though he had swallowed two Sublimaze for the pain in his groin, he knew this was not some false consciousness. The world was crying, and he was meant to lie still for it.

He took a glass of Veuve Clicquot from a passing waiter and nodded his hellos.

His intention was to have his presence registered by as many people as possible and then slip out. The party meant the offices back in the city would be not exactly empty but empty enough. Somewhere inside Leviathan's steel and glass tower was a file marked FIREBIRD, an electronic dossier that contained an array of holdings and account numbers that would be swept into the thumb drive he carried. Alfa Bank, Paradise Financial, the URLs originating in the Caymans. Leviathan's 19% stake in the Russian oil giant Rosneft.

He sipped his champagne and was walking toward the tent when he felt his phone go off.

A text from Dietrich.

where r u?

party, Hugh typed back.

all ok?

fine

chat at 330?

yes, he replied.

From three-twenty to three-twenty-eight Leviathan's ubiquitous CCTV cameras paused to download the last twenty-four hours to the hard drive. It was a flaw in the system, but trivial enough that it had never been corrected. Beyond a few principals and their immediate assistants, no one knew about it.

But Hugh did.

He looked up to see an attractive middle-aged woman detaching herself from a circle of younger women and making her way over. Susan Logan. Willowy and teetering on heels, the glass of chardonnay, the Hermès scarf. He hadn't seen her since the funeral.

"Hugh Eckhart isn't it?" she called. "I think we've met before."

"Hello, Mrs. Logan."

5

"Susan, please," she said, and then looked around as if embarrassed, her free hand fluttering up to hide whatever she was about to say, though she said nothing. Still, there was something manic about her, the way she kept twisting her head, the way she kept flexing the cords of her neck.

"A beautiful day for a party," Hugh said.

"It is, isn't it?"

"You have such a lovely home."

"Yes, well, we're packing it up, of course. Everything in boxes. Boxes everywhere. But I suppose you know that."

"Bratislava?"

"I'd never heard of the country, for God's sake, let alone the city until Erskine said yes. But then Erskine has never been one for consultation, now has he?"

Hugh offered a tight smile. The Logans were on their way out, Erskine the newly named U.S. ambassador to Slovakia.

"It's supposed to be one of those undiscovered gems," she said. "And Erskine tells me I can shop in Vienna. He means that as a consolation."

"I think you'll enjoy it, old Europe."

"Yes."

"And Vienna really is lovely."

"It feels like the place for me. The land of the leftover, the might-have-been. You have," her wine glass floated up in front of her, as if of its own accord, "you have a purple aura, Mr. Eckhart."

Hugh laughed.

"Is that good thing?"

"Almost indigo," she said, and put her hand over her mouth.

Hugh turned toward the lawn, toward the celebrity chef and his chafing dishes, the senator and the CFO commiserating over chilidogs. All these men who had become saintly through the purity of their greed.

"You've heard, I suppose," Susan Logan said, "about my daughter?"

"I am so very sorry."

"Yes, Christ, of course you have. You were there, after all. The funeral, I mean."

"It was a moving service."

"I'd forgotten. That day…"

"I understand."

"Erskine tells me I have to quit talking about it, and he's right. He's always right. You can set your clock by it, Erskine and his rightness."

"Speaking of your husband."

"He's somewhere I'm sure. Probably…" She put her hand back to her mouth and bit her fingers. It was only for a moment, but it was unmistakable. "If you'll excuse me, Mr. Eckhart. I just need to…"

"Certainly."

When she was gone, he looked for her husband and, spotting him, began to look for Randy.

Randy was, of course, Randy Garcia, an elder brother in the Covenant, a Reagan appointee in the State Department and, most relevant, founding co-principal of Leviathan Global. Garcia's partner, the Czech dissident Colonel Tomas Venclova, had left for academia, but Garcia had stayed on, cashing out just ahead of the Great Recession. Two years ago, Garcia had flirted with running for president but decided to put some distance between him and his financier past. It was a wise move. He dealt in resource extraction—minerals, oil and gas—and recently had positioned one of his associates to be the future U.S. ambassador to Cuba, just as he had positioned Erskine Logan to be the next ambassador to Slovakia. Garcia would drop oil rigs along the Florida Straits and frack natural gas in Eastern Europe with the same efficiency he'd mined Iron Ore and bauxite in West Africa.

Hugh served as his chief of staff. He tried to think like the man, but that seemed impossible. Garcia owned a luxury-bunker in a converted ICBM silo in North Dakota and an airstrip in New Zealand. On his daughter's eighteenth birthday, he'd bought her eighteen zebras, a flock of them, a herd. He spoke Spanish, Russian, German, Polish, and Czech. He spoke Good Ole Boy and Wall Street, was fluent in Langley and E-ring of the Pentagon. Obama had been reelected in the fall, but the future belonged to Randy Garcia.

"Hugh Eckhart!" a voice called. "Here in the land of milk and honey!"

Hugh looked up to see Ray Shields walking over with a young woman he recognized as Colonel Venclova's granddaughter, Rachel. Ray Shields was Garcia's public face, a true believer. Maybe thirty and—Hugh thought the word might be—telegenic. His hair was cut precisely. He smelled faintly of leather. Garcia had hired him away from a right-wing news outlet operating out of Orange County and here he was, eating a stars and stripes cupcake.

"How are you, Ray?"

"How am I? I'm absolutely delightful, my friend. I'm in excellent company today. Not sure," Ray said turning, "if you've met Rachel."

Hugh had, briefly, years ago. They stood on the lip of a sand trap by what appeared to be a putting green and made the requisite small talk. The lovely day. The lovely estate. Ray was cheery, talking about lawn tennis and the fireworks at dusk, but Hugh found his eyes drifting to Rachel. Maybe it was his growing instability, but he detected a readiness about her that frightened him. Not just to act, but to become. The need for some definitive statement. To live in a yurt and consider her breathing. To become fiercely vegan. She had just finished her first year in a graduate program at Yale, and appeared both younger and far older than he knew her to be.

"I was just trying to lure Rachel away from academia," Ray said, and licked away the frosting. "Get her on board with us."

"We'll see," Rachel said.

"Yeah, we'll see for sure," Ray said, smiling. "Tell me again what it is exactly you're studying?"

"Governmental applications of social media in the post-communist world."

"Governmental applications of—yes, Jesus Lord. We'd gobble you right up. The Colonel would love it. Isn't that right, Hugh?"

Hugh knew the Colonel better, of course. In his Covenant days, he had been under the Colonel's spell, just as they all had. The prayerful study of Bonhoeffer and Arthur McGill's *Death & Life*, all the talk of the Bronze People.

"America's birthday," Ray said dreamily. "It's stupid, I know, but it's like I look out here and I see—what do you see, Rachel?"

"Money."

"Yeah, money, true." He folded the cupcake wrapper into a tiny triangle and stuffed it in his pocket. "But more than that, I feel like I'm looking at all the men and women heading out to the mission fields, you know? Like it's 1875 and we're all on our way to the Ottoman Empire or somewhere."

"God's work," Rachel said, and caught Hugh's eye.

"God's work, exactly," Ray said. "You know, given the occasion, perhaps we should?"

He took Rachel's hand and reached for Hugh's. Hugh watched Ray's wide palm approach, uncertain if this was a joke. But then Ray was interlacing his soft fingers with Hugh's. Rachel's hand was smaller but harder, almost rough.

"Lord," Ray intoned, "we come to you most humbly from the frightened and wrecked whoredom of your fallen kingdom to ask your blessings on your loyal servants Rachel and Hugh as they venture forth into the wilderness of spiritual warfare wearing the armor of God and carrying the cross of your son Jesus Christ, born in Bethlehem but raised up here in this once-red-blooded city on a hill we know still as a light unto all nations, these United States of America. Be with them, Lord. Amen and amen."

"Amen," Rachel said.

"Excuse me," Hugh said, and stepped away to swallow a Sublimaze with his champagne.

IT HADN'T ALWAYS been like this.

He thought of that in the Uber back to the city.

Just four days prior he'd been clean-shaven and sober, standing with Ray Shields outside the studio of a right-wing talk show syndicated in 43 markets while, behind the acoustic glass, Randy discussed the criminality of the Obama administration.

"He's always wanted to be a hero," Ray said, smiling.

"He's always wanted to be wanted to be a demi-god, is what he's wanted."

The show went to commercial. Precious metals and water-filtration systems. A cancer doctor selling liquid vitamins in a bottle capped with silver foil. When they came back, Randy started talking about China and currency manipulation.

"He does shit, you know? The rest of us," Ray said, "we just bitch about the world. But Randy has that long-term vision. There's a body of thought that says that's everything." He put one hand to the glass, a wistful gesture. "He's got his eye on the Great Barrier Reef. Did he tell you this? He wants to buy it, move it here."

"He told me he's having dreams."

"For his grandchildren. Like an aquatic park."

"Nightmares about snakes."

"He sees it as a legacy thing. Clownfish. Brain coral."

They'd gone to lunch after that. The three of them in the private room of a Lower East Side bistro that had once been a Bulgarian discotheque, the trace of a great hammer and sickle still visible on the wall. Randy staring as if he could see through Hugh's skin to the gathering betrayal, his intentions as evident as the clump of cells metastasizing in his right nut.

"Kiss those boys for me, Hugh," he'd said when they were back in the car.

"Yes, sir."

"Kiss that wife. Give her my special love."

Randy and Ray got out at a heliport near the Port Authority Terminal and Hugh had the car take him north past the park to St. John the Divine. He'd intended to pray but something was wrong. When he looked up at the crucifix, he realized it wasn't Christ on the cross. They had changed it. Jesus had climbed down, it seemed, and now it was someone else. It wasn't Hugh. That would have been too much. But it wasn't Christ either.

Something had failed.

Something had come undone.

He could see the fragile joinery all around him. It was a wonder things hadn't already fallen apart. But he also knew they had. What he was seeing, what was left, was the afterimage, the heart's desire. The real world had died sometime in the recent past.

The thought had been unsettling enough to make him desirous of home. His boys watching Nick Jr. His wife doing Bikram in baggy clothes, everything gauzy and draw-stringed and hemp. He wanted the familiar. Instead, he'd gone to his sublet in Bushwick and swallowed two Perc 20s. It had been all downward spiral since then. Something that must have reached terminal velocity halfway between wiping a man's spit from his forehead and watching his apartment walls weep.

OUTSIDE LEVIATHAN'S HEADQUARTERS, Hugh avoided the temptation to look at his watch. He had an eight-minute window—3:20 to 3:28—and needed to be precise, but he didn't need to be noticed.

He waited, and at three-fifteen entered the lobby.

Past the swipe-card turnstiles stood a wall of sheer water coming down a face of polished black rock. It had been part of an art installation once, something purred over at the Venice Biennale, but Garcia had bought it, crated it, and unpacked it here. It was an alpha move, something to convey not simply wealth but a willingness to apply such, the shipping fees alone equivalent to the GDP of some insolvent island nation. It altered weather patterns. Redirected air currents. You could feel the mist the moment you entered.

Three-sixteen.

For the third straight day the lobby was full of bodies, maybe three dozen protesters, flat on their backs and arranged on the marble tile like malformed starfish. It was the most he'd seen, and that was the holiday, he supposed. People off work, people feeling particularly civic.

A few were peeking up or checking their phones, but most maintained some form of discipline, eyes shut, limbs still. Their sleeveless tees and poster-board signs all read the same things

#GaysAgainstGuns

#Divest

#GunSense

Clusters of them had been cordoned off like spills, traffic cones and yellow biohazard tape, and around these clusters moved a few associates, younger folks who realized their invitation to Logan's estate was less formality than test: they were expected to politely decline while working through the holiday. You needed at least three years before you could expect to sink into white wicker with your vodka lemonade.

They moved quickly and Hugh moved with them. Men and women but mostly men, in their Brooks Brothers suits and Thomas Pink shirts. Tag watches and the Cole Haan shoes with blue laces. The women wore Christian Louboutin heels and wearable tech, Garmin watches and Fitbits, chunky eyewear. Everyone was staring at a phone.

Security stood near. Burly men with earpieces and blue blazers. A few Iraqis scattered among them working as whatevers. As well-paid doormen, Hugh supposed. Translators for Garcia's people and he'd taken care of them just like he'd said he would. Put them on C-17s with their families. Baghdad to Ramstein to Dover to an apartment in Queens and 52K a year with health and dental. Everyone knew that about Garcia, that he kept his word.

That he still ran the place—that was the other thing they knew.

Hugh swiped his badge and nodded politely.

He got on the elevator with three other men, all younger than him, and watched as they got off at various lower floors. When he was alone, he inserted a key card and touched 32. It was three-nineteen and he stared into his own eyes. Forty-four years reflected in the steel of the doors. The face lined but handsome. The suit rumpled but expensive.

He stepped out at three-twenty, just as the cameras flickered off.

The floor was empty and dim.

He moved quickly past his own office, past Erskine Logan's office, and then past Garcia's antechamber with its L.L. Bean dog beds and the British flintlock that dated to the eighteenth century. Though technically retired, Garcia maintained a vast suite, the rear wall glass so that with the curtains drawn the view was broad and arresting, the East River and the Williamsburg Bridge, Brooklyn gloaming in a haze of ozone. A world of water and sky. But the office was ceremonial, a place to greet the occasional dignitary since everything said made its way via wiretap down to the FBI's field office at 26 Federal Plaza.

Hugh wasn't going there.

Outside an unmarked door he slipped on a pair of microfiber gloves.

Garcia's real office was a windowless perch not much bigger than a custodial closet and equally dim. He used his key to enter and moved to Garcia's desk where he booted the vintage Dell, logged in as GARCIA.RA, and inserted the thumb drive marked COSY BEAR. Six months prior someone had approached Hugh, exactly as he had hoped they would. A few days later, he'd rented a P.O. Box in Newark and started driving out twice a week, always at different times, and always to find it empty. All spring Leviathan had repelled a series of cyberattacks, each more elaborate than the one before. Then, two weeks ago, a month after the last attack, a padded mailer had arrived, the thumb drive labeled in Sharpie. Hugh took it as an admission of defeat: successful penetration would have to come from inside.

A window appeared and he clicked OPEN FILE and watched as COSY BEAR began to download, its progress marked by a right moving arrow. Somewhere on the hard drive was the FIREBIRD dossier and COSY BEAR would find it.

Then something happened. Something failed.

The telescoping line stopped abruptly.

He clicked OPEN FILE and watched it fail again.

He was sweating harder now.

Three-twenty-three.

He took the thumb drive out, reinserted it, and watched it fail a third time.

His scalp was damp and suddenly he could feel it in his armpits. Cool—it started coolly, and then began to streak down his ribs and into the waistband of his pants.

Three-twenty-four.

There was no way it could not work. The code was specific. Someone would have had to anticipate it precisely, to have loaded a very specific security response, and yet…

Fail.

Fail.

Three-twenty-five.

The screen flashed and then locked and Hugh found himself tapping the keys uselessly.

He had to go and jerked out the thumb drive.

Sweat and more sweat. His scalp and armpits and now it was moving down his inner thighs. He was halfway to the elevator when his phone went off.

Another text from Dietrich.

IRC?

He put the phone in his pocket and stepped into the elevator at three-twenty-seven.

He was in the lobby by three-twenty-nine—the bodies still strewn about—and it was only when he was outside, more than damp now, wet and almost panting, that he took his phone back out and replied.

give me 30 min

He walked south to Madison Square Park, faster than he intended, and sat on a bench by the dog run. Put his phone on his thigh and tipped his sunglasses into his hair. The park was crowded and loud and though he assumed he was being watched no one seemed to be paying him any attention. That was fine. They would come for him now or later, it didn't matter. The dying didn't have to be absolute, only the attempt. Though his wife didn't yet know it, he was ending—had already ended, he supposed—their marriage. That was the move three weeks ago to Bushwick, the penance, the self-mortification. She was at home on the Upper East Side, grooming, as he imagined it. Their boys with her parents on the Cape. A tidy scene. Harmless, if only it had been. All of them, even his wife's good-hearted liberal parents, under the ready-made impression that Hugh was just having a rough go of it lately, a little mid-life stumbling, nothing that some time and space wouldn't solve. They'd given him the summer to sort his life. He could take what he needed and then return.

But he wasn't returning. He was taking everything and running. He logged into an IRC as <corp> which, he liked to imagine, was short for corptocracy. A moment later Dietrich appeared.

<Dietrich>: ok?
<Dietrich>: u there?
<corp>: yes im here
<corp>: but it didnt work
<Dietrich>: what?
<corp>: didn't work
<Dietrich>: how didnt work?
<corp>: idk. just failed
<Dietrich>: wtf?

He looked around him at the young couples, the families with quilts and lawn chairs. Sun-ripe people, honeyed and happy. The Bronze People. He'd sweated through his shirt and felt it plastered to his back.

<Dietrich>: corp u there?
<corp>: still here

Hugh had started lurking in chat rooms almost a year ago. It was a gnawing boredom, but a boredom he knew would eventually manifest itself as the Word of God. He dreaded the moment, knowing that when it came he would be compelled to act. He'd been a believer once, and though he'd long ago shed the dogma, in his way was a believer still. So he went on lurking.
#ChristianAnarchy
#Anti-Globalization
#JesusTheSocialist
Eventually, he'd met Dietrich and over time, just as he knew it would, that gnawing boredom had solidified into something like a moral indictment. It was the same thing he'd felt as a younger man in the Covenant, a purer time, as he remembered it, and while it frightened him, he was also grateful for it. To live without

purpose was to become foreign to yourself. The alternative was to do something. The alternative was to acquire the dossier. Dietrich represented—or claimed to represent—an online collective called *différance*, Christian anarchists united in their opposition to the sort of casino capitalism that had made Randy Garcia very rich and much of the rest of the world very poor.

Since the collapse of Lehman and Bear Stearns and the near-collapse of everyone else, Leviathan had engaged in a particularly aggressive form of activist investing, grabbing 9% of this company, 11% of that. They'd fire everyone in sight, watch the stock price rise, and then sell their interest. Their cash reserves were tremendous, as was their geopolitical influence.

That was where the Wojtyła Society came in.

Publicly, the Society was nothing more than a charity, a humanitarian NGO doing work in Eastern Europe. More accurately, it was Leviathan's direct-action wing, its funding laundered through the PAC of Marco Torres, a Republican Congressman in Florida Hugh had once loved. The dossier contained details of such. Account numbers, holdings, contracts. Everything. Except Hugh didn't have the file. What Hugh had was nothing.

<Dietrich>: going to see a movie 2nite
<corp>: what
<Dietrich>: now the nickelodeon?
<Dietrich>: *know
<corp>: in east village?
<Dietrich>: goddard film about simone weil

They'd exchanged a number of emails that confirmed to Hugh that he was being recruited. But he hadn't needed recruiting, and in a single unmitigated rush had told Dietrich everything about himself, everything except Baghdad, everything except the Angel. Dietrich's name was some sort of homage to Dietrich Bonhoeffer, the pacifist German theologian executed by the Nazis. His real name was David Lazar, something he hadn't revealed, something it had taken Hugh a great deal of effort to discover. That he was, like Hugh, one of Colonel Venclova's boys had been easier to surmise.

<Dietrich>: you might enjoy
<corp>: ok what time
<Dietrich>: 820

He logged out of the chatroom and shut his eyes so that the afternoon sun pinked his eyelids, the finely drawn veins there. He started breathing again. He didn't remember stopping, but clearly it had happened somewhere in the recent past.

THE THEATER WAS off an alley on St. Marks Place.

The film was *In Praise of Love.*

A cart sold overpriced beers in aluminum bottles, silver, blue. Box wine and soft pretzels. Hugh sat alone in a love seat with maybe a half dozen other people scattered about on couches or recliners. The floor was uneven—ply-board poorly graded. Glue abrasions. He had a tub of popcorn and kept two fingers of his right hand in the bucket, thumb hooked along the rim, melted butter, salt. The light flickered, the projection wavering in a way that signaled a previous era, Hugh's childhood, the *Star Wars* and *G.I. Joe*, listening to Bible stories in Mighty Mouse pajamas. His favorite being the Tower of Babel. Also a fan of the parting of the Red Sea. Those monumental events, operatic in their demands. Sleeping on the pew during Sunday night services, never any doubt he'd been chosen by God Almighty. His election the single thing that persisted from childhood. That was the message he had left on the bathroom mirror. His intentions lipsticked into a quote from Emerson, a message to those who came looking for him.

GOD WILL NOT HAVE HIS WORK MADE MANIFEST BY COWARDS.

They'd find it when they raided the apartment. The FBI, Leviathan—it amounted to the same thing. They'd come for him. They'd find him. Still, he would not be a coward.

The film started.

French with English subtitles, a lot of anti-American screeds in a rustic kitchen.

He ate his popcorn all the same.

He had, after all, seen an Angel once, a great radiant thing standing over the dead children, their wraithlike bodies on the cool concrete, the long spills of their mud-colored hair.

It was the closest he'd ever come to a vision.

He needn't come any closer.

SOMETIME LATER HE was back in the lobby, the movie concluded, the drink cart shuttered. He tried to wait without appearing to be waiting, to appear occupied by his phone, by the vegetation. Around the lobby were banana plants, elegant leafy things in plastic planters. He moved between them, lingered.

But the lobby emptied and eventually he walked out and up the street, too exhausted to be disappointed.

Things were still festive, the evening still warm. Sidewalk diners. Faintly realized Dave Brubeck. Diesel and baking bread.

Near the intersection of First Avenue he sensed someone approaching, a black man, tall and languid and closing at an angle.

"Hey, now," the guy was calling, "hey, brother."

Hugh stopped and turned, hands in his pockets, sweating again.

"Do I know you?"

"I don't know," the man said, "you do any time in the man's army?"

"The man's army?"

"Uncle Sam and all."

"I don't think so."

"You don't think so?" He was older. One tooth capped gold, his beard a patchwork of gray. "I did eleven years before I got busted back to buck sergeant. That sound right to you? That sound like liberty and justice?"

"I don't know."

"Hey, listen. You think you might could help a man, out?"

"With what?"

"You waiting on somebody or something?"

"I don't think so."

"You don't think so?" He removed a toothpick that Hugh only now noticed. "You don't know a thing, do you, boss?"

"What do you need?"

The man returned the toothpick.

"Whatever a brother can spare."

Hugh gave him a ten and the man nodded.

"You think you could hit me like ten more?"

"Just like that?"

"I'm asking strong and sober. Not an intoxicant in my system." The man cocked his head. "What? You want the whole song and dance?"

"No," Hugh said, and passed over a twenty. "Take it."

"Strong and sober I'm asking humbly."

"Take it. Please."

He took the money and nodded again. Except Hugh saw now it was more like a tic, and as the man walked away Hugh called after him. *God bless you.* No idea why he said it, but the man pivoted and spread his arms, walking backward.

"Wherever He's gone," he said.

When Hugh turned he saw the man watching him. A white man this time, early thirties in a starched shirt and Chuck Taylors, small rimless glasses. Sideburns like a Civil War General. He'd unbuttoned his sleeves but hadn't bothered to cuff them, on his narrow wrist a Seiko from 1985, the band gold. Hugh started walking and the man fell in beside him.

"That was interesting," Dietrich, David Lazar, said. "I like the way you blessed him."

Hugh was silent.

"You like the movie?" Lazar asked.

"I'm not sure. It confused me."

"The plot?"

"The timeline. I tend to be linear."

"You're older."

"That seems to be the case."

"I'm not blaming you," Lazar said. "That would be ridiculous."

"You think I screwed up."

"I think it's foolish to blame someone for something they can't control."

"It's a thumb drive," Hugh said.

"Right."

"You stick it in, you take it out."

"That would be the accepted practice, correct."

They were headed toward Tompkins Square Park.

"The place was empty?" Lazar said.

"Fourth of July. They're all out celebrating."

"They're all out building their bunkers for dubya-dubya-three is what they're doing. You get your hydroponic vegetables, a big tank of carp. You know how to clean a deer, Hugh?"

"No."

"Me neither. But I think I'll learn." He stopped walking and stroked one sideburn. "Everything else was good?"

"Except for it not working," Hugh said, "yeah, everything else was great."

"Tell me how you mean 'not working'?"

"I mean it kept saying 'system fail, system fail.'"

"That doesn't seem possible."

"Then the computer locked."

Lazar nodded and started walking again.

"Somebody was waiting then," he said. "They had prepared."

"You'd have to go in there, right? To the actual computer. It's this ancient thing from the Clinton administration." Hugh shook his head. "No one would go in there."

"Someone did."

"I've kept watch. I would have known."

"There is one other possibility," Lazar said. "Let's suppose someone was already running a sweeper."

"How do you mean?"

"I mean if someone had already compromised the program it would lock you out. We sent you with a very specific code. It seems far more likely someone just beat us to it. So who would that be, Hugh?"

"Not the FBI."

"No."

"We'd know if it was the feds. These Russians maybe."

"Guys in tracksuits."

"They're consulting, a team of them."

"Adidas, Fila. Which, correct me, do they even make Fila anymore?"

"Friends of Randy."

"L.A. Gear just to go crazy old school on you."

They waited for the light to change and then crossed. The park was quieter.

"He's supposed to be off being happy," Hugh said, "retired."

"Men like Randy Garcia aren't made for retirement."

"He's trying to buy the Great Barrier Reef."

"He thinks shit like that is okay."

"There have been talks. Nothing firm."

"He thinks shit like that's just fine and dandy." Lazar shook his head. "A man like Garcia, this is biology I'm talking about, not politics. You start and finish with biology. Politics are what you get in between. But maybe I'm being apparent?"

"Maybe."

"The hole they bore in your skull out of which flows paid vacation and college savings. This sort of thing." Lazar put a finger to his forehead. "Jesus, now I know I am."

"I still don't understand how someone could have gotten in. You'd need Garcia's credentials, his password."

"You managed to get them."

"They're all out in the country," Hugh said. "Fireworks. Ice-cream sundaes."

"We'll have to find another way."

"The past two years they had a waterslide."

"It's trickier, but it can be done."

"By you?"

Lazar went quiet again, and Hugh watched the muscles of his jaw that in chewing nothing appeared to be chewing his own tongue. There was a basketball court ahead and you could hear the metal catch of the chain net. Someone posted on the block, calling for the ball. They stopped at the last edge of darkness. Hugh would have to disappear. Somehow they would know, and then they'd come for him. He'd resign. Medical reasons. Treatment for the cancer in his groin. But he had no intention of taking any treatment. He'd go back to the sublet for his pain meds but that was all. He had work to do.

"I'll find a way," Lazar said. "I'll talk to the Colonel. I'll get over there."

"Over where?" Hugh asked.

But he wasn't listening anymore. Walking along the path, for only a moment, he had seen something out of the corner of his eye. For the first time since that day outside Baghdad, he had seen his Angel, watching him, and he felt something gathering inside him. His Angel. It had come back for him, and as he watched it flutter up into the darkness, he shouted at it. *It is not upon you alone the dark patches fall,* he told it, defiantly, angrily.

Because he might well be many things, but he would not be a coward.

THE WOJTYŁA SOCIETY FOR PEACE AND INTERNATIONAL COOPERATION

August 2013 to April 2014

THERE WAS A truck in the road.

Chris Berger had made the drop three times and never had he seen anyone or anything aside from the men in the hangar. Not a soul between the highway and the drop-point—impossible that there could be—and yet there they were: a truck, two men.

"Shit," the young man said to Berger. "This is what?"

Berger eased off the brake, decelerating slowly so that the crates in the back wouldn't shift. They were twenty kilometers outside of Slaviask in Eastern Ukraine and two kilometers down a dirt road that was nothing more than twinned tracks that reached and bent through the birch and pines. Just past the curve he could see the hangar that was more a giant corrugated shed than anything else, aluminum on a concrete slab, vast and empty but for a few chairs and an electric space heater run off a generator. But that had been in the dead of winter. It was summer now, and the airfield appeared waist-high and golden with rapeseed. Butterflies and bees. Birdsong.

And now a truck.

The road was too narrow for either to pass.

Berger and the young man beside him—his name was David Lazar, but he was *the young man* so far as Berger was concerned—sat in their idling box truck, windows down, and waited. Berger was slower reacting than he should have been. The braking was automatic, but his thoughts came listlessly. Even in the moment he recognized this, his dulled perceptions, his absence of focus.

It wasn't forgivable, but was possibly understandable in that they'd driven eighteen hours from a decommissioned airbase outside Lviv, past wheat fields and on through a series of checkpoints with blast barriers and orange construction barrels, waved forward by soldiers with facemasks and chemlights. Past the Donbas Ceramics Factory with its lattice and rust, past the coke plant with its gray haze, on across the North Donetsk River, brown and sluggish with rain, and finally—*finally*—into the forest.

The airbase six hundred miles behind them was a holdover from the Cold War. It had the three-kilometer runways for the old Tupolev Bears with their red stars and forty-kiloton bombs. Hardened bunkers. A network of tunnels. It had belonged to the Soviet Union and might someday belong to NATO, but for now it belonged to no one but Berger.

He blinked several times.

The truck in the road made no sense, but then again it was just a truck.

"Explain this to me," Lazar said.

"I don't know."

"You've seen this before? Someone out here?"

"No."

"Maybe we back out?"

"Let's give it a minute."

Lazar had arrived a week earlier with a black diplomatic passport and the blessing of Colonel Venclova. He carried the credentials of a freelance photojournalist and Berger had seen the camera and telephoto lens in his bag even if he'd never seen them out of it.

"You see them in there? They're watching us."

There were two men in the truck, a heavy Russian-made Kamaz maybe thirty meters in front of them. Another fifty or so meters behind the truck stood the hangar.

"This isn't right," Lazar said. "Something isn't right here."

"Be cool."

"Let me talk to them."

"Let's be cool a minute."

From the corner of his right eye, Berger saw Lazar's vision shift. On the seat between them sat a short-barreled SIG 515, paid for by their employer, the Wojtyła Society for Peace and International Cooperation. The Society was registered in Kiev as a Catholic NGO. The website talked about clean drinking water and medical care, but in the back of the truck, behind a pallet of grape Pedialyte, were sixty Strela-3 anti-aircraft rockets packed in crates and cushioned in wood-shavings.

Berger watched Lazar's hand crawl toward the rifle.

"Let's be cool here," he said. "He'll walk out here and tell us something."

The man on the passenger side did appear to be moving, the door opening. He stepped out and when he showed one open palm Berger saw he was missing the last link of his right index finger—his trigger finger. When his sleeve rode up it revealed a constellation of puckered scars that might have been cigarette burns but might just as easily have been fry grease.

Berger raised his left hand in greeting, careful not to lean forward. He wore a thin North Face jacket that barely concealed the Glock strapped beneath his arm. If you leaned just a bit, it was possible to shoot a man without ever removing it from the holster.

"I don't like this," Lazar said.

Berger looked at the SIG. "Cover that," he said, and the young man slid his jacket down over the rifle he now held between his legs.

"He's coming over here."

"Probably playing lost," Berger said. "A poacher, maybe. Or he's cutting the timber. Let's see what he has to say before we get ourselves on the nightly news."

The man was dressed like one of the loggers that worked the linden and beech forests. Work boots and dirty coveralls. He had a scratch of silvered beard and a watch cap pulled low.

"You can't log these forests," Lazar said. "This is supposed to be protected."

"Probably exactly what he's thinking."

The man stopped three steps short of the box truck and greeted them in some barely understood Slavic pidgin the young man interpreted. They were lost, he said. He pointed behind them. Trying to get back to the highway. Was this the way? They thought this was the way, yes?

"They ain't lost," Lazar said quietly.

The man was gesturing at the surrounding forests. Berger caught the word *owl*.

"What's he saying?" Berger asked.

"The other guy keeps looking past us. The guy in the truck."

"Tell me what he's saying."

The man behind the wheel of the Kamaz had not moved.

"I don't like sitting like this," Lazar said.

"Just be cool."

"Let's back up. Let them pass."

Berger gestured at the man, at the narrow shoulder.

"Pull onto it," he told the man in English. "Tell him."

Lazar spoke whatever it was he spoke—Ukrainian, Russian—and the man shook his head. He pointed with the stump of his finger. There. The shoulder. You back up and we pull forward.

Lazar reached for the door handle.

"What are you doing?" Berger asked.

"I want to see what's back here."

When the door opened, the man took a step back and put his hands in his coverall pockets. Going to look, Berger said. Back, he gestured. To back up.

The man nodded and stepped onto the loose shoulder that fell away into the ditch.

Berger could see Lazar in the truck's wide side mirror and then he stepped around the edge of the box truck and Berger couldn't see him at all. The SIG was still on the seat, mostly covered by the jacket. The man—the Russian, the Ukrainian, whatever he was—had his hands back in his pockets, but Berger saw no discernable bulge. Whatever he was carrying, assuming he was carrying, was back in the Kamaz.

He checked his watch. It was almost noon and the hangar was in clear sight, the flashing along the roof catching sunlight. Inside were two, perhaps three men who would help unload the crates. The weapons went to Ukrainian militias, farmers and factory workers who spent their weekends training in the eastern forests. There was no war, not yet. But war was only a matter of time. Which was more or less the point.

He saw Lazar in the side mirror, coming up the driver's side.

"How's it look?" Berger asked.

He was sweating, his shirt matted to the plastic upholstery. His left hand, stretched on the side panel, twitched as much with the residue of caffeine as nerve damage.

"There's a little room if you go back and cut hard to the right," Lazar said. "Not much, but enough."

"Watch for me."

Berger motioned to the man in the coveralls. *Back, back.* The man nodded, walked to his truck, and spoke to the driver through the passenger door.

"Hand me the SIG," Lazar said.

"You don't need it."

"These guys are Spetsnaz, Russian special forces."

"You don't need it," Berger said again. He looked at the two men, one standing by the cab, the other in it. "I don't want them to see it either."

"I don't like any of this."

"Just make sure I don't go in that ditch."

Lazar moved to the rear of the truck, made eye contact in the mirror, and motioned for Berger to come straight back. Berger kept one eye on the mirror and one eye on the Kamaz. He could smell the exhaust—clouds of diesel in the otherwise piney air.

Easy, Lazar was mouthing. Easy.

Berger couldn't hear him, but his lips never stopped moving.

A little more. Okay, cut it.

Berger cut the wheel, sharp and then sharper. He wanted this over. He'd drunk gas station coffee all the way from Lviv, but had sweated it out hours ago. The energy was gone and what was left was a very precise throbbing just above his left eye that beat with a low and wet certainty. Everything felt weighted. The shift of the tires. The softness of the shoulder. In the mirror, Lazar held his hands shoulder-width apart.

Deep, he said. Two feet.

Berger still couldn't hear him, but read his lips. He was nodding, right hand motioning, and then—almost quicker than Berger could register—he was falling backward as if yanked by his hair. The report sounded a half-second later, a shattering that started breaking apart before it even arrived. The birds lifted. A screaming out of the trees—ravens tucked into the low boughs. Berger ducked and when he did, his foot came off the brake. The truck lurched back into the ditch, pitched, gave a hard bounce—the passenger door flung open, the cab light flashed—and was still.

Move, he thought.

But before he could move the passenger window exploded and Berger felt his face catch fire. He tumbled into the floorboard, scrambling, and then he was on his hands and knees, crawling over a fine shower of glass.

In his hair. On his arms. Down the neck of his shirt.

He crawled toward the passenger side, knees burning, scalp bleeding, groped across the seat but the rifle wasn't there. He let himself fall out just as another burst hit the engine block.

He eased forward on hands and knees and when he went to wipe the mud from his eyes discovered the pistol clutched in his right hand. He lay flat on his stomach and looked back. Beneath the listing truck he could see Lazar's legs stretched straight out, toes up and unmoving. Past that, he could hear the sound of men coming out of the woods and onto the road. The engine hissing. The birds again, coming back into the upper boughs of the trees. Cordite and spilled diesel thick enough to taste.

Three sets of legs—no: four.

He could see them beneath the canted undercarriage. They stood on the opposite side of the truck, not ten meters from him. Then they parted, one moving behind the truck, the other in front. He pressed his body against the tire, mud cleated in the shallow tread, and managed to fire just as the man rounded the front—center mass, two shots—and then spun and fired at the second. The second man fired back, puncturing the fender and hood and sending a plume of ditch water into the air, but Berger was already into the forest. Ten quick steps and he dropped behind a tree and fired three rounds. Breathing through his nose. Calm—as calm as he could be. Head down while a thicket of bullets brought a soft rain of shredded leaves.

Wait, wait—now move.

He crawled backward down the slope, deeper into the forest. They were firing at him, but they were firing high and didn't appear to be coming closer.

He crawled and waited, and at the bottom of the slope, he ran.

There was a copse of trees on the far side of a creek. Eighty, maybe a hundred meters off the road now. He could no longer hear them, the truck a dull shape in the far trees, buried in shadow. Either they weren't coming for him or they were already behind him and it didn't matter.

He looked around.

This was good ground with a view toward the road and a backtrack too dense to cross without his hearing. High ground—he'd been in slot canyons in Waziristan where all you had was the high ground and your rifle. You put the sun at your back, remained patient. If you thought clearly it could be enough.

He checked the Glock and went back to watching the forest. If they came he could do no better than this. But he had the feeling they weren't coming and he was right: eventually, he heard the sound of the box truck being towed out of the ditch and then the sound of the Kamaz pulling it toward the highway.

When it was gone, he waited a half hour and went in the opposite direction, toward the hangar, coming out of the forest on the far side of a meadow of sunflowers. The thing was, it was a beautiful day. He could hear the birds again—a pheasant thrumming, the russet fletch of its wing visible in the boughs—and he came slowly out of the tree line to approach the building from an angle.

Closer, he saw that the big roll-up door was raised.

Two men were inside, one sprawled in a lounge chair, hands bound with Det cord before they shot him in the chest. The other must have run. He was face down in his own black blood, the glossy spill just beginning to congeal. The TV was on—a cooking show out of Kiev. A woman held some sort of tart up to the camera. It appeared to be feathered in rosehips, but about that Berger couldn't be certain.

*

HE MADE HIS way back up the road toward the highway. If some-one was waiting, they were waiting. But it turned out they were gone. The site of the ambush was barely discernable: heavy tire tread angling back and forth where they'd towed the truck, an incision in the bank. They'd picked up the shell casings and all that was left besides the tracks was a dripping line of diesel that ran up the gravel, each drop slightly smaller than the previous until the trail was altogether gone. No sign of the SIG.

Lazar was gone, too.

Berger could see the drag marks brushed lazily with a bough. No hurry. No concern. There was a darkness that indicated blood, but even that had faded so that it appeared little more than a shadow.

There was something inevitable about it all. Lazar was a brother in the Covenant, a believer like all the rest of them, which was to say he was no believer at all. He thought God sat atop a great ladder. You could climb to Him. That was what he was doing in Ukraine—climbing.

That was the shit the Covenant fed you.

Crowds with candles. Music and martyrdom.

But belief was a descent, a shedding. Whatever you clung to died. Whatever you let go of died, too, but out of that you might be raised.

Maybe.

BERGER CAUGHT A ride with a trucker back to the city, bought a train ticket for Kiev and in the station café dialed a number that routed its way through a strip-mall exchange in McLean, Virginia, and on eventually to Leviathan's New York office. Roissy 1 played on the screens and the walls were covered with old black-and-white photos of coal miners, shear-headed shock-workers climbing into the dusty light. But among these now hung an antique tin-type of Stalin. Someone had even bothered to polish the frame.

After a series of connections, Berger was put through to Ray Shields.

"We lost the cargo."

"You lost it?" Shields's voice was halting and fractured.

"Your man, too."

"How do you mean lost it? You don't mean—"

"Exactly that."

"And the…the man?"

He thought of Lazar's body floating in the Dnieper, headshot and stripped to its Mammut hiking socks.

"Jesus," Shields said. "You're serious, aren't you?"

"I won't say more. But I wanted you to know."

"I have to make some calls. Can you get back in touch?"

"I'd rather not sit in one place."

"Half an hour and call me back."

Berger paid ten hryvnia to an old woman to use the station bathroom. Outside it had started to rain and water fell through the ceiling in long braids, the floor pooled and flashing with the pale flicker of the overhead lights. His hands shook almost in time with it, the manic twitching of the shattered day. He stood at the sink and washed the glass from his face and hair. His hair was blown and unkempt, his beard dark and shaggy. He looked like something better caged, or better still left untouched. Better avoided. The sort of wild animal you might trap by mistake. Shooting it would make more sense than setting it free.

Shields was frantic when Berger called back.

"The Colonel wants you to come in. There's concern."

"I figured as much."

"This is more than simply an optics problem. This is potentially a signal event."

"I'll need to see Rick first."

"All right, but listen to me," Shields said. "Hugh is around. There's reason to believe he's looking for you."

"Hugh Eckhart?"

"He isn't with the organization anymore. Something happened."

"What do you mean he isn't with the organization?"

"I don't know what exactly. He got sick. He left. Just stay away from him."

"Where is he?"

"If he contacts you let me know immediately, all right?"

The train ground past an emptying downtown, the church with its Orthodox cross and golden dome, the Hotel Taler with its bowling alley and bar. There were vacant lots and an ANTEKA drugstore boarded up as if ahead of weather. A Lada dealership. Techno beside a Japanese teahouse. The thunderstorm had rained itself out, and past the edge of town came the slag heaps green with clover and then fields of new wheat and rising sunflowers, the heads like eyes not yet opened.

It reminded him of Virginia, and Virginia was all manner of memory. He and the Colonel had spent one summer visiting the battlefields around Richmond and up into Maryland and Pennsylvania. I-95 in the green heat. How bright it had been. Gettysburg. Fredericksburg. Antietam. Everything the light touched, he remembered the Colonel saying, belonged to God, and everything else, that was God's as well.

Petersburg. Cold Harbor.

If you were attuned, you could feel the ghosts.

It wasn't hard to feel them here either.

Starved kulaks eating ground hogs and horse tack.

Jews machine-gunned in gullies.

Berger bought a plastic jug of beer from the passing trolley. Sat upright and alone, his head against the seat, his hands in his lap. In Afghanistan, he'd hung from his wrists for a day and a night and some indistinguishable part of another day, and now his hands were like individual beings, of him, but not. At times he thought they signaled him, and in those moments, he tried to be still, to listen to what the vibrations might reveal. Sometimes he would be woken by their shaking, the barely perceptible tremors that he felt certain was God, lifting him up.

Out the window the sun went down. Village after village with their clotheslines and satellite dishes. Between them vast fields. Irrigation canals beside narrow highways. Abandoned factories beside sludge ponds. The train kept stopping and starting. Old women getting on, babushkas with their headscarves and hard candy, on their way to the capital to visit grandchildren.

He woke just outside Kiev. Dawn scattered, seemingly unable to gather itself. Old fields and garden plots now planted with houses.

The porter came around with a pot of tea and Berger thought about Ray Shields. *This is potentially a signal event.* Sixty shoulder-fired rockets in the hands of arms dealers, or maybe pro-Russian separatists. If he was sent here to start a war he might have just done it.

The Colonel would know. If he was going to talk to anyone, he wanted to speak directly to the Colonel. In many ways, the Colonel had made him. There was no shame in admitting as much. Everyone was made by someone or something. You could belong to another the same way you belonged to God.

BERGER MET RICK Miles that evening on the roof of the Sofitel in Kiev. The bar overlooked the flower market and beyond that the Dnieper where gray barges pushed loads downriver. It was humid and crowded and people were eating oysters off beds of shaved ice, drinking lazily while Al Green sang love and happiness on the stereo. They'd be going to clubs but not anytime soon.

"Hugh Eckhart came slinking around looking for you," Miles said.

"That's what Ray Shields said."

Berger had known Miles for fifteen years, at Benning and at Bragg, and later at Bagram. In Marjah, he'd killed with a precision matched only by its glee. *Known him*, Berger thought, though you could no more know him than you could know a rattlesnake. Still when he had gone to work for Leviathan he had brought Miles along, though he could never quite say why.

"He's got it in his head I go to Bratislava," Miles said, "show up at the embassy and keep watch over the flock by night."

"Don't."

"He thinks we're getting played."

"Eckhart's running his own game."

"Ray say that too?"

"He said Eckhart was off the team. You get tied up in that shit."

Miles shrugged. "I hear what you're saying. But the thing is, if I'm getting set-the-fuck-up, I'll likely feel compelled to cut somebody's balls off."

"If someone were to ID you—"

Miles touched the sachet that hung around his neck, a cloth pouch that lay against his throat.

"My medicine's strong," he said.

"Just know that it's a one-way ticket."

"Then tell me not to do it."

"He's out of Leviathan, but he's still in touch with someone," Berger said. "Possibly the Colonel."

"Red light it if that's what you think. Cause shit, otherwise I'm game." Along with the sachet, Miles had a small topknot and bad skin, the soft craters of childhood acne. JUIF ERRANT floated down his left arm. "You're off to the States?"

"It may be we shut things down and get out."

"What happened out there, chief?"

"I don't know. Somebody talked."

"Somebody was waiting is what it was."

A ragged paperback of *Death & Life* sat beside Miles's bottle of Chernihivske. Berger recognized it as the copy Colonel Venclova had given him that summer in Virginia. The book they had studied together. The skeleton key to being, as Berger had once understood it. As they had all understood it, he realized. All the Colonel's boys.

"So who was it talked?"

Berger touched the book.

"Where'd you get that?"

"That's your copy right there," Miles said. "All marked up and underlined. Inscribed by the Colonel."

"I remember."

"The Bronze People." Miles slid it away, as if possessive. "You know," he said, "if I knew what happened—who talked or whatever—that's not the kind of thing I'd keep from a friend."

"Is that what we are now, friends?"

"Shit, man. That actually hurts."

For a moment Berger regretted saying it. Miles did look hurt. But then again, that was just another way to play it. He lifted his beer and looked into the gathering dark. Heat lightning broke and the smell of rain blew west over the distant fields of wind turbines and on across the river. Rain would be a relief. It was raining pleasantly somewhere in the countryside, but it wasn't coming here.

"Hey, fuck it, though," Miles said. "It had to happen like this. All that delightful American money to buy all those delightful American guns. Shit like this is just another logical extension."

"Maybe. But Eckhart."

"Yeah."

"Things fell apart on his watch."

"The center did not hold. I hear you. Still." Miles shook his head in wonder. "You think he talked to the Colonel?"

"I don't think anything about the Colonel," Berger said. "Not anymore."

"Yeah," Miles said, "but that ain't the same as the Colonel not thinking about you."

Rachel Venclova, granddaughter of the great Czech dissident Colonel Tomas Venclova, left the Yale Hall of Graduate Studies and started up the sidewalk to Koffee. She ducked the beggars congregated around a shopping cart filled with aluminum cans, passed the food trucks parked semi-permanently across from the School of Management, and leaned into a skirting breeze that blew the smell of peanut oil and jerked chicken. At the intersection of York and Elm, a woman sold flowers and recited passages from *Macbeth*.

In her buried heart—without really meaning to—Rachel hated her.

But then in her buried heart she hated so many things.

Koffee was packed with students hunched over their phones. Undergrads sprawled on a couch by the window, buried in a sea of course packets and tablets. Rachel gave her order to a white guy with dreadlocks and green-yellow-and-red Rasta cap. A sticker on the door read SAFE SPACE.

Anne waited on a patchy velour love seat beneath a charcoal of Chelsea Manning in a raspberry beret.

"This is so utterly insane," she said. Like Rachel, Anne was a teaching fellow for Dr. Amman Sanneh's course "Oppression in the Americas: A Twenty-First Century Perspective," and seemed as hurt as she was astounded that Rachel was dropping out of the Political Philosophy's doctoral program just days into the semester to take a position with the Wojtyła Society.

"I mean it's your grandfather you're working for," Anne said. "The job isn't exactly going anywhere."

"I won't be working for him directly."

"But why not wait? That's what I don't get."

"We've talked about this."

"Oh, God. I know." Anne threw herself back into the cushions. She was dressed in thigh boots and a black skirt, an old lamb's wool sweater on which she had fastened a giant butterfly brooch. Her hair was shorn to the length of a fingernail and to Rachel she looked like nothing so much as a petulant child. "'Because what is happening is happening right now.' I know. 'What's happening won't wait.'"

"It's true no matter how you say it."

Anne nodded, sullen, and then seemed to brighten.

"Look," she said, "At least wait until after the semester and go with Amman and me to Palestine."

"How is that an enticement?"

"Hello? Gaza."

"On some bullshit fact-finding trip."

Anne looked distraught. "You know it won't be like that."

"You're staying at what, the Intercontinental? Playing show and tell with Hamas. No thanks."

The look of defeat on Anne's face—Rachel reveled in it. For all Anne's pretensions, for all her quoting of Frantz Fanon and Eldridge Cleaver, Rachel knew her to be a child of the American suburbs. Playing Candy Crush at a private high school in Montclair. A yearly iPhone upgrade and a new Lexus when she turned sixteen. No university-sponsored field trip to Palestine was going to change that.

"What does Amman say?" Anne asked.

"He's on board.

"Please."

"He loves it."

"That's what he said? That he loves it?"

Rachel was silent.

"Look, I'm opposed to tyranny too, all right?" Anne said.

"Good for you."

"I am personally and—listen to me, Rach. I am fervently opposed to the exploitation of all peoples."

"And look where your fervent opposition has gotten you."

"What's that supposed to mean?"

"It means we're sitting on a couch drinking five dollar lattes while Assad drops barrel bombs on Aleppo and Putin murders journalists in Moscow."

"I know this."

"Boko Haram's kidnapping girls and we sit around with our hashtags and syllabi."

"Rach, come on," Anne said, "I mean I know this, I get it. We make sit-coms and cruise missiles. You want to be part of something larger. I understand. But listen, your grandfather's group, they're religious, right?"

"It's incidental."

"Does Amman know?"

"Does he know what?"

"That they're like Opus Dei."

"They aren't Opus Dei."

"Well, does he know they're all evangelical or whatever?"

"He knows they're relevant," Rachel said. "He knows they're doing something real."

"Okay. I understand. I guess I just thought we were like in agreement that it's religion itself that creates these structural constraints. That religion is at the heart of oppression in the two-thirds world?"

Rachel blew ripples across her drink.

"It's incidental, Anne. I promise."

Anne's head lolled against the wall. Around them Lana Del Rey was singing *my pussy tastes like Pepsi Cola*. The door jangled and a mouth of warm air blew in. It was Labor Day weekend and they were cutting the town green ahead of the evening's concert; you could smell the mown grass.

"I've got to go," Rachel said. "Did you finish reading those papers yet?"

"I don't know. Maybe."

"Maybe yes or maybe no?"

"I'll finish them tonight. God. Trotsky would beg to be hacked to death all over again if he knew what undergraduates were writing about him."

"Please just get through them so I can give them a read and get them back to Amman."

Rachel stood, straightened her blouse, pulled at her skirt.

"I admire you, Rach," Anne said. "I'm sorry I'm such a bitch."

Rachel touched Anne's cheek with the tips of two fingers.

"Those papers. All right?"

In Prospect Park, a circle of attractive young people sat in the grass, each patiently clipping the stitching of an expensive handbag, medical gauze sealing their mouths. *Mindful of our sisters and brothers in Micronesia* read their banner. Rachel walked past them. She walked past the law school and past the music hall, turning by the cemetery into a neighborhood of two-story Tudor-style homes. Just past Prospect Street stood the ghetto, the crack houses and corner bodegas, single moms carrying their lives in plastic Stop-&-Shop bags and waiting for the M-line bus. But that was another two blocks away, across Dixwell Avenue and beyond the bend of her knowing.

She stopped outside a house flying an African National flag by a set of bamboo wind chimes, climbed the fire escape and used her key to enter. Amman Sanneh sat with his back to her, bent to the screen of his computer, his desk a scatter of paper and books, his wide hands in a span of yellow light.

"Rachel," he said without turning. "Come here, love."

She shut the door with her foot, crossed the cramped office in three long strides, and before he could look up she was in his lap and sliding off his sweater. She bit at his ear and he directed his attention to her shirt, peeling it, and unclasping her bra. They trailed clothes across the room on their way to the day bed that sat beneath shelves of paperbacks, where she settled in his lap.

When they were finished he lay back on the mattress, his head against C. Wright Mills's *The Power Elite* while she padded around the room naked but for a pair of green socks. She deliberately lingered by the two windows at the rear of the office.

"Are you going to fuck Anne in Palestine?" she asked her reflection.

"Would you care?"

When she turned she could see shimmers of sweat iridescent and drying on his smooth chest. He had one leg in his pants, his sweater bunched beside him.

"Little Anne of Green Gables," she said. "The two of you making love in the glare of IDF spotlights."

"Would it bother you?"

"Little Miss Gap Year."

"It would, wouldn't it?"

"Children running wild in their *kaffiyehs* but oh wow, look, there's Anne with her lacrosse stick."

His mouth curled toward a smile.

"She's a child," he said. "Did she give you those essays?"

"Not yet."

He tossed her panties at her and she hooked them with one finger.

"So you want what, Rachel? My blessing? Well, you've got it," he said. "Go to Kiev. Start the revolution. It should please the Colonel if nothing else."

It would please her grandfather, but something about the way Amman mentioned him filled her with a disproportionate anger.

She walked to his desk and sat naked in his chair. Her skin was cooling fast but she wasn't yet ready to dress. To dress would be to abandon the magic, to let it slip into the past tense. To dress would be to dissolve five years of deception, an entire epoch hiding in the land of the carbon offset. All the prison memoirs and bullshit theory. The online petitions and Lena Dunham marathons. Late night rants on social justice delivered by trust-funded babies, their language as empty as it was rote. *We're in agreement that religion is at the heart of oppression in the two-thirds world.* In Poland, they had shit on her parents' bed. That was the heart of oppression.

She tapped the mouse and the screen flashed to life. Amman was writing a book on the rise of post-Soviet oligarchy, and had lifted entire paragraphs from the seminar paper she had written on the Kremlin's use of social media, cutting and pasting them into his draft. She had been too flattered at the time to object.

"You can always come to Gaza," he said.

"Why? So we can have a threesome? Get drunk on date wine and feel each other up?"

"Would you like that?"

When she looked again she saw he was dressed, something not unlike a smile hung on his lips. Suddenly she was cold.

"Rachel," he said, but she was already pulling her clothes on in ragged thrusts. She knew it was time to go. That things had spun themselves out. That she had reached a certain end. And that was fine.

It was what she had come for, after all.

ON THE DAY David Lazar failed to come home, Sara Kovács woke in the communal bedroom of a communal house in Pelham Gardens in the Bronx, a house of Christian monastics, though she was no longer certain of her Christianity, let alone her monastic devotion. David had been on the move lately, trip after trip since their return from Greece, and while Sara had seen little of him she'd thought of him constantly. But today was somehow different.

He had never felt so near, so urgent, so—

She sat up.

Dietrich Bonhoeffer's *Letter & Papers from Prison* lay on the floor, and staring at the book she realized she had slept all night on David's side of the bed. They'd slept like this in Lesvos, crowded onto little more than a cot. A half-dozen aid workers in a room cluttered with crucifixes and dirty running shoes, a few photos of spiritual adepts. It felt like something they should be finished with. David was thirty, five years older than Sara, and grayer and thinner by the day. She had noticed it six weeks ago as he left, his encroaching age, the way he hesitated a half-second before pushing up out of the passenger seat of the cab and disappearing into JFK.

She put her feet on the floor.

The room contained four beds, but it was late and she was alone with only the Bonhoeffer. It was David's book. What little else he owned—a laptop, an athletic bag of clothes—sat beneath the bed, barely unpacked. They had spent a year working for International Peacekeepers on the island of Lesvos, before coming home to New York a few months prior. It had seemed fitting. Sara had met David in New York, moved in with him, lived with him, loved him, done everything, she supposed, except marry him. Marriage had always seemed beside the point, because the point was to pray, to work, to usher in the Kingdom of God and if you couldn't usher in the Kingdom at least you could work with the homeless vets and the HIV-positive mothers and the lazy-eyed children, everywhere the children, hungry and underfoot with their rotavirus and SNAP benefits. The church basements in Fort Greene and food pantries in Mount Eden, the black coffee and metal folding chairs, the serenity prayers and second-hand coats. She had given everything to David, given everything to their work, and that had been their marriage— their work. When David had decided to return to school she had gone with him, spending two years in New Haven, and then *that* was their marriage. Taking classes with the great Tomas Venclova, taking photographs with his antique Nikon F.

Then one day, he told her he was thinking of dropping out of school to join a pacifist organization called International Peacekeepers. There was never any question of her going with him. They were assigned to Greece where it was all bright lifejackets and bottled water, pulling ashore lurching dinghies overcrowded with dehydrated families from Syria and Mali and Libya. The only time in her life she'd ever felt useful, the only time she'd ever felt clean, like she could feel bits of America shedding from her like dead skin cells. The softness, the cynicism. Eventually it had ended, of course.

Eventually, they returned to the States so David could begin his fundraising work. He was a photojournalist, after all, and his photographs from Lesvos or Colombia or Palestine—lots of toothy children, smiling in rags—were the sort of low-grade exploitation necessary to underwrite an organization like International Peacekeepers. It was something everyone in I.P. did eventually, raising money and awareness in church basements and VFW halls amid the folding chairs and ping-pong tables, lecturing on the Christian necessity of pacifist intervention in war zones, a red banner on the wall, a few hymns in the air. There were potlucks and love offerings and earnest speeches while visiting congregations of Mennonites in, Indiana or Quakers in Kentucky. But for Sara, it was separation, and separation unnerved her. However irrational it felt, she knew letting him make these trips without her was a mistake.

He'd come back from his first trip—how to say it?

His word was *ruptured*.

Her word was *scared*, not that she ever used it in his presence.

But she thought this time she would. This time she would tell him very directly: *don't go back. Whatever it is you're doing*—she knew it wasn't just fundraising—*you have to stop. You have to stay with me.*

Sara dressed, brushed her teeth, washed her face on a hand towel stiff with use.

There was a woman in the kitchen—Sara couldn't remember her name—scratching butter on burnt toast. They were letting she and David stay out of Christian pity and Sara wasn't sure how much longer she could stand it. The social worker with his ears gauged as if in devotion. The public defender with the tattoo of Bayard Rustin on her left calf. All the folks who had taken what they called their secular monastic vows, pooling their money and gathering for marathon sessions in which they discussed white privilege and cultural appropriation and environmental racism and…

She got it. She was on their side. The greater part of her was very much on their side, but that part was also exhausted. The other part thought every effort to be vanity, well-intended bullshit that would inevitably be ground down if not by the machine of late-industrial capitalism then by the sheer number of filters available on Instagram. It would all die in a sea of innocuous bullshit posted to Facebook, the Holy Spirit neutered and cataloged alongside the online petitions and selfies from Coachella.

"Good morning," the woman said, looking up. "Sleep all right?"

"I did. You?"

"Like a stone. Really deeply and joyfully, you know?" The woman was smiling, lit, Sara assumed, if not with the Holy Spirit then some passable ghost. "Hey, big day, right? David comes home?"

"Seven-ten."

"You excited?"

"He doesn't land until this evening."

"Oh, okay."

"I mean I'm excited," Sara said.

"Sure, yeah."

"Absolutely excited."

"So what are you doing till then?" the woman asked. "Just, like, wandering?"

Sara poured a cup of coffee.

"Maybe."

"What's the book?" Joyce—Sara remembered her name was Joyce—asked.

It was the Bonhoeffer, David's Bonhoeffer. She hadn't realized she was carrying it.

She held it up and Joyce nodded vigorously.

"Intense."

"Yeah."

"Super intense," Joyce said. "Hey, if you're just like strolling or whatever till he lands, want me to come with?"

"That's okay."

"Cause I'm more or less totally free."

"That's okay."

That's okay because she needed time to think. *That's okay* because while she knew she should be happy, all she felt was dread. Since David began making these trips, something had changed and suddenly everything was guarded and cryptic. She knew he had been sending long emails to Colonel Venclova, *reports* he called them. But when Sara got into his "sent messages" she found them password protected. She knew he was talking online with his old anarchists friends, their mutual friends. But she was no longer welcome.

"What did you do over there, David?" she asked every time he came home

And every time he would simply lay there on their narrow bed, his copy of *Letters & Papers from Prison* beside him, and gently touch her hair. His laptop was under the bed and yet again she was swamped by the urge to dig through it.

Instead, she took the elevator down and walked out into the warm morning.

She thought she might take a taxi somewhere. Taxis were going by, off duty, off duty, off duty. But go where? She started walking toward the water, ahead of her the sound of traffic on the Hutchinson River Parkway. She stopped by the park, the book in her hand like an attachment, like the better part of her, and took a seat on a bench across from the honeycomb of a church, its angled shadow sheltering the intersection. Everywhere walkers and joggers and leashed dogs, the happy motion of lived lives bending around her like water.

I've been reading the Bonhoeffer, she told herself, *those last few letters from Tegel, they're being bombed and he prays for the bombs to fall on someone else. Do you remember this? I read it and I think...*

She stopped when she realized she was composing a message to David, something subtle that might plant the idea of staying. But she was past subtle. David would have to quit. It was really that simple. She wanted a place of their own, a life of their own, to go back to school, maybe, to get her MSW, and he had to go with her, because where else could she go?

Not home. Home was an ongoing critique, her life there a rearguard action against judgment. She was too skinny. Her clothes—always poorly chosen—never seemed to fit. *Honey*—her mother saying this—*maybe something not from Goodwill, you know, just this once?* People remarked on her hair as if noting a rare migratory bird. *Remember the blue shimmer, the pink, the streaks?*

She was too serious.

She didn't smile enough or the right way or something.

Her mother was a refusenik from the old Czechoslovakia, a Jew of spiritualist bent currently studying *A Course in Miracles* and opening her chakras. Sara had grown up working-class poor in Central Pennsylvania until her daddy stroked out one night sitting in the cab of his F-250, his central nervous system preloaded with enough Viagra and cocaine to float him through whatever affair he was conducting. After that, her mother took her to Florida where they exchanged their working-class poverty for poverty of the unadulterated kind. The ketchup sandwiches and I-4 motorcourts kind. The good-hearted shoplifting at the Orange City K-Mart.

This was, as it was explained to Sara, her father's fault.

In the wake of his death, in wake of his *abandonment* (as her mother came to call it), in the wake of the disaster that was probate (there was no will, but there were back taxes), after the yard sale and the drive south, the interstate traffic barrels and construction mesh and thirty-nine-dollars-a-night no-tell motels, her mother began to live on her knees. Every moment save those she wasn't cleaning toilets or whisking the carpet at the Knights Inn on LPGA Boulevard or plating strawberry crepes at the IHOP she was praying, dopesick for some sort, any sort of love.

Sara wasn't immune to it. That God-tug—she knew it well.

It had pulled her across oceans. It had pulled her here.

But here felt wrong.

Everything felt wrong.

It was only when David failed to arrive that she realized everything was wrong.

She waited and waited and eventually had the airline check the manifest: he hadn't boarded his flight in Athens. He wasn't answering his phone. He wasn't responding to texts or emails. She tried to be patient, but patience seemed impossible. She kept calling, texting. An emissary from the airline came out to appease her.

Where is he?

Ma'am, if you'd just—

Why isn't he here?

I understand your concern, ma'am—

But they didn't understand anything. The next morning she took a cab to the Brooklyn offices of International Peacekeepers where there was something of a scene. *Did anyone know anything?* Apparently, they did not. *Did anyone even fucking care?* They did, but she needed to quit throwing things. She went back to the communal house and swallowed two Valium.

She returned to the I.P. offices the following day, calmer and apologetic, but no one there had seen David in months, and what fundraising was she talking about? She got out his laptop, started searching online. It was three days later when she found first the Facebook news item and then the memorial page. David had been in Ukraine, reporting a story on human trafficking, when a pimp shot him in the face with such precision his body was identified only by dental records.

It made no sense.

David?

In Ukraine?

She stared at the page for what felt like days. She read the comments, the platitudes, the strings of emoji tears, and reading them, something opened inside her, as if the door of a vault had swung wide to reveal an area empty as space, and as she stared into this abyss, she knew it would be a long time before she felt the door close, and even when it did, she would now know of its existence. Which meant she would never quite be free.

A CAR TOOK Berger from Reagan National to the Columbia Country Club outside D.C. where he sat with the Colonel, Ray Shields, and Rachel Venclova. Berger hadn't seen her since she was a child. Now, no longer a child, she disconcerted him. That David Lazar had equally unsettled him meant it was perhaps something within Berger, that sense of gathering irrelevancy, of believing in ideas as antiquated as they were discredited. This, he understood, was what was meant by getting old.

"Christopher?"

He looked around the dining room. A table of middle-aged women lunching without their husbands. Pearls and iron gray hair. Handsome women, laughing. White wine and the house salad, everything on the side. The menu had a page for bourbons and a page for gluten-free. The meat was grass-fed and sourced, the wait staff tireless and black. One of the women stabbed a tomato with her fork.

"Christopher?"

His unease must have been as evident as the Colonel spent much of the meal reassuring him. All was well. Everything was as it should be. Yes, there had been an unfortunate event, but nothing that should be of too much concern. He offered a series of lively affirmations along with the mixed greens and vinaigrette, but Berger felt the undertow of panic. The Colonel seemed a different man, older, pale. He drank his lunch, and the drinking seemed to diminish him. He slumped against the tablecloth, and Berger thought it to be the exhaustion of having lived if not the wrong life, the life not-exactly. They parted by the valet station, the meeting brief and unsatisfactory. No talk of Virginia or the Bronze People. Nothing surprising, but for the mention of Congressman Marco Torres. Berger didn't know the man, and didn't ask. Otherwise, it was wholly superficial. Otherwise, it could have been aired on C-SPAN for all that was said, and Berger assumed that was the point: the Colonel was playing his public role for all to see.

Ray Shields drove Berger back to D.C.

Berger wanted to know what the hell had just transpired.

"That?" Shields said. "That was lunch."

"What about the girl?"

"Can you use her?"

"Use her? What is she, fifteen?"

"She's a doctoral student. Twenty-four, if you need a metric."

"What I don't understand is what she's doing here."

"You know the story? Her parents were part of the Solidarity movement in Poland in the eighties. Someone actually physically defecated on their bed, like right there on the quilt or whatever. The Colonel has no objection about her joining if that's your concern."

Berger was silent and Shields leaned forward, elbows planted on his knees.

"Tell me something," Shields said. "Serious question. When they strung you up over there—"

"What are you talking about?"

"In Helmand. When they strung you up."

"No one 'strung me up.'"

Shields raised a placating hand.

"You know what I mean. When they tied you up like that, raised you, whatever. What did you think?"

Berger looked at him.

"What did you think, Chris?"

"What the hell do you think I thought?" he said finally. "I thought I was going to die."

"Bullshit"

"I thought they were going to disembowel me on YouTube is what I thought."

"No, sorry. Not to be rude, but that's bullshit. You knew you were going to live, didn't you?"

"I didn't know anything."

"You knew you were going to walk away. You didn't know how. You had no idea when. But somewhere way down deep, you knew."

"I suppose I did," Berger said after a moment.

"And you know why too, don't you? Because guys like us, we're agents of something greater."

"The Colonel tell you that?"

"The Colonel didn't have to." Shields looked at him. "What the hell happened over there?"

"They took the body."

"The body. The rockets."

"But who?" Berger said. It came out angrier than he intended. "Who was it? Who else knew?"

"I don't know who. Me and you and the Colonel," Shields said. "And Hugh Eckhart."

"Eckhart."

"When he finds you, you have to let me know. Something's gone wrong."

"But what? What's gone wrong?"

"I don't know," Shields said. "But Hugh does."

Berger got a room at the Mayflower Hotel, changed into shorts, and went for a run along the greenway that paralleled the Potomac, eight or nine miles in the evening heat. As a cadet at VMI there had been routine trips to the District and he had loved every one of them. The statuary, the monolithic granite buildings. It spoke of something older. It spoke of something you could believe in, and that was what he'd been searching for. The Absolute. In some regards, he was searching for it still. At the Institute, they had spoken of the Three Legs of the Whole Man: the intellectual, the physical, and the spiritual. One sought a sort of ascetic purity in all three.

Study, exercise, pray.

They strived to be Stoics.

Once the Colonel had taken Berger with him to a conference on the theologian Arthur McGill at Saint John's College in Minnesota, and there, in Marcel Breur's great cantilevered abbey, Berger had seen a statue of John the Baptist cast in bronze. But it resembled an alien more than a man, stripped of flesh and impossibly lean, like something constructed from wire and string and a great disavowal of all else. It had frightened him because seeing it he had realized what it meant to go through the eye of the needle, how spare he would have to become, and what a great demand, even for a man as austere as Berger, it would be.

Which was why he'd wanted to hang by his wrists forever.

He'd been operating a joint-CIA/Afghan team out of Kabul, when it happened, his capture a blurry fuck-up, a pressure-trigger rigged to an artillery shell buried beneath some busted concrete. He woke sometime later in a burning Humvee, then—hours had passed, or maybe only minutes—woke again, bound and bagged in the back of a Hilux, the world a washed-out copper, the sky a cloudless blue. Another day you might otherwise call beautiful.

Ultimately, he spent over twenty-four hours suspended by his hands in a sand hovel, the world compacted to the purely physical, and for the first time since he had stood with the Colonel in that abbey in Minnesota, he'd felt himself growing thin and taut and pure, all finger and wrist, narrowing until he was being given a very small taste of what it meant to lose your life in order to find it.

It wasn't possible to survive it, yet that was exactly what it reduced to: the inevitability of his survival. Later, they would shoot him or behead him, but hanging there, his life no more than the roped pain in his wrists, he knew he would live, and he would do it very precisely in his hands and arms and shoulders.

But then they cut him down.

They cut him down and locked him in a shed until a team of SEALs helicoptered in and shot everyone. Berger was flown back to Bagram where, besides a throbbing headache and the nerve damage to his hands, he was dehydrated. Nothing more. He got an IV, met with a debriefing team, and a combat stress nurse. A week later he was back with his team. It was like being reborn. But he had never asked to be reborn.

He was transferred to a desk at Foggy Bottom where he served as liaison to State, and it was there he met Hugh Eckhart. Who Eckhart was or what exactly he did was never clear to Berger. But then that had been a time of confusion, a winter of dense wet snow swirling against the glass, little twin tracks leading from the sanded sidewalk up to the construction mesh surrounding the Washington Monument. He drank Jack Daniels in a commemorative 9/11 mug, quit exercising. Half the desk officers at State thought he was some sort of shaman, the tortured mystic who had sat at the right hand of the Devil. The other half thought he was a drunk. He did what he could to encourage the latter, and ultimately drank himself right into legend and right out of the Agency.

Eventually, he found himself doing contract work at Fort Bragg, forgotten.

Except he wasn't, and eventually Ray Shields and Hugh Eckhart came looking for him, driving down to Fayette-Nam with its strip clubs and tattoo parlors. The day-glo pawnbrokers financing their day-glo shit. The gun shops and barbershops. The $3-HIGH & TIGHTS with military I.D.

Berger was renting a single-wide ten miles off post and two miles down a graveled fire road. They found him there with his books and his regret, grim and unshaven, Eckhart carrying a bottle of PX Johnnie Walker as peace offering.

The Colonel had sent them. The operation would be in Ukraine, running guns to freedom fighters. The Colonel wanted him there. So what could Berger do but go? What could Berger do but allow himself to be stripped down? It would happen whether he sought it or not.

Which didn't necessarily mean God would someday lift him up. But it didn't preclude it either.

He met the Colonel the next morning at the Hotel George. Venclova looked worse than he had just a day prior, tired and conflicted and coughing into his fist. The righteous anger, the talk of God's will—it seemed to sit just behind those gray eyes. But it never came forward.

"I suppose you read David's obit." The Colonel lifted his Bloody Mary, the glass rising, while the rest of him slouched beneath. "I liked him."

"I didn't know you knew him."

"A very intense young man, very focused." He rubbed his eyes and fell silent. For a few days, David Lazar would be celebrated as a hero of freedom and human rights, then, in a few more, he would be just another dead reporter.

The waiter brought out another Bloody Mary.

"Colonel," Berger said finally, "what do you know about Hugh Eckhart?"

"He's been dismissed."

"From what exactly?"

"From Leviathan, from Randy Garcia's staff. I'm not sure why exactly."

"Ray Shields wasn't sure either."

"He's been sick. It may be that he left on his own. It amounts to the same thing, I suppose."

The Colonel sagged into his cloth napkin.

"Do you ever think about the old days, sir?" Berger asked. "Jogging in formation, singing 'C-130 rolling down the strip.'"

It was possible the Colonel's eyes were teary. But he kept looking away.

"The food in those big ceramic serving dishes," Berger said. "The prayer before the meal. I think about it sometimes. Sir?"

"Yes?"

"I was talking about the Institute."

"Of course, yes. It's natural to remember the past. I often find myself thinking of my father. He led the partisan fighters in Kosice. *Ten Medved*, they called him. The bear. Crawling out of his cave to strike, crawling back to heal. He was a hero and was to receive the Order of the Anti-Fascists Fighters. Forgive me. I've told you this story."

"No, sir. Not really."

"He went to Moscow. But instead of a medal he was taken to Butyrka and received a bullet in the head. I imagine a neat entry wound behind the right ear, such as the Cheka did so well." He seemed to be addressing the drink in his hand. "My mother froze to death in one of the camps and I became a ward of the Great Soviet State."

The Colonel coughed and drank.

"You are indulging a very sick old man," he said.

"Please go on."

"I was in the second year of my military service before I learned my mother had died in Kolyma. I was writing my dissertation when I was recruited by the Third Directorate of Intelligence in Prague. What was called then, simply enough, State Security." He drank and smacked his lips. "In Kolyma, everything froze, and then everything died. It was so cold one's breath froze in the lungs and tinkled out onto the ground. They called it the whispering of the stars."

"Hugh Eckhart is looking for me, sir."

"Stay away from him."

"Something happened out there. They knew we were coming."

"Don't trust them, Christopher. Garcia especially."

"Then tell me what I should do."

The Colonel fingered the stem of his drink but did not lift it. It could have been his first glass or his fifteenth. None of it seemed to bear on the rotation of the earth.

"There have been talks, this trade deal, the Slovak gas—are you aware of this?"

"No, sir."

"For months now there have been talks between Brussels and Kiev involving a trade deal. This is largely viewed as a precursor to joining the European Union, a very large, very important first step. NATO membership would likely follow. The geopolitical ramifications are substantial. You understand me?"

"Yes, sir."

"Garcia is involved, Leviathan, the State Department. It is effectively a fait accompli—the only thing left is to sign the papers. When that happens Ukraine will drift into the orbit of the west, a place the Ukrainian intelligentsia has always imagined it belonged. At the same time, it will pull further away from Russia. Yet when the time comes, the Ukrainian Prime Minister is going to refuse to sign the very deal he has negotiated."

"Why would he do that?"

"Because he's a puppet. Because Moscow will tell him to. Of greater importance is the result."

"Instability, I would guess."

"Instability. Anger. Imagine the riots, the demonstrations. Imagine a possible coup. If that were to happen the Russians would have pretext to invade."

"That's what the rockets are for?"

"Very much that is what the rockets are for."

"But who would want an invasion?"

"Are you aware of the natural gas fields in Ukraine? Vast deposits. There has only to be the whiff of instability, and that gas stays in the ground. Meanwhile Leviathan acquires gas concessions in Slovakia."

"And sells its Slovak gas to Western Europe."

"While Rosneft sells their gas to China. If the Ukrainian gas is inaccessible the price stays inflated. Both sides wins."

"So they start a war for profit."

The Colonel dismissed this with a wave of one trembling hand.

"Don't act naïve."

"Over gas concessions?"

"You needn't act naïve."

"What about your granddaughter?"

"We invent the world—you know this—and everyone else lives in it."

"Tell me what to do about Rachel?"

"Keep her out of it if you can. But you won't be able to."

"Colonel?"

"I've made so many mistakes, Christopher. I imagined it was all ordained. It was a charge, a sort of Pentecost: go out into the world and re-create it."

"Tell me what to do."

"I am grateful, at least, that my father was shot in Butyrka," he said. "It was the finest of the three Moscow prisons. I imagine that to have been solace of a sort."

When he spoke again his eyes had filled with tears. Berger was certain of it now.

"I am speaking physiologically," he said, "when I wonder how long it took my mother's lungs to freeze."

BERGER TOOK THE overnight to Vienna and waited at the departure gate for the KLM flight to Kiev. It was just after dawn, the room full of Hasidic Jews on pilgrimage to Bratslav, and the only seat was across from a slim, green-eyed woman, a little older than Berger, her white hair cropped to her skull. She wore an insulated vest and the sort of well-made hiking shoes without which Westerners couldn't exist.

She caught his eye and sniffed, a tissue wadded in one hand.

He opened a Ukrainian primer on his lap, and took out his iPod. Held the earbuds but didn't yet insert them. He could tell by looking at her she was with one of the NGOs, sincere if world-weary, carrying an actual clipboard on which was some actual field report. He could tell, too, that she was going to speak to him, lean in with her sensible shoes, all big-heart and head cold.

She was still smiling when he looked again but it wasn't friendliness exactly. It was meant to disarm him. It was meant to signal the weight of being morally right and knowing it. She sat straight-backed, the sort of woman who ate the compartmented airline food with dutiful resignation. The pat of foiled butter. The vacuum-sealed dessert. He knew better than to talk to her, but sensed from her posture she was religious and that was hard to resist. If she said anything about having been called he knew he'd believe her. It was the same sense he got from Rick Miles, just as he had once gotten it from the Colonel.

"Ukrainian," she said finally. She had an Irish brogue. Boston, he thought. "You must be serious. Have you been to Kiev before?"

"In and out."

"In and out." She sighed and for a moment her posture collapsed. But only for a moment. "Lot of Americans in and out. You know how many Americans I've sat here beside in the last six months? For years nothing but Slavs, Israelis on pilgrimage. But suddenly here come you Americans. Of course, no one seems to want to say why. No one seems to want to elaborate on anything anymore. I don't suppose you want to talk, do you?"

Berger gave the slightest of smiles.

The door to the jetway was closed.

"I understand," she said. Her laugh was a like a bird escaping a cage, that quick. "This was what it was like in Bosnia during the war. Or right before, at least. I remember you men going in and out of Sarajevo, always so serious. You look old enough to remember, if you don't mind my saying."

Berger nodded. He'd been there too, but didn't say this. A blue-helmeted first lieutenant in a Stryker brigade. He remembered long trains of refugees, sometimes walking, sometimes sitting on ox carts like something off the History Channel. It wasn't a memory he went back to.

"You're an aid worker?" he asked.

"An engineer with ICG. The International Crisis Group. You know them?" She laughed. "Of course you do. A middle age American headed to Kiev. You've got the beard, maybe an American flag tattooed somewhere. You probably know the whole lot of it, the entire alphabet soup."

"What was Bosnia like?"

"What was it like?" She laughed her flighty laugh. "My God. I don't know what it was like really. We kept trying to bring pumping stations online and they kept shooting us is what it was like." She gave another laugh, more strained than before. "We finally got one going inside the tunnel to Kiseljak and…"

She looked at him and he noticed her ragged fingers, the skin scalded pink and peeled around the nails, the tissue shredded. The door to the jetway remained closed.

"You could always smell it," she said, "the river, I mean. In Sarajevo, I'm talking about. Always diesel the smell." She looked across the room and back down at her hands. "One time they brought in several cases of good whiskey on trucks from the airport. Top shelf you would call it. Just case after case. You wouldn't believe how much. So we sat in our little office listening to the shells fall.

The little—" She waved her fingers in front of her, a motion not unlike the way heat shimmers. "The little shivers in the glass, the rattling panes. It's crazy to talk like this, isn't it? I know it's crazy, but sometimes…"

She shook her head as if waking.

"But there have to be limits. We have to recognize the need for limits in this life. We—" She was still shaking her head, but slower. "It might be a good thing," she said, "I think it would be a good thing if you knew what it was you were doing. Before, I mean, you started, doing those things."

She stared down at her lap.

"We had the pumps running once," she said. "First time really, and what comes out is this God-awful mud, this stinking mud where we're taking it straight from the Miljacka, and a gout of this mud, a gout the size of your fist hits my boot and I swear to the Lord on high there was a piece of finger in it. A tiny finger. A child's finger. Just the last link actually, but there it was. The little nail, all neat and trimmed." She spread her hands flat on her knees. "A moment later the clearest water began to run from that pipe. Absolutely crystal. But that finger," she said. "Someone had crossed that line. As they always do."

Berger said nothing and the woman went back to whatever report was on her clipboard.

It would be human trafficking numbers, or forecasts of child mortality. *Those things.* The dogs shot out of boredom. The rivers of street sewage. He'd seen a kid once, maybe seven years old, with what appeared to be a length of rebar through the dim interior of his skull.

Still, you liked to think it wasn't you.

You liked to think you were somehow separate.

A few minutes later they began to call boarding zones. The gate agent scanned his ticket and he walked down the jetway. He was crossing the tarmac when he realized that Hugh Eckhart hadn't simply left or been dismissed. Berger had heard a rumor once about Eckhart, something involving dead Iraqi children and an angel. Absurd, yet he'd never been able to wholly dismiss it. It occurred to him now that the rumor was probably true, that Hugh had started in one world only to wind up in another. Years ago he had crossed that divide. And now he had crossed that line.

As they always do.

BERGER RAN A truckload of sniper rifles to Eastern Ukraine, alone this time. When he returned to his airbase in Lviv he learned that Tomas Venclova was dead. The Colonel had suffered a stroke, and then another. He had asked for Chris at the beginning of the end, and then, at the very end, he hadn't asked for anyone. He had simply shut his glazed eyes and gone to wherever it was he was going.

The day was bright and hot and Berger walked out onto the abandoned runway.

Everything the light touched belonged to God, and everything else, that was God's as well.

IT WAS COLONEL Tomas Venclova who was dead, but Sara Kovács was going for David, who—she had no need to remind herself, but there are certain habits, she was starting to realize, you might never outgrow—was also dead. The memorial service—the *celebration* it was called in the email invitation—was to be held at the St. Thomas More Center on Wall Street, a narrow pedestrian lane of cobble- stones and gas lamps that ran through the center of Yale University.

Though she was still living in the communal house in Pelham Gardens, she hadn't been in New Haven in years, consciously avoiding any link to the past. But the invitation had caught her in yet another weak moment and on impulse she had taken the Metro-North from Grand Central. Now, walking past the town green with its flowers and shrubs and tent city of homeless, she was already regretting the act.

Venclova was David's professor, after all. David had met him at the student Catholic center and Sara wasn't Catholic. She hadn't even been enrolled in courses, but had somehow gravitated into Venclova's orbit. Or not *somehow*. It was a discernible conscious process. In the plainest terms, she had simply refused to leave David's side. Though, she reminded herself, that had done nothing to keep him from leaving hers.

She waited for the light on Elm.

Early October and the sky darkening with what was surely the last thunderstorm of the season. The wind picking up. Trash skittering.

She stopped again when College intersected Wall and took the printed email from her pocket. *You are cordially invited to a celebration of the life of Tomas Venclova, Chair of...* It went on for another half page, time and place, a bio, photographs of the beloved professor with former students and various luminaries. Smiling with Madeline Albright, Bill Clinton between them, arms thrown over their shoulders. In a flak jacket and helmet with General Wesley Clark. In some brown desert with Richard Holbrooke and Randy Garcia. Venclova was known to be generous and kind, and Sara had stuck around long enough to experience both. It was why she had come.

But what sort of reason was that?

It was no reason at all, and a part of her knew she was there searching not for what had happened to David but for what had happened to her faith, which was another way of searching for what had happened to herself. She thought for the thousandth time since David's death how something had dissolved, her purpose, her sense of direction. Without God this is what you get. You stand on a sidewalk and hold not your lover but a piece of paper, the weight of your soul equivalent to whatever object you happen to find at hand.

She put away the invitation just as the first drops began to bang against the sidewalk.

THE SERVICE WAS in an upstairs library, metal folding chairs crowded into a room of beige carpet and walls of books. Maybe a hundred people in an overheated space meant for half that. But it was nice in its way, warm and welcoming, everyone nodding and smiling the way you smiled in the presence of subdued grief giving way to *hey, good to see you, how long's it been?*

Handshakes and hugs. Rain coats in the foyer. Ugg boots and silver scarves.

The windows were up and it came back to her, this world, the smell of it, overstuffed with attractive young people who swallowed their CoQ10 with expensive brain tonics. Everyone happy and self-congratulatory, giddy to be reunited.

Everyone but sullen, moody Sara, she thought.

Sara with her self-pity.

Sara with her cloud of drama.

She sat near the back, far right, nearest the wall so that she could slip out if need be. There was a 10:35 back to New York she intended to catch, but there was also an 8:55 if it all proved too much. You get up quietly, walk to the exit, ease shut the door. She could take a cab, be at Union Station in seven minutes. Coming was a mistake—she already knew that—the question was how big a mistake. Manageable, she hoped. The worst behind her.

The worst being the nostalgia thing. She had already done that. Had taken a cab from the train station to Chapel Street and from there preceded to revisit their old life, or at least what was left of it. The Malaysian place with two-dollar drafts. The library where they sat reading their Tolstoy or memorizing the Port Huron statement.

She had walked past it all. Past the bookstores and boutiques, past the blocks of Section 8 housing where they had run an after-school program, black kids loitering on the concrete stoops. The beauty supply shops with their hair extensions and two-inch press-on nails. She had walked past it all to find there was very little left. She remembered no one, and no one seemed to remember her. That was the worst part. She thought the rest was endurable. But just in case it wasn't, the idea of escape calmed her.

The milling crowd began to take their seats. Mostly people like herself, men and women who had graduated in the last five or so years, did their time in the Peace Corps or Teach for America, and had now returned for graduate and professional degrees.

A few younger faces—undergraduates.

A few older—colleagues.

Along the front sat the silver and balding heads, Venclova having sired an entire generation of diplomats and NGO-niks.

"Excuse me."

She looked up into the face of a man about David's age, vaguely familiar, she thought, but then everything about the day had the glow of the vaguely familiar.

"May I?" He gestured at the aisle beyond her and she uncrossed the leg that was blocking his passage.

"Of course, please."

"Thank you. Do you mind if I—"

He smiled and edged past. There were five empty seats beyond her, but he sat directly beside her. It wasn't exactly annoying, but it wasn't exactly welcome, either. The chairs were pushed tight and his shoulder and right arm were close enough for Sara to feel the heat coming off his body. He smelled like wet leather.

"If you'd rather," he said, "I can..." and he pointed at the empty seats. But then a group excused its way by and there was nowhere else to sit. Sara smiled down at her hands. There was always that train at 8:55. Meanwhile, a man she thought might be the Dean of one of the residential colleges had taken his place at the podium.

"Here we go," the man beside her said, and winked.

Sara kept her eyes on her hands.

THERE WAS A solid hour of praise—former students turned tenured professors, remembering their old mentor's charge to *respect the intellectual ambition of every student*, a human rights lawyer speaking of *the precision of his moral compass*, a journalist who, embedded with U.S. Marines and face-down in a Tikrit firefight, had locked his mind on something Venclova had once said about courage. Sara knew the Colonel's thumbnail bio as well as anyone, but heard it again and again: born in Czechoslovakia in 1944, a ward of the great Soviet state after his father was executed in the basement interrogation cell of a Moscow prison. Defected Colonel, dissident, Commandant of Cadets at the Virginia Military Institute, Chair of Slavic Studies at Yale, and lately—lastly— a partner in the Wojtyła Society, a subgroup of the EurAsian division of Leviathan Global.

Finally, Venclova's granddaughter rose from the first row, uncertain and wobbling until a hand reached up and steadied her. It appeared to be as much an issue of balance as grief, and Sara felt the room hold its breath as the girl made her way to the podium where the Dean put his arm over her shoulder and turned to the room.

"Rachel Venclova, as I'm sure most of you know, was the light in Tomas's life. I know he took care not to pressure her to matriculate here. His counsel, as you all know well, was never anything but wise and fair. But when Rachel was graduated from Branford College and entered the doctoral program I know Tomas felt the circle of his life had drawn full. I know he loved that sense of symmetry. But mostly he loved Rachel."

He stepped back, the room applauded softly, and Rachel Venclova stepped to the microphone.

"My grandfather," she began.

Meanwhile, Sara's wet boot had shaped a small pool in the weave of the carpet.

She felt the man beside her nudge her shoulder.

She ignored him. He nudged her again.

At the front of the room, the girl was talking about a trip she had taken with her grandfather back to her late parents' home in Gdansk, tears hanging along the edge of speech. Sara felt the man tap her knee and finally looked at him. He was smiling again, pointing at her boot.

"What a drip," he whispered, looking now at Venclova's granddaughter and then at Sara, waiting for her to what? get the joke? nod appreciatively?

Instead, she stood as quickly and quietly as she could, folded her jacket over her arm and turned for the door. The last thing she saw was the look on the man's face, a confusion bordering on panic. And then the arrogant smile she associated with everything about the university, the knowingness, the sense of entitlement. When they built the place, they buried the roof tiles in the floor of the Long Island Sound so they'd appear as weathered as anything at Oxford or Cambridge—that was the look on his face, and it said everything about the sense of privilege and power you could physically smell. Which she hated, but had also, she realized, never managed to forget.

*

OUTSIDE WAS A dripping dusk, the rain having blown itself out, the day cooler for it, and she stood for a confused moment, alone and momentarily disoriented. Which way was it to—think Sara—and then she was walking. She knew the way back to the town green, back to Chapel Street where she could catch a cab to the train station. It wasn't about direction, her little panicked pause, or at least not about physical direction. It was suddenly finding herself back in this place, this life, but without David. Had there been any service for David, any celebration?

If there had she wasn't aware of it.

There had been no talk of Ukraine or human trafficking, of that she was certain. But then she thought of Colonel Venclova, about the emails David kept exchanging with him after he'd come back from his first fundraising trip, about David's gathering obsession with Dietrich Bonhoeffer's martyrdom, and she began to wonder not what had happened to David in Ukraine—he was dead, she understood that—but *why* it had happened to him. Which lead to the question: had she ever really known him? Which—in the darkest of moments—regressed to: had she ever really known anyone?

She stopped at the intersection, out of breath but not from walking, sweating despite the cool. Why had she come? For David, she freely admitted as much, but what did that even mean?

For David.

How for David?

Earlier in the day, doing her nostalgia thing, she had walked past the cottage they had shared. A converted pool house, it sat behind a rotting fence on the back of an estate on Alston Avenue, and she had stopped on the street to study the small concrete patio where they had spent so many evenings drinking PBRs and talking about everything. There was always so much to say, those nights when fifteen people would crowd into their tiny place, all of them talking at the same time. There were Catholic Workers down from Hartford and Christian anarchists over from the divinity school, militant veterans of the Occupy movement micro-dosing on LSD and EarthFirst! reunions. Sara had never felt so alive, following David to Russian classes and then to underground parties in abandoned churches or old theaters that gradually evolved to planning sessions, someone slapping a map saying *here* and *here*. This was just after the imperial reign of George W. Bush and everything was turning violent, or was about to, at least. You could feel it like changing weather. Columbia dropouts sizing up police checkpoints and clothiers in need of assault.

The drug of choice that spring was Molly and Sara loved it. It took the bad out and brought the good in. Happiness entering the brain via an unbroken ray of light. She would swallow a tablet and dance and dance while David and his ridiculous sideburns moved around the room snapping photos of would-be revolutionaries barely removed from making artisanal jams or small batch whiskey, now mail-ordering Bushmaster rifles and quoting Chomsky.

They were accomplished hackers, devoted anarchists disgusted by empire but good at nothing that didn't involve a keyboard and IPO address. Some were members of online collectives, hacktivists, the transparency movement—all the step-children of Anonymous, THIS MACHINE KILLS FASCISTS printed across their iPads. They specialized in denial of service attacks and made the occasional raid on Citibank or SIPRNet, but did little else. Still, David kept shooting them, his circle of art friends steadily replaced by a circle of anarchist friends, one group as hapless as the next.

All those vampire weekends in the city, sleepless and frayed, and then Sunday night he would carry her back to Grand Central, home to New Haven on the Metro-North, home to their block cottage. She always seemed to be passing out in cabs or on ferries or in someone's Subaru on the BQE or the Van Wyck out to JFK to pick up this visiting monk in town to construct sand mandalas for bored sixth graders or that Palestinian protester-in-residence arriving for a panel at the New School. Somehow she'd find that cool damp place between toilet and wall, moist and bacterial, that place of regrets. And then David would find her, hold her head in his lap until they could sprawl across the bed where he would stroke her hair.

"Tell me something," she would say, her voice like a balloon forgotten in the corner, leaking helium and, though still floating, unable to rise, "something beautiful."

And there were beautiful things. There were many things, and so often they were beautiful.

Other nights they sat with people and discussed what was not. They were all opposed to the government, opposed to the wars, the torture, the multi-nationals. They'd get high and sing gospels, and then at some point, strewn about the room like wet laundry, the questions would start.

Would you fight?

Would you actually kill someone?

At the time David was systematically working his way through both the Psalms and the nonviolent theory of Gene Sharp and had only one answer: I would bear witness. My job is to bear witness.

But there was no witness. In the end, there was only David and his rupture. David with his righteous anger, and then, eventually, there was no anger, because there was no David. But that was never here, she told herself. That was later. So maybe that was what she meant by *for David*. *For David* actually meant *for me*. *For David* was a sort of indulgence, a window back to when she was happy. Though even now she wondered how much of that happiness was a backward projection, happiness as the blistering need to have felt she had once been happy. It was the sort of tortured logic that was making her crazy, rereading Dietrich Bonhoeffer's *Letters & Papers from Prison*. David's name printed on the inside flap in the blocky letters of a little boy.

She had to stop this, she had to—

She heard someone coming up the cobblestones and turned toward Elm and started walking. She didn't need to see his face to know it was the man who had sat beside her.

"Excuse me," he was calling, "hi, sorry! Could you maybe wait? I—" He raised a palm, smiled. "Just a sec here."

She stopped, but said nothing.

"I hustled," he said.

"I see that."

"You speak! Wonderful, that's a start. But listen." He pointed back toward the St. Thomas More Center. "I'm sorry about that. I was being stupid, I know. I didn't mean to upset you or—"

"You didn't upset me."

"Right, sure, or offend you or whatever. Colonel Venclova meant a great deal to me. I know if you're here—"

"I didn't really know him."

"Right, but—could we maybe go somewhere? Get out of the wet? Some people were going to the Cuban place over near Bar. They rented the place out actually so—"

"I'm on my way to the train station."

"Perfect," he said. "You can have a drink on the way."

"No, thanks."

"Well, at least let me drive you to the train. I'm Ray Shields, by the way. And you're..."

She looked up the street and back at him. It was starting to rain again, lightly, but then thunder sounded.

"Sara," she said finally.

"Sara. Perfect. I'm glad I caught you."

"I should be going."

"Let me drive you, Sara. This weather."

"No, thanks.

"Sara," he called.

But she was already walking, headed for the lights of Chapel Street.

Where she failed to find a cab, failed, in fact, to find anything open. Passing the green, she had watched the lights ahead of her wink on and off with the surging power. A blackout, and even the restaurants were closed or closing. A storm was coming, this from the Somali janitor who shooed her from the foyer of the Anchor. Go home, be dry. You have no idea, she wanted to tell the man, how complex that would be. She walked a loop of several blocks, the rain coming harder now, the power flashing off and on. She was wet and growing cold but thought she could outwalk both.

Crown to Park to George, and then back to Crown.

She told herself she was looking for a cab, but really it was about motion. It would do her good to be drenched, to strip her of whatever it was that had brought her here. Coming was a mistake, sure, of course, what had she expected it to be? But it was also instructive, what Venclova—were Venclova alive to say it—might have called a teachable moment. Buck up, Sara. It isn't all that. Get back home, get back to work.

Yet she couldn't.

She was heading up Crown and suspected herself of knowing what she was doing—ahead she could see the light from the Cuban place so really, who was she kidding? One drink. Light. Warmth. She could get a cab from there. She could summon an Uber. But if she was going to summon an Uber wouldn't she have done that already?

She couldn't trust herself, not anymore.

She pushed open the door of Soul de Cuba, stomped her feet, brushed the rain from her sleeves. The tight restaurant was packed, folks at the high-top tables and in the booths, three-deep at the bar. Loud and happy in a room of mirrors and wood and Edison bulbs dangling on wires. She looked for a place to hang her jacket, finally slung it over her arm, and waded in half-heartedly. She was almost to the bar when someone put a hand on her upper arm.

"Sara? Oh my God. I was so hoping I would see you."

She turned toward a tall woman about her age, maybe a little older. Frizzy red hair. The kind of woman who probably grew up being told she looked like a boy and never much cared.

"I'm Penny? Penny from Advanced Russian. Oh my God, you don't remember me. That's okay. I'm totally forgettable. What are you drinking? Do you have a drink? Jesus, you look soaked." She put her hands in the air. "God, it's good to see you. But really, what are you drinking?"

They sat in a corner booth and sipped mojitos. Penny from Advanced Russian seemed to know a great deal about Sara. She had so so *so* been hoping to run into her and catch up.

"Do you remember the guy who sat near the front, dark-haired, cute? You remember?"

Sara nodded her head. She didn't, but could almost believe she did. Just like she could almost believe she remembered Penny. She had followed David to two years of Russian courses, but Sara had never taken Advanced Russian. She didn't know the cute boy with dark-hair. She didn't know Penny. She was confused about a lot of things, but about this she was certain.

"Listen." Penny had one hand on Sara's forearm, leaning forward conspiratorially. So close their heads almost touched. "I know maybe it's weird to bring it up, but I just want to say how sorry I was to hear about David." She leaned back. "Is this weird for you, me saying this?"

"No."

"Because I don't mean it to be."

"It's okay."

"You're okay?"

"I'm fine."

Penny took a drink and nodded vigorously.

"Because what I'm saying is that he was such a good guy. Doing such important work. I would see his photographs and think 'wow, this guy is crazy brave.'" She put her hand back on Sara's forearm. "I want to get us two more."

Sara watched her disappear back into the crowd, a glass in each hand. She could have known her, she supposed. It could have been Intermediate Russian. It wasn't hard to confuse classes and it had been a weird year. The course was supposed to have been taught by one of Venclova's doctoral students but something had happened and it looked like maybe the section would be canceled, but then the great man himself walked in the door and took over.

"This is so crazy." She looked up to find Penny in front of her, a fresh drink in each hand. "It's kind of insane actually, but there's like the whole crew playing some serious nostalgia in the back. I know I shouldn't have said anything, but sorry, yeah, I said you were out here and they are dying to see you. Is that cool?"

It was cool. Cool because Sara had given up on whatever logic the night carried, given up on any sense of order. What had she expected, after all? She'd known not to go to the service, but had gone anyway. Known to avoid the bar, and yet walked right in. The crew from Advanced Russian. David's friends, to the extent that David had friends. Not that she had been any better. Some anarchist friends from when she was living under the delusion she might become Dorothy Day. Some activist friends in New York when she was pretending to be alive.

She shrugged, smiled, took the drink from Penny and followed her past the crowd and through the back room where they stopped outside a small door.

"The inner sanctum," Penny said.

It was quiet inside, dim. Votive candles. Bottle service. Maybe a dozen people, but not the crew from the class she never took. The crowd was older, all male but for Penny and Rachel Venclova, the granddaughter, who slumped into a banquette, barefoot and bored. She wore what appeared to be a cocktail dress, a satiny yellow cut low enough to show her thin shoulder blades and the deep hollows around her clavicles.

"Hello, Sara." Beside her was the man who had followed her out of the service. Ray Shields, she remembered. "I was hoping I'd see you again. Thanks, Penny," he said turning, "I've got this."

"Shall I come with?"

"No need. I'm just going to show Sara around." He watched Penny move off to sit by Rachel Venclova and turned to Sara. "I met David in Poland and then it was this crazy thing where we realized we must have met once at the Colonel's."

She said nothing.

"I didn't say that on the street, obviously. It seemed a little, I don't know."

"Aggressive?"

"I was hoping you would take me up on that ride. But you made it. That's what matters. Let me introduce you to a few people. Friends of David." He took a step forward, stopped and turned back to her. "I guess if you were wondering why you were invited this is your answer."

THEY KNEW HER, knew David—that was the thing. Knew about the time in New Haven and Greece, hinted at the low-grade pharmaceuticals she'd taken in, Jesus, how many different Brooklyn lofts where they'd sat around high and contemplating revolution?

The tablets of Ecstasy and occasional benzo.

The centering prayer.

The men in the back room laughed, they smiled indulgently, *what a pleasure to see youth not wasted on the young.* Ray Shields led her around the table where the men, slouched before bottles of Patron, each came to life, stood, shook her hand, looked her in the eye to say how wonderful it was to finally meet her. Two gentlemen from Leviathan. The DCM from the Czech Embassy. The Slovak ambassador to the U.S. Blue suit. Grey eyes beginning to glass.

"Are you familiar, Sara, with the Wojtyła Society?" Ray Shields asked. "David was one of our most enthusiastic members and did wonderful work on behalf of the Society. He mentioned this?"

"This is a religious society?"

"Of sorts, I suppose. But we have broader interests as well."

That was how it started.

Or at least that was how she told herself it started, weeks later, sitting in the flat three blocks off the Maidan in Kiev she had rented while dialing the number she had been given. That night in New Haven, Ray Shields had explained the Society's broad interests in the broadest way possible. Words like *autonomy* and *sovereignty*. Their context so hazy as to be meaningless. Penny kept bringing her mojitos and afterward she and Shields walked her to the Hotel Duncan on Chapel Street where they had booked her a room.

It was late and she should have been drunk but wasn't. Strangely, she found herself both calm and hyper-sober, relaxed yet acutely aware of her surroundings. The way the sound of their steps changed as they moved from sidewalk to street back to sidewalk. The moisture gathered in her eyelashes. The chap of her lips. A box of real estate magazines had spilled from the dispenser into the rain, yellow ink tinting the wet street. They escorted her up to her room and sat her down on the bed like a child.

What did she need to know? What could they tell her? *What do you need to hear to make this right, Sara?* Shields speaking, standing by the window. The room had two beds and Penny sat on the one opposite, hands in her lap, looking solicitously at Sara. Of course there was much that couldn't be said, but yes, he really had known David, admired him, loved him like a brother if you wanted to get down to it. Penny admitted she had never met David, but knew him by reputation.

"A lot of people were starting to talk about his work," she said. "He was turning heads."

"His photography?"

"In part, certainly," she said, "and also other things."

Like his work on behalf of the society. The Wojtyła Society for Peace and International Cooperation had been formed to carry forward the concerns of Pope John Paul II. Shields had met David at the annual society gathering in the Liptov region along the Polish-Slovak border. They had been friends since.

But what exactly did he do for the Society?

What exactly did the Society do?

"The Society is dedicated to the promotion and protection of at-risk populations in what we generally regard as the northern block of Eastern Europe. Poland, Slovakia, Ukraine, the Baltic States," Shields said, quoting, Sara guessed, some official mission statement. "What exactly David did," he shrugged, "it's a cliché, I know, but a little of this, a little of that. The more you can do, the more they ask you to do, being the general principle."

"But what did David have to do with Ukraine?"

"David was devoted to freedom," Shields said.

"But we were in Greece," Sara said. "Never there."

"Sara, let me just—" Penny's cell rang and she excused herself, stepped into the bathroom to take the call, and returned a moment later. "Rachel's here."

"She's coming up?" Shields asked.

"I'm going to meet her downstairs." She looked at Sara. "Be right back."

Penny returned a few minutes later, hands at her side in surrender.

"He's with her," she said quickly.

"Who?" Shields asked.

"Him," she mouthed, but didn't say, because already entering behind her was Rachel Venclova, hanging off the arm of a good-looking man somewhere in his thirties.

"Congressman Torres," Shields said, hopping off the bed. "Ray Shields with Leviathan." He came over with an open hand. "Good to see you again, sir."

"Good to see you, too," the man said, hand extended. "But please, just Marco. Hello," he said, turning to Sara who still sat on the bed, too exhausted to rise, had the thought even entered her mind. "I'm Marco Torres. You're Sara Kovács if I'm not mistaken.

It's a pleasure." They shook hands and he moved behind Rachel where he stood with his hands on her shoulders. She wore a man's Burberry coat over her pale skin, her hair the color of wet sand. "I'm leaving Miss Venclova with you. You'll take good care of her I trust?"

"Of course," Shields said.

The man, Marco Torres, Congressman Torres, whispered something in the girl's ear. When she nodded he smiled at the room, took Rachel's hand, and said, "Let's all bow our heads." But whatever prayer he uttered was silent: the next thing they heard was "Amen." The next thing they saw was that smile again, and then he was gone.

Penny shut the door.

"I didn't know he was down there. Sorry."

Shields shrugged and walked over to stand between the beds. Rachel sat opposite Sara now, neither looking at the other.

"It's late," Shields said finally, and looked at Penny. "We should go."

"You two are all right?" Penny asked. "Sara?"

"What?"

"You're all right?"

"Yeah."

"I left something for you by the sink? Just don't forget." She looked at Rachel. "You're good?"

"I'm fine," Rachel said. "We're just going to talk."

"Sure, of course." Penny kissed Rachel's cheek, leaned over and squeezed Sara's hand. "We'll be in touch, all right? And remember by the sink."

Sara didn't look up until she heard the door shut. The silver safety bolt. The cartoonish exit map. Whatever clarity she had possessed had dissolved into fatigue: she was exhausted. The girl across from her appeared equally tired. Lanky and limp, she slouched on the edge of the bed like an expensive rag doll. White skin and a Chopard watch. Sara could smell her, not her perfume but her deodorant.

"I asked to see you." Rachel Venclova didn't look up when she spoke. "I thought I wanted to say something, but now I think I just wanted to meet you."

"I was sorry to hear about your grandfather," Sara said.

The girl shrugged. "That's the evening's general theme, how sorry everyone is. Not that I don't appreciate it."

"You were close to him?"

Again, she shrugged. "He was all the family I had. He raised me, and then one day when I was sixteen he asked me to do a favor for him." She looked up. "That's what they're asking you to do now."

"A favor."

"That's what everyone calls it."

She lifted her bare feet up onto the bed and smoothed the yellow crinkle of her dress. The soles of her feet were dirty. "You can lose like eleven pounds in four days with this sort of calorie restriction and extreme exercise. Like 360 calories. Lots of water and electrolytes. Six hours a day walking, just walking, and everybody can walk, right? All for this dress. Now I'm thinking about sleeping in it."

"Did you know David?"

"Would you mind if I stayed here?"

Sara was silent.

"I did meet him once," Rachel said, "but not really. This was maybe a year ago in Warsaw. I can tell you that my grandfather loved him. They were working together. I'm not sure on what exactly."

"I don't understand any of this."

"I do know it was important, whatever it was." She touched Sara's hand. "If you let me stay I promise not to make a sound."

Sara got up and walked into the bathroom. By the sink was an envelope. Inside were reservations for a flight out of JFK to Boryspil. A sheaf of euros was paper-clipped to the ticket, a phone number scrawled on a post-it note attached to that. She put it all back in the envelope and stared at herself in the mirror for a long time. She had some Russian from her time in New Haven. A pidgin of childhood Slovak courtesy her immigrant mother. She was going to do this favor, whatever it was, and they were going to tell her what happened to David.

But instead of David, she thought of Bonhoeffer. A pacifist German pastor and theologian, he had decided to take part in the plot to kill Hitler, and in doing so had believed that he was sacrificing his personal salvation. He would go to hell. The Bible was clear; there was no way around it. Yet he pushed on, eventually to be hanged in a concentration camp, a failure as a conspirator, a failure as a pacifist.

All of it no more than a gesture.

But my God, what a gesture.

When she walked back into the bedroom Rachel had plugged her iPhone into the wall dock and curled beneath the sheets, eyes shut, the lamp still on. She snored lightly as a child while Nina Simone sang quietly. It was ridiculous, but also strangely moving, and Sara couldn't bring herself to stop the music.

She got in the opposite bed and clicked off the lamp. She thought she had never felt as exhausted as she did that night. Still, it must have been near dawn before she fell asleep. She woke late the next morning wondering if any of it was real. Rachel was gone, but the sheets were rumpled, and the envelope was still by the sink.

It wasn't until she was in Kiev that she called the number on the post-it. No one answered. She dialed it again, and must have dialed it twenty times over the next few months before someone finally did.

IT WAS LATE October when Hugh Eckhart found Berger in a meat locker in Kiev, the store converted to a church and buried deep in a Stalinist ghetto of high-rise concrete and dying trees. Barred windows and empty shelves, the rust rings of old cans still visible.

"I didn't come here to give you shit." Eckhart was drinking something green and weedy. "So you missed the memorial services. No problem there. I did, too."

"Rick Miles said you'd come slinking around."

"'*Slinking?*'"

"What do you want, Hugh?"

"First, I want to say I'm sorry about the Colonel. I know he meant a lot to you."

"You don't know anything."

"I know he got in your head. How about that?" Eckhart said. "He got in all of our heads. Agents of a God *totaliter aliter*. All of us sitting around reading our theology. All of us thinking we were on some divine mission."

"You don't think we are?"

Eckhart smiled.

"You can't rattle me, Chris. I'm past that."

"Crossed that bridge, did you?"

"You can't rattle me so don't even bother."

"You probably already know they're looking for you," Berger said.

"He had such good intentions, the Colonel. That's all we've had since 9/11, you know. We've been so magnanimous, nothing but the best intentions for the whole wide world. But look at the world now. It doesn't love us anymore. What happened? Why doesn't it love us anymore?"

"I would guess finding you is just a matter of time."

"I would guess you're probably right," Eckhart said. "So maybe shut up a second and listen."

The Ukrainian Prime Minister was about to refuse to sign the trade deal he'd negotiated with the EU.

"The Colonel mentioned this," Berger said.

"Did he mention what happens next?" Eckhart asked.

"Instability."

"Instability indeed. There'll be rallies, the streets filled with righteous protesters demanding a new government."

"Folks chanting."

"Chanting, waving flags," Eckhart said, "hanging around talking to the BBC. The government will tolerate it for a while. But at some point they'll refuse to disperse, and that's when the shooting starts. Snipers up on the McDonald's in the Maidan. The Berkut coming out of coffee shops with their lattes and zip-strips. Imagine it. The Ukrainian government is helpless, so Putin has to react, protect the people, defend order. He rolls over the border and takes Crimea, moves Spetsnaz teams into the eastern provinces. You familiar with the Spetsnaz, Chris? Sometimes I watch the training videos on YouTube. Brutal motherfuckers."

"Isn't that what we've been preparing for, moving weapons to fight the Russians?"

"Except you're saying it exactly wrong. It's the one thing the Colonel didn't figure out. Or maybe he just couldn't believe it. But those rockets aren't going to fight the separatists. They're going to arm them. They're for the pro-Russian folks, to make sure they have weapons enough to start an actual war. Think about this. We arm the separatists in the east, and then the Russians come in and organize them. That load of sniper rifles you carried? Those are to shoot protesters."

"Bullshit."

"Those rockets are to take down Ukrainian aircraft."

"Not even an outfit as big as Leviathan would try something like that."

"All they want is a dust-up—like the Colonel said—a little instability. Just enough to keep all that Ukrainian gas in the ground." Eckhart looked at him. "Did he really use the word *slinking*?"

"Tell me what you want."

"They've been running the money through the PAC of a congressman in Florida."

"Marco Torres."

Eckhart smiled.

"Just tell me what you want."

"There's a dossier that outlines the holdings, the transactions, all of it. I couldn't get it in New Yok, but there's a woman in Bratislava," Eckhart said. "Susan Logan, the ambassador's wife."

"I thought you sent Rick Miles to keep watch."

"Forget Rick. Rick is—" He fluttered one hand into space. "Rick is I-don't-know-what. Obi-Wan Kenobi off his Abilify or something. But this woman, Susan Logan, she put a request in a few weeks back with a hiring agency for domestic help. If I could get someone inside, a young woman."

"You can't stop something like this."

"She lost a daughter. There's an opening here. We find the right girl, get her inside."

"Did the Colonel know about any of this?"

"I think he was sniffing something out. But the Colonel was a what, a centi-millionaire? That didn't really cut it with Randy."

Berger was silent.

"Garcia's got a nineteen percent stake in Rosneft, Chris. It's through a series of shell companies, very difficult to source. But if I could get my hands on that dossier it would bury him. That Garcia colluded with the Russians to start a war, a financial stake on both sides. He'd spend the rest of his life in federal prison. Otherwise, you're looking at our next president."

"What happened to her daughter?"

"An overdose. She'd be twenty-seven if she'd lived."

"Shields said if you contacted me to let him know."

"He didn't say to shoot me?"

"I think it'll be more subtle than that."

Eckhart shook his head more out of exhaustion than disagreement.

"Do this one thing for me, Chris. Go find Marco Torres."

Berger found himself looking just past Eckhart's shoulder.

"Look. Eventually, Garcia will get to me," Eckhart said. "I have no doubt of that. But before you completely write me off, go find Torres. They set him up just like they have you. Find him. Talk to him. Then you make your decision. We all set out to do right."

"Jesus—"

"Truth, justice, and the American way, Chris. We all believed in it. I still believe," Eckhart said. "As ridiculous as it sounds. I still do." He almost touched Berger's sleeve then seemed to think better of it. "I think deep down you do, too."

In November, Berger flew to Tampa and followed Marco Torres to a fundraiser in St. Augustine, the city wind-swept and empty, the fundraiser in a college reception hall beneath an ornate rotunda of gilt and glass. Berger sat silently at a table of lawyers and accountants and their wives. Conservative suits. Talk of the good old days. Torres spoke briefly and uninspiringly, Berger thought, and then they all sat down to lamb and herb-roasted potatoes.

That night, Berger made no effort to meet the Congressman. He needed to watch him first, to get a sense of the man, and what he sensed was impatience. What he sensed was frustration. Torres was likely the smartest man in the room. Yet he had to glad-hand his way from table to table, and for that he was barely able to restrain his disgust.

A man like that would be willing to take chances.

A man like that might very easily overextend himself.

A few days later, Torres flew up to the District. Berger got there a day ahead and accosted him in a museum gift shop. It was the same as St. Augustine: the impatience, the barely bridled anger. Something else, too: fear. The way Torres kept putting things between them. And it wasn't just that Berger was presenting himself as some vagrant conspiracy theorist, bearded and homeless. The menace was deeper. The man knew something was coming. Maybe he didn't know what, exactly, but he knew it would be bad.

"You're Congressman Torres, correct?"

"I am." And that long hesitation, as if collecting himself for what came next. "And you are?"

"Just a photography nut. But I've been hoping to meet you."

"Are you one of my constituents?"

"No, but I've certainly kept up with your activities."

"And what activities would those be?"

Berger was gone after that. People were coming up the stairs toward them, but more importantly, he knew what he needed to know. Representative Marco Torres, man of the people, was going down.

That was the point at which Berger should have left town. Had he the discipline he'd carried as a soldier, he would have gone back, he would have taken up his rifle and died on the battlefield. Instead, he stayed. First, because he saw a performance of Shostakovich's Symphony No. 7 was being performed at the National Cathedral. The "Leningrad" Symphony. It was the worst sort of sentimentality. The music he had listened to as a cadet, the music he associated with stoic virtue. The standing at attention on the parade deck. The quiet shiver that came hearing the National Anthem. Because he had believed. He had been carried by belief.

As if he could recover such. As if that was even desirable.

Still, he bought a ticket and combed his hair.

Then he got a message from Rachel Venclova asking if he could meet. That it was the same night as the Shostakovich seemed more than a coincidence: it seemed like a sign.

He sat through the concert, one trembling hand wrapped in the other, as if for solace. He wept only briefly, alone in the men's room, and for that discretion was grateful. Coming had been a mistake. The past is behind us for a reason. Only a fool turns back.

He was headed to the Metro stop when he saw Marco Torres following him. He couldn't believe it at first, the blatant stupidity of the man. Berger took the train to an Irish pub in Arlington where Rachel Venclova waited at a table. He walked toward a young woman about Rachel's age, and then turned abruptly and walked to Rachel. He motioned her up and out the back door and she came without a word. On the street, she took his arm. The wind was up and it was getting colder.

"You're going to hear all sorts of things," she said. "The craziest rumors. Me and the Russians. My God. If my grandfather wasn't already dead that thought alone would finish him off." She leaned against him. "But I'll tell you this, I'll go to them if I have to."

"Where's your family?"

"He was my family."

Berger said nothing.

"Do you know about them?" she asked. "My parents?"

"I've heard stories."

"Stories, right. Because that's all they are."

Her parents had emigrated from Czechoslovakia to Poland in time for the Polish Solidarity movement, her father an economist with the state shipyard in Gdansk, her mother an accountant. They had been Party members—the only way to be granted any freedom of movement—and when their allegiance switched from the United Workers the repercussions were bitter. Her father had been beaten on two occasions, her mother constantly threatened, stalked, followed. Still, they had refused to leave. It was their country and they intended to rebuild it.

Then one day they came home to find someone had shit on their bed, a mound of human feces centered atop the chenille bedspread. By then the Wall had come down and it all felt somehow unnecessary, all the useless heroics more vanity than sacrifice. Rachel's mother was pregnant with her and with the help of Randy Garcia they very quietly arranged for the baby to be born in Virginia where Rachel's grandfather was Commandant of Cadets at VMI. Her parents spent a year in the States but apparently felt a greater sense of duty toward their country than to their year-old daughter. So they left her in the care of her grandfather and a rotating field of live-in nannies and returned to Gdansk. Her father died of a heart attack the next year, and her mother, wasting no time in following, passed a few months later. By then Rachel and her grandfather had moved to New Haven and there were no thoughts of going back.

"Stories," she said.

Berger put his arm around her, unsure where this solicitousness came from. Some paternal instinct never activated, perhaps. Or maybe she just felt so fragile, hanging off his arm like a half-forgotten Christmas ornament.

"I could probably be of use to you," she said. "I speak Russian and Polish. I've got decent Slovak."

"They offered you to me once before."

"They offered me?"

"That lunch at the country club. The Colonel was there. Ray Shields."

"And they *offered* me? That was their verb?"

Berger said nothing.

"Well, you should have said yes," she said finally. "I'm going to be a part of this one way or another."

"There's nothing to be a part of."

"I'll do whatever Randy wants. I'll lure him to sleep. I'll tuck him in at night with his rockets and his spreadsheets. But then, when he thinks everything is in place, when he's assured of my loyalty, I'm going to fuck him. I'm serious. I'm going to blow up his world."

"Rachel."

"He killed my grandfather. And don't even say it sounds crazy. They have ways. They call it fairy dust. Dioxin. Polonium-210. You even think about it too long and you wind up with renal failure. Garcia poisoned him just like he'll poison you. He uses you and then he gets rid of you. You act like it's ridiculous and then one day you find out you have leukemia. You don't believe me?"

Berger was silent.

"It'll be subtle and slow," Rachel said, "and then it'll be over. You'll all be dead and he'll be president."

They were passing brownstones, the street quiet.

"I'll go to the Russians if I have to. I'll go against you, Chris. But I'd rather not. I'd rather be on your side."

"Why is that?"

"Just your rugged masculinity, I guess. Shaving with a straight razor. Always setting your watch to local time." It took him a moment to realize she was making fun of him. "I don't know," she said, her voice quieter. "I think maybe you remind me of my grandfather. I know he trusted you. Maybe you seem like someone I can trust, too."

"Don't," he said, and caught himself, realizing he was consciously imitating the Colonel. Then going ahead with it anyway. "Don't trust anyone."

She let go of his arm and faced him.

"If we meet again," she said. "It won't be like this."

"You need to stay out of it."

"If you try to stop me—if you try to stop me, Chris, I promise. I'll kill you."

"Rachel."

"I promise you I will."

He left her at the Metro, took the train back into the city and walked to the Cannon House Office Building where he picked the lock on Marco Torres's office. He didn't know what exactly he was looking for, and certainly didn't expect the man to return, but there Torres was, stumbling into the dark while Berger sat behind his desk, remembering things. Lost in those lost years. The things he had believed. The things he still did. He put his hands between his legs to hide their trembling.

Torres kept the light off. There in the dark, he no longer looked afraid.

Berger wasn't afraid either. He felt it first in his hands, and when it spread to his arms he knew, without the slightest doubt, it was the presence of God, preparing to lift him up. This was certain, God's presence. Only one question remained unresolved, and he asked it: are you one of the Bronze People, Mr. Congressman?

ALL THE WHILE, Ukraine continued to buckle. There were protests and counter-protests and the streets filled with young people hiding their faces behind *kaffiyehs* and ski masks. The Maidan was full of walls of tires and then the new year came and those tires were burning and things had devolved in a way Sara hadn't thought possible. The revolution had begun and everywhere were ambulances, people hauled onto gurneys or having their tear-gassed eyes flushed with saline solution. Zip-cuffs and CS fumes. Burn barrels in the freezing nights. Big Russian-made armored personnel carriers tore up the streets hauling in the Berkut and then hauling away those the Berkut had beaten and arrested. A nationalist group called Right Sector fought the police with bats and pitchforks up and down Hrushevsky Street. There were snipers on the rooftops. People used words like *autonomy* and *freedom* with an earnestness that embarrassed Sara.

From her flat three blocks off Khreshchatyk Street, she could run down and snap photographs and video and run back to upload the files to her blog and Twitter feed. In the months since arriving in Kiev, she'd rented a flat and made herself into something of a journalist. Of course, journalists were disappearing, but she wasn't a *real* journalist. She was a lost American real-timing the implosion of the Yanukovych regime, who just happened to start finding her posts getting picked up by the BBC and the *New York Times*.

Now and then, she would call the number on the post-it but there was never any response. She hadn't heard from any of the people she met in New Haven, either, so maybe they had forgotten her? Or maybe she was doing what they needed, being their eyes? Maybe the crisis had changed things?

She tried as best she could to go on with life, to make her nightly visits to the Maidan, to file her stories, to eat her oatmeal.

In January, she went to the ballet with Carolyn Reynolds, a Slavic Studies professor at NYU, and her husband, Timothy, a former chess prodigy with a crest of gelled hair. She'd met them at the U.S. embassy the autumn before when they were visiting the city on their honeymoon. Now they had returned for the year, Dr. Reynolds on some rarified fellowship from the Institut für die Wissenschaften vom Menschen in Vienna. Timothy learning Russian and hanging out in barbershops by day, castling in Italian restaurants by night.

Sara met them in the cold street, dead Christmas lights still hanging from abandoned tramlines.

"This is going to be a waste of time but what else is there?" Dr. Reynolds asked the evening.

"No," Sara said, "not a waste."

"They're shooting people down in front of the McDonald's yet here we are."

"Wait, what?"

"Are they not, Timothy?"

"I didn't hear anything about shooting."

"Near the McDonald's. Someone was shot today."

"Someone on the Maidan?"

"A sniper, I imagine. He was sniped. Is that the correct usage?"

Her husband shrugged. He carried everywhere a silver vape loaded with cannabidiol oil and lifted to his mouth as if it were a recording device.

"I would have heard about shooting. Someone would have said something." Sara looked at Timothy. "Does that do anything?"

"It calms me."

"The cannabis?"

"More that I bite the tip."

"He chews it," his wife said. "It's disgusting, but I live with it."

"I was into ketamine for a while," he said.

"This was a tragic time. The chewing, the gnawing, this is disgusting, yes. Unhygienic. Vulgar. But not yet tragic."

"My ketamine period."

"The great theater of the drug-addled lover."

"This is over."

"The wailing, the gnashing of teeth."

"This is behind us."

"The private room at the Center on the Hudson over which one fought an ongoing rear-guard action with Aetna—how glorious. Now we've entered a new epoch." She was emaciated and brilliant, Carolyn Reynolds, running on Cymbalta and nerve. "Now he chews the tip and I somehow live with it. I wish you'd take him on a trip east, Sara."

"I've become very spiritual," he said.

"Show him poverty. Show him mass graves."

"I've cultivated a practice of meditation."

"Cultivated?" She shook her equine head. "I find him so precious of late."

They passed a construction crane.

They passed a man in a panda costume.

"I think I would have heard something," Sara said. "If there was shooting."

The ballet was Stravinsky's *The Firebird*. They sat in the loge and looked down on the babushkas cutting sausage in their laps, the old intelligentsia in their polyester suits. Sara had waited for the second bell before going in and halfway through had looked across the hall and thought she'd seen David sitting with a young woman that might have been her. On stage, the dancers fell under the Firebird's spell, helpless but to dance their endless goddamn dance. Tears then, shivering in the cracked light. It might have been grief, but it might also have been the Dilaudid. Since New Haven, she'd found herself dabbling in it and it wasn't really something to dabble in. It was, in fact, a gratuitous fucker of a drug, almost like it was personal, almost like it was the part of her she'd spent her life going without, the missing piece that would see her dead. This was intriguing, this theory, and she told herself her interest was philo-sophical. But that didn't make her any less ashamed.

She passed the Maidan on her way home to her flat. Someone had indeed been shot, but instead of filing a story she swallowed a 4 mg Dilaudid and tried to pray.

It was later that night that God came to her.

She had drifted off, but gradually woke to sense the walls of her flat breathing, pulsing as if she were within some giant bellows. Was this a dream? Was such fear possible in a dream? But the fear washed out of her and she was left with an abiding comfort. She felt warmth, and tasted—for it was a taste—a gauze of blue light, radiant and clean, that washed like cool water and brought with it an overriding sense of safety, as if she had finally arrived where she had always been: cupped in the hand of God.

She understood then that you could simply lean into the pres-ence, unite with God simply by accepting that unity already existed. It was merely the recognition she had lacked. It seemed absurd, it seemed like something she would have mocked had she heard someone else say it. But that night it felt frighteningly real. Some-time later she found herself swimming in the indoor pool at the Marriot.

But how had she gotten to the pool?

Sara only asked this question later and that was a mistake because by the time she got around to examining the moment, the moment had dissolved. She did remember the pool lights lit the water a ghostly aquamarine, her body the darker shape, a fluid shadow, and here was where the confusion came in, because the light—she could remember at least this—the light in the pool was no different than the light in her flat. So it had been real? And if so, which part?

That was January.

IN FEBRUARY, YANUKOVYCH fled. The streets filled with cheering throngs and rumors of Russian tanks. John McCain arrived along with more earnest talk of freedom. The U.S. Secretary of State arrived along with promise of a massive bridge loan to sustain the economy. Sara watched him lay a wreath at a giant memorial where you could still taste the charred tires, the burnt rubber in the air. She hung around the embassy, trying to see who she could see. All she wanted was a face, someone from that night in New Haven, eye contact, a nod.

But she saw no one. No one associated with the University. No one from the Society. She told herself she was no longer needed, the situation had evolved and so had their needs. She wanted to feel profound relief, but what she felt was disappointment.

A few weeks later Congressman Torres paid a visit—lately, she saw him almost nightly on BBC World, raging against Russian aggression—and though she was refused an interview ("I'm sorry, the Congressman has no recollection of meeting you"), she did receive a stack of Torres's 14th District (FL) cardstock stationary.

It wasn't until after Torres had left that she admitted just how intensely she had convinced herself she would learn something about David. Not that he was *alive*, not that she would *see him*. He was dead; she understood that, accepted it. But what had grown within her was the wild hunger for any scrap of knowledge. Rumor, hearsay—it didn't matter. She wanted something. An inactive Facebook memorial page—that was all she had, and that wasn't enough. None of it was. The world, she meant. The flimsiness of it all. Not just David's death, but the entire universe built around it.

The emojis while the bombs fell—it wasn't enough.

The selfies while another CEO selling financial instruments escaped with his golden parachute. The homegrown shooters attacking elementary schools—it wasn't enough. Not against the migrants drowning, the elephants going extinct. She was maybe going a little crazy and felt the early tipping of her life, a graceless forward lean, like she was standing on some precipice and the direction she was headed was down. She had felt it that day in New York when she'd learned of David's death. She'd ran to Kiev after that. But where would she run this time?

Her flat consisted of two rooms, a fold-down table situated around the stove and sink. A fold-out couch that swallowed the whole of the second room. She kept her clothes in a carton stored beneath the small bookshelf. Gloves and hat, a coat with a fur-trimmed hood.

A box of pu-erh tea.

Olives. Nuts. Wine.

She stopped calling the number. She stopped posting articles. A photographer friend kept messaging her, practically begging her to accompany him to Donbas in the east but she ignored him. An important U.S. journal wanted three thousand words on the role of youth culture and social media in the revolution. An online magazine wanted a reassessment of Pussy Riot in light of resurgent authoritarianism in Russia. She didn't respond to either.

Outside, somewhere to the east, little green men were moving through the streets of Sevastopol, but inside Sara's flat the world was very gray and very still, because only within that gray stillness could she come to terms with the fact that a human being, someone you had touched and held and loved, could disappear so completely as to make existence more the stuff of conjecture than memory.

But it wasn't David, not really. What had disappeared from her life was purpose, the possibility of doing something useful. The more she tried to think of David the more she thought of Bonhoeffer. She found herself walking around with his book, unable to remember what it was she was supposed to do with it, or for it, or to it.

These were dangerous thoughts.

These were not thoughts she needed to be having.

Suddenly everything seemed confusing and unnecessarily complex. Frozen pizza came with instructions in eleven languages and three alphabets. Her hot water heater seemed a mercurial lover that might be wooed so that Sara stood there and pushed the same reset button over and over, talking to it, touching it, trying to divine its ways.

That was February.

*

IN MARCH, SHE bought a bottle of 2 mg Klonopins and something happened to them. She took them, she supposed, over the course of some number of days, though after the fact had no direct memory. Just the smell of her unwashed body, the whatever that had dried in her hair.

Her phone had died.

Someone had left the refrigerator door open.

Time began to blur and one morning she woke to find herself back in Split—this after David's first fundraising trip, after his *rupture*. Woke to find they had taken a room in the old quarter, halfway up the hill with a view of the harbor and Diocletian's marble palace. Outside were terracotta roofs and flower markets, giant stands of bright fruit and Italian cigarettes. Every building some degree of once-white and above and below it all the shattering blue of the sky and sea. Cloudless Croatian days. A room overlooking palm trees and yachts and old men in fishing caps peeling oranges with their thick fingers while from somewhere inside the palace walls someone was playing Daft Punk.

They found a club in an abandoned bus station and for four straight nights went there at her insistence. When she danced he watched her hair, her hair and the spot in her throat where her heart beat.

"Tell me what happened, David."

There was an outdoor market that sold ashtrays and flags and cheap dive masks.

There were androgynous boys with kohl black eyes.

"Tell me where you were."

Instead of telling her, he drove her up the coast to Opatija, a seaside town that terraced down the mountain to palms and boats and cafés open to the Adriatic. They took a room at the Grand Hotel Palace by the jewelry stores and giant dogs in silver collars. The St. Bernards and Mastiffs. The late night dinners consisting of nothing but vodka and quartered limes.

They walked along the promenade, her feet in straw flats, her fingers ringless.

"Please, David."

Slovenia then, crossing and re-crossing the clear cold of the Sava, the river winding its way out of the mountains to tangle with the narrow road. They took a room at a small house—a two-story A-frame with flower boxes of red roses, two single beds pushed together—and walked to the lake's shore. It was a thread of valley here, green grasses and small farms tucked behind fences with their sheep and cords of firewood.

They kept waking to bells, the village church ringing.

The alpine wind. The rough chap of her lips.

"Tell me how this ends, David?"

It ended at Lake Bled. Another small room overlooking the lake. Window sashes and a porcelain bidet. Benches and bicyclists, cafés and spas.

That evening, they ate alone in the dining room, a single table set on a parquet floor patched with mismatched wood. The water visible through the bay window. The monastery islanded in the lake's center.

"We'll row out there tomorrow," he told her. "I'd like to row you out there."

"I'd like that, too."

But the next day they didn't row to the monastery.

They flew to New York and had no more settled into the communal house than David was gone again, his second trip, his third—and then no more trips because there was no more David. David was a news item, a data point. David was a Facebook memorial page.

She was sinking.

She was sinking, spiraling—there were any number of verbs for it—and decided to go east with Carolyn Reynolds's husband, Timothy. There were rumors that an asylum had been shelled, no images, no footage. But his wife thought he should see it.

"He's playing chess eighteen hours a day." She bought the tickets and stuffed 20,000 hryvnia into Sara's hands. "This really isn't acceptable."

They took the overnight train, buckled into a jostling sleeping car. Morning found them in fields of lifting fog, the ground sketched into rectangles of black earth. A Lada taxi took them from the station through the ramshackle town of stray dogs and scattered masonry to a hotel beneath the bright golden dome of an Orthodox church.

A man waited for them in the hotel dining room.

"You're a little early to see the war," he said. "Maybe come back next month."

"Just show us what you can," Sara said. "This asylum."

"Sure."

"Maybe take us there."

"It's a great way to spend an afternoon."

She'd gotten his name from a contact in Kiev. An ex-Royal Marine who, having done two tours in Iraq, had studied Russian and got a job with the EU's office of Security Policy doing post-impact analysis.

She paid him 200 euros and they rode in a silver Audi out through shriveled trees, his driver Yuri at the wheel, the sky a flat dead gray, the grass matted and brown. There had been scattered acts of violence, a few thugs calling themselves militias, shrapnel in the aluminum siding of a Skoda dealership, the wind singing through the frame of what was once a greenhouse. Here and there a government checkpoint. They followed a long straightaway past sludge ponds full of heavy metals, chlorine tanks outside a water filtration plant.

Yuri pulled into the opposite lane to pass a convoy of gas trucks.

"It takes a fine eye, actually," the Brit said, turning in his seat to face Sara and Timothy, "to distinguish neglect from actual damage."

The asylum was a three-story white brick monstrosity set by a complex of apartments. State TV was reporting an explosion from a gas leak but it was evident the building had been hit with artillery. Inside were seas of broken glass, a desk blown into the hall, plaster dust. Sara walked through silently while Timothy snapped photos. She wasn't sure what she was doing here. She was a tourist, she supposed.

"Take a look at this," the Brit called.

She found him in a blasted room of scattered clothing. Coats, pants, underwear. A black bra, twisted so that cups formed a sine curve.

"You writing about this?" he asked.

"Maybe."

"Just keep my name out of it if you would. I'm not supposed to be freelancing."

On the floor was a Snoopy toothbrush.

Outside, kids in puffy jackets rollerbladed by.

"Police," the Brit called eventually. "Just pulled up. We should probably be, you know."

Sara and Timothy wound up buying benzodiazepines at a teahouse from a green-haired girl and her boyfriend, swallowed two pills each with their verbena, and walked back to the hotel. She didn't want to touch Timothy but then, when she finally did, realized it was exactly what she wanted. Human warmth, the tensile friction of his hands beneath her clothes. His slim body howling above the fork of her legs. She woke sometime later to the dim awareness of someone else in the room, some flare of confusion that steadied into recognition. Timothy was in the corner with the green-haired girl and the man from the teahouse, shooting up.

When she woke again he was crying, both hands wrapped around his lower leg.

"I found their menu," he said.

There was no one else in the room.

"What?"

"Tomorrow's meal," he said, "at the hospital or the asylum or whatever it was."

"What happened to your leg?"

"Or the next day's meal or whatever. They were having beef."

"Let me see."

He had heated a coat hanger and burned a three-inch curve into the meat of his right calf.

"I can't translate it," he said, and held a stiff card out at her. "Can you read this?"

"Let me see your leg."

"I recognize the word *beef*."

The flesh was white and puffy and hot to the touch.

"It's supposed to be an S," he said.

"Christ."

"For Sara, for you."

She was disgusted with herself. Stupid. It was all, for lack of a better word, stupid. The small joys, the pleasures—all unfathomably stupid. She found a tube of expired antibacterial cream and wrapped the whole thing in a Maxi-pad, regular absorbency. Neither said a word on the train back to Kiev.

If her life had been slipping, it had now slid, off to the side of whatever place she had once occupied. She was depressed, maybe addicted, maybe had just a little bit of a habit. But then a week later Ray Shields called and she felt everything suddenly and blessedly restored. It was like going from black-and-white to color, and she felt ridiculous to be so happy, to sway so wildly. She felt like a child, smiled upon by an adult, and hated herself for this. Hated herself, but still met him at a back table in an Italian-Japanese chain called Mafia.

"We do appreciate your patience, Sara. Things have been fluid and in some respects we've been holding back, trying to assess the situation." Shields had three entrees spread before him—chicken, sushi, some sort of pasta—but none seemed to please him. The place was loud and crowded, but not as loud and crowded as it had been a few weeks prior. Most foreign journalists were in the east preparing to cover the invasion everyone knew was coming. "But we do have a request."

There was a man named Hugh Eckhart, an employee of Leviathan. Shields had reason to believe he was looking for Sara.

"So what do you want me to do, exactly?"

"Wait for him to contact you seems to be our current position. Once he does, keep us apprised of what he's up to. It's really that simple."

"But he's working for you?"

"He is, but these things are tricky. We'd like an extra set of eyes, that's all. There's no proof he's gone off the reservation."

Shields lifted his beer but didn't drink.

"You like it here?" he asked. "I mean in this country? I'm having difficulty buying fruit. I feel like I don't know the secrets."

"This all seemed so urgent in New Haven."

"I keep getting these brown-spotted bananas. It's like eating a tiny whale shark."

Sara could feel her lips unconsciously forming the word *David*, but dared not say it.

"Look, these things." Shields twirled a finger in the air between them. "It's like the old Polaroid pictures if you ever knew those. There are stages of waiting, you might say."

"So what stage is this?"

"This is where we wave the picture back and forth, maybe stick it under our armpit if we're superstitious, which we're not. But we are waiting," Shields said. "Still there's this feeling the wait is almost over."

"You think he's gone off the reservation?"

He smiled brightly.

"It's an expression," he said. "And probably not even true."

When she got home that night she dialed the number on the post-it for the first time in weeks: no answer. She undressed, checked her email, and had no more gotten into bed when her cell rang.

"We need to meet."

"Where?"

He gave her a place and time and the next day she took an Uber to a scruffy bar called Under the Asphalt, the Beach, where she sat for two hours in a banquette, alone with a dry martini and her gathering despondency. She felt ill-used, pissed off and done with it.

She left 100 hryvnia on the table and imagined walking home in the cold as a sort of antidote, though she had no idea for what. Down through an unlighted park, raining now, the cobblestones flooded, the linden trees bare. Past the VAPE SHOP HOUSE, past the WEST BARBERSHOP, the espresso windows. Stray dogs and skateboards and the way the traffic never seemed to slow at the intersections. She could see the bus stop, the cars passing on the highway, but for all that it felt as if she was in a dark forest and she wanted it that way. She wished for the night to be blacker, colder, wished for the kind of cold that can shatter. She liked the idea of a sudden deep freeze, liked the thought that there were things that could not survive it, yet she would.

She got home and shut herself off again.

Lay on the bed with two Klonopins on the bare flesh of her stomach.

She expected nothing. But that night, her phone rang.

It was the same voice, and this time he said the name she needed to hear.

He said *David*.

IT WAS MARCH when they picked Berger up at a checkpoint a half mile from the airbase outside Lviv in Western Ukraine, two national police officers at a blue sawhorse who motioned for him to step out of the box truck he was driving. The day was wet and cold, the road, he saw, rutted by the tracks of passing vehicles. An agent from the Ministry of Internal Affairs came out from a Nysa van parked on the shoulder to offer him a cigarette.

Berger declined.

The man spoke English with a British accent.

"Any idea what this is about?" Berger asked him.

The man wore a rain suit and a skullcap on his shaved head.

"I was hoping you might tell me."

"Looks like I'm not the only one who's been through."

"You Americans," the man said.

"Singular," Berger said. "Just me."

"Well, there must be a thousand of you gents now. I was hoping perhaps you could explain it to me."

He rode in the back of the Nysa van down the road and through the front gates.

"You see them?" The agent gestured at the men wheeling back a wall of chain-link, new concertina wire along the top. Americans, rifles slung across their backs.

"Yep."

"And this means what, exactly?"

"I guess we'll find out."

He got out in front of the hangar that for the last year he had used as his command post. The place had been empty when he'd left, just Berger and a few Ukrainian nationals with their wool hats and back-braces. Now eight-wheeled Strykers sat in line by a wing of Blackhawks and a few scattered shipping containers that appeared to house commo equipment. What looked like an infantry platoon jogged by, blue guidon, PT sweats. Grain-fed American youth, shaved and scrubbed pink. Over the hangar hung the flag of the 173rd Airborne Brigade.

"Jesus Christ," Berger said.

"So you know then?" the agent asked.

"When did they get here?"

"A few days ago. I probably shouldn't say."

"You probably shouldn't."

"But you know?"

"I know absolute shit."

TWENTY MINUTES LATER Berger was seated in a room with the brigade S2, a Major with a cowlick and a scrunched face. A guard sloped in the corner, hulking with a thin mustache, his uniform sterile. Name, rank, and unit insignia removed.

"We didn't exactly expect you to just waltz in like this," the Major said.

"If I'd known you were here."

The Major nodded.

"It is sort of amazing, really. Do you realize we found probably forty javelin rockets in packing crates here?"

"Probably more like fifty."

"Fifty. Incredible. So tell me, Mr. Berger, did you set out to become an international arms dealer in violation of any number of U.S. and international laws or was this just one of those interesting turns of fate like, say, figuring out you love to rollerblade?"

"I think you know how it goes."

The man looked down at the folder in front of him.

"Well, let's see here. I see time in a Ranger Battalion. I see time with Central Intelligence. I see your severance from the Agency in 2012." He looked up. "This is your service sheet, by the way."

"Lucky you."

"What I don't see is the point at which you decided to violate the Arms Export Control Act. Section 36(b) just to cite chapter and verse. But, again, maybe that was just happenstance."

"I think you should probably send me up the chain."

"Also, ever wonder—because I'm not going to lie, I certainly find it curious as to why I just happen to have in my files—unbeknownst to me—the service sheet on a guy who separated from the U.S. government almost two years ago?"

"I think you should call your CO."

"My CO is in Eastern Ukraine. Which is where I suspect these weapons were headed."

"I didn't know you boys were coming. Otherwise."

"Otherwise, yes, you could have made arrangements."

Berger shrugged.

"Right, of course, Mr. Berger. So, is this the point I apologize for having disrupted your criminal enterprise?"

"What are you doing here, anyway?"

"What are *we* doing here? This is called NATO, Mr. Berger. This is called a treaty of mutual defense, founded in 1949. I'll spare you the acronym."

"Call your CO."

"Personally I say we let the Russians have the entire country. Twenty, twenty-five million dead. They paid for it in blood."

"From Stettin in the Baltic to Trieste in the Adriatic."

"Hey, look, I hear you. But the fact is, we showed up late. We barely showed up at all. I don't care what Tom Brokaw has to say."

"Call your boss."

"Besides the rockets, we found crates of Dragunov sniper rifles. Russian-made right down to the Cyrillic on the walnut stock. I honest to God don't even know where you'd find such short of eBay."

"Have him contact Leviathan Global."

The Major leaned back and drummed his fingers on the metal table.

"You might have just said the magic word right there."

"The New York office."

"We don't have to call, Mr. Berger. And I'll just say once more the whole of this baffles me, but Leviathan has a rep here on base. They're probably listening to us right now."

Berger nodded and the Major stood.

"Goddamn it," he said. "This is not the America I signed up for."

"I guess none of us did."

THEY PUT HIM in a walk-in pantry with a cot and an industrial sink.

"Am I under arrest?" he asked the guard who accompanied him.

"I think more like a guest of the U.S. government."

"But I imagine I'd find this door locked?"

"Yes, sir. I imagine you would."

"Are you boys Tenth Group?"

"You know I can't answer that."

"I was at Bragg for a while. I probably taught you how to put stainless steel needles under the fingernails of a non-compliant."

"I'm sure the Major will be in touch."

"I'm sure he will."

The guard came back an hour later with a plate of hot chow on a compartmented lunch tray, steaming, wet food. Gelatinous green beans and meatloaf. Dying carrots. It all came back to Berger, the dining hall at the Institute, the time at Benning and later at Bagram. All the Homer and Clausewitz they'd read, everything the Colonel had taught him. It was like a marker to measure drift, who he had intended to be, versus who he had become. He ate quickly and tried to meditate, his back against the empty shelves, his hands trembling.

He wanted the holy.

Never had he wondered why kids blew themselves up. When you're young, you want to matter, and then you realize you don't. It was a blow, but for most the saccharine bullshit sufficed. The sports and celebrity sex tapes, the happy hour drinks. Maybe it did for everyone, at least for a while. But then the self reasserted, that need to belong to something larger because the world didn't fit. At least not like the butt of a rifle, or a suicide vest.

You needed the Holy. When the sound of those Velcro straps was the only thing to speak the name of God, and God was the only thing to speak the name of the boy strapping it on—it wasn't hard to understand.

He shut his eyes. He'd been reading theology again.

You have to destroy something to release what it contains.

He was reading McGill and Bonhoeffer and Mircea Eliade. He had taken a room on the grounds of the Sviatohirsk monastery where he drank goat's milk and swam in the river. There was a sauna nearby in what had been a synagogue before the war and a kolkhoz after. Birch branches. The smell of forest rain. In between, he read his theology. In between, he ran guns east.

It was night when the guard came back for him.

"The Major give the word?" Berger asked.

"Somebody did."

The guard took him back to the room where the Major waited.

"Goddamn it," the Major said. "You aren't going to believe this. Actually, you probably are."

"You talked to Leviathan."

"I feel like someone should be taken out into a cornfield and shot."

"So they confirmed?"

"I had to get someone on the line in Brussels but make no mistake, confirm they did. Not only are you being released. Not only are you to take every bit of your weaponry with you that you can manage. It's been made clear we are to help you load it."

"It's all profit margin," Berger said.

"Is that supposed to comfort me?"

"So I'm free to go?"

"I feel like a CPA for goddamn K-Mart."

"It goes that way sometimes."

"It's motherfucking Bank of America bullshit is what it is. Yet we're still calling it democracy."

"Can I walk?"

"Yes, Mr. Berger, as of." He slipped his sleeve up onto a bare wrist. "Goddamn it, Bruce, what time is it?"

"Almost 2230, sir."

"As of almost 2230 yes, goddamn it, Mr. Berger, you can walk. I understand a truck is being loaded for you as we speak."

A DAY LATER, Berger sat at the bar of the Hotel Taler waiting for the commander of a local militia, a brewer in his previous life. Not a Leviathan contact because Berger was in the process of disappearing from Leviathan's reach.

When the man arrived, Berger followed him down the steps into the streets of Slaviask. The day was gray, the sky low, and they walked between blocks of concrete towers banked with air conditioners and window boxes of dead flowers.

The man was tall and exceptionally thin. Nikes and a denim coat.

In the square by the administrative building were pigeons and Ukrainian flags, a pay-lot renting battery-powered cars to children. Two girls rollerbladed off the asphalt and into the dirt.

They moved quickly through a street market of disemboweled chickens and the fleshless head of a cow, eyes glossy and set. Then boots and heels. Jars of honey and pressed sunflower oil—Berger had largely stopped eating. He could feel himself narrowing and this was a good thing, it signaled a return.

Once, in central Bosnia, he'd seen a man crucified to a barn, his body soaked in pitch and burned. Or at least what had appeared to be a man.

Those things, the woman at the KLM gate had said.

When they reached the highway they crossed into a park.

The man walked a step behind Berger, the grass matted and dead where a thread of trail cut its way past benches and swing-sets. In the rear of the park sat an abandoned amusement park. Carnival rides, a Ferris wheel, spinning teacups. Everything vined and rusted and stripped of copper.

Berger's van sat just beyond the bumper cars. He opened the rear doors and pried open one of the crates. The rifles were cradled in foam.

"Negevs," Berger said. "Israeli-made. Five-five-six so it won't be hard to find ammo come judgment day."

The man took the rifle.

"And how many of them?"

"Sixty here. But I can get another sixty."

The man nodded and returned the rifle.

"I can have the money transferred," he said. "But cash is harder to come by."

Berger was already sealing the crate.

"I don't want your money."

He only wanted to hurry. His hands were shaking, and he could feel His nearness.

Sara met him at a coffee house off the Maidan. It was late March, and though the square was still filled with tents and tarps, the revolution was over. She walked past the walls of tires burned to their steel cords, past the discarded shields made from plyboard and car parts. Past the memorial candles and the men in bear suits, the endless Europop. Around her, people were texting, snapping selfies in front of bullet-ridden walls. Finally, she descended into a vaulted cellar of exposed brick and mortar, a glass case of pastries with cabbage and rosehips and globs of black poppy seed.

Boy George was singing *Do you really want to hurt me? Do you really want to make me cry?*

"Sara?"

Hugh Eckhart sat straight-backed and silent, fingers knitted in his lap as if in contemplation.

"Sara?"

She realized he must have said her name more than once.

"You said David on the phone," she said. "That you knew him."

"We met once in New York."

"When?"

"Fourth of July last year it would have been."

"So you're part of them? The Covenant. The Wojtyła people."

"Did he ever call himself Dietrich around you? Or talk about a group called *différance*? This would have been in New York."

Along the upper wall was a small rectangle of window that opened onto the snow-plowed street. Sara directed her eyes there.

"Look at this," he said, and put a photograph in her lap. A man in his mid-forties, she thought, his beard flecked gray around his chin. Hair short above his ears, but longer and brushed back on top. He put her in mind of some ill-trained bear, some large animal given up on just before domestication could take hold.

She picked it up, held it closer.

"His name is Chris Berger," Eckhart said. "His job was to help foment a Russian invasion in the east. He thought he was running money and guns to a group of Ukrainian commandos through a front. Actually, they were going to pro-Russian militias." He took the photograph back from her and put it in his bag. "But now he's realized he was, let us say, rather ill-used. There are some who think he has gone what they call rogue."

"That's what someone told me about you."

"Ray Shields."

"I don't trust him either."

"You shouldn't. But he's right. About me, at least."

"Did you really know David?"

Eckhart was silent for a moment, as if measuring a possible response, and then cleared his throat, softly, if a bit theatrically. "What David discovered was that arms and money weren't just going to the Ukrainians, they were going to the Russians, too. We were gathering information. Me inside the inner sanctum, David on the ground."

"Here?"

"It didn't work in New York, so yeah, here. Donetsk. Slaviask."

"And that's why they killed him," Sara said. "Not some accident like they said, not some pimp."

"Maybe the GRU, maybe a Spetsnaz team working with Randy Garcia. But no, not some pimp."

"I don't understand what this has to do with me."

He looked at her for a long moment.

"Did I know some of these people, in New York?" she asked.

"Probably."

"So you're a spy for these Anonymous people or whoever they are? All those fools we used to sit around with talking revolution, those rich kids catfishing bankers."

"Some of them grew up."

"They were mostly stoned. A bunch of hackers on Adderall."

"They grew up, some of them."

Sara sat for a moment.

"But even if you knew David," she said, "why would I help you?"

"Because you loved him," he said, "and this is what love is, Sara. This is what it looks like."

"What it looks like? Are you making fun of me?"

"God will not—listen to me."

"You are."

"God will not have his work made manifest by cowards."

"You're making fun of me."

He said nothing and she sat waiting for an answer.

"So what do you want?" she asked when it became clear no answer was coming.

"I want you to go Bratislava, to the embassy there. There's a dossier called FIREBIRD, a file that outlines all of Leviathan's holdings. They're negotiating shale gas concessions, so somewhere everything has been drawn up, asset disclosures, contracts. It's what we couldn't get in New York. You get that to me and I pass it along." He took an envelope from his bag and gave it to her. "Take this with you."

Inside was another phone number, another sheaf of euros—it was just like before, another favor, another something besides what she wanted. She reached beneath the money and found an application for domestic work with a staffing agency at the U.S. embassy in Bratislava. The ambassador's wife, a woman named Susan Logan, had requested a personal assistant. Below the request was an EU residency card and resume that identified Sara as Erin Horváthová, a Slovak-American with dual citizenship, fluent in three languages and in need of employment.

"They were watching you for a while," he said. "They thought I'd come looking for you."

"You did."

"I did, but I waited till they'd lost interest."

"But I still don't understand why me?"

"Because you're exactly what she's looking for," he said. "Not hired help so much as a substitute daughter."

Sara picked up the residency card. The photograph appeared to have been taken with a telephoto lens the night of Colonel Venclova's wake. Erin Horváthová. A woman in need of employment, in need of purpose.

A favor, she thought.

That's what everyone calls it.

RICK MILES GOT so loaded that by the time he landed in Havana he didn't know what planet he was on, let alone what country he was in. The flight originated in Kiev with a refueling stop at Lajes Field in the Azores, a Leviathan Gulfstream G650 with a substantial mini-bar Miles had nearly emptied by the time he landed at Jose Marti.

Still, he managed to pass through customs and out to the crush of taxis and families where he stood for a moment in the warm air, beneath the blue sky, and tried to get his shit together. It wasn't easy. People were grabbing at him, palm trees were swaying, and when the wind picked up he could hear the dead fronds scrape across the parking lot like rakes.

He needed to breathe.

That four-count shit he'd learned years ago from Berger.

Slow breathing lowers cortisol levels, brings clarity of thought.

Clarity of thought made his medicine strong. Except there was no clarity of thought. What there were, were people, and they were all around him. He was fending them off—*don't need no taxi, man, no girls, no drugs, get on, asshole, don't need shit from you*—pushing his way through the crowd. But when Ray Shields touched his elbow he was suddenly becalmed. They got in Shields's Peugeot, a car Miles found disappointingly plain, and took Este-Oeste toward the city, bumping over storm grates.

"Mr. Garcia is pleased you're here," Shields told him.

"Who?"

"Randy Garcia. The man whose plane you rode."

"Okay."

"The man whose liquor you just drank," Shields said.

"Yeah. I got it."

They passed fields of trash. Beyond them cathedrals. Schoolgirls in plaid skirts. Kids playing baseball by a tethered goat. Miles had a Makarov pistol on his lap and was mindlessly taking it apart and putting it back together. Inserting the barrel into the slide. Flipping the slide-stop lever. When the slide snapped into place, he popped in the magazine, released it, and started over again.

"You probably shouldn't have that out," Shields said.

"Yeah," he said, and slipped it back into the waistband of his jeans. "Walked right through customs with it, but whatever, it's cool."

"If you walked in with that thing you can thank Mr. Garcia."

"Well, obviously I did."

"Then you can thank Mr. Garcia."

"Maybe I will."

Randy Garcia was the man who had sent the invitation. That Garcia was strung high on the great chain of being was clear. That things were off balance was equally evident. Miles suspected this had something to do with Berger's erratic behavior, that he owed the trip to the sudden emergence of Berger's can't-do attitude. The boss had been off his game of late, disappearing for long stretches into the eastern region of the country, living in a monastery and fasting. It was almost like he'd lost his nerve which was a hell of a thing to lose. But Miles had seen him play it that way before. False sense of security—that would be the state Berger sought to lure others toward. Then he would zap you. It belonged in the hierarchy of instinct. Rattlesnakes do the same thing.

"Chris Berger," Shields said, because obviously he had some of sort of mind-reading software emanating from the cell phone planted on his thigh.

"He don't know."

"You had no trouble getting away unnoticed?"

"Berger don't know fuck all about me and mine. He's out living with a bunch of peacocks these days."

"Is that a euphemism?"

"No, man. It's a bird."

Berger had been Miles's company commander in the 3-75th Rangers until Miles was drummed out on some bullshit charges having to do with selling U.S. property to U.S. civilians, chiefly night vision goggles and a crate of M4 rifles to a redneck militia in the mountains of North Georgia. That it was bullshit didn't mean it wasn't true. But Berger had stood by him through the court martial, and when he later went to work for Leviathan saw to it that Miles was brought into the fold.

Miles fixed Shields with a stare.

"What?" Shields wanted to know.

"You got you a haircut."

"You don't know me."

"I liked it better long." Miles shrugged. "That's all I'm saying."

They stopped at a house on Avenida 23 and Miles dropped his bag in an austere room of bed and nightstand, desk but no chair. It did have a lizard, a frill-necked thing that hung inverted from a corner of the ceiling, a little dinosaur son of a bitch, unmoving even when Miles sang to it first the national anthem and then "God Bless America."

"All right then," he told the lizard. "Be that way, you sorry bastard."

He was wearing Diesel jeans and a Hawaiian shirt, good Ariat boots, the Makarov still tucked in his waistband when he came back to the street where Shields waited behind the wheel.

"You're a squirrely motherfucker, aren't you?" Miles asked.

"I see you dressed to impress."

"Where we headed, boss?"

"To see Mr. Garcia."

"Naturally."

They parked behind a four-story wedding cake of a mansion with a small American flag discretely signaling some sort of official U.S. presence. A party was happening on the roof and two men with high-and-tights and matching blue suits came out to frisk Miles. This was private muscle which signaled private money, despite the government associations. They took the pistol but told him he'd get it back, just be cool, and he was. But when one man spoke into his mic, Miles started singing again, the logic being just because some Cuban lizard don't appreciate don't mean others won't.

"Are you with State?" one of the men asked.

"No, man," Miles said, "I ain't with no State."

He wasn't with no Brickell bank neither, nor any of the trade groups looking to put a manufacturing hub in the countryside or a series of cell towers around the city. Don't speak the patois of offshore drilling neither if that's your next question.

The man looked at him.

"Shit," said Miles. "You think I'm joking?"

He wasn't no missionary, no Baptist in hip-boots. He wasn't here to clear mangroves and break down the gospels in a third language. Ain't no sociologist on a Fulbright nor doctor on loan from *Médecins Sans Frontières*. He's just here, brother, happy, singing. Man just likes to sing. Man loves his country is all.

"Ain't a man allowed to be a patriot no more?" he asked.

One of the men looked at Shields.

Ray Shields shrugged.

"Come on, then."

They took the elevator where Miles started giggling. Shields nudged him, but like a good island rain, once it settled in there was nothing to be done but wait for it to stop. He collected himself in the hallway and was led into a room of rattan and glass that looked out onto the rooftop party where people clustered along the rail, the sun not yet set over the Malecon. Three narrow dogs slinked between long bare legs. Everywhere suits and open-backed dresses cut to there.

He knew them even if he didn't, the Boston bond lawyers and Manhattan financiers wearing their guayaberas and looking wistfully at the water. Imagining some romantic past in which they fought for human rights instead of being born the grandson of the governor of Connecticut. Marching out of the Sierra Maestra with their donkeys and dreams instead of out of Harvard Law with their J.D.s and simple greed. A different life. Sending their young to fight in Angola while they cut cane in the fields.

"Who those motherfuckers?" he asked.

"Mr. Garcia's guests," Shields said.

Miles looked out between the potted palms and the slender women moving giraffe-like around their ancient husbands. Framed between the resort hotels spread a horizon of sea and sky. It was a sight. It was a party—it was twenty or so people on the terrazzo tile staring over the rooftops of Avenida 17 out toward the darkening sea while a half dozen Cuban servers weaved between them delivering glasses of rum—and he wasn't invited, but that's cool. It is what it is, right? Quoting either Confucius or Donald Rumsfeld.

A few minutes later Randy Garcia lumbered in ahead of his cortege wearing chinos and a golf shirt from Mandalay Bay. On his feet were the kind of Velcro tennis shoes meant for the infirm. On his face was a drooping oatmeal-colored mustache meant for the O.K. Corral. One of the dogs was beside him.

"Rick Miles." He offered a meaty hand. "Good of you to come."

"Yes, sir," Miles said. "Absolutely."

Garcia stared at him a moment and then began introducing people. Ray Shields from Leviathan—you've already met Ray. Two sweaty Cubans with bad skin and corduroy suits. Another name Miles didn't catch though he had the distinct feeling the man was Israeli, having, as he did, that Mossad shine.

"Let's have us a talk," Garcia said, "me and you."

They sat on the rear balcony in the fragrant evening air. Just the two of them, the party no more than distant noise. Miles could see the parking lot with Shields's car and past that a swimming pool where a woman swam laps. Something in it made him start to giggle again.

"Hell, son," Garcia said. "You're drunk as a lord."

"Roger that."

"Public goddamn inebriation, this is your position?"

"It appears to be, yes, sir."

"Well, I hate to see a man suffer alone." He tapped the glass and out came a bottle of whiskey, ice, and two glasses. He poured for Miles and poured for himself. Laughter came from the party.

"You know what they're here for?" Garcia asked.

"A good base tan?"

"You're funny as shit. Which—let me say—it's a little surprising seeing as how I heard you were vicious in Afghanistan."

"I take the fifth regarding all things Asia Minor."

"A silver star in Helmand as I recall."

"Long time ago, sir."

"No need to be modest. You were a patriot. Now those fuckers out there, they're nothing but grabbers. The telecom companies, the Miami banks. But here they've all come down with the same revolutionary fever. They want a print of Che for their boy's bedroom. A beret for the daughter up at Brearley. As soon as the Castros kick off they'll come charging in and turn the whole island into *Pirates of the Caribbean*."

"And you'll be here."

"You're right about that."

"Waiting to run train on every last one of them sons of bitches."

Garcia looked thoughtfully into his glass.

"You're goddamn right about that."

Down below the woman glided under the surface of the pool, around her floodlights and the pink stucco of the hotel, bougainvillea climbing ladders of trellis, the walls vined magnificently. Watching her, Miles thought of home in Tennessee. The church suppers and car trips to see the shut-ins, the homebound, the unchurched. The way his uncle toppled in the aisle, slain in the spirit.

"Hold on," Garcia said, and slid open the glass door. Out came one of the dogs, a lean bottle-nosed thing that rubbed its face against his thigh. "Francesca," he said, "my best girl. You like dogs?"

"Every man likes dogs."

"Not every man."

"Then he ain't no man," said Miles. "Quoting my daddy."

"Sounds like a wise fella."

"He was an asshole and a drunk, but otherwise tolerable."

Garcia rubbed beneath the dog's muzzle while it eased down to lie at his feet.

"We've had a fuckup, son," he said finally. "Though I guessed you'd figured as much, coming all this way. We're looking to you to make it right."

"Yes, sir."

"You didn't know Colonel Venclova, I guess? A good man, a friend. But he led a lot of folks astray. Got a boy killed in Ukraine which sort of just set the shit all in motion. Your boss, Chris Berger, he came highly recommended to me, but now I hear he's disappeared. You know anything about this?"

"He's out in the east somewhere," Miles said, "praying."

"What about you, you praying?"

"I'm doing what I'm told."

Garcia nodded.

"Hugh Eckhart is finished. I've let him run a while out of affection, I guess. Thought he was harmless. But now I hear your old boss has been chatting with him."

"Is Berger off the team, sir?"

"I don't know. This is complicated shit and got more complicated the day that boy bought it in Slaviask."

"Yes, sir."

"Berger was supposed to deliver a load of Negev rifles but he never showed. Just up and disappeared with a mess of hardware. I can't tolerate that sort of sloppiness, not with these Russians involved."

"Roger that."

"These Russians—you know what they're doing right now? They're sleeping in the snow."

"I hear you."

"Living off tree bark just because."

"Getting hard."

"Getting hard in a way Americans can no longer be. Rugged, independent." Garcia shook his head sadly. "Your boss was drifting around the District asking questions. Suddenly got himself a conscience. Suddenly got all sensitive and nuanced. I tell you, it's always complicated shit until it isn't." Garcia hefted himself out of his chair just as the woman made another turn in the pool. "So long as he shows up with those guns all is well with his world. But if he goes sideways, if you have the slightest reason to believe he's working with Eckhart."

"Yes, sir."

"You whisper in his ear, you understand?"

"I'll talk him right into paradise."

Garcia nodded slowly.

"You think you can do that, being your old boss and all?"

"I wasn't never one for no regular life expectancy."

"You know he's the one wrote you the citation for that star?"

Miles touched the sachet around his neck.

"I'll put him in my magic bag."

"Use the girl if you need to," Garcia said. "You know who I'm talking about, the Colonel's granddaughter? She hasn't found you yet?"

"Not yet."

"She will, rest assured she will." He nodded toward the party. "And she's damn capable, make no mistake. Just don't trust her, and remember you work for me."

Garcia stood a little uneasily and looked at him for a long moment. The dog stood beside him. When Miles reached to pet it, it jerked back its tapered head.

"I don't think she likes me," Miles said.

"Usually she's a good judge of character."

"I'm strictly proletariat. She's pure-bred, ain't it?"

"One hundred percent borzoi."

Miles nodded knowingly.

"Yeah, I reckon my blood ain't blue enough."

Ray Shields waited by the elevator.

"Have a nice chat with Randy, did you?"

"I'd say we're pretty much asshole buddies at this point."

Shields smirked.

"So what did he say?"

"Only that he's sending me on the hajj."

"You got that great green light, did you?"

"All the *federales* at my beck and call."

SARA WAS BACK on the street, Sara who was also Erin, walking too fast, because maybe someone was behind her. Someone from Leviathan, someone from the embassy. It was just after noon and a soft rain was blowing off the river, so fine a mist she thought at times she imagined it. Not that it mattered.

She had the FIREBIRD dossier in the liner of her coat, the pages flat in a brown envelope, and was on her way to the drop. She had already circled it three times—a pedestrian underpass in a park by an abandoned petting zoo overgrown in brambles, its *Finding Nemo* merry-go-round fish-scaled and tipped beyond hope. She was headed back now. She would leave the dossier behind a girder and make her circuitous way to the hotel where Hugh Eckhart would meet her later that day.

She hadn't intended for it to happen so quickly.

Only a few hours ago she'd been in her room at the ambassador's residence, an attic garret that looked out over the houses that stair-stepped down the slope, ending eventually in the high-rise hotels and green parks of Bratislava. She had been lying on top of the duvet when Susan Logan knocked because Susan Logan was always contriving reasons to knock.

"Erin? Are you up, darling?" This on Erin's single day off. "I'm going soon, darling. Are you awake? I'm sorry to bother you, I'm just having a time with the espresso machine again." Then she would catch herself, as if swamped by a wave equal parts grief and shame. "I'll be downstairs."

Her crushing neediness stunned Sara. This woman's loneliness so powerful it overwhelmed her better judgment so that there was Susan Logan, stately, wealthy, attractive Susan Logan prodding the espresso machine when Erin entered the kitchen.

"There you are," Susan said, voice awash in gratitude. "I'm so sorry to wake you, but this thing…my God. For something that cost as much as it did you'd think…Can you?"

She could, and a moment later a thin, aromatic stream began to fall into the porcelain cup.

Susan rolled her eyes and smiled.

"I'm a fool."

"It's tricky sometimes."

"I've only had this thing for a year. What are your plans today, darling?"

Sara had shaken her head meekly, an expression meant to convey self-doubt, but anything approaching doubt was gone.

"I'm sorry to have woken you."

"It's okay. I was up."

"I know it's your day off."

"I'm glad to be of help."

Susan Logan smiled again. She was dressed in a skirt and blouse, something soft and expensive. Her hair coiffed, her earrings small and discrete. Off shortly to shop. Off shortly to sleep with Liam Davies.

Susan put the cup in the sink and patted Sara's shoulder, allowed her hand to rest a moment longer than it should. Allowed for contact, allowed for warmth. Her eyes were moist, not wet. She wasn't exactly crying.

"I'll see you later today." Her voice on the edge of breaking. "Thank you again."

It was that *later today* that put Sara in motion: the certainty of seeing Susan Logan, the certainty of knowing she couldn't bear it.

Now, she was on the street, winding back toward the drop sight. It would be over then, for her at least. That was what she'd decided, that was the deal she had made with herself: drop the file and get out, go—not home, go…she had no idea where.

Syria?

Palestine?

It didn't matter.

She was along the river, the wind ticking through the linden trees that were just beginning to leaf. Around her men and women pushed giant strollers and talked into earpieces. The thirty-something programmers and designers. The men with trim beards and pointed shoes. The tattoos of the women tasteful and obscured by bright scarves.

It was possible someone was behind her, but she didn't think so. Still, she couldn't bring herself to slow down. She was walking too fast. Face cold, lips chapped. Her nostrils were raw yet—*Jesus, Sara, slow down.* She was near the intersection, could see the hotel's gray stone, its vined ivy extending into fog and disbelief, could see the park behind it, snow swept and browning.

The hotel was safety.

The hotel was a different, future life.

Slow down.

She turned east on Spitalska, south again toward Medena, unnecessary turns but she was scared. The Russians she'd seen at the Eurovea Mall and again outside the Hotel Bratislava. They were following Susan Logan, she guessed, but that didn't mean that weren't also following her.

Slow down, Sara. There's no one back there.

The river bent and the castle was to her left now, the ocher towers visible through the airy fog. Jesenskeho Street ahead. Jangling trams and wet cobblestones. You look up at the tangle of electrified lines, except don't look up.

Keep moving, slowly, calmly.

She was ten blocks from the drop sight.

If there was someone behind her she wasn't aware of it.

But honestly, there's no one back there.

Six blocks. Around her storefronts and restaurants and down near the national theater a copper Christ gone green with oxidation. The Ritz Carlton. Pizzeria Bella Napoli.

Walking fast now. Four blocks to the drop.

Please, Lord, don't let them be back there.

But it seemed like they had to be, if only because it had been so easy, entering the ambassador's office with the swipe badge taken from the bedroom, opening the safe with the combination taken from the tablet left lying beside the bed.

Then she was back on the street, walking great circles just as she had been told. The drop was just ahead, beyond that a maze of warehouses and railroad lines paralleling the Danube. The shells of unfinished buildings, concrete and rebar and a murdered dog, stuffed into a drainage pipe. Gantry cranes offloading barges carrying Chinese everything.

She moved beneath an underpass of lichen and damp concrete, and only then did she look back. There was no one there and she prayed, or meant to pray, a quick word of thanks.

Then she was walking again, the folder tucked into a girder behind the embankment. She walked faster, felt herself lift off the sidewalk. It had been that way in Kiev, swimming in the Marriott pool. The walls of her flat breathing blue.

That lift.

That buoyant lift.

It took another half hour to walk to the Carlton where she sat in the hotel bar and tried to collect herself. She had a key for a room on the fourteenth floor, but she had moved so quickly there felt some danger in going straight up, as if she might leave behind the self tailed behind her like the train of a dress.

She asked for a glass of red. Around the room stood antique carousel horses said to have been commissioned by Franz Joseph and carried east from Vienna. Behind them flat-screens played on mute, text blocked along the bottom. Hovering in the high corners was music, piped quietly as if from another room. Mahler's Symphony No. 2 in C Minor.

The piece, she remembered, was called "Resurrection."

She had a second glass, calmer now, and a little after three took the elevator up.

In the room, she took off her heels and rubbed the puckers of pinched skin that roped her ankles, called room service to order a bottle of Dom Perignon. There was something celebratory about it all, the finished nature of things, and when the cart arrived, she drew a bath and soaked until the water cooled.

More hot water, more soaking.

She had spent a week in Kiev with Hugh Eckhart. Hot showers and good food, bottles of Pinotage, bowls of borscht. The strappy indentations on her heels. She couldn't quite remember what had happened, only that something had, though not *to* her exactly. Around her, maybe. She had dyed her hair blue, a *weaponized* blue, as she thought of it. An *impervious* blue. Something to protect her, though she didn't know from who or what.

She did know she didn't love him.

She reached for the champagne.

She didn't think she loved him, at least. But when you're lonely enough, and together that loneliness is assuaged—might that not be a working definition of love? If the loneliness is deep enough, and the love tenuous enough, might not that be enough?

Three, perhaps four glasses, a bubbly lightness while she toweled off and donned the hotel robe, put David's book beside the bed, David's Bonhoeffer.

Four-thirty now, almost five.

Hugh was late.

She'd gone dark since signaling him that morning, but now she checked her phone—there were no messages on WhatsApp. Nothing in the encrypted email account. Still, she didn't worry. In twenty-four hours she would be on a plane to she didn't know where, only that she would have done what she set out to do.

She stood at the window, prayerful, but not quite praying.

Outside the city was blanketed by a low ceiling of clouds, gray and ponderous.

She didn't love this man. She didn't think she loved him. But she had been lonely for a long time, and there by the window her loneliness came to her, its realness, its nearness. She pressed first her face and then her entire body to the glass, stamped herself against a skyline of high rises, the dish cities with their flags of drying bed sheets and drooping clotheslines. Evidence of other lives. But only the damp imprint of her shape to record hers.

She was thinking of this when the door opened.
Hugh, she started to say—
Only it wasn't Hugh.

BERGER WAS IN his shabby room on the grounds of the monastery outside the city of Donetsk in Eastern Ukraine when Eckhart found him. Late April and the town, once a husk of the dead coal industry, was now animated with tents and men in fatigues, unshaven and drunk. Ukrainian and Right Sector flags strung like pennants.

Berger sat in an airless upstairs room piled with what appeared as discarded camping equipment. Metal canteen cups. Little butane stoves with fold-out legs. Citronella candles and sleeping bags thick with the leafy funk of too many nights sleeping on the ground. There were boxes of Celox gauze and IV bags of Cefazolin, all of it strewn about. The rifles had mostly been handed out to local commanders, but he had kept a few, and they were here, too.

It was a mess. But there was a way this was preferable, the way the unfinished kept complacency at bay. Wall studs and exposed wiring. A man left to drift in a part of the world that wasn't his own. The technicolor of away versus the black and white of home. There were any number of clichés available. How it was easier to be a stranger in a strange land than a stranger at home.

Alone, he tended to things just as he once had as first a cadet and later a soldier. Swabbing the interior of a belt buckle with a Q-tip and Brasso. Correcting the gig line. At attention with your thumbs aligned smartly along the seams of your trousers. It reduced back to these things, the habits, the routines, and how without them it was all drift. A man with his goat's milk and river, a man with his guns. This was how sainthood began, the duties, the daily offices. This was how you sketched the cartography of sacrifice.

"I've been waiting on you," Berger said.

Eckhart smiled, a leather messenger bag slung over his shoulder. "Why don't we go talk someplace else?"

Alone, it had eventually come to Berger what it was the Colonel had been teaching him at the Institute. The whole man. The spiritual, the intellectual, the physical. It was how to die well. That was all. But was also enough, this thing barely regarded in the twenty-first century.

They walked outside. Everywhere peacocks. House sparrows in the trees.

The day was gray, the sun a white disc somewhere overhead.

"Shall we?" Berger asked.

The fields were greening, but still it was cold. A heatless glare on the buildings. Tramlines but no tram. The old wrapped in blankets over shawls over coats, heads down. Along the street were children in soccer jerseys, the occasional woman with her nude lipstick and mobile phone, six-foot-one with cheekbones, strolling as if she had just stepped from the car of a Moscow oligarch.

Berger drove them past abandoned coal yards, through the checkpoints marked DONBASS BATTALION, and into the countryside, the van retrofitted with metal plates and a band of gold tape marking them as friendlies.

"When's the last time you saw Rick Miles?" Eckhart asked.

"What is it you're here for, Hugh?"

"What is it I'm here for?" They were driving past ragged hedgerows, houses like garden sheds. Heavy trucks with the launch tubes for Grad rockets mounted in the back. "Everything I said would happen happened, did it not?"

"Instability."

"You're goddamn right instability."

Men sat on stoops or congregated beneath overpasses, volunteer battalions drinking beer and waiting on the war. Berger was meditating again. He could feel himself narrowing, growing thinner, the thing that had begun in that sand hovel, suspended by his hands. The whisper that's left when everything else is gone. Nothing twitching but his nerve-damaged wrists.

"So I guess the question is," Eckhart said, "what are *you* doing here?"

"I came here to die."

"To die? Do you have any idea what you sound like?"

The countryside was flat and bleak, the road lined with ditches filled with snowmelt. A technical school, red brick façade and turquoise windows—a gift from Stalin. They stopped at another checkpoint of barbed and sand bags. Ukrainian soldiers were feeding kindling into a burn barrel while down in the forest artillery and fighting vehicles sat in hardened bunkers.

Hugh Eckhart's hair was coming out in clumps.

"You sound like some third-rate action hero in case you've lost all self-awareness," he said. "I saw Rick Miles in Cuba."

"Rick's in Donetsk."

"Strange then that I saw him having a little pow-wow with Randy Garcia. Guess who else was there?"

The thing about the Institute, it wasn't that nothing had frightened him after his time there. It was that nothing had surprised him. He'd been seventeen and impossibly naïve, rolling out of the squad bay to stand inspection, the brass on his belt buckle, the Kiwi polish on his shoes. You Heel-N-Soled your belt until it was disco fever. Berger had loved it, the precision. The hairless patches on his legs from the shirt-tuck stays. No one had a shirt-tuck like him. The creases. The Scotchgard on the collar. It was a moral thing, like good posture, the way his shirt never wrinkled.

It made sense, such order.

It was the violence that had confused him. How it came with neither notice nor logic. Seventeen and struck repeatedly with a dowel rod so that little red slashes marked the back of his thighs and calves. The gut-punches. The toe in the ribs while panting in the front-leaning-rest. What a gift they'd given him, introducing him to pain while his mind was still supple.

He looked at Hugh Eckhart. What did Eckhart know of violence? Nothing, Berger suspected. The guy with the stammer and the .38 outside the bodega at two am. The drunk staggering into the superette round midnight with a stolen Beretta and a Phillies Blunt. Ridiculous. Violence as internet meme. Violence as surveillance footage on the NBC affiliate. The kid on the LIRR with a paring knife and bad eye? It never touched him. It was child's play, the thrown shadow of suffering. If he had seen an angel, Berger figured he must have conjured it. Or else it was the devil.

Ahead was an old Soviet graveyard where people sat beneath a wooden awning made to look like an old-fashioned well, shingled and quaint. They turned by the gate.

"Rachel Venclova," Eckhart said.

"She thinks Garcia poisoned the Colonel."

"Would that surprise you?"

Berger parked the van and they stepped out onto the gravel.

It wouldn't have surprised him. Surprise seemed a quaint thing he couldn't quite recall, something simple and foolish. But then he'd always been a simple fool.

"They're all turning on each other. That little raid, that little ambush," Eckhart said. "David Lazar was working with us and the Russians found out."

"What about the Colonel?"

"This was always Garcia's show. You really think he'd let the Colonel hang around for it?"

"Fuck you."

Eckhart shrugged. "What were you like as a boy, Chris? Because me, I was in church all the time, praying, studying scripture, singing hymns, all those great old-time gospel favorites. Homeschooled. You might not have known that about me."

"I know you had a vision," Berger said.

"What?"

"I heard something once."

"You didn't hear shit."

"Something about an angel."

Eckhart slung his bag over his shoulder, looked at Berger, and walked into the headstones. Carved faces and crucified saviors. The occasional Orthodox cross. A jumbled mess of impossible density. Statues, plinths, beech trees. A giant plaster-flecked Smurfette.

"You remember I said I needed someone inside, a woman," Eckhart said finally. "Well, I found someone. Sara Kovács. David Lazar's girlfriend. Look at this." He took a German passport from his bag. The name read Dietrich Schmidt but the photograph was of Hugh. "I made it for David. It was sort of a joke—Dietrich. He died before he could use it."

"Now you're using it. Just like you're using his wife."

"She wasn't his wife," Eckhart said. "She wasn't hard to convince, either."

"I should shoot you."

"She's gone missing, Chris."

Eckhart shrugged a second time and eventually Berger took out his pistol, the same Glock he'd used to shoot the man that day with David Lazar. It seemed an exhausted gesture, but no less necessary.

"She was in Bratislava," Eckhart said. "She got the dossier and made the drop. But she wasn't at the hotel. I was supposed to meet her for the extraction. She's a good person. I sort of tricked her into helping, but really I didn't. She did it because she's a good human being."

"What happened to her?"

"Put the safety on."

"I don't think it has one."

"Put the safety on and quit messing around, all right?"

"What happened to her?"

"All right," Eckhart said. "Then don't. I've prayed about it. Actually got down on my knees and took it to the Lord. Didn't think I was even capable of it anymore, but there I was. So fine, pull the trigger if that's what you have to do, but promise me first you'll go to Bratislava and find her."

"Otherwise there's more innocent blood on your hands."

"Look at this, all right?" He took a file folder from his bag. "Imagine it splashed all over the internet, no different than WikiLeaks or the Pentagon Papers."

"What's in it?"

"Everything. All Leviathan holds, all they've done. The stake in Rosneft. The fund that was buying the guns you've been hauling. We have the account numbers. We have everything."

"Including the girl's blood on your hands."

"Our hands."

"I should shoot you."

"Don't act like you aren't a part of this."

Berger pushed the barrel closer to Eckhart's face.

"Standing here right now, I should shoot you and be done with it."

"You should do a lot of things, I guess."

But Berger felt too tired for any of them, and when he lowered the pistol Eckhart touched his arm as if to console him.

FROM THE BALCONY Rachel Venclova watched Rick Miles go meandering down the sidewalk, his movement half-drunken stagger, half-arrogant tilt. She put her drink—Coca-Cola and Club Habana, a strawberry frozen into the ice cube—on one of the wrought-iron tables and a moment later was on the street following him, walking first toward the headstones and angels of Cemeterio Colon and then back toward the ghettoes of San Rafael. He was weaving, drunk and likely lost, but she kept her distance all the same, patient.

The path was littered with confetti fallen from the effigies of the morning's parade, Raul and Fidel, but also Obama, who, everyone knew, would be arriving soon. If not this week then the next, or the next still. It was why they were here, the people on the roof. Because Obama was coming and what he was bringing with him was the free market. It was why Randy Garcia was here, too. Not that it would help the Cubans, and not that Rachel Venclova cared.

Money was no consolation. Her grandfather had been wealthy, but it was clear that the trauma of the Colonel's life had stayed with him. He had coped by turning inward, toward God, straining to hear the wingbeat of angels, which was, as Rachel understood it, nothing more than the sound of his own heart. Rachel's faith lay with a different god. She believed in power. She believed that if not justice at least authority came from the barrel of a gun. This was the

God of Job, of Moses, of plagues and boils and dead children. The world belonged not to the weak, but to the well-armed.

If you wanted to shit on someone's bed, you'd damn well better bring firepower.

When the parade had passed her hotel that morning, she'd slipped into the crowd to march with them, women mostly, up Avenida 23, along the sidewalks and through the margins of the parks, past the banyan trees and the teenagers leaned against hotel fences, arms tangled through the wrought-iron as they tried to steal Wi-Fi.

Bus stations behind churches.

Children swimming in municipal pools.

Everyone barefoot and fever-blistered, everyone happy.

She didn't know the march's purpose, something about lost sons, the disappeared or maybe the forgotten. The reason wasn't clear. Only that they had chanted and prayed, the effigies at the front, papier-mâché gods shedding glitter and paint, the women behind, palms raised, empty but for the rosaries they rubbed. The boys had disappeared in the way that boys always did, which was to say no particular way at all.

She'd been on the island for three days. Her intention had been to buy a gun off the street and shoot Randy Garcia through his robot heart. But when she learned of Rick Miles's coming she had a better idea. Still, she wanted to see the man, and she had.

Their meeting was infuriating. Garcia had already given her a severance of two-hundred K, and when she reappeared he treated her like something unusually pathetic, a little lost lamb, the grand-daughter of dear dead Colonel Venclova. Garcia's study was lined with expensive leather-bound books, prints of old maps on sandy parchment. The curtains damask and the wood teak. A shiny Schomacker baby grand. On the mantle was a photograph of Randy Garcia and her grandfather, the men flanking Jeane Kirkpatrick at the National Press Club sometime in the late eighties.

There was a bed for each of the three dogs.

She had waited dutifully in the foyer until summoned. When Garcia kissed her cheeks, she blushed on command. It had taken her years to perfect the act but now it was as automatic as breathing, a crack of electricity through the central nervous system, a little swelling of the facial capillaries. It had its uses.

"I'm proud of you, Rachel. Honest to God I am. I was just telling Julia we should have had you down months ago. But then when Tomas…"

"Yes."

"I'm sorry this invitation is so late in coming."

"Your willingness to see me now—"

Garcia laid one meaty palm over his heart, a gesture so delicate Rachel was almost fooled into believing its sincerity. As if Garcia's grief was ultimately bigger than the frozen heart that contained it. As if the act of poisoning his old friend was a misunderstood blessing. "I've done nothing, my dear. Nothing any man wouldn't do given my place."

"What you did for my parents," she said, "for my grandfather."

"Your grandfather." There was something like reverence in his voice. "Truly, I loved that man."

"And he you."

They were bound by history, yet sitting there in Garcia's study she could tell it meant little more to him than the cocktail party anecdote he could wring from it, and the lives of the Venclovas had long since been twisted dry. In seeing her, Garcia was doing nothing more than keeping his enemies close.

"Are you going back to school, Rachel?"

She wasn't going back to school. Her plan was simple: she would do whatever was necessary to earn Garcia's trust, and then, at the last moment, she would destroy him. Chris Berger had refused her offer and in doing so betrayed her grandfather's memory. She suspected Rick Miles would not. And then there were always the Russians. She'd already been in contact with the ex-GRU, ex-Spetsnaz men who had worked for Garcia but now worked for her. It was a simple act of wiring the money Garcia had given her, handing it over to perhaps the same men who had dosed her grandfather with the fairy dust that had shut down his organs. They were looking for the woman who had disappeared, the assistant to the ambassador's wife. They were looking for Hugh Eckhart. More importantly, they were preparing for the meeting at the Hotel Bratislava.

She smiled, but there must have been something defiant in her eyes, something that made clear what she knew, because on her way out of his study Garcia grabbed her arm rougher than she expected.

"We're on the right side of history," he told her. "Don't you forget that."

She was headed to the kitchen door when his wife invited her back for the cocktail party the following evening.

SHE WAS PAST the Avenidas de los Presidentes when someone called to her in English, a man's voice, the accent a faded southern. The old imperialist having spent too much time in the Greater Levant or Okinawa or, as the case stood, eastern Ukraine.

"Hey, gurl. Wait up."

She turned to see Rick Miles coming behind her like she had lost him or maybe he had doubled back on her, which was exactly the case.

"Might as well just walk together if you're going to do such a shitty job of following me," he said.

"You have any idea where you're going?"

"Do you?"

They started walking again, but slower this time, past the old women selling beads and scarves. The cabs sliding by were all vintage, Edsels or Stylelines, tricked out with running lights and handsome drivers.

"I could probably stand a drink," he said.

It was full dark, the street calm but for the rustling of dogs in the garbage. A few young men in olive uniforms carried mosquito sprayers that looked like the sort of suburban leaf blowers she'd grown up with in Hamden. They turned near the university and walked in the darkness. Hot but not oppressively so. Dry and rainless so that the palms and ficus trees appeared dusted with the same fine particulates she felt bedded in her hair and beneath her eyelids.

They got a table at a café behind the Gran Teatro and ordered Bucaneros and a bottle of Chilean red. It was all tourists here, Germans and Canadians strolling up the avenue with their well-made sandals and expensive phones.

"So you're the Colonel's granddaughter," Miles said. "I heard about you."

"My grandfather's dead."

"Got the tight jeans and crazy SAT scores."

"He was poisoned."

"Think I heard that too." He raised his beer. "Hey, you got any Tylenol or something on you? Maybe like Advil? I'm coming down off something awful."

"You look awful."

"That's pretty much what I just said."

But instead of giving him a pill she reached into her purse and loaded one acrylic nail with a bump of Colombian Gold.

"Let me tell you how this goes," she said.

"I wish you would."

"We're going back together," she said. "On your plane."

"I was just about to invite you."

"And you're going to work for me."

"All right."

"You know when Randy Garcia said you were working for him? What he meant is that you're working for me."

She was milk white, almost radiant in the darkness.

"I was just about to suggest it," he said, and bent over the table and snorted the cocaine from her hand.

They wound up back in her room, naked beneath the sheets.

He lay in bed, hands crossed behind his head while she told him about someone shitting on her parents' bed. This in Gdansk approximately one lifetime ago but it was like it was yesterday. After, he'd gone out looking for a quiet place, a cathedral or church, but everything was closed and that was a bad sign. The problem with these people, Miles thought, these Christians, was that they had lost the mystical part of their faith. You lose the mystical part and you start doing shit like going to bed early. Walking, he thought of home. The porch swings and Sunday dinners. The hand-me-down Fisher-Price toys. God and the Devil—back then everyone knew they were real. Back then, it was war.

He kept walking.

His body ached and motion helped. He'd found a mixed martial arts gym in Lviv where he went to get the shit kicked out of him. It was limitless, what he could endure. Broken fingers and floating ribs. The nail flipped off each big toe like the cap off a bottle. Burst capillaries that came in contusions of red starburst. He figured Berger had narrowed into some private death spiral, holed away with his books and prayers and guns. Miles would help him. Give him the gift of oblivion. He owed his old boss that much at least. It was reason enough to help the woman, not that he much gave a damn about reasons. His instinct was migratory. He walked until daylight and the next day was dozing on the roof, blissfully drunk and reclined in an angle of sun, when she shook him awake.

"We have to go," she said.

"What?"

She had her phone in her hand, the mesh of her chair embedded in the soft of her shoulder. "They have her."

"Who you talking about?"

"The woman, the assistant to the ambassador's wife."

"Who has her?"

When she smiled, he saw there was something hanging around her, not a shadow but dark matter. Bad energy.

"Who has her?" he asked again.

And this time she answered him.

This time, she said, "The Russians."

WANDERING CLOUD

May 2014

MARCO TORRES HAD pushed his way off the plane, through the jet-bridge, and into a hallway of descending switchbacks before it came to him what he had actually done.

Which was what exactly? Escaped? Disappeared?

Or was he simply running?

That was what he was doing now, or near enough, trotting past the windows overlooking the runway, past the bathrooms and trash-cans and a custodian in a blue jumpsuit, until below was an expanse of tiled floor and a sign that read *Welcome to Tampa International Airport*. People were beginning to mass around the luggage carou-sel, a little punchy, a little pissed off, because—and here was the way of the American world—every last person was too busy for this shit, every last person had somewhere else to be.

Including, most definitely, Representative Marco Torres, U.S. Congressman from Florida's 14th District, who, had he time to consider it, was disappearing, at least to the extent a gentlemen of the House could.

He shoved his way past the car rental counters and banks of tourist brochures out into the Gulf heat. No media, no staff. He felt like he was alone on a life raft, and for the fifth or sixth time that morning took his phone from his pocket and studied it. It was turned off, but it worried him no less. At one point he'd thought about discarding it, considered removing the battery because couldn't these things be activated remotely? At the least he should remove the SIM card, but what the hell was a SIM card and did his phone even have one?

It had a GPS, of that he was certain.

So what now, Mr. Congressman?

So get home, get what you need. Write down the necessary numbers and destroy the phone. He had wood-working equipment in his garage—a gift from his wife Vendela that he'd never cared for, but she had an eye for The Brand and years ago had commissioned some photos of him running the Skilsaw. That she never bothered to do anything with the images meant even his wife recognized how false an already false man looked. But he'd use the tools now, break the phone into component parts and run a hand drill through them. Get in the car and go.

But go where?

He had with him a small carry-on of toiletries and his laptop, the little he was able to throw together when he got back to his Arlington townhouse and found it ransacked in such sloppy fashion the message had been not so much that they were looking for something as *we were here*. Books on the floor. IKEA couch cushions razored and spilling synthetic stuffing. Everywhere a granulated dust, meant, he supposed, for fingerprints.

He hadn't paused to consider it. Instead, he'd ran, taken toothbrush and computer and summoned the good sense to have a cab take him directly to Reagan National where he just managed to catch the next direct flight south. All of it in an ill-considered rush. He might be, per *Time* magazine, one of the Republican Party's "Five Rising Stars," but that didn't mean they hadn't scared the shit out of him. The optics problems. The cable traffic and redacted memos, the mistakes-were-made—he felt it all around him.

On the curb he turned on his phone to find it twitching with texts and emails, a vibration that felt as dangerous as nearing footsteps. It would be only a matter of hours before someone came knocking, and while it might be someone from Leviathan, it might as easily be someone from the FBI or the DOJ. At this point he wasn't sure which was worse, only that in the intervening hours he had to figure out what had happened. If he could survive until tomorrow, he could meet Randy Garcia at his estate. Randy would have answers. Randy would know what the future held for Marco Torres.

As to what would happen with Marco's wife and girls—he put his hand up to flag a cab, hopped into the backseat and gave the driver an address in Pinellas Park. As to his wife and girls—his two girls, beautiful girls—well, he knew better than to let his mind wander there.

HE'D BEEN ON his way to chambers when one of his staffers bounded up the stairs to pull him aside and say his chief of staff needed to see him immediately. The boy was young and well-scrubbed with curly hair and pink ears, his chubby neck flushed with color. An obedient pup who had spent his days at Trinity arguing against Obama's birth certificate, a blow-up of Reagan on his dorm room wall. *Please, Mr. Congressman, if you can just wait absolutely right here for just like one minute.*

A moment later his chief-of-staff Bill Waters arrived to dismiss the boy and tell Marco Mr. Garcia needed to see him.

Like when?

Like now. Like I was shitless I wouldn't catch you before you went in.

That had been this morning. What seemed lifetimes ago was—he checked his watch; the cab was in St. Pete now, almost home—a mere four hours in the past.

It wasn't necessarily surprising, Randy's sudden need to see him. Garcia's web was as vast as it was longstanding. He'd began life at the U.S. embassy in Costa Rica in the early eighties back when the Sandinista were circulating their blacklists. But *voila*—everybody got out, because Randy was there. Randy was, in fact, everywhere.

In Vienna in '86.

In Berlin in '89.

In '91 he was at the Spaso House in Moscow with James Baker, and there was Gorbachev, and there was the newly elected Yeltsin, and there, lingering quietly in the back of the room, wine in hand, was Randy, watching the evil empire unravel to the tune of what? Six thousand ICBMs scattered over a dozen different republics. *I invite you, Mr. Secretary, to imagine the shittiest little corners of Central Asia sitting flush with their own mobile launchers.*

It was the sort of thing that was handed to Randy, the sort of thing Randy took care of. Talk to a friend in the OMB, move the money through Swiss Interbank Clearing system, take a meeting in Georgetown, call an acquaintance in Hialeah or Zurich or Paris.

He was in Port-au-Prince in '94.

In Sarajevo in '95.

There were routing numbers and holding companies and money moving through the Caymans because such was the way of money. Such was the way of Randy. An adept of the free market, its inner locutions, the spiral circuits of wandering capital. What had Hugh Eckhart once said? *Randy gets up in the morning and the Invisible Hand brushes his hair.* He'd stepped aside as founding principal of Leviathan, but not before negotiating the concessions to a Tier One Iron Ore field in West Africa, the same deal on which Marco—then a junior brother in the Covenant—had cut his political teeth. It wasn't exactly a known thing. There was, in fact, a way in which Garcia's life was hearsay, a collection of pool reports and microfiche stored in climate-controlled rooms, some brief mention beneath the fold on page 14A. You could find him, but what was it you found? A civil servant? A businessman? Garcia was all of these and none. Most recently, he was the Congressman's patron.

Marco had walked with his chief back toward the garage where Bill Waters had touched his shoulder and leaned in to whisper, "Marco, Congressman, strictly in confidence, you need to understand what's happening here. They're cutting you loose."

Waters's physical closeness had prevented Marco from speaking. His chief was not a toucher. His chief was a private shark.

"What do you mean cutting me loose?"

"Please listen to me when I say things have evolved."

"Evolved in what way?" Marco asked, but already he knew. That seed of betrayal—it had always been there, and the look on his face must have said as much.

Waters had leaned back to adjust his jacket. They were in the underground garage where it was all cool concrete and the little numbers painted by each parking space. Pale cancer light. A distant stairwell.

"Sir." Waters had recovered. No trace of emotion. He could have been talking about the wax job on his Mercedes for all Marco could tell. "There's been an incident at the embassy in Bratislava. At this point details are thin, but it looks like our man was involved."

"Are you saying for me not to meet with Randy?"

"I'm saying Mr. Garcia isn't alone in his concern."

"You talked to him?"

"I most certainly did not."

"You're confusing the hell out of me here, Bill. You say they're cutting me loose and..."

Marco stopped. His chief was looking out through the yellow lighting, watching. Somewhere, an elevator pinged opened. Waters stepped closer.

"Someone got into the discretionary account," he said finally, quietly. "The money's gone. So are some internal documents. This was two or three days ago. We thought maybe it was a mistake, but now a woman is missing—"

"A woman?"

"So long as the situation is fluid you have to remain in play."

"What woman?"

"She was an assistant to Erskine Logan's wife. You recall he's the ambassador over there now."

"I don't recall anything."

"She had false papers, but...you know."

"No. I don't know. In fact, I have no idea what you're talking about."

"Mr. Congressman—"

"Did you talk to Hugh Eckhart?"

"If things blow up publicly somebody has to take the blame, you understand?"

"Did you talk to Hugh?"

"Maybe collect yourself before you drive over. Maybe go home first."

"I want to talk to someone before—"

Marco was taking his phone out when his chief reached out and palmed it from him. He held it for an awkward moment, looked at his hand, looked back at Marco, and returned it.

"Please," Waters said, "just go home first. Before you do anything else."

Which was how Marco had discovered his trashed apartment.

It occurred to Marco only later that perhaps his chief had known about the ransacking? That perhaps his chief had a hand in it? An attempt to warn Marco, to convey the seriousness of the situation? Money was missing. A woman was missing. The personal assistant to the U.S. Ambassador's wife. She'd somehow slipped into the embassy in Slovakia and there gotten her hands on a dossier containing both the account information and whatever internal documents were necessary for the meeting. *The meeting* being, of course, the discrete signing over of Slovak shale gas concessions to Leviathan, a deal that would take place in two days' time and was worth somewhere in the vicinity of 4.2 billion U.S. The G-20 was currently taking place very loudly in Vienna. The meeting in Bratislava was meant to happen very quietly seventy kilometers away. But now someone, some woman—

It looks like our man was involved.

"Oh God," Marco said, because it had all started to come together in his mind, the meetings, Garcia's sudden patronage. The parallel plan, already in motion.

Are you one of the Bronze People?

"Oh, Lord, please, no," he said.

Not because he didn't know the man's identity.

But because he did.

HE GOT OUT of the cab and walked through the acacia and lavender-scented heat. He was at home in St. Pete, surrounded and safe, the bay a moat against the aggressions of the larger world. Here was the good Cuban food and the Dali museum. Dolphins playing chase in the surf. Here, you had the sunset over the Gulf, you had the stars, you had the tiki torches along the sand. There, to the east, it was all strawberry fields and migrants hunched in clouds of pesticide. Past that, the resorts. The clowns, the rats, the roller-coasters built around movie franchises. The motels full of folks making six bucks an hour under the table at Denny's.

He was home here, yet he found himself keeping his head down. Paranoid but so what? The vague warning, the trashed townhouse coated in pink dust—he had reason to be paranoid. At least his wife Vendela and the girls were in Connecticut with her parents.

In the glassy cool of the foyer, he took out his phone to see he had seven missed calls, thirty-one texts, and God only knew how many emails. He was AWOL, due by now in Garcia's D.C. office. Tomorrow, he was expected at Garcia's Davis Island mansion, Boca Grande. It had been the spot of any number of fund-raisers and parties, a politically ecumenical gathering of the powerful. It was supposed to be celebratory. The papers signed. The shale gas concessions in hand. Everyone off to the private island of his choice.

But not now. Now his disappearance would have his staff in a quiet panic, freaking out but taking great care that no one realized they were freaking out. He thought of calling, just a quick word to have them clear his schedule, tell them he had decided to fly up to see the family in Litchfield County. It might buy him some time, but to hell with it. He would—

He stopped when he heard it.

Someone was crying in the kitchen. Barely audible over the hum of the air conditioner, but it was tears, and it was the housekeeper Yesenia. She stood at the sink, gasping, a dishtowel in her mouth. He called to her and she shook her head and burst into another round of sobs. Out the window her husband Alfonse was trimming the hedges.

He tried to calm her down, to coax out what had happened. It came in fits and starts. Someone was here earlier. Immigration. Two white people with badges. Man and woman. They had not seen Alfonse, but she knew they would be back.

"You're sure, immigration?"

"Yes, Mr. Torres. The ICE."

"They said ICE?"

"They do not say, but I know."

"Did they come inside?"

"Alfonse they did not see. I hide him."

He looked out the window at her undocumented husband, cutting greenery with the precision of a neurosurgeon.

"They ask for you, Mr. Torres. I tell them no."

"You told them no, I wasn't here?"

"I tell them you are away in the nation's capital doing the business of the people."

He stood for a moment at the granite-topped island. It was almost three in the afternoon. He had been due in Garcia's office around ten. They were here, then, after he had failed to appear? Not the FBI—there would be no cause for that, and even if they were he couldn't imagine the Tampa field office moving with such dispatch. Garcia's people, then?

"They never came inside?"

She'd turned back to the window.

"No, Mr. Torres. I stop them."

"You did right, Yesenia. You did great. Listen. They won't come back."

"They say—"

"I understand, but don't worry. They won't come back. I'll take care of it."

She threw her hands in the air as if suddenly remembering something.

"She left a card for you. This woman left a card. I remember now."

But it was one of his cards. Marco Torres. U.S. House of Representatives. *Hoping to hear from you very soon* was written on the back. Below that was the name *Penny* in looping letters and a phone number with a D.C. area code.

"This was the woman, Penny?"

"Tall woman, Mr. Torres. Red hair. Very curly."

"You did right. You really did."

Upstairs, he put his laptop in an overnight bag, and packed some clothes. Took an envelope that contained a thousand dollars in hundreds he kept for emergencies and used the landline to call Mike Lee. An evangelical of unquestioned provenance, Lee had been homeschooled by Moral Majority parents, held degrees from Liberty and Duke Law, and chaired the Greater Tampa chapter of the Federalist Society. He and his wife had even adopted two daughters from Botswana, girls with beaded braids and Bible verses they recited on command.

For the last three years, Lee had managed Marco's political action committee. More importantly, he had offered entrée into the *ancien regime* of Old Florida, laying and then thickening the bedrock of fundraisers and contributions that were the ground on which Marco had built his political life. Marco was just beginning his second term, initially elected on the ferocity of his denunciations of home foreclosures (much of Tampa had been in financial ruins) and his ability to lay the blame at the feet of the *liberal elite* of Obama and Wall Street (that his wife was at McKinsey at the time was a fact his Democratic opponent, a retired Eckerd College English professor, had failed to capitalize on). For weeks he'd driven out to places like Tampa Heights and Carriage Pointe—neighborhoods ravaged by the fallout of sub-prime mortgages—to appeal to Rotary Clubs and the Hillsborough County Commission. But it was only when he took to the airwaves, becoming an occasional guest on *Ray Shields's Morning in America*, that his star began to rise.

Lee picked up on the first ring.

"What level of panic should I be at here?" he asked.

"Did someone call?"

"Did someone call? Lord have mercy, Marco. Please tell me you know what on God's green earth is going on."

"I was hoping you could tell me that."

"I had someone here this morning from the Hillsborough Sheriff's Department asking for documents."

"What sort of documents?"

"Bank statements. Donor lists. The usual. Then I got a call from someone claiming to be with the DOJ. I'd rather not talk about it on the phone."

"What did you tell them?"

"What do you think I told them? I told them to come back with a subpoena."

"We need to meet."

"I think they're coming back, too. I don't think it's any kind of bluff."

"Can you come out to the beach?"

"Give me an hour," Lee said. "Right now I'm praying."

Marco stood with the receiver in his hand. When it began to bleat he hung up and grabbed a bottle of the Scotch his wife loved. Sentimental, maybe. Or maybe the forethought that he was going to need something to fortify himself.

After that, he spent a few minutes in his oldest daughter's bedroom. It was a dangerous use of time, just sitting there on the lime green comforter. But all the urgency that had driven him from chambers to his Arlington townhouse to the airport and on to their Florida manse was draining. Sitting there, he felt it go out of him, energy, purpose, leaking through the warm soles of his braided loafers.

That he'd felt the same thing in Iraq was not lost on him. It was the sort of deflation he hadn't felt in a long time, and occasionally wondered if the birth of his daughters had lifted it. He liked to think that it had, and sometimes, running on the treadmill in the House gym, he spent the better part of his seventy-five minutes of cardio telling himself it was gone.

He looked around the room. The canopy beds and miniature vanity with its tiny mirror and tiny chair. Stuffed animals. Both his daughters cute, independent things fast outstripping the limits of his comprehension, already viewing him with a measure of pity, as if they were privy to his secrets, the private failings he fingered like prayer beads. The owls on the curtains. The glow-in-the-dark stars on the ceiling. The Hello Kitty everything.

His stomach cramped and he doubled forward.

He was still sitting there, arms circling his gut, when his phone went off. He panicked, looked down to see it was Hugh Eckhart calling, and panicked a little more. He wanted to answer—a part of him said it was the most rational thing he could do—but he knew he couldn't. Hugh had been on Garcia's staff. Hugh, to some extent, *had been* Garcia's staff. But Marco had heard rumors of some falling out, of Hugh's dismissal, of some advanced stage cancer left too long untreated. So far as Marco knew, no one had seen Hugh Eckhart in months. Still, if anyone knew what was going on it would be Hugh.

But then there was the question of divided loyalties, a more complex question than Marco currently had the brainpower to unpack. There was a time he'd been closer to Hugh Eckhart than anyone else on earth, but then Hugh had told him about his Angel, about the dead children in that Baghdad school.

God did this, Hugh had said. Because God gave us dominion over the earth.

Marco knew this was true because Marco had been there, too. Or at least close enough.

As a young man, he'd deployed with a civil affairs battalion in the Green Zone—what had seemed at the time a completely safe post, physically as well as psychologically. It hadn't been the case. Even within the blast walls, it was a world of Lidocaine and gauze and red chuffs of Clotting Factor clumped like concrete dust. Fentanyl lollipops and IEDs. That he came home as mind-fucked as any other soldier shouldn't have been a surprise.

But at least he came home, enrolling at the University of Florida where, in his senior year, he worked in the regional office of Randy Garcia. When he graduated, Marco was invited by Garcia to Washington, or if not by Garcia then by his new chief-of-staff Hugh Eckhart, whom Marco had gotten to know over the course of the previous year. Hugh, however, hadn't been offering him a job, rather something better than a job: a connection, a way in. He had offered Marco a place within The Covenant, an eccentric and secretive collection of ambitious Christ-centered Christ-believing young men.

For years Marco had heard persistent whispers. Some Special Forces Captain with an MA from the Kennedy School of Government who couldn't believe this lowly E-4 could recite the Psalms with the same ease he discoursed on the Koran might make mention of it. Or a Major who had the ear of the battalion commander. *This kid has an IQ of probably 150 and they've got him working in a supply tent? Handing out tubes of Plumpy'Nut like some Shriner? Hey, Torres, you ought to think about relocating your skinny ass to the*

District when you get out. They all had friends in D.C., they all knew someone who knew someone, and always it led back to The Covenant. *You ever get to D.C. you track me down.* And eventually Marco had, eventually Marco tracked them all down. Spent the next two years praying and working with his Covenant brothers, and it was because of that, because of the manual labor, because of the Bible study in the shadow of the Potomac, that he was where he was now. And that was good, he thought, in so many ways that was very good.

The phone in his hand had stopped ringing and he put it down on his daughter's pillow.

In so many ways it was wonderful.

Of course, it was also terrifying.

YESENIA WAS STILL in the kitchen though whatever storm had possessed her seemed to have subsided by the time Marco came back downstairs. She stood at the sink, her husband still in the backyard out among the lantana and palms. Marco had his laptop, some clothes and toiletries, the Scotch. What he didn't have was a way out. Then he saw Alfonse's battered Chevy pickup parked by the pool house, his own Jaguar in the garage.

"Yesenia," he said, "momento, por favor."

Ten minutes later he was pulling the truck to the curb in front of a Wells Fargo ATM. Stick shift. Split upholstery. There had been some confusion, Yesenia not understanding, or refusing to understand his trade of the keys to the Jag for Alfonse's pickup. He tried explaining it in both English and Spanish, begging with gestures. Finally, he'd walked out the door. To hell with it. *No immigration, no ICE. Listen to me, Yesenia. It's fine. Está bien, okay?*

Though it wasn't. Whoever had come knocking would come back. A red-haired woman named Penny—he thought he knew her, but couldn't quite place how or where. The FBI, someone from Leviathan—it didn't matter. It would be ICE agents soon enough. Yesenia had papers, but her husband would be deported, poor Alfonse back to packaging cut flowers in some Maquiladora sweatshop in two weeks' time. He told himself that if he made it through this he'd do something for them, make a call, get Mike Lee's firm to handle it.

If he made it through.

He parked and walked to the ATM.

It was difficult to reckon how seriously he should take things, but discretion—given the state of his townhouse—was starting to feel like the better part of valor, and discretion meant cash. Someone could trace the withdrawal, but thereafter he would be safe.

He punched in his PIN, mistyped because of nerves. Reentered it only to find that no, he had typed it correctly, only his account had been frozen. ACCOUNT LOCKED PLEASE VISIT WELLS-FARGO.COM/HELP FOR ASSISTANCE ... ACCOUNT LOCKED PLEASE VISIT ... It took a moment for comprehension to register, and when it did he realized he was freezing, standing in the Florida heat on the edge of shivering.

He tried once more and when it failed a third time he folded the card in half, bent it back the other way, back and forth until it tore. He dropped it in the garbage with his cell battery, walked to another trashcan, and left the actual phone there.

It wasn't real exactly, but he was certain it had just happened, and what it was like was an untethering. He felt himself rise up a few inches off the concrete, heedless and almost floating. That he'd felt it when his father died, that bright afternoon he was summoned to the school office of St. Peter's in Ybor City, wasn't lost on him. That day, slumped into the block wall, something he had never known was holding him suddenly released him. He was free, weightless. A moment later, he'd felt himself scratch against the ceiling.

It happened, would happen, years later in Iraq when the All Clear sounded after the stray mortar or rocket had landed.

Everything brighter, crisper.

Something precious saved, and you knew it.

HE MET MIKE Lee at an air-conditioned raw bar in Pass-a-Grille. Lee drinking sweet tea in the cabana shade, big cracker finger swiping the screen of his phone. Past him sat the shimmery blue of the Gulf. He clapped Lee harder on the back than he intended and tea spilled over Lee's hairy wrist. He wondered if the man would lick it, if he was capable of something that human. Apparently, he was not.

"Marco. Sit down." He shook his head. "I tell you I've been absolutely—why are you smiling?"

"Am I smiling?"

"I can't eat."

"Were we planning on that?"

"I mean physically," Lee said. "My indigestion's all wrong. Now sit down and tell me what's going on here. I've had two more phone calls since we talked."

Marco really was smiling. He probably could have helped it but he wasn't going to bother trying. Something had happened to him driving from the ATM to the raw bar. An airiness had begun to gather beneath him, as if the breeze moving over the families camped beneath beach umbrellas might be enough to lift him. He smiled again, almost laughed. He'd taken it all so seriously, the buffet luncheons and captain's choice golf tournaments, the five-hundred-a-plate dinners, and here Lee was just another sunburned cracker with remarkable LSAT scores. How had he never realized that?

"Marco?"

"I'm listening." Lee had been describing the visit he had been paid by the Hillsborough County Sheriff's Department, followed by two more phone calls. One caller refusing to identify himself. The other claiming, yes, he was with the Justice Department, but offering nothing beyond that.

"But that's all?" Marco said. "They just wanted financial papers?"

"Lord God, what more do you expect? Money is missing. Money is unaccounted for."

"How much?"

"Let's just say enough, all right? I talked to Larry Medicine and he says you opened a secondary account and have been moving money into it and now—"

"That I did what?"

"Opened a secondary account."

"Me?"

"Well, somebody sure as shooting did. You're telling me you didn't?"

"What do you mean a secondary account?"

"Larry says it's like a ghost. You see it out of the corner of your eye, but then you're going looking for it and it isn't there." He sipped his tea. "I tell you, I was calm today, very composed, but this has gotten to me."

"That isn't like you, Mike."

"Like me? Good Lord. We're the good guys here, you remember? We usually ask for the papers from the *other* guy." He put down his tea. "What are you doing here anyway? I thought you were in the District."

"Let's imagine I am."

Lee stared at him for a moment. "Well, whatever the heck I'm supposed to imagine, let's remember you have to be at Garcia's tomorrow. I want you to see Larry Medicine before then. If this is a mistake—"

"I don't want to see Medicine."

Lee raised a pink hand.

"If this really is a mistake Larry can clear things up. All right?"

"I'll give him a call."

"Not a call, Marco." Lee took his handkerchief and mopped his face. Larry Medicine was the PAC's accountant, a Mormon who refused caffeine with the same conviction he refused life. Everything about him repulsed Marco. "Not a call," Lee repeated.

"I'll go see him."

"Today."

"Yeah, sure, today. I appear to have cleared my calendar."

"I'll say you have."

Marco put his arm on the back of Lee's seat and looked around. "It's nice out. Maybe I will order something."

Lee turned to appraise him.

"What on earth happened to you between now and you calling?"

"What do you mean?"

"Well, pardon my expression, but on the phone you sounded like you were about to shit your britches."

"Did I?"

"I hate to use language like that."

"You know what, I lost my phone."

"You sure you didn't lose your goddang mind along with it? Because here I am worried by something like embezzlement—"

"Don't say that."

"I'm serious—"

"Don't even speak its name."

"I'm serious as a heart attack and here you are making light of it."

"Mike, come on, please." Marco stood and rested his hand on Lee's shoulder. "You need anything while I'm up?"

"No. I don't suppose I do."

"I want you to relax, Mike. How about you breathe?"

"How about you take your hand off my shoulder?"

Marco laughed, squeezed Lee's shoulder, and crossed from the bright beachside into the cooler shadows of the bar. A wall-mounted TV played ESPN. Somewhere, perhaps on another station, was a report from the G-20 in Vienna. There would be nothing from Bratislava. News from Bratislava would come in a more direct manner.

At the urinal, his stomach cramped with nerves, and he stood there panting, suddenly soaked with sweat. When it passed, he zipped up and walked out. The bartender was a blonde with an ear full of loops and a sleeve of intersecting tattoos. He asked for a shot of Patron, and another, slammed the second and dropped on the bar one of the ten bills in his possession.

To hell with Lee.

To hell with them all.

He stood waiting for the thought to take root, for the tequila to take root, to burrow its way into his bloodstream. He would go find Larry Medicine and tomorrow he would go to Boca Grande and find Garcia. He thought about going over and telling Lee everything, the funneling of money, the back channel movement of men and materiel. He would lay it out, laugh about it. What a sucker he'd been. He had known absolutely nothing about any secondary account and saw now that they'd set him up perfectly. *Yeah, they cut me loose. I'm the dupe hoping for eight to ten at some low-security prison in Maryland. Basic cable and a starchy diet.* Because it was coming to that. The best he could hope for was a sentence suspended down to a few years of cutting grass in denim slippers. What was the worst? He had no idea, but given he was—or had been—party to a plot to arm a small insurgency in Ukraine, to manipulate the world energy market and—to hell with it.

That was the tequila talking.

He passed on a third shot.

The blonde had brought over his change, four twenties and a few singles, but he left it all on the bar, and without ever looking back at Lee—old friend, though he wasn't, really—Marco Torres walked out into the afternoon heat.

AN HOUR LATER he was in a hotel room in north Tampa, air-conditioner cranked, laptop open, determined not to call Hugh Eckhart. It was possible, Marco had realized forking over fifty-nine dollars at the front desk of the Sand & Palm Motorcourt, to use the hotel phone to call Hugh's cell and then simply pack up and go to another place. It wasn't a good idea, but it was possible.

He stood at the window.

Presumably Vendela and the girls were still with her parents. Litchfield County. The land of heliports and racquet sports. A ridiculous place, but at least they were safe.

Marco thought of calling her but knew he wouldn't. There'd been a panic a couple of years ago, minor against what was happening now. But it had been enough to clarify certain things. His mother—his estranged mother—had summoned him to Nicaragua where she lay wasting at the hand of some rarefied cancer, alive but only barely.

His first thought had been *well, we're all dying, now aren't we?* He was maybe ashamed of that, though he didn't want to be. He'd definitely been disoriented enough to call Vendela at work, something he knew never to do. She was, if not married to her work, in a very committed relationship, and had forbid him to call her there. The weekends were for emotions, that cushioned world of art auctions and au pairs. She was her own sort of rising star in Treasury, having bounced over from private equity. When she bounced back, she'd be worth millions. But Marco was shaken at the time and had called her.

It was—he was already formulating his defense—something people did. Vendela was less receptive. Did he think she had time for this? What information did he have? Had he actually talked to anyone and did Marco have any idea of how much work there was to be done on the brief she'd be delivering in 60—no, make that 57 minutes?

No, he hadn't. He was sorry.

Look, Marco—

No, I'm sorry. I know better.

She softened then—*Marco, honey*—how could she not soften?

But the damage was done. From that point forward, he knew he would receive her counsel, but never her compassion. So he asked her for advice: What should he do? and she was all cooing softness: They'd talk about it tonight, everything would be fine, she loved him, the girls loved him, everything would work out, and could he please put his chief of staff on the line before he hung up?

When he'd gotten back to his office his chief was waiting on him.

"I don't think you've ever told me about your mother," he'd said.

"Yes, I have."

"Not properly you haven't."

What was to tell? A lot, it seemed. The bare bones of Marco's life were public record, indeed much of his campaign had been built on it: his arrival in the United States via the Mariel boatlift, his early years in Tampa where his adoptive parents were (*for the purposes of campaign narrative let's call them*) missionaries, his father's death, his mother's work in Nicaragua where she had reinvented herself as the well-meaning American you found propped in the corner of every poor country.

"What is it exactly she's doing?"

"She's at a healing center," Marco said. "There's a guy some people think is a prophet. They call him Wandering Cloud."

"Wandering Cloud." His chief stood, walked to the window and back. "Look, Marco, how long have we known each other? Forever, right? And I know this is your mother—I'm entirely sensitive to that—but we have to think big-picture here."

When he'd gotten home that evening Vendela was waiting for him with take-out Ethiopian. The nanny had the girls for the night.

"I'm sorry about today," she said, and at that time, in that moment, he'd believed her. "Tell me everything."

He had. What little there was to tell, and in telling her he found himself mildly surprised at how little she knew of his life, which was partly the fault of his revealing so little, but partly the fault of her simply not knowing. They'd been married almost four years at that point and while it might be seen as a convenience, the proverbial Washington power-couple, they were also in love, or if not in love, fond of each other, or surely had been at some time in the past. Strange then, that talking to Vendela he found himself thinking of Hugh, those years in Gainesville and later in D.C.

She led him to the bedroom.

The sex felt vaguely predatory, and was it wrong to think that was how she preferred it? She finished in his lap, thrusting her hips and biting an earlobe. She was thirty-four and constructed from green tea and Pilates, built, it sometimes seemed, by a team of Cross-Fitters in a lab at M.I.T.'s Sloan School of Management where it was all Milton Friedman and no carbs after two p.m. Later, they showered and sat in the kitchen, picking over the last of the *injera* which he noticed she wasn't actually eating, just moving around.

"So," she said, and let it hang there between them. "I talked to Bill and he voiced some concerns."

"About what?"

"Come on, baby. You know about what."

"And how is this any of Bill's concern?"

"I've read up on this guy." She stood, came back with her robe falling open on nothing beyond her panties and the gloss of her skin, and put a printed article from Wikipedia on the table, another from *O. Magazine*.

"Nube Errante," Marco read.

"It's about as New Age crazy as it gets. I have more besides that."

"This is enough."

And it was. Not because of the strangeness of his mother's life, but because they had conspired against him, Bill his chief and Vendela his wife, and he wondered if this wasn't a frequent thing, this planning of his days and ways. Gauging missteps, making subtle corrections. In public he was *no* but in private he was something else, the frightened soldier, the child of Focus on the Family American exceptionalism, too busy trying to be of use, too busy trying to be *loved*, to notice he was losing his faith, had already lost it, had maybe never had it in the first place because—

Utter bullshit.

He stopped himself. The doubt, the questioning, it was utter bullshit, the sort of thought he couldn't allow to germinate because where would it end? If his mother dying in a New Age healing center had been enough to trigger his wife's abject and manipulative fears over his political future what would be the fruit of his *involvement* with the *situation* in Eastern Europe?

How would Vendela take to his being *cut loose*?

He pulled back the orange curtain.

By the time he was installed in Washington he was being touted as a new breed of populist, young and good-looking, a family man, a veteran, the rare non-white member of the conservative and quasi-secret Covenant. He had entered the establishment via his help negotiating a trade agreement on the Iron Ore field, a deal that may or may not have been legal, but had happened simply because all involved had said *yes*. After that, once he was elected, he developed a penchant for *no*. Whatever came before him—immigration, regulatory policy, gay marriage—he simply said no. Lantern-jaw. Firm-handshake. *NO*. Though he never yelled it, yelling wasn't necessary. He simply did not waver.

The motel was a horseshoe of cracked asphalt and aging Town Cars, Alfonse's borrowed pickup, a few plastic lawn chairs on the concrete stoop. Neon palm flickering in the glare. Past the parking lot stood a Laundromat and a bodega with iron bars and old men. The smell of hair oil and cocoa butter in the ninety-degree shade.

He let the curtain swing shut.

The plan was to wait until sundown, drive over to find Larry Medicine, and get his hands on whatever spreadsheets Medicine had. He'd take it all to Garcia tomorrow night. Or maybe he'd make copies and FedEx it all to the *New York Times*. Give it to *Politico* and implode fantastically.

Or maybe not. Maybe he was imagining things. Allowing the situation to run ahead of him. He tried to recall every word of his conversation with his chief that morning in the garage and found he couldn't. *They're cutting you loose. Someone has to take the blame.* Marco would be the natural suspect. Garcia would have covered his tracks, hidden behind walls of paper and dummy corporations. Ambassador Logan was simply carrying out official duties. Colonel Venclova was dead. It was Marco's PAC that had held the necessary funds and, apparently, funneled them through some ghost account. And it was Marco who had stood in the empty chambers of the House and thundered against Russian aggression in Eastern Europe. Ukraine, Estonia, Latvia, Lithuania, Georgia...It would make for good B-roll footage during the indictment: Marco at the dais, finger raised, while the flavor-of-the-month anchor tossed her vanilla hair and talked about a far-right conspiracy to—to what?

That was what he was hoping Larry Medicine could shed light on. If the money was simply missing, it might come off as no more than embezzlement. A whimsical if misguided plan to move weapons into Ukraine? The act of a patriot. Iran-Contra in a minor key. He could survive that, maybe even emerge better for it somewhere down the line. But if they went after Garcia, Marco had a feeling he wouldn't be alive to find out.

He opened the scotch and sipped until his stomach clenched.

He vomited in the shower, but kept drinking, waiting. It was after six but the heat remained oppressive. The street all shutters and shade. Grandparents raising grandchildren in the nub of shadow, entire clans asleep behind bed sheets hung for curtains.

He thought again of his wife. There was a notepad on the bed and on it he wrote *Dear Vendela*. But then nothing else. He wadded the paper, changed his mind and smoothed it.

I want to explain...

I am writing to make clear...
But what it was he was making clear he didn't know.
I am so sorry, he started to write, but eventually he gave up.
Eventually, he left.

IT WAS DUSK by the time Marco knocked at Larry Medicine's block bungalow. Medicine didn't seem surprised to see him. He had handled the PAC's finances from the start, and had been associated with Mike Lee for God only knew how many years before that. There must have been moments, crises, Marco thought, that eventually drew everyone to his door.

They sat in the front room, Medicine on a metal folding chair, Marco on the couch.

"I understand we have a serious problem."

"That would be a subjective assessment," Medicine said. "We have numbers that fail to balance. We have asymmetric columns."

"How bad is it?"

"Again, Mr. Congressman, you're asking me to engage in a subjective analysis outside my purview. If you're asking about imbalances—"

"How much money is missing, Larry?"

"Eleven point one million dollars."

"Christ. When did it disappear?"

"I'll have to contact the bank, but I would say sometime in the last two days."

"Where did it go?"

"Where did it go, Mr. Congressman?" Medicine spread his big knuckled hands. He was probably in his late sixties, but so emaciated it was impossible to tell. Maybe fifty but just as likely eighty. Six-foot-six with a scarecrow's build. "Where does any of it go? All I see is a large withdrawal. This is not uncommon. What is uncommon is to have Mr. Lee call, to have you, Mr. Congressman, show up asking these questions."

"Mike said a ghost account."

"I regret the term. I only meant an account beyond my purview."

"You mean you don't have access to it?"

"I'm not even certain it exists."

"Except it has our money."

"Had, Mr. Congressman. So far as I can tell this secondary account was accessed. Money was transferred—"

"Eleven point one million dollars."

"And then the account was closed."

"Closed as in?"

"As in I can find no trace."

"A ghost," Marco said.

"I do have one thing that might interest you." Medicine walked to his computer and returned with a printed sheet. "I couldn't download anything. But I managed to get a screen shot. This was just yesterday. Does this mean anything to you?"

The sheet read: ACCOUNT# XXXXXX-XX THE WOJTYŁA SOCIETY 000.00. The account appeared to have been routed through a Ukrainian bank but the transfer had been made in Slovakia. That was all.

"Mr. Congressman?"

"No," Marco said, looking up. He felt the nausea returning. The sweat. The cramped stomach. "I'm afraid it doesn't."

"That's unfortunate."

"Did you—"

"Look them up? They're a 501(c)(3) doing work in Ukraine. But I can't find anything beyond that."

"A ghost." Marco folded the paper lengthwise. "May I keep this?"

"Of course."

"There's probably going to be other folks showing up too."

"Probably?"

Marco stood, turned to the empty mantel behind the couch.

"What is it you want to know, sir?" Medicine asked.

"I don't know. A lot of money moves through the general account." Marco shook his head. "'A lot.' I know, a relative term. But you watch the account, Larry. You've watched it for years. What do you see? What's different?"

"You mean beside the Wojtyła business?"

"I mean regarding patterns. Can you detect any patterns?"

"Money has been moving rapidly in and out of the account. That would be the pattern. It goes out, is quickly replaced by another deposit. Quicker than usual, I would say."

"Except not this time."

"No, Mr. Congressman. Not this time. At least not yet."

"What does it mean, legally speaking?"

"At this point, absolutely nothing. Money has been withdrawn. By law, as I'm sure you know, that money is intended for specific purposes."

"But when it disappears…"

Medicine opened his clasped hands, palms up.

"At that point there would be the possibility of legal issues, certainly. An audit."

Marco sat back down.

"If you were looking at the books what would you see? What would be your general impression?"

"My impression, sir, did I not know better, was that someone had been moving very large amounts of unaccounted for funds through your account simply for the sake of moving it—"

"You mean laundering it?"

"I'm more comfortable with *moving*. But then, something happened, maybe the account was compromised, let's say, and they stopped."

"They cashed out."

"That appears to be the case."

"But who?" Marco asked. "Who would have access?"

But of course Marco knew who.

The larger question was why?

HE FOUND A pay phone outside a Sav-A-Lot and dialed Vendela collect at her parents' in Connecticut. She sounded more pissed than concerned, but then caught herself and over-corrected toward motherly worry. She wanted to know where he was.

"You're supposed to be in D.C. Bill drove up here—"

"To your parents'? Why the hell is Bill there?"

"He's here because he's concerned. We're all concerned, honey."

"About me?"

"Don't act like that, all right? I've been trying to reach you all day."

"I lost my phone."

"You lost your phone? What are you, six?"

"Put Bill on."

"I want to talk to you before you hang up."

"Just put Bill on."

"Vendela called me after Garcia's office called *her* trying to track you down," his chief said when he came on. "This after they called me, having already called the field office in Tampa. Which all came after they tried to call you directly."

"I lost my phone."

"Mike Lee called. He was upset."

"The place was trashed. You were right. They've cut me loose."

"You need to come in, Marco. For everyone's good."

"I went to see Larry Medicine. They set the PAC up. There was a secondary account we didn't know about. They emptied it, but left just enough evidence that Justice can pick up the scent. What it will look like is very basic white-bread embezzlement—"

"Marco—"

"The meeting, the one in Bratislava—"

"Let's not talk about this right now. Just go home. Get a good night's sleep. In the morning get on a plane and get back to the District."

"I've got everything with me," he lied. "Spreadsheets, notes. I'm going to copy everything."

"Don't do anything rash, all right? We can open a dialogue here."

"Medicine knew what was up."

"Are you listening to me? We can still land this thing." There was some noise, some jostling and muttering, and Vendela came back on the line. "Marco, baby, listen to me. I talked to Yesenia and she said you stole Alfonse's truck."

"Christ, I didn't steal it."

"I'm worried, all right? The girls are worried."

"What did you tell the girls?"

"Call Randy. Please."

"Don't say a word to the girls. Jesus, Vendela."

It would be just like Vendela to leverage their concern. *Daddy's had a little breakdown girls. Try to be extra sweet around your crazy father, kay?*

"You hear what I'm saying?" he asked. "Not a word."

"You're not thinking clearly. Go straight home and call Randy? Promise me that."

"I have to go."

"Just promise me that, okay?"

But he'd made too many promises already, and hung up before he slipped into another.

IT HAD STARTED with promises.

For the last year Congressman Marco Torres had been making promises he never thought he'd have to keep, if only because he was making them to an empty chamber. It was a familiar trick: provide the press with a copy of your speech, make sure the C-SPAN cameras were rolling, and thunder away. He could be as belligerent and unbending as he wanted with no worry of repercussions within the Beltway as it was understood that any speech delivered in the absence of the actual members of the House was intended as theater, something to be rehashed on Fox News and gain traction with voters back in his district. Representative Torres was a rising star, true, but to better ensure his continued climb he needed an *issue*, something he owned. Something everyone from reporters to retirees would instantly associate with the Marco Torres Brand.

Condemning Russian aggression had been an easy fit. Putin had already fought a war with Georgia over South Ossetia. It seemed likely he might fight over the Baltic States. It seemed certain he would fight over Ukraine. Marco posed the issue in the good versus evil rhetoric of the Cold War, drew on the trauma of his own Cuban heritage (he'd been adopted by well-meaning white parents who, though they taught him the gospel of Reagan, couldn't be bothered to teach him the language of Spanish.). He pitted brave freedom-loving Ukraine against the tyrannical aggression of Vladimir

Putin. It wasn't, he felt, that far from the truth. More importantly, polling showed it resonated with voters.

He became a fixture on the Sunday morning circuit of *Meet the Press, Face the Nation, This Week*, became a darling of conservative radio. He talked about Powers and Principalities, suggested fast-tracking NATO membership, raised the specter of sending weapon systems and military advisers to Kiev. It wasn't going to happen, so he could speak with impunity. It didn't hurt to bolster his foreign policy credentials, either. No one outside the echo chamber was listening, and that, after all, was part of the point.

Then one day his office received an email from a Professor Tomas Venclova, a former defector and current Chair of Slavic Studies at Yale University. The Colonel, as he was known in foreign policy circles, admired the Congressman's championing of the region, admired the nerve, the commitment, and suggested, should the Congressman ever find himself in New York, they have lunch.

A week later they met at Tavern on the Green, Venclova everything Marco had hoped he would be, white-haired and continental in his bespoke suit, lisping gorgeously as he quoted Hannah Arendt. He was planning a study trip to Kiev. He would visit with pro-democracy leaders, travel to the threatened border and take the measure of the soldiers garrisoned there. Perhaps the Congressman would like to join him?

His chief liked the idea immediately: Marco photographed exhorting the troops from atop a tank. You raise a megaphone and yell invective across the border, back on a Lufthansa flight before the images air. *This can be your area, Marco. You can own this.* A politically risk-free bonanza of coverage. The opportunity to invoke the founding fathers and drag up the specter of Castro. To carry the gravitas of distant war into future televised debates.

How could he possibly resist?

Two weeks later, Marco was changing planes at Charles de Gaulle for the hop to Boryspil, Venclova at his side, Venclova's pretty granddaughter at the Colonel's. It was thirty hours of photo ops and applause, of standing in the Maidan and raising his fist in salute. He visited the parliament and had his picture made with a few soldiers, their indifference impervious to his double-clasp handshake and lapel pin of crossed U.S. and Ukrainian flags. As promised, he was back on a plane before anyone knew he was gone. Except this time, he was on a Leviathan plane, headed to Bratislava for dinner with the U.S. Ambassador, *and an old acquaintance,* Venclova said, *I'm sure you remember Randy Garcia.*

Marco remembered him—how could he not?

What unsettled him was that Garcia remembered Marco.

Ambassador Logan was the former CEO of Garcia's Leviathan, Venclova told him. A capable if unimaginative man.

"I prefer his wife," he told Marco. "A lovely woman. They lost their daughter, an overdose out in California. She was in one of those tanks—what are they? Dear?"

"A sensory deprivation tank," Rachel said, without looking up.

"Yes, exactly. She sort of lost it for a while, Susan Logan, sort of cracked up, I suppose. Now she is a pretty woman who has about her an air of melancholy."

Marco caught Rachel's eyebrows go up at that, *an air of melancholy.*

"Seriously?" she asked over her paperback of Joseph Brodsky.

Venclova laughed and slapped Marco's knee as the jet descended, the lights of Bratislava's airport barely piercing the fog.

"Also your friend Hugh," Venclova said. "What is his name? He works with Mr. Garcia."

"Hugh Eckhart."

"Hugh Eckhart, of course. How could I forget?"

THE MEETING WAS on the roof of the Tulip House, a penthouse atrium of lollipop trees and a coursing stream, the glass beaded with condensation. He saw Venclova holding court with the Ambassador and a circle of eager Slovaks. Drinks were mixed, introductions made. The Slovak Minister of Energy. Someone from the State Department's Bureau of Energy Resources. A professor from the Colorado School of Mines. He was introduced to a ferret of a man named Liam Davies, said hello to his former champion, the talk-show host turned

Leviathan adviser Ray Shields. Finally, he saw Hugh, reluctant Hugh, chatting with the Ambassador's wife, Susan Logan, the pretty woman with her air of melancholy, straining to be taken seriously.

Marco downed a scotch, took another from the bar, and walked over.

"There he is," he said. "Hello, Hugh."

"Mr. Congressman."

They shook hands and Marco was equal parts giddy and skittish, but also inexplicably pissed off. It was, he knew, his wounded ego. Marco had revered Hugh, but then one night Hugh had confessed to Marco—the dead children, his angel—and thereafter avoided Marco at all cost, embarrassed, which made sense, but also angry, which didn't.

"Where's—" Marco asked, looking around for the wife he'd never met.

"Michelle," Hugh said.

"I know her name. I was hoping I could meet her."

"Afraid not."

"Finally, I mean."

"She doesn't do the business trips."

"So that's what this is then? Business and not pleasure?"

Hugh gestured with his drink.

"Does this scene bear the faintest resemblance to pleasure?"

"You know," Marco said. "I'm still not sure I believe in her."

"My wife we're talking about?"

"Like, is she real, this woman?"

"We have two children together. An apartment, a mortgage."

"You pay building fees together, this is what you're telling me."

"I'm fairly certain she's real."

"The family Christmas card."

"I'm trying to be glad to see you."

"These very adult things," Marco said. "The matching sweaters. The season's greetings."

"I'm trying to be gracious if you care to realize."

"Marching up and down the courthouse steps. Sign the papers. Get the fireproof box." Marco scratched his nose on the cuff of his jacket. He knew he was rambling, but that didn't mean he could stop. "Does that exist, fireproof plastic? I want to believe that it does. Excuse me for a moment."

He wandered to the bar for another scotch and then one more, spent a few minutes charming the ambassador's wife who kept laughing with her hand over her mouth. He had a white aura, she told him, and this was a good thing. It signaled purity. To celebrate, he had another drink before he walked back and started in with his shit. He was mildly berating Hugh, not meaning it, but yes, actually he did mean it, every word of it, when Hugh interrupted him.

"If you could shut up for a second I could tell you that Garcia wants to meet with you later, privately."

"How flattered I must be."

"You see that man over there, Ray Shields?"

"I did his radio show a few times."

"Oh, how lovely. Are you drunk, by the way?"

Marco felt the light in the room, the blurry shapes, the way he was leaning, a little wildly, a little out of control, while around them came lobster puffs, beef wellington, trays of tooth-picked things shouldered by Slovak girls.

"Shields is one of Garcia's chief lieutenants," Eckhart said.

"Ah, dear Randy, the czar of extraction fees.

"Hilarious."

"The king of Conakry."

"You could take it on the road, this act."

"The sultan of silicate." He leaned into what he intended as a bow, stumbled and caught himself. "How much did they give you, Hugh?"

"Come on."

"Two, three million? Enough for the place on the Upper West Side, I guess."

"Come on, Marco."

"The moneychangers, I'm talking about."

Hugh nodded as if amused. He had been healthy then, at least so far as Marco knew. A different time.

"I see you haven't forgotten how it's played," Hugh said.

"'Randy thinks *this*, Randy thinks *that*.' But how much did Randy pay?"

"That would be the game, sober or not."

"Fuck those bastards." He wiped his mouth on his sleeve. "That's my statement to the press. This is what we sat around studying the Gospels for? To cheat a bunch of peasants out of their natural resources?"

"We call it extraction resources. It's empowering, geopolitically speaking."

"Fuck their geopolitical empowerment then."

"You know who you sound like, all that eloquence? You sound like Billy Graham."

"I wanted to *be* Billy Graham," Marco said. "As I recall, you did, too."

Hugh took Marco above his elbow and led him to the balcony. "Let's get some air, all right?"

It was a cold night, the city a tangle of light climbing toward the castle. You could sense the river somewhere near, a generalized dampness, a collection of marine fog, scrapped and drifting.

"So what is this about?" Marco asked. "I'm being serious now. Ukraine versus Russia? Somehow I don't see Garcia coming out for a minor border skirmish. I thought he wasn't running Leviathan anymore?"

"He sold his interest, but he's still the man behind the curtain."

"Is he our next president?"

"You haven't kept up, have you?"

"I guess I haven't." Marco downed the scotch and instantly regretted he hadn't brought another with him. "So why was I invited?"

"Are you familiar with the Global Shale Gas Initiative?"

"Shale gas as in fracking?"

"That would be one name for it."

"Tell me another."

"Hydraulic Fracturing as market response to Climate Change. A clean, affordable alternative that fosters geopolitical stability."

"And this is what we're after, a clean affordable alternative?"

"You drill the well sideways from the borehole. Pump it full of whatever toxic chemical you can get your hands on."

"I know what fracking is. It just seems too low-rent for such a hefty gathering. Besides, what's Leviathan doing in shale gas? I thought that was Koch's area."

"Koch won't touch it. It's too volatile, the geopolitics of it all."

"But Randy will?"

"Water, chemicals, and sand. It breaks up the shale and makes everyone rich."

"Richer. I get it. But Garcia? He can't possible care about the money."

"You've read up on Rosneft, right?"

"A few hundred mil to a guy like that? That's pocket change."

"Rosneft, yes or no? With all your thundering about Ukraine?"

"I've heard a little."

"Well, tonight you're going to hear a lot. The great Russian bear that is Rosneft." Hugh looked at him. "They're going to make it sound like Rosneft is this big evil thing. Probably it is. I don't know. But just remember the real bear in the room is Randy Garcia."

DINNER WAS AN intimate affair: Randy Garcia. Marco and Hugh. Venclova without his granddaughter. The Ambassador without his wife. Ray Shields. Six men around a table eating pheasant and drinking goblets of Slovak red. They were back at the ambassador's residence in the third-floor dining room. Two cars had brought them up the road from the hotel where a Marine in a windbreaker greeted them at the security gate. The ambassador's wife had come in with them and while her husband sat at the piano, she led them in a hymn of thanksgiving.

All the world is God's own field
Fruit unto his praise to yield

The words were on the paper she had handed out. *Raise the song of harvest home!* It was a song about gratitude, of course, about thankfulness for the bounty you have gathered, and the bounty the

Lord will someday gather. But it was mostly about taking. First the blade and then the ear. Singing, Marco had felt a thought gathering, some genuine insight, but by that time they were on to "My Country Tis of Thee," and then the ambassador was saying Grace and his wife was gone and gathered around the table were the six men charged with remaking at least one little corner of the world.

All the while Marco was leveling out. Not exactly sober but not exactly drunk either. He sat there listening, taking in the grand simplicity of it all because it really was very simple. Half of all natural gas entering the EU came from Russia at three times normal market value. Yet Slovakia had a vast untapped store of shale gas. You pump water in one end and money comes out the other.

"Do you know how many cubic feet are in the ground here?" Shields asked the room. "Exactly. Nobody does. Right now the Slovaks are sitting on who knows how much gas. Hungary has been tapped. Romania has been tapped. Royal Dutch Shell has concessions in Ukraine. The Czechs—God bless em—are short-sighted enough to have put a moratorium on drilling. We're patient there—certainly, we are willing to be patient.

"But let's suppose this, gentlemen. Let's suppose we could open these Slovak fields and get the gas out of the ground. Oil is finished. Natural gas is the future. Amen? So what if instead of back-flowing Russian gas the EU was buying Slovak gas. Cheap Slovak gas that undersells everyone else. Think of the kind of message that would send to Putin. Think of what energy independence—a clean source, incidentally—would mean to this part of the world. We force the Russians to send their gas to China. Putin's tail between those fat KGB legs. Think about this, gentlemen. We should all be thinking about this."

GARCIA RELATED THE rest later that evening, stalking the balcony overlooking the front courtyard. It was too cold to be outside but the view was too good to be inside. The white tabletop castle to the right. To the left, thrusting out of the linden trees, a memorial to the Red Army. A winged figure atop a column, at her feet a grave-yard for the liberating dead. In between spread the city, necklaces of glittering highway and squared monoliths of glass high-rises. The curled darkness of the Danube twisting through it all like a snake.

Garcia had an unlit cigar in his fist.

"There are some elements here, naturally, that Ray failed to engage," he said. "But Ray is a salesman. Hell, he's *my* salesman, and his role here is to sell the vision. Not to address what elements have, historically speaking, failed to materialize."

Poland. What Shields had failed to mention was Poland. Nearly a third of the country had been handed over to Leviathan in shale gas concessions. But when the gas finally started coming out of the ground, Royal Dutch Shell had flooded the market with Ukrainian gas and the price had collapsed.

"It hurt the Russians as bad as it hurt us," Garcia said. "Neither side wants that to happen again, all right? The Russians can sell to China while we sell to the EU. But neither of us can do shit if the bottom falls out. So let's suppose the provocations of the West were so great the Russians were justified in rolling over the border?"

"Provocations in Ukraine, you mean?"

Garcia made a little gesture that might have concerned his cigar but might also have signaled his dismissal of so facile a question. That was the thing Marco was slowly learning: everything relied on a nod of the head, a handshake, some vague referent that would eventually manifest as policy.

"If they crossed the border," Marco said, "if there was a war, it would also keep anyone from drilling in Ukraine. Cheap Slovak gas would own the market."

Garcia said nothing. Down below a Marine walked out from the guard shack, exhaled a plume of silver, and walked back inside.

"But would this happen?" Marco asked. "Could it?"

"Could it?" Garcia laughed, delighted.

A parallel plan was in motion, a plan to bolster the Ukrainian response to Russian provocations, to help *encourage* a Russian inva-sion, to *incentivize* a low-intensity guerilla war. *Novorossiya*. We lure them toward the prospect of New Russia, Crimea, Donbas, all that they lost when the Soviet Union dissolved. A man—our man—was already moving materiel to Eastern Ukraine.

"So that right there," Garcia said, "is one line—shale gas. The other is war."

What if these two parallel lines were to meet? In Western Europe, the price rises. In Ukraine, chaos reigns. There is the faint whiff of desperation, yes, but *voila!* Here's the Slovak gas. How many trillion cubic feet? Russia turns east, sends her gas to China and all of us, everyone gathered that night, retire to our own private islands.

"And when I say private island, don't for a minute imagine I'm speaking figuratively, Mr. Congressman."

"And you're telling me because?"

"Because you've demonstrated a talent for helping to broker such deals. Because you've demonstrated loyalty. Because you are perfectly positioned to grow your career." He looked less like the bear Hugh had warned him about and more like a wolf. "You have gravitas on the issue, Mr. Congressman. When you hold forth people listen. That matters to us."

"And of course I'm not averse to wealth."

"It's common as dog shit, I grant you. But I have yet to meet the man who turned his nose up to it."

"And your man on the ground—"

"Our man."

"Our man," Marco said. "He can do this?"

Garcia seemed to consider this for a moment.

"Hell, son," he said. "He's doing it already."

AFTER THAT, DOORS began to open.

Not so much doors that had been shut, but doors about which Marco previously had no awareness. Garcia invited him for lunch at the Columbia Country Club in Chevy Chase where they ate crab cakes and drank Elijah Craig and all the legs were long and all the fairways short. *I'm sure you recall the parallel plan already in motion, Marco. Not something either of us should probe, but...* Yes, yes, of course, he was aware, and of course he had the sense not to ask questions. It had become the company line, this parallel plan, and he had become a company man, not unlike the kept women of centuries before. It all delighted Garcia. The billionaire back-slapping and squeezing elbows like a glad-handing robot. *By God, I am glad to have a man like you with me in Florida, Marco. An insane asylum if ever I've encountered one. But what do you expect from a state shaped like a gun?* Naturally, Ray Shields wandered over to say hello, to check in, to make sure things were *happy and happening*, and naturally they were, and just as naturally a few weeks later a hefty check arrived from a Leviathan shell company made out to Marco Torres's Political Action Committee.

Suddenly, there were receptions and fundraisers and drinks. Come on, Mr. Congressman, join us *après* this or *après* that. We'd love to talk about our future together. A future which was, of course, radiant.

Please tell me you don't have plans for the Friday cook-out...Saturday's bloody mary brunch...Seer Sucker Sunday...Monday dinner at the club...lunch next Tuesday with Martha and me at Café Milano?

Tell me, Mr. Congressman...

Tell us, Marco...

...where do you see the next ten, twenty, thirty years of your suddenly auspicious life taking you because we want to be a part of it, understand?

Tampa was the pawing ground of Generals, both Central Command and Special Operations Command were headquartered at MacDill AFB, and suddenly Marco was arriving at some waterfront mansion with Major General this or Lieutenant General that. Men who treated Marco in a fatherly way, proud elders whose chests were splattered with a fruit salad of medals. At least when they weren't dressed for some Halloween or masquerade ball.

Marco wore a patch and carried a sword for the Gasparilla Fest, Vendela his captured booty in a dress that showed off her hard legs. The band was called Casual Sex ("the name is aspirational, folks"), and they all came as pirates and ate cotton candy from carts set up around the pool overlooking Hillsborough Bay, the kids home with their iPads and West Indian nannies.

He floated between Tampa and the District, trips to country clubs or prayer breakfasts, local business forums where he railed against Obamacare or taxes or femi-nazi-Islamo-radicals. It didn't matter. He got up and said *No* publicly because when it had counted, privately with Randy Garcia, he'd said *Yes*.

But it was the *No* that carried. He had a district full of aging middle class white men who had watched their 401(k)s melt while their daughters got high-paying jobs in far-away cities. They had suffered the country molting from lily-white to some indeterminate chattering brown and they were angry. Angry and nostalgic for a past that had never existed, or if it had, had existed on the backs of the poor, the black, the non-male non-white non-whatever it was they were or had been or might yet be if only someone in Washington would *stand up for America*. So that was what Marco had done. And every time he said *No*, every time he raised a finger to blame the takers who were draining the makers, they cheered in a voice that spoke greenly of Money.

As for the parallel plan, there was no more talk of that. It was in motion. It was in play. Meanwhile, Marco found himself making a circuit of parties. Vendela on his arm at Garcia's Davis Island palace, Boca Grande, where everyone sang "God Bless America," dewy-eyed and swaying, while behind them the bay glittered like a toy they had all failed to outgrow.

Money flowed through the PAC, but beyond that it was as if that night in Bratislava had been only a happy dream. Then Colonel Venclova died suddenly and there was a last gathering of the tribe in New Haven. In hindsight, that was the point Marco should have realized something had already gone wrong, or at least that something was in the process of going wrong. First, there was Garcia's conspicuous absence from the service coupled with the presence of another young woman—her name was Sara Kovács—who was to be kept under watch.

But Marco never asked why because to not ask was the single thing he'd learned.

What he did do was stumble to the Duncan on Chapel Street where he drunkenly blessed the room. Or at least that had been his intention. It had seemed, at least in the moment, marginally nobler than praying for himself.

It was November when he flew up to attend a meeting at the Museum of the American Indian with several tribal chiefs, including a local delegation of Seminoles lobbying to build a casino and resort on Treasure Island. It was a sudden trip, a disruption from an extended holiday break devoted to celebrating himself, and he took a cab straight from Reagan, as impatient with the Nigerian and his too loud Sports-talk and a Baha'i air freshener as he was with everything else. The Congressman wanted warm mornings in the Florida sun, his daughters breakfasting in the kitchen. But instead he had a cold and immaculately clean cab, the radio talking Giants versus Eagles, the cabbie talking the unity of God. *There is only one source, monsieur.* Marco put his eyes on his phone and didn't look up until they arrived.

He was early and climbed the stairs to the third floor gallery. *VOICES UNHEARD* scrolled over the door. An early snow had fallen and so far as he could see, besides a homeless man looking to warm up, he was the museum's only guest.

He moved dutifully past photographs of nameless men and women, only the tribes and geographical locations given.

Tapirapé, Mato Grosso, Brazil.

Kiowa Tribe, Oklahoma, USA.

Tohono O'odham Nation, Arizona, USA.

The photographs were black and white and heavy with the burden of history, of time both felt and suffered. On any other day it would have moved him. It would have made him think of his parents. But that day all he felt was resentment, as if their solemnity had intruded upon his holiday, dragging him out into the wind and ice.

He was in the gift shop when the homeless man approached him and stood so close Marco could hear the breath rattle in his nose. Dripping boots. A parka that on closer inspection was an ancient army field jacket. The smell was wet and warm, body odor with an overlay of cologne. He went to move away, but the man moved with him.

Lord, one of these. You got them now and then. 9/11 Truthers. Anti-Fed conspiracy theorists. The D.C. homeless who otherwise spent their days on public library computers researching the role of the Trilateral Commission or the establishment of the coming caliphate.

Down in the lobby, Marco could see one of his staffers standing with the Seminole delegation and tried to catch his eye. Then the homeless man moved closer still. A wild beard, black hair spilling beneath a Redskins watch cap. They stood in front of a wall of photography books.

"Amazing, aren't they?" the man said. "I have a friend who thought I should see these. He said it would 'refashion the lens through which I imagine the world.' A bit much, I know, but I'm always interested in altered perceptions."

Marco said nothing. He sensed the man looking at him, his eyes moving up and down Marco's frame.

"You're Congressman Torres, correct?"

"I am." Marco turned to him now. Eye contact, very direct—it was how you handled these sorts of things. If you hesitated, you were finished; they latched on; started their spiel. You never show fear. "And you are?"

"Just a photography nut. But I've been hoping to meet you."

"Are you one of my constituents?"

"No, but I've certainly kept up with your activities."

"And what activities would those be?"

Marco was making a mistake asking a question, but couldn't help himself. It was the holiday despondency, he thought. A chink in the armor. Still, he had the sense to move from the bookshelf to a display of pottery and fist-sized figurines. Brave Wolf and Yellow Dog. Chaac, Guatemalan God of Rain. There was a heavy vibe of menace coming off the man, and he needed something between them when the gun came out or the knife was unsheathed. Whatever it was the man was going to pull, because it had just occurred to Marco that something was coming out, if only some single-spaced manifesto in ten-point font regarding the Reptilian Elite. Across the room was a security guard, but too far away. Then Marco saw the delegation coming up the stairs toward him, his staffer smiling. MITSITAM! read the banner over the cafeteria.

"And why is it that—" Marco started to say to the man, but realized he was gone. He felt strangely crestfallen. It was like reaching for your water glass late at night only to find it empty. The disappointment seemed disproportionate.

A few days later, at the National Cathedral, Marco saw the man again. He had gone with a campaign donor and his socialite wife who had stopped in town on their way back from a visit to their son, a pianist at Julliard. They were old Florida money—phosphate mining parlayed into real estate—and what of it they hadn't used to fund a series of endowed professorships in musicology they were giving to Marco's PAC.

That night they went to hear Shostakovich's Symphony No. 7 and in the vast space of the Cathedral, Marco found himself distracted and unmoved, looking around at profiles and the backs of heads until just down and to the left someone caught his attention.

He thought for a moment—but no, it couldn't be.

He thought for a moment it was the homeless man he'd seen at the museum. But this man was well-dressed, hair so black it appeared oily, long and brushed over his ears. Beard trim. He wore a gray suit and appeared lost in the swell of strings, head back and eyes shut. You're wrong, of course, Marco told himself. You can barely see his head let alone his face. You're dead wrong. Yet he knew he wasn't.

At the intermission, Marco excused himself to follow the man toward the restrooms, and just before the man stepped in, Marco was certain: it was the same guy.

What had he said?

I'm always interested in altered perceptions.

Now he was locked in one of the stalls, weeping.

At the concert's end Marco begged off a nightcap and rushed out into the windy night to find the man gone. But then, up the walk, he saw him making steady progress past the drifts of dirty snow toward the Metro station.

They got off in Arlington, not far, in fact, from Marco's townhouse. He waited for the man to descend a series of steps into an Irish pub and followed him inside past a crush of people pressed toward the stage where someone played "Scotland the Brave" on bagpipes. The crowd was three-deep at the bar and finally Marco slipped through to see the late Colonel Venclova's granddaughter.

Then the crowd shifted again and for no more than a minute—it couldn't possibly have been more—Marco's view was blocked. When he could see again, the man was gone and it wasn't Venclova's granddaughter at the table but a young woman who appeared similar to, but most certainly was not, the girl he'd met on the trip to Kiev and later in New Haven.

He made a long head-clearing ramble and eventually walked back to his office to find the man sitting behind his desk. The lights were off and Marco made no move to turn them on. He wasn't scared. In fact, he was relieved.

"You followed me," the man said as he steadily began to take grainy shape. The wide shoulders. The thick hair. "Poorly, I might add."

"How did you get up here?"

"How did *you* get up here, Mr. Congressman? Referring not just to this physical space, but, let's say, the larger universe in which you find yourself."

"There's security in the hall."

The man's hands were flat on the desk and he showed two empty twitching palms.

"Would you rather I leave?" he said. "You have only to say the word."

At that point Marco thought of turning on the light, but knew that somehow it would end things, that the moment hung on dim perceptions. Whatever revelation was coming could only be made in the near dark.

"What do you want with me?" Marco asked.

"I want to ask you a question, Mr. Congressman. In some sense, I suppose I'm seeking reassurance."

"For what?"

"We have a number of associates in common. Over time I have—not exactly lost faith. But there are things that trouble me. Patterns, certain scenarios I play out when I'm alone, and lately, I guess, I'm too much alone."

"I don't know what you're talking about."

"I think probably you do. But I wouldn't say much if I were you either."

"Tell me what you want."

"I already told you. I want reassurance. When I'm left on the battlefield," the man said, "and I will be, Mr. Congressman, of that I have no doubt. But when it happens, I need to know what kind of man you are. I need to know if you're one of them."

"One of whom?"

"'Whom' is a nice touch, sir. But I think we both know who I'm talking about." The man hesitated and looking back later Marco would wonder if he'd actually sighed. If he had, Marco thought, it would have betrayed something human, which would have signaled the possibility of some weakness, something that might break. But he was no more certain about the sigh than he was about the weakness.

"Let me put it in simpler form, Mr. Congressman," the man said. "What I need to know is this: are you one of the Bronze People?"

A few weeks later, as if summoned, Russian forces began to mass on the border of Eastern Ukraine, almost as if they'd been summoned.

Which, of course, they had.

IT WAS EASY enough for the Congressman to finish the Scotch, slugging from the bottle and chasing it with sips of energy drink. He was back in the hotel and needed to think through his possible options.

He could hand over everything he had in his possession to some enterprising journalist who would—what? Publish, yes. But what did he have besides a screenshot of an empty account and his own unreliable testimony? But, okay, hand it over and then what? Obviously, his political career would be over. He would also be prosecuted. So maybe he should go to the DOJ and cut a deal, but no—ridiculous.

The truth was, he believed in what was being done. Something had happened, something had clearly fallen apart in Bratislava. But that didn't change the simple fact that Marco wanted them to succeed. He wanted the gas to flow. He wanted the Russians to bleed.

So what other choices existed?

Turn himself in. Take the blame. It was evident he'd been brought on board for this very purpose. His position high enough to appear culpable, a lone actor working out of conviction; but not so high that he could protect himself or threaten larger interests. This appeared the greater possibility. He was the fall-guy, after all, so couldn't he simply take the fall?

What would happen were he to stroll into the Tampa branch office of the FBI and ask to be arrested? *I acted alone. I did it for*

Truth, Justice, and the American Way. Eventually, he would be prosecuted, yes, but whatever sentence he received would be bargained down. He would do his time and walk out a few years later a hero to the Freedom-Loving Right. Perhaps he'd even be pardoned by President Garcia. What had happened to Oliver North? A talk show and a book deal. Commemorative t-shirts.

Couldn't he do the same?

We can open a dialogue, Marco. We can still land this thing.

He felt another wave of prickled sweat and made it to the bathroom just as the vomit came up his throat.

He washed his face, brushed his teeth.

What the hell was he doing?

He thought of praying.

His mother had prayed the sun right of the sky, prayed cancer into remission, prayed dying babies back to life. Had prayed, ultimately, the faith right out of Marco's heart. She'd ruined him, in a sense. A child shouldn't be exposed to such pure uncompromising spirit. Her wild unflagging faith so great it had eventually swallowed itself—that had been his undoing.

Yet he'd gone to Nicaragua to see her. Nube Errante. Her wandering cloud.

He was fifteen the day his father was shot behind a Sunoco station on Ninth Avenue. Three weeks later his mother was off to Chiapas to join the revolution, Marco left behind with his grandmother in Tampa. His parents couldn't help themselves: they were compelled by God.

He was—what was he?

There was no way of describing it that made it seem anything other than his job, his life. But his life as separate from him, an abstraction. He thought again of his time inside the Green Zone, going to work two doors down from the Viceroy, Paul Bremer. The Any Soldier care packages with their toothpaste and PowerBars, their Lee Greenwood good intentions. Fucking Iraq, fucking Mesopotamia: It was seven months of poolside BBQs and Filipino maids and the occasional Senator doing a windshield tour. It was many things, but it wasn't exactly a war. The insurgency had been in its infancy so besides the occasional rocket or mortar attack it was like being at camp: sleeping in a dorm, eating in the KBR cafeteria. He joined a Bible study, ran on a treadmill, and over time became a sort of mascot, loved the way you love a housebroken puppy. The Ivy League staffers running entire departments because daddy gave big to Bush-Cheney '00—guys twenty-seven, twenty-eight, barely older than Marco yet running *entire departments*—they absolutely totally could not get over this freakin kid.

Outside, a war had broken out. But inside, so long as Marco worked editing documents and writing scripts for press conferences—work far beyond his pay grade—he could dismiss the violence as God's inscrutable will. It was a form of self-preservation, tucking his faith into some buried pocket of self, and though he prayed daily for the people beyond the wire, he tried as much as possible not to think about them.

A worthy distraction was talk of the Covenant. One of the oldest staffers he knew, a thirty-one-year-old MBA from the Wharton School, started riffing one day about Warfare, the necessity of Warfare, and how the War was going to be carried back to the States by all of them. It took Marco some time to realize he was talking about Spiritual Warfare, the kind, he said, fought with prayers rather than guns. They were out by one of Uday's pools, drinking Rockstars and leaned against the mosaic tiles, maybe six of them, and every last one nodding, yeah, for real, we carry it home. Marco doubted the guy even knew his name, but Marco stuck around after anyway. He wanted to talk to him. He needed to know how real this really was.

"How real is it, brother?" the staffer asked. "Tell me this: how real do you want it to be? Because that's what it comes down to, doesn't it?" His face was soft and pale which sort of amazed Marco. Marco had become lean and bony and to carry such give, through the world, through *this* world of sand and sun and the muezzin calling the faithful to prayer, seemed the greatest of luxuries.

"I'm sure you know that quote from Mr. Rove about creating our own reality, and yeah, that's come in for a lot of laughs from a lot of people, sure, whatever. But let me tell you: those people simply don't get it. They're incapable. Because the truth is, we *do* create our own reality. That's not only our birthright, that's our charge as Christians, our responsibility. God demands of us that we create our own reality, which is His reality. So how real is it?" At this point he spread his hands and smiled. It was no longer the conspiratorial whisper but a wide grin, every square inch of his body open. "That's what you have to decide for yourself, brother."

Marco nodded, and found his body, in crude imitation, leaning back and opening up. He felt exhausted, but it was a good sort of exhaustion, the kind that follows real work.

"My name's Evan, by the way." He stood and put out his arms. "Let's hug this out, all right?"

Four months later Marco flew out of Baghdad with a campaign medal and a letter of recommendation from Bremer himself. He had spent much of his time filling out college applications, and to his great surprise, everyone seemed to want him. He prayed about it, and God told him, maybe, to go to the University of Florida. So the following August he went, happily, it should be said, though it was only then, settled into an apartment complex with three hundred undergrads that Marco fell apart.

Maybe it was time to reflect, he thought later, or maybe it was the monumental triviality of *every-fucking-thing*. The decisions being made around him, being debated, being suffered over by the eighteen-year-olds through which he waded, involved what frat to rush, or from which Midtown bar to begin the Thursday night crawl.

Other kids their age were daily leaving the wire of FOBs, or living outside the wire, Surge-style, getting shot at, getting blown up. Trying to decide whether the old woman walking obliviously toward your checkpoint was carrying eggplants or wearing a suicide vest. Which was trying to decide, if you want to get right down to it, am I going to shoot granny or not? Mostly it was not, and when you didn't blow up, you thanked whatever God or god had seen fit to abandon you to this hell.

So maybe Marco simply didn't have much patience with the bickering, with the entitlement, with the *deliberateness* of it all. Or maybe he was far enough away from Iraq to actually begin to consider it. He'd rushed from the Green Zone to Gainesville and it was every bit as confusing as it sounded. This confusion made him angry. Or more to the point: it pissed him off. Everything did. The way dumbasses double-parked along West University Avenue. The way the soft serve ice cream machine in like *every damn* dining hall was always out of order. The way the girls—these otherwise slender, sleepy-eyed things—reeked of too much body spray or fruity shampoo or whatever the hell it was they seemed to marinate in.

Marco had always been a quiet, calm guy, a back-of-the-classer, silent and focused, the guy you never even considered until he got the highest grade in the class. But suddenly he could go apoplectic at the drop of the proverbial hat.

You want Mutually Assured Destruction? Try bumping the cat one night down at Fat Daddy's, try spilling a little beer on his shoes. He was a popular guy, a vet, older and wiser in a cynical sort of way. The Cuban-American right-wing wet-dream doing the anti-Castro thing, sure, but more concerned with the liberal agenda sweeping the nation.

Then it occurred to him one night that maybe he was so popular because he was so easily pissed off. And naturally that just pissed him off all the more. Which resulted in the night Marco-Smashed-the-Window. Actually, a twelve-foot window of plate glass in a particularly crowded bar.

No shit. Epic, bro. Absolutely epic.

He spent the night in the drunk tank and the next day was released by the Magistrate. All charges were dropped—even the bar owner was sympathetic—on the sole condition that he pay an overdue visit to the campus counseling center. He didn't want to go, didn't want the stigma, the cliché—here comes the damaged vet, didn't see that coming!—but had no choice in the matter.

He expected the worst and got it: an animated earth-mother in toe-rings and a silver ankh. But he did walk away with a clean record and prescriptions for Ambien and Klonopin. He went zombie after that, but at least he was doing well in class. Emotionally, he was a mess, but if he kept moving, club after meeting after lecture, it might just stay at bay. That was the thinking in the spring of his junior year when he attended a lecture by Randy Garcia, who was stumping for local Republicans while raising his own public profile. Garcia was folksy and unabashedly conservative, a businessman who prayed before every public event and conflated small government and a flat tax with the Sermon on the Mount. He'd once hated communism and now he hated Islamo-fascism. People were excited. Marco was not. But imagine, just imagine, how he felt walking into the auditorium to see Evan—*let's hug this out, all right*—Evan from Baghdad, Evan from afternoons by the palace pool and evenings drinking craft beer at the BCC, Evan sitting just behind Garcia, applauding softly.

Marco tracked him down afterward and they had a beer at the Salty Dog. Marco had the fleeting suspicion that Evan didn't remember him, but he was too excited to allow that thought to develop. The words started falling out of him, his story, everything that had happened since the day they'd parted. That Evan was trying to disguise a look of mild confusion, that he was clearly glancing over Marco's shoulder to see who else was in the place—none of that mattered. Marco felt alive for the first time in years.

He told Evan everything.

"So what I'm hearing," Evan said. "What I'm hearing is that you're suffering, and the cure for your suffering has thus far been chemical. Hey, and listen, don't think I'm faulting you here, from what you've told me—from what I already knew—you saw some horrible things, Marco. We all did, right? What I'm also hearing, and I want you to correct me if I'm off base here, but the other thing I'm hearing is this solution isn't a real solution. You're treading water."

Marco nodded.

"So let me tell you, if I may. May I give you some advice, my Baghdad brother?"

"Please."

"It's pretty simple, actually. You've got to hand it over. You follow me? By the look you're giving me I'm not sure you follow me." He smiled, glanced once at his watch, and fixed his eyes on Marco. "You can hand it over to something like Zoloft or Paxil or whatever. You can hand it over to," and he lifted his glass, "the King of Beers. I've seen it happen. You could even hand it over to some woman. I'm sure there are plenty around here that might take an interest. Or—"

And he let it hang there between them, that *or*.

Marco was determined not to repeat the word but in the end he did, so clearly was Evan waiting for it, and so badly did Marco want to please him.

"Or?"

"Or," said Evan, "you can hand it over to the Lord Jesus."

Evan was responsible for cultivating donors for a future Garcia campaign, and it was later that night at a fundraiser in Jonesville that he introduced Marco to Garcia's regional director, Hugh Eckhart.

"You know," Hugh told him, "if you're interested we could really use you."

It was on maybe their third drive across the great state of Florida that Hugh mentioned he was a Brother in the Covenant. By then, Marco knew exactly two things: Hugh was his spirit brother, and that he wanted badly to become a Covenant Brother.

A year later, degree in hand, he was.

He'd heard things about the Covenant for years. It seemed half the CPA staffers in Baghdad were Brothers, but what did that mean exactly? You could say it was a secret club, maybe, an evangelical Skull & Bones, and to some extent that was true. But you could just as easily call it a Bible study, or a select dormitory where certain young men were groomed for a certain future. You might call it, as one investigative reporter had, "a neo-con nursery." But that only scratched the well-buffed surface.

Hugh was a Brother. Two years he'd lived there. Straight out of law school and questioning everything. The secular demonic world undermining his Will to Power, his Will to Believe. He told Marco all this over those long drives fundraising for Garcia, crisscrossing the state from local campaign offices to town halls to fire departments to church basements. Sometimes Marco driving so Hugh could sit and do absolutely nothing but answer the unending flow of text messages. Hugh saw in him, or about him, or maybe he just *saw him* in a very particular light, a light Marco wasn't sure he'd ever felt before. High-beam, yes. And very knowing. And while Marco was sometimes made uncomfortable by it—here they were lost somewhere outside Jacksonville, on and off I-95 and Marco looks up from the wheel to find Hugh staring at him as if entranced—

while he was sometimes unnerved by it, he also came to love it, to need it, actually, and to suffer very acute withdrawal pains when Hugh was absent.

So they were in Tallahassee or Orlando or Fort Myers or some tiny panhandle fishing hamlet not yet overrun with condos and the *nouveau riche* trying to solidify donors, and Hugh is spilling this out, his childhood as an isolated homeschooled genius and how he'd done everything he could possibly do at Wheaton except question a single thing he'd ever been taught. And then came Yale Law.

"And I guess you could say"—big smile here—"I guess you could say I started hanging out with the wrong crowd. These social gospel pseudo-Christians."

"Pseudo like how?"

"Pseudo like white guys with dreads. Girls who thought female masturbation had something to do with the incarnation."

And they both blushed at the word *masturbation* so maybe that was it, that despite everything they both were capable of blushing?

"Anyway," Hugh said.

Anyway, he'd been working seventy hours a week as an equities trader in New York, not even studying for the Bar, so lost at this point, so confused by what he'd heard these Christians—*Christians!*—talking about. Like how Noah's Ark was a metaphor for Creation Care which was just left-wing misdirection for the environmental movement. And don't even get them started on Jesus as a socialist.

Then one day Hugh had met Evan at a Young Republicans conference, and it was Evan who eventually invited Hugh to the Covenant.

But what exactly was the Covenant? That was the subject of many a car ride, Hugh speaking in parables because how else could he describe it? Fundamentally, it was fifteen or so young men, the youngest nineteen, the oldest maybe thirty, but most in their mid-twenties, living in a slightly exhausted manor at the end of an Arlington street.

"At its most basic," Hugh told him the day they were on Amelia Island, relying on an out-of-date GPS to find a VFW hall, "it's prayer and Bible study. We gather every morning for group prayer

and every evening for Bible study. Second to that is work. First, taking care of the house: painting, cutting the grass, repairs, whatever.
But lots of us work outside the house for elder Brothers who have
gone on to higher positions."

Like Senator, Congressman, Attorney General.

"You get it?"

"Yeah, I get it."

Except he didn't, Hugh assured him. Because taking care of,
say, the House Majority Leader's clogged toilet was meant more as a
Practice, in the sense of Buddhist practice, than a job. The network-
ing didn't hurt, either.

"There are lots of elder Brothers on the Hill," Hugh said.
"Sometimes their entire staffs are younger Brothers, guys who
maybe two years ago were washing their windows or picking up
their dry cleaning."

Marco started on a lawn mower. He cut grass. He prayed. It
was beautiful. It was pure. Then one day he got up and went down
to the kitchen to find Hugh waiting for him. Marco hadn't seen
him in the two months since he'd arrived, but Hugh acted as if not
a minute had passed. All the Brothers present were smiling when
Hugh motioned at Marco's grass-stained sweat pants and t-shirt.

"Go put on your church clothes," he told him. "You're with
me."

"For the day?" Marco asked him later as they were driving
toward the Cannon House Office Building.

"For all days," Hugh said. "As of 0900, soldier, you are in the
employ of Randy Garcia."

Marco was staggered, but tried to play it off.

"I thought I was in the employ of Jesus."

Hugh smiled.

"Who did you think Randy works for?"

A year later, Marco and Hugh were in the Keys, scouting a
fundraising location. It had been an astounding year, a year of rapid
ascent, but a frustrating day. There had been confusion, delays, cup
after cup of coffee, and it was late when they finished, lost on some
nameless key amid the conch fritters ½ off with the coupon on
the back of the car wash receipt. The Key Lime pie available for

shipping. Finally, they found the Best Western on Islamorada where they had booked a room with two double beds. Except when they got to the room it had a single Queen.

"I can go down and get it changed," Marco said.

"Forget it."

"It's not a big deal. We paid for two beds."

"Do it if you want to," Hugh said, already pulling off his shoes, "but I'm too tired to argue."

So Marco didn't, and they crawled beneath the cool sheets and lay there, the air conditioning rattling beneath the window. The curtains, sheer and bulk, pulled back so that the light from the parking lot triangled the room. So maybe it was the exhaustion, maybe the intimacy, maybe the fact that despite the fatigue they were both very consciously awake.

"I need to tell you something," Hugh said eventually.

"All right."

"Something serious." Hugh turned on the lamp, and then he did something else: he reached down and wrapped one hand around Marco's right ankle.

Marco's instinct had been to jerk back as if stricken, but something had stilled him.

"I'm asking you to reserve judgment," Hugh said.

"Okay."

"Actually I'm asking you not only to reserve judgment, but not to comment at all, all right?"

"What's this about? Is this about Randy?"

"Just say 'all right.'"

"Yeah, all right, of course."

Hugh let go of his ankle and clicked the lamp back off.

"I was in Iraq, too," he said. "Briefly. I guess you didn't know that."

"No."

"It's crazy," Hugh said. "I've only told one other person. What happened, I mean."

"What happened?"

"I told Randy right after."

"What happened?"

Hugh was silent and Marco found himself wishing badly for Hugh's hand back around his ankle.

"It was just," Hugh said eventually. "I don't know. Shit over there."

"Yeah."

"Excuse my language but the goddamn motherfucking shit over there." His voice broke, and Marco thought he was going to cry or scream, but when he went on his voice was steady.

"I was just out of the Covenant," Hugh said, "and so insanely thrilled to be doing anything."

It was for Randy. Randy had hired him, saved him, given him purpose. So when Randy asked him to go, he went. His privilege was to oversee a number of reconstruction projects financed by Leviathan. He had no involvement with the Iraqi people, no attachment whatsoever, and imagined himself a sort of financial mercenary. He was scared, but he was also grateful. Here he was, barely in his thirties, and already entrusted with a string of no-bid multimillion-dollar contracts.

He did the work and he did it well. Four months later it was time to go home. He was glad. Glad to leave, but, more than that, glad he had proven worthy of Randy's trust.

"You have to remember how young I was," he said. "It's such a cliché, I know, but how young we all were."

"Naïve."

"Naïve, innocent. The entire country."

So: it was time to go home.

A military convoy would move them from the Green Zone to the airport along Route Irish: four lanes and six miles of scrubby palms and piles of trash. He put on his body armor, and sat there, the ceramic plates of his vest steadily rubbing him raw. He'd only traveled by helicopter before, out to distant construction projects, but here was something suffocatingly intimate. Here was the smell of machine oil, the chatter on the radio. He exhaled just as the vehicles started moving, headed to the airport.

Then something happened and suddenly they weren't.

Later—but only later—he learned there had been an ambush that turned into a major firefight, a company pinned down, a Humvee burning by a river of sewage. They shouldn't have gone. He learned that later too—there was a quick reaction force for such— but they did. The neighborhood had accepted American aid, a school was being built, a medical clinic, and Hugh supposed they knew that made it particularly vulnerable. The lieutenant up front must have known the same because he wheeled the entire convoy around.

A running gun battle had spilled through a string of concrete buildings. It was over before they got there, but Hugh didn't know it at the time. Hugh didn't know anything. The Bradleys circled, the soldiers poured out, and Hugh and two other contractors were left alone in the back wondering why in God's name they weren't already getting on a flight out of this hell.

But after a few minutes, they stepped out, too.

"I remember the ditch."

The open sewer and the smell of raw sewage. The neighborhood was a collection of block buildings, two and three stories, roofed in corrugated tin. Rebar stuck up like stray hairs. The streets dusty and uneven.

"It was so quiet. You could hear the soldiers moving around, occasionally one of them calling. A helicopter flew over on its way somewhere else, you know? But that was all."

His eyes were watering. The dust, or maybe the sewage as he walked through the empty village. Because for some reason Hugh Eckhart had started walking.

"I could tell you every detail. I passed the huts and a soccer field, headed toward the building that was situated on the edge of the highway—the half-completed school, the target."

As he approached, the smell grew. The air deadened.

"There were soldiers clearing houses, I guess. But they stopped, froze. Everything froze. It was just me, walking. Nothing else moved until I got to that school."

It was there that he saw the children, their hands bound to their desks, the older ones shot execution-style in the back of the head, the younger ones with their throats slit. A torture room, they called it. Electrical wires. A hand drill. Three girls sat on the concrete back-to-back-to-back, legs spread on the floor as if assuming the shape of a flower, throats cut so that they appeared to smile.

"There were nineteen in all, and I kept thinking: we did this. By being here. And then I thought: No, God did this. You know what I mean?"

Marco said nothing.

"God did this. Because God gave us dominion over the earth. Us. Me and you and Randy and all the rest of us."

Marco was silent.

"I was reading Whitman then," Hugh said. "Whitman had sort of sustained me, I guess. Do you know that line about the dark patches?"

The light was off, the room still.

"It is not upon you alone the dark patches fall,
 The dark threw its patches upon me also."

Outside, he walked around the building, and it was there that he saw it, his vision, his emissary from God. Massive and brilliant, the angel was hunched in the lee of the building, its wings scraping the eave of the roof. It looked at Hugh as he approached, angry, he understood, to be interrupted at such grim work, then turned its radiant face back to the task at hand, back to the children who lay face down in the mud. It was gathering them, collecting the newly dead into its bright arms.

"I ran back to the Bradley and said nothing. What could I possibly say? Nineteen dead children and an Angel, stacking them in its arms like firewood. I guess it was on CNN the next day, but the next day I was in Germany, waiting for the hop back to the States."

"That's just…"

"Yeah."

"I don't know what to say."

"Please don't say anything," Hugh said.

"I just—"

"Please."

"All right."

"Just forget it," he said, and put his fingers back around Marco's ankle. "Please."

And that *please* was the final word on the subject, the final word that night and the final word the next day as they made the endless trek back to D.C.

It occurred to Marco now, late at night in his Tampa motorcourt, that he should have taken Hugh's call, sitting on his daughter's bed, he should have answered his damn phone. But it wasn't too late, was it? Dawn was near, the caffeine fading, and all at once the exhaustion washed over him. The nausea, too. He was sweating again and sat perfectly still until it passed. He had to sleep. But when he woke he promised himself he would do the one thing he should have done from the very start: he would call Hugh. He'd call Hugh and then go to Boca Grande. It wasn't too late. He could still land this thing.

A part of him believed that.

A part of him believed it was never too late.

MARCO WOKE THE next morning late and sick. Sunlight bisected the bed through the part in the curtains: it was after eleven by his watch. He'd thrown up once during the night, emptying himself, though his body seemed not to be aware of its emptiness as he dry-heaved his way across the room back to bed.

Now his stomach was less cramped than caved.

Still, he managed to get up. He managed to drink water from the tap and finally, reluctantly, turn on the TV. There was no cable and what he got were the morning talk shows, the celebrity cookbooks and aggrieved actors. When the news came on there was no mention of him and he suspected there wouldn't be, not yet.

It was no comfort. If he was wanted, if he was missing—there was a certain protection in this. So long as his disappearance remained private he knew he was in trouble. Anything could happen to a man cut loose.

He dressed and walked up the highway until he found a pay phone. He still intended to call Hugh, but the conviction he had felt just hours before had faded. Marco wanted to talk to him, *would* talk to him, but he had to figure some things out first.

He hadn't touched the business card since Yesenia had given it to him—Penny and the D.C. number—but he called it now. A man answered.

"I need to speak to Penny."

"Penny?"

"I have a message to contact Penny."

"You have a—wait, this is—Congressman, don't hang up—"

But he already had.

He fished several quarters from his pocket and dialed the next number from memory. Mike Lee sounded scared.

"I'm willing to meet you, Marco. I will despite everything, but I have to let the FBI know if I do."

Marco looked out on a lot of plastic bags and busted glass, the day already hot.

"They were here when I came back from meeting you," Lee said. "Which, by the way, where the hell did you go?"

"It wasn't the FBI."

"Local office, Marco. I saw the badge."

"It wasn't the FBI, Mike. Believe me."

"I'm going to have to report this conversation. You know that, right?"

He hung up and called his chief Bill Waters's cell.

"Mike Lee wants to turn me into the FBI."

"You need to come in, all right? If you come in now we can settle this. I've been in touch with Garcia's office. We can sit down and talk."

"Simple as that, huh."

"They want this resolved as badly as we do."

"Except I can't come in and you know it. Not yet, at least."

"Why the fuck not, Marco? Why not right-fucking-now?"

"Because I don't have what I need yet."

"What you need is to come in. Please. They want this to work out. But there's a point at which it passes out of Randy's hands."

"Nothing passes out of Randy's hands."

"Marco—"

"I've got to put all this together first. The woman in Bratislava. The secondary account."

"We can't be having this conversation." His chief sounded on the edge of tears. His chief was about to cry. "You're making me an accessory."

"You *are* an accessory. In the very least you're an accessory, same as me."

"Marco, please," he said. "Come in, okay? We sit down and talk to Garcia's people. We work this out."

"I need to see Hugh Eckhart first. Without the FBI. I need you to arrange it."

"What the hell makes you think he'll see you?"

"He'll see me."

"He isn't even in Tampa."

"I have a feeling he is. I have a feeling quite a few people are in town."

"Marco—"

"Just call him."

"Why don't you call him yourself?"

"I can't do that."

"Why goddamn it not?"

"Bill, please."

There was a long pause on the line, long enough for a hooptie full of teens to cruise by. He watched them turn around at the end of the street and come back toward him. He was sweating again, almost trembling.

"If I can arrange it," his chief said, calm again, "you'll come in?"

"You arrange it and after I go straight to Randy."

"I can't promise anything."

"But just the two of us, me and Hugh. No calls, no tricks. Set it up and I'll come in. I'll go to jail, I'll take the fall. I'll do whatever they want."

"Give me his number," he said finally. "He seems to have dropped off the planet of late."

Marco did.

"Now give me a number where I can reach you."

"No, I'll call you."

"Christ, Marco."

"Five minutes."

"Give me ten."

The hooptie ambled past, low slung, rattling. The boys inside seemed more bored than dangerous. A Puerto Rican flag. Clouds of white smoke. He called Waters back in seven minutes.

"One-thirty at Bern's Steakhouse."

"I knew I could trust you."

"You just keep your end of the deal. You meet him and tonight you go see Randy."

"All right."

"We can still fix this, but right now you're in the shit."

"Yeah," Marco said. "We all are."

BERN'S WAS A white stucco compound, a pre-fab Moorish dream, windowless and just off the Lee Roy Selmon Expressway. Marco parked the pickup and checked himself in the rear view mirror. He'd walked back to the hotel and pulled himself together as best he could, but it was largely hopeless. He drank off the last of an energy drink and rounded the building.

Hugh waited for him at the top of the steps. He looked emaciated, starved into a tight-fitting gray suit, his hair smoothed back in a gelled pompadour that made him appear vaguely antique. It took Marco a moment to realize it was a wig. It took him a moment more to realize Hugh looked sick. But he also looked clear-eyed.

"Shit, Marco."

"Good to see you too."

"This is the best you could do?"

"I seem to be on the run of late."

"That's what you're calling it?"

"My bank account's frozen. My apartment was trashed."

"In the District or here?"

"The townhouse."

"I'm not surprised." Hugh took his phone from his pocket and swiped the screen. "Let's get a table. I'm not sure how much time I have."

They sat in the dining room along a wall of picture windows Marco hadn't seen from the street, ushered quickly through the walnut and velvet dining room by the put-upon captain. Marco was waiting for some canned remark—*perhaps you'd be more comfort-*

able in the lounge?—but it never came, just the quick brush-off, the heavy wine list with twill bookmark, the curt nod to the man who came over and took their drink orders.

They drank bourbon in silence while outside, off the edges of the deck and out in the trees, a storm gathered. Hazy green shadows. Dark thunderheads impossibly low. Marco touched his fork and sensed some assemblage of wave or light, some slight electricity. Only the current not yet strong enough to be realized. But soon enough.

"Can you tell me what's happening?" he said finally.

Hugh looked at him for a moment without speaking. It was a pained look.

"Want to know what I think?" Marco asked.

"Your interpretation of events?"

"What I know," Marco said, "is that things are moving along, everything going according to plan, and then one day—yesterday, let's say—I go home and find my apartment trashed. Like I'm getting some cryptic warning sign. Then my back account's frozen. Someone comes by my house—"

"Someone came by your house?"

"The housekeeper saw them."

"But not you?"

"She thought they were immigration."

"They weren't immigration."

"No shit they weren't. Now Mike Lee tells me the FBI just paid a visit."

"That doesn't seem possible. At least not yet."

"Then who?"

"Come on, Marco."

"Tell me who?" ·

"When the global order falls apart, when all the institutions of liberal democracy have crumbled—"

"Are you delivering a speech?"

"When the entire post-second world war inheritance of order goes—"

"You are, aren't you?"

"Just listen to me. When that's gone, who do you think is going to be left standing?"

"So Randy sent his boys knocking?"

"He doesn't answer to Congress," Hugh said. "He doesn't answer to voters or donors."

"I know I'm not innocent. But I thought I was part of something here, a larger plan. Some sort of global strategy."

"You were."

"I *was*?"

"You know what I mean."

"Actually, that's the thing. I completely don't."

The waiter brought out another round of drinks. Hugh drank his in one long swallow, batted his watering eyes, and waved over another.

"Things evolved suddenly," Hugh said. "They didn't believe it could happen, but it did. She got a dossier called FIREBIRD."

"This is the woman in Bratislava you're talking about?"

"She left it at the drop but then she disappeared."

"The assistant or whatever?"

"Sara Kovács. She's a good woman."

"So you're a part of this?"

"She was working for the ambassador's wife, but then—"

But then he did this thing with his head. Marco caught it, the way Hugh looked quickly over each shoulder. It was barely a brush—he could have been flexing his jaw for all it encompassed—but Marco caught it.

"Who's watching us, Hugh?"

"For the thousandth time, I'm trying to help you here."

"Then tell me what happened in Bratislava."

"Nothing happened. That's what I'm telling you. She got the dossier and disappeared."

"Then I find my apartment trashed."

"It wasn't supposed to fall on you. I didn't think it would fall on you like this."

"Who was it supposed to fall on then?"

"I had to empty the account."

"Jesus. The eleven point one million."

"They were using it to buy weapons, rockets, sniper rifles. It was the only way to get their attention. But it wasn't supposed to fall on you."

"Who was it supposed to fall on?"

"I was trying to do something right for once in my life. That's all."

"All God's creatures great and small," Marco said.

"I don't believe in that anymore."

"I think maybe you have to."

Hugh waved over yet another round.

"Not anymore I don't. I—"

Marco felt his stomach knot and doubled forward, one hand flat on the tablecloth, the other around his waist.

"Are you all right?" Hugh asked.

"I'm fine."

"You need to see a doctor."

"I'm fine, goddamn it."

"Fine? You show up here dressed in rags, hiding."

"What did you expect me to do?"

"All right. I get it."

"Sit on my couch?"

"I said I get it."

"Sit on my couch and wait for Randy's boys to show up with the pliers and blowtorch?"

"I get it, and I'm sorry."

Marco attempted to nod, but the gesture proved too much. He was a whisper of his past self, a notion, an unfed Lazarus brought reluctantly from the tomb. He was also drunk.

When Hugh stood he appeared equally drunk.

"I have to," he said, and staggered away.

Marco kept his eyes on the front door but they were alone, for all intents and purposes just a couple of businessmen boozing on the company dime.

A few minutes later Hugh staggered back, dropped into his chair, and tipped forward.

"I've been reading about the Bronze People," he said.

"What?"

"The Bronze People."

"What are you talking about?"

"You never heard the Colonel talk about this? About *Death &
Life*? The Bronze People are us," Hugh said. "We are finally being
revealed."

"Revealed as what?"

"The Colonel honestly never told you what to think about the
Bronze People? I thought the Colonel told everyone what to think."

The Bronze People were the well-fed, the insured, the American
strivers who saw Being as a ladder to climb. They were the safe, the
smug. They didn't fear the world so much as ignore it.

"But God demands risk, Marco."

"I think you're full of shit."

"On earth as it is in heaven—it's our charge."

"I think you're full of absolute shit."

"No, listen. Without risk, God is their projection. They won't
embrace a God that is *totaliter aliter*. Which means they can never
know love. You hear what I'm saying? I couldn't live like that anymore."

He tried to wave over another round of drinks but the waiter
ignored him.

"This thing you're holding onto," Hugh said, "you call it identity,
your essential self, your essence, whatever you call it, I—I've only
now realized it. My whole life I missed it. We all did. The Covenant,
the campaigns. How did we miss it?"

"Tell me what happened in Bratislava."

"It isn't real. We are re-created every day if we allow ourselves to
be. It's like manna from heaven. There's always enough."

"Bratislava, Hugh."

"Don't ever stop moving. Rilke said that. Be open to everything, radically open."

"Did you set me up?"

"In a few minutes—"

"Hugh."

"Please listen. In a few minutes," his voice was beginning to
slur, "you're going to go to the bathroom and when you walk back
out you are going to be in possession of something."

"I'll tell you what I think."

"There's still a way out, Marco."

"I think you're full of shit, and I think you set me up."

"Just go take a piss." Hugh's eyes had bleared into some manic grace. But his voice was clear. "And be sure to wash your hands. Come back with clean hands."

"Clean hands."

"It might still be possible, Mr. Congressman."

"Hugh."

"Please," he said, and reached across the table to circle Marco's wrist with his fingers. It was only for a second, quick enough that Marco might have imagined it. Only he hadn't. Clean hands. He stood and nodded.

The bathroom was a narrow, marble affair. Mirrors. Sconces of malnourished light. He'd been here once before, a luncheon with donors or would-be donors years ago, but hardly remembered the place. The amnesia of upward mobility squared by the sneaking suspicion you'd remember everything on the way down.

He managed a few nervous splashes of flax-colored urine, checked himself in the mirror, washed his hands and splashed his face. It was when he reached for a paper towel that he saw it. Stuffed crudely in the bottom of the dispenser was a brown envelope, the corner badly bent in order to fit. It read *FIREBIRD* in what he recognized as Hugh's frightened scrawl. Inside he could feel a sheaf of paper. He put it beneath his t-shirt, flat against his stomach, and walked back out.

Hugh was still at the table, eyes on his phone, and all at once Marco was reminded of the months he had spent in Davos trying to put the Iron Ore deal together. Hanging around the lobby of the Bad Ragaz sipping expensive coffee. Carrying a messenger bag and sending lonely texts. But more than that it had been the feeling of nearing the end of something, the wildness of that. The fear, too.

Outside the day was hammered gold, the rain-light weak and weakening as it stretched over the far roofs and trees. But inside, it was all fear. Still, he was alive.

He sat down without complaint.

"It's a shame I can't stay," Hugh said. "I understand it's very good, the food."

"The chauteaubriand is actually one of those rare things as good as promised."

"That's good. I'm glad for that at least."

Hugh stood, straightened the trim gray suit, and all at once Marco realized that he was dying. The rumors of cancer—they weren't rumors. The emaciation, the gray pallor. His friend would be dead soon, and Marco felt some great regret rise up within him.

Hugh watched him. He seemed about to say something else but then didn't.

Instead, he pocketed his phone and walked out.

Marco watched him go around the corner past the bar and captain's stand, a pencil line in the dimness, graphite and smudge, and then nothing at all.

The day was inky with rain and alcohol, and Marco sat for some time after Hugh left, long enough for his eyes to fully adjust to the failing light. Then he touched the envelope flat against his stomach. He was going to walk out the front door and maybe it would work out, though most likely it wouldn't. Still, it was nice to think of his old friend floating down the front steps, as free, at least in that moment, as a wandering cloud.

IT WAS WELL after midnight, but Marco was still awake. He'd left the steakhouse and driven the pickup back to the Sand & Palm Motorcourt, composed himself, and driven to Boca Grande where he found Randy Garcia sitting in the solarium.

He had walked out of Bern's feeling buoyant, gliding on a warm cloud of possibility, and it wasn't so much that he had the dossier in hand as it was the fact that Hugh had given it to him. This was a signal of what exactly? Marco couldn't say, only that it marked for him the possibility of a different life. Probably, the information offered some sort of security, something he could bargain with. At the least, it offered some small measure of revenge: he could simply hand it over to the media just as it was handed to him. But that was beside the point. The point was the act itself, that another human being had put himself at great risk to offer Marco the possibility of escape.

And here was how he was going to do it: he was going to take the blame.

For the last few hours Marco had sat with his laptop open and composed a narrative of all that had happened. Not just the unfolding of events in Ukraine and Slovakia, but his entire life. Or almost all of it. He had made a few key deletions, a few tactical changes, and the result was that the plot appeared to be completely his own. There was no mention of Randy Garcia or Colonel Venclova, and there was most definitely no mention of Leviathan's stake in Rosneft. Congressman Marco Torres was the proverbial lone wolf, moving money from his PAC to pro-democracy forces in Eastern Ukraine because it was the right thing to do.

He moved the money because he loved freedom.

He aided anti-separatist forces because no one else would.

Eleven point one million U.S. because freedom isn't free.

He was a veteran, after all, a patriot, a believer in Kennedy's charge to *pay any cost, bear any burden*. There was no mention of any of his ambiguities or hesitations, only the necessary routing and account numbers.

Alfa Bank.

Paradise Financial.

The URLs originating in the Caymans.

He emerged from the document as an American hero, and would be recognized as such by the political right. The liberal elites—many of the very people who had stood to profit from the entire affair—would condemn him as a criminal, a political vigilante, and that was exactly what Marco wanted.

When he was finished he would destroy the originals, send the narrative to various media outlets, and sit back to face the congressional inquiry, the DOJ, the federal inquisition. In the end, Garcia would be elected president and Marco would do a couple of years of light detention at a low-security camp. And then his new life would begin. For so long he had deluded himself, for so long he'd repeated things that weren't true. He'd never believed in God—he knew that now. He'd never believed in anything but himself. And that was okay, that was fine. He wasn't made American by birth. He was made American by the power of his self-delusion.

In between all of this, he puked into the trashcan. Bourbon and Red Bull and then nothing beyond stringy bile. He could feel the strength going out of him—and knew he had to hurry.

Around eight, he'd saved the file and tucked his laptop behind the grate of the air duct. It was an amateur place, but he couldn't locate another. He dressed, prepared himself as best he could, but on the way to the door something caught his eye. It was the letter he had started the previous day, the letter to Vendela wadded into a ball at the foot of the bed.

It wasn't salvageable. Not the paper, but the sentiment. He had been in another place then, preparing for a different future, and it appeared to him as a relic. He thought of destroying it, but felt a certain pity that extended not just to the man who had written it, but to the very message itself.

The failed message. The failed life.

If it was a relic, it was also a reminder.

He left it on the bed and drove to Boca Grande.

GARCIA'S HOUSE WASN'T so much a house as a compound of buildings, something that started before you realized it and continued long past what seemed possible. Gray stone sprawling over three or four lots. One giant variance request flush against the seawall. Cars lined the street along the latticed iron fence all the way down to the blue Davis Island P.D. sawhorses.

Marco approached the gate on foot.

The storm that had whipped all afternoon was gone now and what remained was the sparkle of dew caught in the yard-lights. Around the corner and nearer the water he could see the tops of white tents and strung lanterns, hear the sound of laughter. The people appeared happy, slim and polyamorous beneath the lights that struck off chafing dishes and samovars holding whatever it was that was wafting across the lawn.

A blue-suited security guard checked his name and spoke softly into his lapel. A moment later two men emerged from the house and came down the walk.

"Congressman Torres?"

"I believe Mr. Garcia is expecting me."

"If you could raise your arms, sir."

He ran a wand over Marco's body and led him through the front entrance, past a fountain, and into the caterers and noise.

The party was out back around the pool and against the dark shimmer of Hillsborough Bay, but Marco wasn't headed that way; he was headed up the stairs. He had a brief view of the living room—the mounted antique rifles, the autographed baseballs in glass cubes. Then, at the bottom landing, out through a wall of glass, he thought he saw his wife in heels and a pussy-bow blouse, Bill Waters beside her.

This wasn't possible.

But—

The man put his hand lightly on Marco's elbow.

"This way, sir."

He climbed three flights of marble stairs up to what was revealed to be a solarium, a glass dome of ornate couches and chairs, a giant tear-drop chandelier burning dimly. You could see the tops of the tents around the lighted pool, the sagged corners where rain had collected. You could see the band. But no sound. The room was sound-proofed.

Randy Garcia sat by the far wall, face turned to the glossy bay, a lean borzoi curled by his feet.

"I thought I saw my wife downstairs," Marco said.

Garcia turned.

"That's certainly possible. Everyone seems to be out tonight. Thank you, Joseph," he said to the man that had led Marco up. "You can leave us."

The door shut and Garcia turned back to the water.

He wore white socks and no shoes.

He hadn't yet stood.

"It appears Hugh Eckhart has up and disappeared on us," he said. "I don't suppose that surprises you?"

"Where is he?"

"I don't know, Marco. That's sort of my point." He turned, crossed and uncrossed his thin legs. "Christ, man, you look like the walking dead. Want to tell me why you're here?"

"I said I'd come. I'm just keeping my end of the deal."

"You're pale as a ghost."

"I came to talk to you."

"Well," and he spread his hands, open-palmed except for a cigar clutched by his thumb, "you're here. Talk."

"I'm going to turn myself in."

Garcia snorted. "Hell, son. To me?"

"To the FBI, to Justice. That's what I came to tell you."

Garcia was shaking his head. "Marco," he said. "Be serious for a minute."

"The Tampa P.D. if I have to."

"I'm sorry, son," Garcia said. "I honest to God am. But that's not going to happen. Why don't you sit, all right?" He motioned at a chair opposite him. "I understand you met with Hugh today."

Marco was silent.

"Bern's," Garcia said. "That's a heavy place. I guess you're aware of the connections to Kennedy's assassination?"

"Frank Ragano," Marco said. "Trafficante."

"Folks love shit like that. Conspiracy theories. The mafia and worldwide Jewry. Except here's the kicker. None of it's true. That they sat there and plotted. No, sir. It never happened." Garcia looked at him. "I don't mean to disappoint you. They were pissed off, absolutely. That much is true. They'd lost their casinos in Havana to Castro and here Kennedy had failed to kill the man. Did you know this? Or maybe you thought it was happening again, you and Hugh sitting around, reordering the universe. Shit, Marco. I've read up on all of it. Ragano was getting dialysis in Miami the week of Dallas. We know that for a fact. We also know Hugh got on a plane a few hours ago," Garcia said. "We don't know where to yet, but we'll know by the time he lands. We also know he gave you something."

"Only his good wishes."

"His good wishes, goddamn." When he smiled he looked like a wolf, something physiologically superior, if a little sated, a little sleepy. But no less dangerous for it. "He was running around on a German passport, completely unknown to us. A smart man, Hugh. But smarts only get you so far."

The dog raised its head and eased it back down.

"He's Stage Four," Garcia said. "He tell you that?"

"There were rumors."

"Refused treatment."

"He was talking about the Bronze People."

"The Bronze People? Shit, that was Venclova talking."

"What happened to the Colonel?"

"Hugh's mistake was listening." Garcia shook his head. "Eschatology. The Last Things. Who the hell talks like that? All the Bonhoeffer he had em reading. That goddamn *Death & Life* he carried till it fell apart. Made poor Hugh think he was on some grand mission ordained by the Lord. You remember our man on the ground?"

"He came after me once. In my office."

"He threaten you?"

"He asked me if I was one of the Bronze People."

Garcia nodded.

"Tomas got in all their heads. Hugh's, his crazy granddaughter. David Lazar. What happened to the Colonel was regrettable. I see now it was inevitable, looking back. But that doesn't make it any less regrettable. For a long time he was my closest friend." Garcia leaned forward, elbows on his knees, face reddening. "We got him out through Vienna. This was in '86. It's still probably the finest thing I ever did. Did you know any of that?"

"No."

"Of course you didn't. So don't for a second think it pleased me." He eased back and addressed the glass ceiling arced above them. "What else did ole Hugh say?"

"He said we won't embrace a God that is *totaliter aliter*."

"Shit."

"It means 'wholly other.'"

Garcia sighed.

"He was always the Colonel's boy. Close to me as a son, but deep down he was the Colonel's. He ever tell you about what happened to him in Iraq, what he saw?"

"His Angel."

"I guess we were the only two he told. Not exactly something you go blabbing about, I suppose." Garcia motioned again at the chair opposite him. "I wish you'd sit."

This time Marco did.

Garcia leaned back in his chair, fingers laced and resting on his stomach.

"He told me right after," he said. "He was a kid and something astounding had happened to him. I guess he thought of me as some sort of mentor."

"We all did."

"What's that?"

"I said we all did. We all believed."

"In what?"

"In you, I guess."

Garcia nodded reluctantly.

"Those weren't bad days," he said. "Lot of promise. Lot of future ahead of us. Soon as he told me though, I knew he regretted it. It makes you vulnerable, telling something like that. You can't take it back. But here's the thing. It never happened. I mean I have no doubt he believes he saw something. Some archangel with flaming sword. But this massacre."

He exhaled, his head slowly moving side to side.

"I looked into it. I mean how could I not? Something like that, it would be an international incident, a room full of dead children, tortured children. But that convoy ran straight to the airport. It didn't stop. It didn't get rerouted. I talked to the lieutenant myself. He dreamed the thing, poor old Hugh did. What do you make of that?"

"I don't make anything of it."

"You were over there. I guess you're sympathetic. Probably a lot of people have worse dreams."

"Probably so."

"I dream every night of snakes. Everywhere snakes, and I never got any closer than Amman, Jordan. Got all my people out, though. Maybe the only other honorable thing I did besides getting Tomas out. The translators, the fixers, their families. Every last one of them."

Garcia took his hands off his stomach and pushed himself upright.

The borzoi stirred but did not rise.

"Let me ask you something," he said. "If you were going to turn yourself in why'd you come here? Why not go straight to the feds?"

"I thought we were the feds."

"You're funny about it, and I admire that. But there's an FBI branch right downtown."

"I guess I wanted to see you. I want you to understand my intentions."

"Which are what exactly?"

"I intend to take the fall."

"That's all?"

"What else is there? I lawyer up, cut a deal with Justice."

"Shit."

"I make the whole thing plausible. People do it every day."

"Shit, son. It's admirable, but it won't work."

"The total blame," Marco said. "The money. The weapons. I have evidence to support my grand malfeasance."

"So that's what Hugh gave you then. Dear soft-hearted Hugh with his make-believe Angel. That's what he spent these last few months doing, running around gathering evidence against me."

"I guess so."

Garcia looked at the cigar as if only now discovering it.

"I hate it, but the truth is it got too big. These goddamn Russians. I don't know what Hugh told you but I didn't want David Lazar killed. That was unnecessary. That wasn't my call," Garcia said. "But the goddamn lamestream media will want their story."

"Let me give it to them."

"You know it doesn't work like that."

"I can give them the closest thing to the truth."

"Wouldn't matter."

"That I acted, that I believed—that is the truth, actually."

"Christ, son, nobody looks to politics for the truth." Garcia looked at him as if disappointed in his failure to imagine. "That is your wife you saw down there. Do you want to see her?"

Marco looked down at the tents. A man with a stick was moving from corner to corner, pushing from beneath and spilling the collected rain. He could see people cheering, but heard nothing. When the stomach cramp came, he managed to keep himself upright, squeezed himself into some tighter version of himself.

"Marco?"

"No."

"What's that?"

"I said no."

"I understand." Garcia stood and seemed to attempt a shrug, some self-conscious gesture. "Everybody's going to blame America anyway. Might as well make it worth their while. I do wish it wasn't like this though."

"You've been good to me. I understand your position."

"Goddamn, son."

"You gave me my start. Way back when. I appreciate that."

"That was Hugh. Hugh's always been the man behind the curtain."

"Still, you dealt me in and I appreciate it."

"In spite of everything."

"I'm being serious when I say it."

Garcia studied him and went back to his cigar. "I won't tell you what to do, Mr. Congressman. But if you try to go public with this, you're a ghost. You know that, don't you?"

"Then give me another option."

Garcia looked at him as if trying to commit him to memory. "Hell. They got to you too, didn't they? You're already a ghost."

"No, I'm alive."

"That's your ego talking."

"Maybe," Marco said, "but it's all I've got."

*

HE DROVE STRAIGHT back to the Sand & Palm, got a Red Bull from the vending machine, and went back to his laptop. He worked another two hours before he felt fatigue settle over the nausea. Only it wasn't just fatigue. He felt jittery with the caffeine, sore from dry-heaving, but it was something deeper, a sort of hopelessness he knew he had to keep at bay.

The sheer amount of information in the dossier was overwhelming. But he kept at it, worked for another two hours, incorporating this file and that spreadsheet, all the while puking into the trashcan. It was a complete history of the last two years and he worked to make it incomplete, to create gaps large enough to fill with his old life. If he could bury enough of his old life here, a new life would emerge in its place. That was what kept him going: the sense that he wasn't so much changing the past as creating the future. The world of Mike Lee and Larry Medicine, the power lunches with trade lobbyists, his wife—there would be no more of that. Nube Errante. To wander free as a cloud. His mother had been exactly right—it was the only thing worth pursuing.

What his wife was doing here wasn't complicated: she was moving on without him.

It was still hours to daylight and he felt certain he would be done by then. He would sleep at dawn. When he woke, he would email everything to every media contact he'd ever had. After that, he'd find a doctor. He was sick, but his sickness would have to wait.

He got another Red Bull from the vending machine and looked out at the deserted street.

It had all started in Iraq. Somehow that had never occurred to him. Sitting out by Uday's pool while somewhere an Angel gathered the dead. He would have liked to explain things to his daughters. To tell them he had tried to embody the good, only the good had never bothered to reciprocate. He had failed, but he had tried all the same.

He would have liked to tell them that.

He turned back to the file.

He woke to the blue emptiness of the room. He'd heard something, a noise, but there was nothing now. He raised his head. Somehow he was on the floor, exhausted and barely able to sit up. There was only the light from the screen, the light from the streetlamp that entered through a part in the curtains. For a moment he couldn't place where he was. He could have been an infant in a boat, an orphaned boy in Ybor City, a soldier in Baghdad. He could have been a father, waking to the sound of a child crying from the shallow bed of her sleep. Except there was no noise.

Except he heard it again.

He pulled himself up to look at the screen. The work was complete and saved. He had only to send it. He put the laptop aside and looked out at the dark street that was just as empty as before.

He tried to stand but was too weak. It was more than just nausea, more than exhaustion. His vision was beginning to fray, his fingers turning white. He thought he would sleep now and send the file when he woke, but then he heard it again, louder, closer too, and it came to him what it was.

He grabbed the laptop from the armchair and sat on the edge of the bed, logged into the Wi-Fi and began to bring up his email. They were outside—he could hear them assembling.

The internet connection was slow. He heard them again, a soft bumping sound as if gauging the heft of the door. He fought to stay upright, logged into his email but instead of his account saw the pyre of himself blaze up and out. All of it beneath the noise. The men readying themselves out on the concrete walk.

COMPOSE

ADDRESS

His guts cramped and he remembered the pink dust in his Arlington townhouse, fairy dust. The fine powder that lay over everything. *They got to you too, didn't they?*

The Russians, Garcia had meant.

They had poisoned him.

He put one hand against the wall for balance and typed with the other. Added three addresses—reporters at the *New York Times*, CNN, the *Tampa Bay Times*—and began uploading the attachment.

Poisoned him.

The men slowly gathering outside his room, the file slowly gathering within—it seemed to take forever, but could have been no more than a few seconds. Yet he heard every bit of it. The sound of these Russians preparing to tear down the door and then the sound of the door coming down just as the filed uploaded.

He looked up for only a second, but it was enough. A fatal hesitation—they knocked the laptop from his hands—but it couldn't have been helped.

He had failed to hit SEND, but didn't care. He couldn't get past that sound of invasion.

That sound of someone coming in to change his life, to end it.

Never in his life had Marco Torres heard something so American.

THE HOTEL

May 2014

THREE DAYS AFTER Erin Horváthová disappeared from her life and world and, more specifically, the residence of the U.S. ambassador to Slovakia, Susan Logan, wife to that same ambassador, swallowed a Valium and lay on Erin's bed.

The point was to try to sleep. The point was to try to force the universe into the sort of small still point Susan might find herself capable of examining.

She wasn't supposed to enter the room. It was, her husband had told her, a crime scene. But the men had already come and gone. The State Department's Diplomatic Security Service, she supposed, or Leviathan's, whatever difference it made.

They had ransacked her closet. They had taken her clothes for God's sake.

Susan and her lover, Liam Davies, had stood in the foyer and watched these frighteningly large men in suits and latex gloves carry out tiny objects, Liam at her side, berating the agents who worked indifferently, silently. *You could show a little respect.* Liam saying this. It made no sense, the respect part—the men were wholly professional, their auras the blue of calm focus—but Susan appreciated it nonetheless. At least he had been there. Where had her husband been?

She'd called him at the embassy and begged him to come home and he had, finally. *My God, Erskine, what do they want with her clothes?* Her husband—when he finally arrived—looking aggrieved, looking exhausted. Looking many things, but not looking at her.

Susan, honey, try to be calm. There was a spot on the floor where he kept his eyes. He shook his head with that resignation he'd carried through thirty-one years of marriage. *You have to consider their—*

This is Erin we're talking about. We know her. We trust her. We—

What Susan didn't say was *we love her.* Because it wouldn't have been true. Not we, but I—I love her. Me, Erskine, your wife, I love her. That would have made things clear to her husband or to herself or to whomever it was Susan was actually addressing. But she hadn't said it. She'd just gone on stammering until her husband finally took her by the wrist.

Susan—

This is her room.

Susan, honey, look at me. Because he was looking at her now, green eyes pinched behind wireless frames. *This is not her room anymore. This is a crime scene.*

What had she felt then? Anger, yes. Rage, certainly. Shame, too. But shame at what? At loving a girl who had only just entered their life, at loving her completely while failing her completely? A substitute daughter. A handout from her husband, Susan supposed. A consolation prize, awarded for accrued grief.

Yet Susan had been grateful.

Now she was simply desolate.

For two days she had lingered near Erin's room, as if by keeping vigil she might reappear. On the evening of the third day, Susan took the Valium, opened the door, and lay back on the bed, a heatless light streaming through the windows so that her eyelids pinked. She wasn't thinking, and in the buoyancy of not-thinking, somewhere between sleeping and waking, she saw a woman pressed against a window, staring out as if into some deeper space.

Jill, she thought, Jill in that awful tank.

And then said it aloud.

Jill? a question, something moving through the house like vapor.

She tried to hold on to it, but it was the whisper of a ghost.

Less than that: dissolving hope.

*

ERIN HORVÁTHOVÁ HAD arrived at the U.S. embassy in Bratislava on April first. April Fool's Day, Susan Logan would later think, but not at first. What came first were thoughts of Jill. That day, for the first time since their move from Greenwich, Susan had actively remembered her daughter. Jill Logan was always there, always at the edge of Susan's thought, but her memory was never welcome, and though that sounded particularly harsh Susan knew it was as necessary as it was true. It was her own form of harm reduction: she could barely survive her daughter as fleeting ghost, let alone conscious thought. The grievous hypotheticals: If Jill were alive, would she be...

In love?

Married?

Making children or making art? (She'd been such a creative child with her portraits and Calder-like mobiles of coat-hangers and yarn.)

Tragic, people said when they heard the story. But *futile* seemed more accurate, the attempt at memory, the attempt at understanding. Like spending a lifetime trying to catch the darkness inside a refrigerator. Which could surely be done, but to what end?

Jill Logan had been twenty-four when she climbed into a Stinson Beach sensory deprivation tank with her heroin and heartache, and there, blind to the Pacific spread before her in all its incomprehensible vastness, neglected to get out. Susan and Erskine had been living in Connecticut when the call came, a driver ferrying Erskine to Leviathan's Manhattan offices while Susan stayed home and did nothing. She had been doing exactly that—nothing—the day she'd gotten the call from the Marin County Sheriff's Department. That had been in morning, but she hadn't told Erskine until that night.

There had seemed no hurry. She already knew a part of her would remain in that moment after hanging up the phone with the Sheriff, the news of her daughter's death so fresh it wasn't so much news as impact. Sitting there, she remembered the beginning of a poem she'd once read:

> Don't die, Dad—
> But they die.

It was exactly like that. *Don't die, Jill,* she'd thought, there on the couch with the phone in her hand. But of course she did, she had.

Four days later, they buried her at the First Congregational in Greenwich.

Erskine seemed incapable of comprehending her suffering. That months after his appointment as U.S. ambassador to Slovakia Susan continued to lurch around the house, sleepless and weepy—a ridiculous indulgence. He never said anything, of course, but she read it in those squinty amphibian eyes, those glasses she wanted so badly to knock off his satisfied face.

You never gave a damn about her growing up. So don't act so high and mighty now.

And was it that he was right?

Had she loved her daughter? She had, she supposed. She knew she had. But that love seemed to have shrunk in the deep shadow she eventually identified as shame. It was that shame that had led Susan to not only welcome a move to Slovakia, but decide that it would be a different Susan making the trip. She'd once been someone else, after all, and realized she could cultivate this former self as surely as one could cultivate a garden. So Susan—child of back-to-the-earth Vermonters who revered Jimmy Carter and Jefferson Airplane with equal adoration—took what had once been her innermost and made it into an act. She quoted from *Diet for a Small Planet* and began to discuss the possibility of the transmigration of souls, made a trip to Berkeley to hear a guru explain the oneness of the universe. There were mantras and books on Jungian archetypes and a trip to Taos where she sat in a sweat lodge until she had to be dragged out. When they moved to the ambassador's residence on a hilltop overlooking the Danube, she diffused lavender oil and arranged the furniture to maximize a room's energy.

She loved it, for a while at least. It was so wonderfully incongruous, Feng Shui as applied to red, white, and blue bunting and a security detachment of U.S. Marines. Salt lamps as proper response to an intricate surveillance system. The house was cream-colored and massive, four stories of quarried Belle Époque grace, and here was Susan, placing a mirror very precisely in order to better enhance the flow of *chi*. She chanted a mantra. She watched a YouTube video where a tattooed talk-radio host warned of the possibility of "death by astonishment."

It seemed to Susan a wonderful thing.

Their friends scoffed happily. *Erskine, your wife! She's in there talking about food security!* Yet they loved her for it, his wild, free-thinking, mildly bohemian wife. They were constipated Catholics, Erskine's circle of friends, evangelical neo-cons, and her potentially unrepressed sexuality, she divined, was the unspoken assumption, realized, as often as not, in the way she would catch them looking at her across the tops of their gin-and-tonics.

She suffered it, was even, at times, animated by it. She was an attractive woman and thought nothing wrong with acting as such. She began to sprawl across furniture, wearing her chakra necklace over massive billowing pleats. Nurturing certain gestures of boredom and amusement.

Her husband seemed happy for her to play publicly the role of progressive whimsical wife so long as their social circle was pleased by her performance. Not that Susan cared. She had long since lost interest in him. So why not play the dreamy wife?

She gave him that in public. It was different when she was alone. There were long somnolent hours while her husband was at work when Susan considered nothing beyond what she might have done to make her daughter so unhappy. Then the evening's tide of regret. Followed by the sleepless nights of trying to determine why the question even mattered. And if it didn't matter, why did she feel so awful for asking?

She chased anti-depressants with sleep aids.

She started an affair with one of her husband's staffers, a trade specialist named Liam Davies who had spent two years wasting away on the Caribbean desk before finally begging his way out of Washington. It was meant to be an adventure.

But nothing changed and nothing changed.

Then Erin arrived.

Susan had asked for help so long ago she had forgotten the request. But a local employment agency with which the State Department contracted had found a suitable candidate. A Slovak-American actually, dual-citizenship, multiple languages. Would Susan like to see her file?

It came over by courier one afternoon, and the first thing Susan noticed was her resemblance to Jill: this woman was twenty-seven, Jill's age, had Jill lived.

She was not unattractive. She was, in fact, rather beautiful, though in a hungry, drawn way. Wiry with cords of muscle, tendons that outlined her neck—a graduate of the Bolshoi school of undereating. Her hair was blue. Her aura—Susan took its measure without ever intending it—the deep red of one grounded and strong.

The day she arrived, Susan was a bustle of energy and greeting, tortoiseshell glasses perched in her hair.

"Erin, my dear," she said, taking the woman's hands, "welcome to our—to your—home. My husband and I are so—"

And she stopped, grateful her husband wasn't there to witness her stumbling, to witness her having no idea why she'd suddenly lost the power of speech. She stood there befuddled, with no idea what was happening to her. Only that it had something to do with the way this young woman was looking at her intently, eye to eye, and while Susan wouldn't call the look threatening there was nothing subservient either. She almost appeared resentful, as if she were making clear that while for the sake of money she would do the wife's bidding, she would do nothing by dint of will.

My God! The recalcitrance! It was so much like Jill. She was Jill made-over.

It isn't enough, Susan thought that day facing Erin, that you do the required work. You must also be grateful. More than that, you must love me.

Later, she admitted this to her husband.

"Oh, dear," he said, putting down his MacBook and taking her in his arms, "that is so—"

"Pathetic, I know."

"No, no. Not pathetic. Sweet, actually."

But it wasn't sweet. There was a childlike greed about Susan when it came to Erin, a sense of possession that grew over the coming weeks. Susan took her everywhere, from Erskine's office at the embassy to the salon, made her less a personal assistant and more a beloved confidant. She talked to her about Erskine and Jill, gave her access to schedules and passcodes—all to win her affection. But instead of affectionate, she was aloof.

This went on for weeks, and Susan was nearing despair when she suddenly devised a new plan. That day she spotted Erin cleaning the master bedroom, a dusting cloth and a bottle of spray polish in her hands.

Susan watched her as she finished with the bedroom and moved into the bathroom.

Disinfectant wipes, toilet cleaner, damp towels.

Susan followed her.

Mirrors, then.

Faucet, handles.

Sconces. Light fixtures. Finally the kitchen, where Susan hustled to meet her.

"Erin, dear." She was nearly out of breath. "What great good fortune to catch you here. I need your advice if you might."

Thereafter followed a week of feedback, asking Erin for her opinion on any and every small thing. China patterns. Curtains. Lipstick. To wear *this* to the reception or *that*? She treated it as a matter of great import and Erin's opinions always seemed weighed and considered, but never revelatory, and that was what Susan really wanted.

She thought of telling her husband about this new plan for approval, this strategy that would convince Erin to love and respect her rather than simply serve her, but knew exactly how he would respond: lovingly dismissing it all as an overspill of sweetness, rehashing it as an anecdote for some perfectly boring dinner party: *have you ever heard of such a tender heart?* So Susan didn't tell, and eventually she felt the wind go out of her plan to burrow into Erin through the sheer aggregate of her opinions.

But not before she followed her.

It wasn't intentional, a crime of opportunity more than anything else. That Susan had been sitting in the bar of the Hotel Bratislava when she saw Erin pass on the street was chance, so why not?

She'd been up to Liam Davies's room that afternoon, and was now waiting to meet Erskine for dinner. The Russians were at the bar that day, three of them this time. Susan had been seeing these same Russians for the last week, always, it seemed, lingering near. Though, honestly, she was probably imagining it. Honestly, it was probably a product of her boredom.

Yet she knew it wasn't. One Sunday two weeks prior, Susan and Erin had been wandering through the Eurovea mall, four stories of escalator and glass overlooking the Danube, when she spotted them. On the fourth floor, beneath a flashing sign marked HERNA, three of them sat at a table, big men in dark coveralls and church shoes. They looked like janitors at rest. But also they didn't look like that at all. There was a coiled violence about them that held Susan. She had stood perhaps thirty meters from them, unable to stop staring until they grew quiet and as a group looked up at her. One of the men had the puckered mouth of a red abscess on his upper arm. Another was missing the last link of his index finger. She had walked away then, quicker than she had intended.

It had to be her imagination.

So what to do that day in the hotel bar but breathe and wait? What to do but watch?

She'd waved over another glass of Armand de Brignac, but when she saw Erin pass in the street, Susan dropped twenty euros on the bar and left. It was chance, after all.

She hustled onto the sidewalk, downhill and through the Old Town, eventually crossing the Most SNP Bridge and the public park on the far bank. She told herself she never would have started had she known Erin was walking this far, but she didn't turn back, either. Susan was almost jogging, but it was a game after all, a lark. So there she was, hurrying across the river while ahead was Erin, ahead was Jill. But no—not Jill, just—Oh, Susan, you're so confused! You're not thinking right! So instead of thinking, she moved.

Follow her, stick close.

Oh, what a ridiculous thrill it was!

Was she crazy or just excited, just alive? No matter. There was Erin, her Erin, turning south toward the Petržalka district, the ghetto, as Susan understood it. But why would she head there?

Susan couldn't imagine her meeting a man, an actual flesh and blood man—no, that seemed far too pedestrian. Erin seemed not exactly human. Erin seemed constructed from some light-weight composite that hadn't yet crossed the Atlantic.

Susan kept walking.

The street was getting darker, physically darker, or was Susan simply imagining that? Definitely dirtier, seedier. My God, she was in the ghetto. The place full of gypsies and exiled Ukrainians carrying their bed bugs and sinus infections. Music came from open doors. Bubbling hookah pipes. Dirty bare feet. It was repulsive, impossible for her to imagine her Erin consorting with such, yet there she was, up ahead passing a café, its iron grille raised, old Turkish-looking men lounging in front on crates and folding chairs.

They watched Susan pass. Oh, how she felt them watch her pass! With her good heels and Coach bag. With her profound sense of decency. She felt an intense desire to remind them of the Marshall Plan, of how America had saved them from, well, maybe not the Germans, but at least the Soviets—if she was remembering her history right, which she wasn't exactly sure, but it didn't matter.

She felt a swell of anger against the people all around her.

She walked faster.

She walked faster and that was a good thing because Erin had turned again. Susan made the turn just behind her only to find the street dead end against what appeared to be an abandoned convenience store. Sitting out front was a lone man. One forearm read *JUIF ERRANT*.

It was late morning when Susan woke, her body arranged just as it had been when she had lay down ten hours before on Erin's bed. Erin had been missing for four days now, and Susan thought such proximity might amount to something. But she had slept a deep and dreamless sleep, and of Erin, there was nothing.

There was no Jill, either, and it came to Susan that there wouldn't be.

Her daughter, dead of an overdose, was gone.

Susan lay there letting the thought settle, the ripple moving out until there was no ripple and the surface of her mind was still and transparent. Things were finished. That was a simple fact. And here was another: tonight Susan would host a dinner party that would celebrate the meeting to be held that afternoon at the Hotel Bratislava. The papers would be signed. The deal—whatever the deal was, the shale gas concessions—would be made official. She was fifty-four years old, married to the U.S. ambassador to Slovakia, and about to be incomprehensibly rich.

She was also well rested. It almost felt like it might be enough, and it came to her that for the first time since Erin's disappearance that she was something like happy. It was a new thought.

The following thought was her realization of how much there was to do. It was after nine. The caterers would arrive at eleven. She was to meet Liam Davies at one. Their affair had lasted months, but after today there would be no more meetings. Today she would end it.

They had met at an embassy reception.

Two days later, they'd had lunch in the splendorous stupidity of the Hotel Bratislava. The chandeliers and tablecloths and waiters recommending the goulash and goat-cheese biscuits. The restaurant was said to have remained unchanged since the collapse of the Austro-Hungarian Empire and even to a woman like herself this was silly and unnecessary. She thought of her parents, of her childhood, the weekends in New England, eleven years old and drifting around thrift shops in Stockbridge, the evenings beneath the stars of Tanglewood—that was her America, the antique America of community gardens and library boards. Bake sales at the firehouse. Old coats tagged with lift tickets from Killington. It was simpler then, washing the chlorine from her hair after a day at the city pool. The toothless marches and chants for the ERA, her mother cooking couscous while her father listened to "world music" on NPR.

Here was decadence, here was the antithesis to everything earnest and civic and upright.

And, yes, it was silly. But it was also gorgeous and disorienting. Venison borscht.

Creamed sherry from the crystal decanter.

Pomme frites and bacon-cured maple green beans.

She almost believed in it, this world. Looking across the table at Liam—how handsome he'd been, a quiet understated handsomeness she had at first failed to appreciate—looking across the table and across the room, she'd believed it.

"When you called," he'd said.

"Yes?"

He'd blushed, that high Irish flooding into his cheeks.

"My heart," he'd said, and made a little beating motion with his right hand against his chest.

But that was over now, she told herself. Or would be soon enough.

She sat up and stretched, clasped her hands and extended them in a way that might have appeared fake had it not been the first real physical thing she'd felt in days.

She felt like a cat, waking. She felt like some previous self you tried on like an old dress you thought you'd outgrown—yet how wrong you'd been because it fit! You were who you once had been.

She lowered her hands until they rested on top of her head. She imagined her husband had found her in Erin's room and hadn't cared. More likely, he'd indulged her. Because he loved her, she realized. And that made her happy.

It was the first Sunday of May and for the first time since Jill had died, Susan Logan was happy.

A HALF HOUR later she was sitting with her husband, the morning sun already over the top of the ancient lime tree planted in the courtyard and tangled above the ivied wall that predated even the house, that had been, in fact, part of the original castle fortifications. She hadn't thought of it in months, but how much pleasure it had given her when they first arrived. The older, courtlier world of Europe, full of its counts and castles and that ancient shaggy lime. That her husband was officially the ambassador but more like a viceroy only added to the sense of wonder that gradually shaded into a sense of proprietorship.

All this had animated her on arrival but she had lost it in her eventual boredom, her fascination with Erin, her affair with Liam, and, finally, Erin's disappearance. Now she felt foolish, having played a child's game when life had been in front of her all along. Life was in front of her still.

"Much to do," she said.

Erskine looked up from his tablet. Hearing, she thought, something different in the honey of her voice. "Yes, darling. I suppose there is. You can manage, though?"

"Of course. You're due downtown?"

"Shortly, yes."

He was still a most desirable man, of course. The silvered temples and onyx cufflinks. When he smiled, his eyes crumpled in such a lovely way. There had been a single moment of unpleasantness in the wake of Erin's disappearance. Someone had gotten into Erskine's office at the embassy. Documents were missing and *who the hell else could it be, Susan?* He had immediately recanted, apologized, attempted to soothe her, and she had let it go. He was wrong, of course. It was a misunderstanding, an unfortunate coincidence—it had to be. There was no way of convincing him, but she didn't need to: it was behind them.

"I wish you had better help," he said. "These past few days—"

"No, Erskine. I'm fine."

"So regrettable, the whole mess of it."

"Oh goodness," and she pshawed! away the specter that was Erin in the way she'd seen so many women do. She wouldn't think of Erin's sudden disappearance, or the way the men had arrived with their questions. "There's never any decent help, dear. You yourself have told me as much."

"Yes, but still." He fingered his screen and looked up again. "Tell me, dear, what can I do?"

"What you can do is absolutely nothing. I've taken care of it all."

"And the caterers arrive?"

"At eleven. I'll be here."

"And you'll call me if I can send anyone over to help? Half my staff spend their days updating our Twitter feed. They could use some work."

That dismissive hand gesture—she did it again, so playful, so coquettishly authoritative. "I have it, darling. It's under control."

"All right, dear," he said. "I love you."

With that, he tapped his screen, smiled, and left.

When he was gone, Susan went to the third-floor bathroom, the place from which nothing, not even the sound of his driver rumbling down the cobblestone street, could be heard.

Against her will, against her better judgment, she found herself thinking of Jill, of the day they buried her. Of Jill in that tank and the way the phone rang only once before Susan had it. And then Jill in the ground behind the First Congregational. But the thought would pass. It would pass and something would form in its place.

She stared at herself in the mirror, waiting for that something to form or settle, some resolve, some hope, maybe. She could do this, a new day, a new life.

She knew she could.

And yet, a moment later, she began to weep.

SHE WAS STILL in the bathroom, the weeping having given way to a teary wheeze, when her phone went off. How stupid, she thought, my God, what a fool I am. Why was she crying? Why had she let herself? Except she didn't regret it. Such a flood of emotion felt purgative. Embarrassing enough that even considering it brought on another wave of sobbing. Susan as cliché, Susan as some creamy suburban bitch, her well-curated, well-appointed life shattering on the rocks of platitude.

On emptiness, too.

On oven cleaner and kebab shops.

On the place cards for a dinner party with the Polish ambassador.

Were these the totality of her days, the sole measure of things? The evening reception and the dead daughter. The infidelity on expensive sheets. You added one to the next and arrived at a self.

But to feel something deeper, to be overwhelmed by it—she was grateful for it. In the wake of Jill's death, in the wake of Erin's disappearance, the desire to feel something had been overwhelming. Pain, grief—grief somehow made things larger. But you could bear such largeness. What couldn't be shouldered was the emptiness.

She turned on the sink to drown the sound of the phone, dipped her hands and splashed her face. Something had happened to the tissue under her eyes. It was more than age, more than crying, she thought. This weight, these gradations of shade.

She saw that it was Erskine who had called just as she heard the landline go off in the bedroom, and ran to find him calling again. She ignored it and walked downstairs to the kitchen. When he called a third time she was composed enough to answer.

"Turn on the news, darling."

"What's happening?"

"Just turn it on."

She did, only to find the screen held a familiar face she couldn't quite place.

"Who is this?" she asked her husband.

"It's Marco Torres."

"Do we know him?"

"The Congressman. He came for dinner once."

"Dinner? Yes, I remember. What's—"

"You're watching BBC?"

"Of course."

"There in Tampa. Some kind of low-rent motel."

"But what's happening—"

"Wait a second," he said. A face was on the screen now, a man in uniform, unsmiling. "Let me hear what he's—"

"Oh God," she said. "This is—"

"Yes."

They both waited.

"Oh God," Susan said. "He's dead?"

"He shot himself. Apparently it just happened."

The Congressman's face was off the screen now, replaced by another image of the motel. Hispanic kids, black kids, lots of brownish people loitering just beyond the circle of emergency vehicles. It wasn't yet dawn there and the reporter appeared to be staring into the blinding glare of a spotlight. There was concrete and palm trees and a low ceiling of scudding cloud. But superimposed over it all was the handsome face of Congressman Torres. She'd met him just once, but she remembered him now, good-looking and kind. Charmingly tipsy and showing her photographs of his daughters while they sang around the piano. *Come ye thankful people come, Raise the song of harvest home!* Such a polite young man, sweet and then suddenly so serious. Like her husband, a Brother in the Covenant.

The camera panned the parking lot a second time and you could see the kids—thugs is exactly what they were, little Mexican thugs, probably here illegally—leaned against the block wall of the motel office.

"What are they saying?" she asked.

"They're waiting on forensics."

"My God, it's so awful. I remember the picture he had of his little girls."

"Yes."

"Marcus."

"Marco," he said.

"Of course. Yes, I remember, I just."

"I didn't mean to upset you. Dear?"

"No, I'm glad you—"

"Dear?"

"I'm here."

"I didn't mean to upset you. I just—"

"No, no."

"I was upset myself, and if you heard anything I didn't want you seeing this and thinking—"

"No, of course. I understand."

The doorbell sounded.

"Erskine, I should—"

"The caterers?"

"Yes."

"Of course, darling."

She hung up and cut the TV.

It was such a relief: they were here, someone was here. Which meant she didn't have to think about Erin as missing, or Marco Torres as dead. It was simply a matter of motion, it was simply a matter of staying out of the way. She opened the door and smiled. Quarter past eleven and already a team of white-suited technicians were shouldering in great quantities of food, silver chafing dishes, samovars, magnums of champagne, cocktail shakers, great mounds of shaved ice.

Susan hoped for fresh fruit. It was difficult to get, and when she did, it was never bright enough. It failed to gleam in a way that made her question the nation's competence. Then she saw a silver plastic-wrapped tray of—was it citrus? could it be?

She stopped herself from checking.

The caterers were in the kitchen, and Susan retreated to the bedroom. She thumbed to her contacts and brought up Liam Davies. They weren't supposed to meet for almost two hours, but she found her finger hovering above the green *call* icon.

She was going to end it today, now, immediately, so that she might live this new, different life.

A moment later Liam was on the line.

"I can meet you in a half hour," she told him.

"Certainly."

"That's earlier than we said, so if it's a problem."

"No, no," he said. "In fact, it's perfect."

She hit the red *end* icon.

Don't die, Jill, she thought.

But of course she had.

SARA SAW THE ambassador through the slits of her swollen eyes. He seemed to want to see her, but only just, to confirm her identity as the woman who'd spent the last month as live-in help, and then walk away, back up the metal stairs she could hear ringing, and then the ringing was gone and what was left was the dull ache of her head, the weight of it on the cold floor. She was in a basement of some sort. Having been deposited here to crawl out of the heavy vinyl bag into which they'd forced her. The beating had been incidental, someone clubbing the sack. But then something had caught her temple and time had flattened and everything felt unbalanced.

The suppository they put up her anus.

The haloperidol they put in her mouth.

Hours or days later she found herself on a hard surface, no longer moving, a prayer hung just above her, there, but not quite falling through the understory of thought.

Dear God...

The way it was suspended in white stars.

Dear Lord...

Little pinpricks of light, so close.

She shut her eyes.

Then came the pain in her head, an eventide of sickness. Pressure in her eyes, mucus in her nose. She'd been on a steady diet of benzos since arriving in Bratislava but had nothing since the morning they took her. She suspected that to have been three days ago. She suspected, with some evidence, she had soiled herself. That she had shit her pants. Then the pain rolled back in and with the pain came the doubt. *Pray,* she thought, the word before her like a hand-hold. But when she reached for it, it was gone. Belief in suspension like the star on her dead father's Christmas tree, the way the sparkle would follow her, the way it would insist without ever quite arriving.

When she opened her eyes again the ambassador with his bald head and rimless glasses was gone. Then the sack went back up and time passed.

WHEN SHE WOKE again she was lucid, somewhat lucid. The sack appeared unknotted and when she stretched toward the light her body hurt. Something had gone wrong. Her shoulder, she thought. Possibly her left arm which seemed to hang against her.

Her nose ran. She smelled herself. She eased forward and put one hand out of the bag, testing, onto a tiled floor, so cold it felt damp.

She knew she wasn't alone. But who was with her?

Not David.

The blue breathing she sensed that night in Kiev?

She thought perhaps yes. But then no.

Then the sliver of light mouthed opened and she blinked against the glare. Hands, two hands, reaching in to pull her out so that she lay curled on her side, cheek by the metal drain.

Standing above her was Rachel Venclova, the toe of her boot very near Sara's left eye. She said something—there was a sound—and Sara whimpered involuntarily. She would have hated herself for it, but there seemed little left to hate.

Then the hands again, sitting her upright like a rag doll.

She saw the two Russians that had entered her room at the Carlton, another man beside them, an American.

"How about that?" the American said. "Little sister woke up."

The face came to her, the man, kneeling, smiling, a top-knot balanced on a skull of cratered skin, a little sachet dangling from his neck. He was the man she had seen outside the—

She vomited.

She vomited when she smelled him—*Fucking, bitch*—felt the spasm, both painful and a relief, as the face jerked from sight and then there was something in her side, a boot maybe. He was kicking her. She vomited again, cheek on the smooth tile, bile and saliva or whatever was inside her coursing the grout, spreading symmetrically along the floor.

They rolled her on her back and she stared into three faces arrayed like a halo.

Venclova and the American.

One of the Russians.

The vomit was warm on her face—in the folds of her neck, on her scalp and in her once-blue hair. Then a hand came down and very gently wiped her mouth, Rachel's hand, Sara's mouth, and she thought of her that night in the Hotel Duncan in New Haven, how frail she had appeared, the smell of her deodorant, her Nina Simone playing like a lullaby.

They pulled her up again.

Do you rec—

The woman was speaking, Rachel was speaking.

She pulled Sara onto her knees, and Sara thought perhaps she wasn't hurt as badly as she might have thought. Wounded, that was all. A small bird with a broken wing. A benzo would fix things. A benzo and she'd rise into her body.

"Do you recognize this?" Rachel was saying.

It was David's book, David's Bonhoeffer. It had been on the hotel nightstand when they'd taken her. Her mouth made a sound, said something, or meant to. Rachel held it open, near enough to Sara's face so that she saw David's name blocked in his childish print.

"Make the bitch clean it up," the American said.

"Shut up," Rachel said.

"I'm calling bullshit on little sister here."

"I said to shut up."

"I just want her to know she hasn't fooled me," he said, closer still. "A great way to spend your twenties, ain't it? All outraged and righteous. Play pacifist and then run home to Fortress America. At least your boyfriend got it. Motherfucker died with a gun in his hands." He looked at her. "Or did you think he was some righteous martyr nailed to a cross?" He held a plastic baggie in one hand. Oxy 80s. Green Goblins. "She had these on her."

"Let me see those," Rachel said. "You were taking these?"

"Girl went and got herself a habit," the American said.

"Give her one."

"Girl's nasty."

"Now."

"Nose running like a faucet."

"I said now."

He did, his hand at her mouth, his ragged fingernails. But she took it, gratefully she took it. The pill on her tongue, swallowed down with the sour burn of vomit.

"All right then." Rachel bent closer, tore a page from the book and took Sara by the wrist, crumpled the paper into her hand and said, very softly, "wipe this up, please."

Sara made no move and with a great gentleness Rachel moved her hand and the crimped page to the edge of the vomit.

"Wipe it up," she said, as if in speaking soft enough Sara might understand.

And she did. Sara moved the page to the edge of the mess, her mess, thin and dark and spidered out in the grid of the tiles. She wiped the vomit. Rachel tore another page and gave it to her.

It was just a book.

She wiped the vomit.

But it was his book.

Rachel pulled apart the spine. The pages lay fanned by Sara's knees and maybe this was a good thing. It had never been about David, after all. It had been about herself.

Bonhoeffer, she said, or meant to say.

"What?" Rachel asked.

"Bonhoeffer," Sara said. "When he was in prison."

"Yes."

"Ask her where her little broke-nut lover is hiding," the American said.

"Shut up," Rachel said. "When he was in prison," she said kneeling by Sara, "tell me."

"Have you read." Sara gasped. "His letters?"

"These letters?" She handed Sara another page as if it were a tissue. They were sopping now, floating or sunk into the puddle of vomit, the remains of David's book. "Tell me about them."

Sara paused for a moment, swallowed, collected herself. Her left shoulder throbbed. She heard the ringing of the stairs again, someone coming down.

"There's..."

"It's okay."

"There's this moment he talks about," Sara said.

He was in Tegel prison outside Berlin and he could hear the bombers coming, American or British bombers—she couldn't be sure if she was saying this or just thinking it—but whatever it was, she went on with it—he could hear them coming and found himself praying that they would hit someone else. They had hit the prison before and the explosions had almost driven him insane. But he prayed they'd hit somewhere else, and they did. And he had never felt so ashamed in his life.

She waited.

If she was saying this, then the question was why? The answer was she'd thought about that moment again and again, on Lesvos and in New York. He had been ashamed, Bonhoeffer. But wasn't it only a prayer that this cup might be taken from him? It had been her prayer too, even when the cup was already in her hand, even as she drank from it.

She imagined David dying with a gun in his hands, fighting. She thought it would repulse her, but the image felt surprisingly right. Maybe it was true. She hoped it was true.

Because, she tried to say.

"Yes?"

"He was a pacifist and thought he was sacrificing his own salvation. But he decided…He decided he was willing to give it up if it meant saving the lives of others."

"Do you believe that?" Rachel asked. "That he sacrificed his salvation?"

"I don't—" *know* she was going to say, but realized the stairs were no longer ringing and whoever had been approaching had arrived.

"You have to stop this shit," the voice said, and she knew at once it was Ray Shields.

"You have to stop this," Shields said. "Hugh Eckhart just landed."

HUGH ECKHART BOOKED a rental car on the overnight from Tampa so that on landing in Vienna he found waiting for him a green Skoda. He handed over his credit card and passport and started east on A4.

Real credit card. Real passport.

It was stupid, but also, more than that, it didn't matter. He'd been traveling for months on the false identity he'd created for David Lazar—Dietrich Schmidt, he'd meant the first name as a small homage, a joke—but Leviathan had finally tracked it and it was useless now. So he used his own name. Less than twelve hours ago he'd been sitting in Bern's with Marco Torres. In another twelve he'd be in the hands of Leviathan. Which only meant Randy Garcia would kill him before the cancer in his testicle could.

He didn't care.

All that mattered now was finding Sara.

Marco had the dossier and that was that. Hugh had debated handing it over, but in the end it was sympathy as much as prudence. He could have given it to any number of news outlets. But the moment it went public Sara Kovács was dead. Still, Hugh had needed rid of it, and then he'd seen Marco sitting there, maybe on the edge of death, maybe not. But whatever it was Marco was approaching, Hugh found it unbearable. Hugh was sad. He was also drunk and ridiculous, spouting all the things he'd heard the Colonel say, if only to determine if he still believed them. Turns out, he both did and didn't. Turns out, it didn't matter. So he stuffed the dossier in the bathroom towel dispenser and sent Marco in after it.

He didn't regret it.

But he couldn't forgive Marco either, just as he couldn't forgive Randy Garcia.

That they knew, that he had told them.

He couldn't forgive any of them, not even the dead children scattered in the tines of sunlight that had lighted that Iraqi school.

He couldn't forgive the world.

He was past the airport now, the road paralleling a rail line, past the clusters of shops and houses and into a countryside of sheepfolds and wind turbines. The border was just ahead, the Danube beyond that. He was driving faster than advisable but what choice did he have?

Sara had left the dossier beneath a bridge underpass four days ago. Routing and account numbers, transaction histories, the 19% stake in Rosneft, everything Hugh had hoped to get off Garcia's computer in New York—it was all there. It had been set up to look like the fund for a political action committee, but what it had bought was not airtime or print ads but guns. Rockets. Mines. The account was closed now.

The account wasn't the problem. The problem was Sara.

He'd arrived late to the Hotel Carlton to find an empty room. She had checked in. The bed was mussed. The tub was damp. But she was gone. It was possible she was in hiding. More likely something had happened. He knew, in fact, something had happened. It was why he had sought out Chris Berger and then flown to Florida. He had intended to offer himself up to Randy Garcia in exchange for Sara's freedom. But then Marco's chief of staff had called.

He made the turn onto the A6.

Twenty kilometers to the border.

He'd be in Bratislava in forty minutes.

A van pulled behind him, too close, its headlights in his mirror. He tapped the brakes and it backed off.

The plan was simple: get Sara and get out.

He knew he was responsible for her, just as he was responsible for Marco. Something had happened to her at their initial meeting in Kiev. Hearing about David, holding the papers that identified her as Erin, she had become very still. She had failed to blink. Yet when Hugh touched her elbow, she had risen and followed him up the stairs and into the street where snow clouds were beginning to bunch.

He asked her where her flat was and she said nothing.

Sara?

Sara?

In the Maidan were tour groups, clots of men and women gathered around guides holding aloft brightly colored umbrellas and signs that read EUROMAIDAN REVOLUTION TOUR and HEAVENLY HUNDRED TOUR. Stands selling tickets for *La Traviata* beneath the three-storied McDonald's where the snipers had perched. Plastic flowers and glassed candles in front of poster-board memorials.

Come with me.

They arrived at his flat soaked and freezing and he lit the gas burner and stood there, warming his hands, while she showered. He opened a bottle of Montepulciano and afternoon fell into evening. She started speaking, but only single words, responses to his offerings.

You can stay here if you like.

Okay.

There are some towels there, dry clothes.

Thank you.

Sleet lashed the windows but the flat was warm. She put on a dry shirt, old gym pants he gave her from his travel bag.

"Do you resent God?" she had asked him.

"Why would you ask that?"

"I do," she said. "Because it was God who made the world, and God who made me care."

They drank a second bottle sitting on the fold-down bed with its thin plastic mattress and thick down duvet. When her hand slid toward him he touched it, lightly, without looking, and felt it cover his own. She made space for him on the mattress, a sliver, a crack. He lay on his side and held her, uncertain if she was pushing him away or pulling him toward her, and then he realized she was doing both.

He held her.

No sex—he was no more capable of such than desirous.

Just contact, human.

He held her.

Now he had lost her.

If he could find her—*when* he found her—he had arranged a series of safe houses. He'd put her on a plane and wait. If they came for him, they came for him. He would live, or not live, as the case may be, with what he had done.

He was ten kilometers from the border when the van began to edge into his lane. He caught it in his peripheral vision, a black Opel. He honked the horn, but it edged closer and suddenly he was in the rumble strip, decelerating but it was still there.

He honked again.

It was happening.

Honked again and again and then simply didn't. He jammed the brakes and skidded into the breakdown lane and to a halt on the grassy shoulder, a popping sound, a long slide. One of the tires had blown, but it didn't matter: he was blocked in by the van. There was nowhere to go, and when the sliding door opened he cut the engine. There was no use trying to run. There was no use regretting anything either, only that they had found him a moment too soon, a moment before he might have found Sara.

He watched them get out, two men in Halloween masks, Ninja Turtles holding compact rifles. He put his hands on top of the wheel so they could clearly see them.

A third man carried a Mossberg shotgun in one hand, and with the other motioned for Hugh to roll down the window.

"Greetings, earthling," he said in English.

When he pulled off his mask, Hugh saw it was Rick Miles.

Hugh hadn't seen him since Bratislava and something ran through his arms and legs and stomach. Something in him turned. It might have been his heart.

"Shit, Hugh! You water-walking son of a bitch." Miles reached in with his free hand to massage Hugh's shoulder. "Long time no see, ain't it."

"Hello, Rick."

With his other hand, Miles kept the barrel of the shotgun near Hugh's face, near the ear, near the eye. He tried not to see it, but there it was.

His skin felt tight, his throat dry.

"What's going on here, Rick?"

"Out loafing and spotted you. Coincidence, right? But I tell you, I think it's the will of the Universe. I think this shit is cosmic."

Eckhart felt a certain rage inside him begin to twist itself into being. Not fear, he realized, but anger.

"You're full of such facile bullshit," he said calmly.

"What's that?"

"This stoic philosophy you got third-hand from Berger. Who got it from the shit the Colonel taught at the Institute."

"What's that?"

"Schopenhauer and the crucifixion."

"*Lama sabachthani*, baby."

"I couldn't possibly tell you how it pisses me off."

"You wouldn't have to, brother."

"I think all of you, you're…you're…"

Eckhart shook his head. Rick Miles looked both happier and meaner than he remembered, his skeletal face grinning.

"That all you have to say?" Miles asked.

Hugh thought it probably was.

"Maybe so," he admitted.

"I guess you better get out of the car then."

Hugh nodded, but made no move.

"Get out, muchacho."

"All right."

"Now, chief."

"All right. I can do that." Hugh opened the door but found himself unable to move, absolutely paralyzed with fear because, turned out, he was a coward after all. For all his talk of God's work, Hugh felt himself alone, and very afraid.

"You're making those boys over there nervous as ponies," Miles said quietly. "Get out of the car."

Finally he did. He stepped out and stood there by the Skoda.

Cars were streaking past but none of the men seemed to mind. None of the cars seemed to either.

"What are you going to do with me?"

Miles shrugged.

Then Hugh looked past him into the van—the door was open and someone was inside, he saw her—and what he felt was not *too soon,* but *too late.* All at once everything was too late, and he found himself crying not in fear but regret.

BERGER SAT IN a café across the street from the Hotel Bratislava with his coffee, waiting. He'd been sober since taking up residence at the monastery, and with sobriety came a frightening lucidity. He felt himself compounded of memories.

Days and nights at VMI.

Afghanistan and the IED.

The way it all fluttered into the dreamy sleep of his life.

His hands shook.

He sipped his coffee.

On the table in front of him were several aerial photographs taken by a drone of Russian forces moving around Slaviask. Putin had already annexed Crimea and now they were in the eastern provinces too. It was where Berger should have been. Instead, he was here, waiting.

But not without reason. He'd already watched Rachel Venclova enter the hotel with two Russians he took to be either GRU or part of the Spetsnaz team said to be operating in the city. He'd thought she was working for Randy Garcia—Garcia probably thought so too—but clearly she was running her own game, exactly as she had told him she would.

The waitress came over—*did monsieur want another café?*

Berger opened his mouth to speak, but felt his throat close. She looked at him and finally he shook his head no. Monsieur did not. He didn't speak because what was it to speak?

The answer was motion, even when it was motion toward death. Which ultimately it all was. Yet another thing the Colonel had taught him.

I came here to die, he'd told Eckhart.

Stupid, melodramatic—but he meant it.

He looked at the photographs again.

The images were blurry and overexposed but clear enough: just across the border were Russian APCs and Uragan-1M rockets. Behind them were forward bases with enough logistics for a long-term occupation. The invasion was about to start. Perhaps it already had. He didn't know what was about to happen inside the Hotel Bratislava but it was evident it was tied to the coming war.

He drank his coffee.

"Yes, sir," he said quietly, as if the Colonel had asked him something two decades ago and he had only now formulated his response. "Yes, sir," he said again, because it was near.

It was all very near.

Riding in the embassy car down the winding road out of the high hills into the Old Town and toward the Hotel Bratislava, Susan Logan felt herself thinking again of Erin. She put her head back against the leather upholstery of the seat as they sailed past the Lidl and the Tesco. The falafel stands along the broad pedestrian area lined with Romanesque shops and cafés and kiosks selling pastries and cake. Louvered windows and street musicians. The Japanese tourist kneeling, smiling, snapping photographs with their giant telephoto lenses. Their windbreakers and pockets of yen.

But Erin—

They had spent no more than a month together, but that month had overwhelmed her, and Susan had been, perhaps, a bit careless, leaving about things that shouldn't be left about. But the idea that Erin was anything other than absent, the idea that she might be—

They turned off Vajanskeho and traffic slowed, the street ahead narrowed to a single lane in front of the hotel. Four blocks but it looked like it might take the rest of the morning to get there.

She took out her phone and saw that her husband had called again, saw that he had also messaged her. She checked Twitter—TMZ was reporting rumor of a suicide note *Dear Vendela*—and again found herself recalling dinner that night, how handsome Marco Torres had been, all of that soft beauty not yet sagging beneath the weight of responsibility. The photographs of his children. His lovely wife.

Susan closed her eyes, and when she opened them found they were now sitting in a snarl of traffic as much human as automotive.

Why was there so much...

"A conference, madam," the driver said.

"Yes," she said, it was her husband's conference. But had she spoken? had she asked? Or had this simpleton read her mind?

"Is there a way around?"

"No, ma'am."

She felt her phone buzz with another message but didn't touch it, just let it vibrate there against her thigh.

"Perhaps up the back street?"

"No, ma'am. I'm sorry." He motioned around them. "Security. The street is closed."

"I see."

"All the streets."

"I see."

Yet she didn't. She tried, though. Closed her eyes a second time and tried. She was going to have sex with Liam today for the last time. She thought rationally that this news would disappoint him, but knew it would not. For months he had no more made love to her than you could make love to a wisp of steam. He was after an idea; she was simply the vessel of some unfulfilled wish about which she wanted no knowledge. She would close her eyes a last time, give him this final thing, and be done with it. Go home to her dinner party, her friends, her life—

They were moving again.

Past the apartment buildings, past the concrete monoliths, a few fading pastels painted during Khrushchev's thaw. Salmon, peach, sherbet. Everywhere satellite dishes.

Everywhere something sloshing.

She felt the salt water sloshing.

Felt herself moving through the deep black tank with its slick sides.

Sensory deprivation. Her daughter a child of western favor, indulged and inoculated with just the proper dose of insularity and NPR. Yet it had gone so wrong, and here was Susan, sitting there with the phone in her hand, thinking don't die.

It was all sensory goddamn deprivation.

She looked at her phone: her husband again. Two, no three messages. She didn't read them. Reading them would be the exact wrong thing to do at this moment. Instead she thought of what lay before her: a drink in the sitting room of Liam's suite, Egyptian sheets of a high-thread count. Music, perhaps. She hoped he would put on some music, Brahms or Stravinsky. Something, anything, to distract her from the sound their bodies would make because if she couldn't hear herself, if she squeezed shut her eyes and couldn't see herself and couldn't smell herself then it wouldn't be so real. If her senses were deprived, it would be happening not exactly to someone else, but not exactly to her either.

"Madam?"

The car was no longer in motion but had stopped two blocks from the hotel—as far as it could advance. She opened her eyes to the driver, his arm across the seat. Out the window a bellhop waited, white gloved hand extended, around him a crowd of hotel staff and dark-suited security.

"Are you?"

"Yes, of course," she said. "Thank you."

She reached for the door and felt it open from outside. The day was warm, finally, and she allowed herself to be helped from the car and into the lobby where it was calmer, all marble and potted palms and polite obeisance, though she felt no less disoriented.

She looked at her watch: she was late to meet Liam but couldn't face him without a drink. The bar was dark wood and polished silver and she drank vodka from a pewter stirrup cup. On screens mounted in the corners the war played mutely. Not the war in the Middle East—Iraq, Syria—that had become so constant, something so familiar you barely noticed it, but the war in Ukraine, which— when did this start? The screen read "REHEATING THE COLD WAR." A solid graphic of thick copper letters against a backdrop of shadowed greens, the word HEAT burning above the ghostly silhouette of Vladimir Putin. Something had happened. Tanks had happened. Artillery had happened.

The Russians had invaded. Or someone had, at least. Men in masks, shooting.

This was Slaviask they were showing. The volume was off but she could see smoke rising from a large building, around it smoking vehicles and a shattered street. The image was from a circling drone and it took her a moment to realize the bright streaks that occasionally flashed past were shots being fired upward at the drone, and at her, at her life, at everything Susan Logan was or ever would be.

She finished her drink and was asking for another when she saw them and stopped.

It was—

Only it couldn't be.

Across the room, sat two giant Russian men and a beautiful young woman that absolutely had to be Tomas Venclova's granddaughter.

But of course wasn't.

Ridiculous. The thought was ridiculous, yet…

Susan finished her drink and waved over a third.

A cold sluice had opened in her throat, and she stood carefully, cognizant of the unsteadiness she felt in her ankles and wobbling high heels. She gripped her clutch purse with one hand and the bar with the other, but the strange thing was that despite the airy tipsiness that unbalanced her, she had never been more sober in her life. Everything was open: her eyes, ears, even her sinuses. Sharp as the edge of the vodka she tasted still.

Was this being alive?

She posed the question very calmly—was it?

There was also the possibility that she was dead and this was what death felt like. There was the possibility that this was what Jill had felt in the tank.

On the corner screen, a news analyst gave way to another drone-feed. The smoldering machines lined with rust. The blowing trash. Piles of crumbled cinders blew across a playground of swings and a winding slide and some sort of jungle gym hung with torn netting, and there! The way the scraps of cloth huddled across an expanse of parking lot—there!—were people!

Or had been.

There! She saw it, a human body!

For a moment she had thought it was her daughter she was seeing, Jill having risen, naked and knee-deep, glistening and whole. Yet jointed with such fragility Susan expected her to shatter into pieces. It wasn't Jill, of course. But it was a body, and it was most certainly dead.

Was anyone else aware? Had anyone else noticed that people were actually dying?

She turned to see Liam at the table behind her.

She almost gasped.

"You're here."

"I am indeed." He was holding a glass of something, smiling.

"And you've been..."

"Right here." He had not yet stood. "I've enjoyed watching you."

"You should have said something. I didn't know—"

"That's what made it so pleasurable, that you didn't know."

Now he did stand, finished his drink and placed it on the table. That smile, that nonchalance. She hated his boyishness, the assumption of his relative youth. She'd never been able to put her finger on it, but did now. He saw her not as a person but a novelty, something one might collect like orphaned flatware or pieces of fine china.

"Your husband is looking for you," he said.

"My husband?"

And here she thought he'd finished his drink, but he lifted it again to let his tongue tap at the rim. It was a vulgar gesture, a bit of adolescent innuendo. Damn his smug confidence, his smirk. His tiny elfin body. She hated him, but in this keen new awareness felt herself interested in a way she'd never realized.

"I must admit I was a bit baffled when you suggested meeting earlier," he said. "The Minister of Energy is here. Leviathan's people."

"What are you saying?"

"This is not exactly a discrete location is what I'm saying. At least not today."

"What did you say about my husband?"

"Only that he's looking for you. That he called."

"Called you?"

That smile again. He looked around them, made a point of looking around.

"Or perhaps nothing could be more discrete. He's out there in the lobby."

"My husband?"

"Darling." He took her hand. "I meant the Minister. But your husband did call. I'm sure you've seen," he gestured at the war on the screen, "what's happening."

"What is happening?"

"Little green men are happening. They're all over the east."

"But this—"

"They've attacked a municipal building, it appears."

"Who has?"

"The Russians, the separatists." He gave an exaggerated shrug, those shoulders that belonged on an eight-year-old boy. "It amounts to the same thing, doesn't it?"

"I saw a woman, dead."

"I haven't seen anyone dead. Perhaps your husband did. Perhaps that explains his worry."

"You're making fun of us, aren't you?"

That *us*, that sense of Susan and Erskine together, was so unexpected. Yet it must have been how they appeared to the world. On the screen were masked soldiers on top of armored personnel carriers. BBC was reporting sporadic fighting, the encirclement of a Ukrainian barracks, the taking of the airport in Donetsk.

"You are, aren't you, Liam?"

He swung her hand playfully.

"Perhaps a little. Is that all right?"

"I don't know. I suppose it is."

"Good," he said. "Then shall we have another before we head up?"

WHEN THE AMBASSADOR'S wife entered the hotel Berger knew it was time. He followed at a distance, out of the café and into the lobby where he moved to the left, away from the reception desk and bar. The place was crowded and he was near the elevator bank before he spotted Rachel Venclova.

Chris, she mouthed, and he followed her around the dining room toward the kitchen, blindly, obediently. It was stupid, but he couldn't help himself. Whatever was going to happen was going to happen. He only wanted it to happen now.

He rounded the corner where several serving carts sat silvered and backed into a corner, and it was there, in the rear hall, that a man put a pistol against his head.

It had a calming effect. He felt himself become very still.

Rachel was smiling.

"Chris," she said. "This is so perfect. Walk with me, all right?"

They went around the kitchen, down another hall, and onto the loading dock, the barrel of the pistol buried in Berger's thin hair.

"What is this?" he asked when they were outside.

A van was coming down the alley past an open dumpster. It was moving slowly, the side mirrors folded back as it pulled to the dock and stopped. A man in a green misshapen mask got out, a second, a third, grabbing out gear like an assault team, which, Berger realized, was exactly what it was. Except for the masks they were in black, head-to-toe, and carried rifles, tactical vests crisscrossed with flash grenades.

Ninja Turtles, he saw. Children's masks.

"See?" she said. "Are you happy?"

He wasn't happy. It wasn't happiness he felt.

But it wasn't exactly sadness either.

It felt more like finality. Five men. Guns. Bombs. It came down to that. But what else could it have come down to?

They were pulling on chef's whites, the double-breasted coats big enough to cover the weapons. White hats over their green masks. *Toques* they were called. No idea how he knew.

"You see?" Rachel Venclova said again.

She looked like a child wanting to please, bright and hopeful.

Berger said nothing.

Here were the men from the forest, the men who had killed David Lazar. Three of them carried heavy bags past Berger through the bay doors. Sacks of sugar or flour but obviously not. RDX, Berger thought. An explosive the Russians called Hexogen. The FSB had used the stuff to bring down entire apartment buildings in Moscow and Volgodonsk, razed whole blocks in Grozny with it, and it looked like they had more than enough to take care of the Hotel Bratislava. The *toques* made sense: they'd wire the building, slip out disguised as staff, and then blow it from a safe distance. So that was it then. Garcia had poisoned Rachel's grandfather, and now Rachel was going to destroy Garcia's meeting.

They had all turned on each other, just like Hugh Eckhart had promised.

The fourth man walked over, screwing the long baffle of a silencer onto a pistol, and despite the mask Berger knew instantly it was Rick Miles.

"Boss," Miles called. "You made it."

"I thought you were in Donetsk."

"And miss the party?" He shook his head. "Look what we got here."

One of the Russians reached into the van and out came Sara Kovács, out came Hugh Eckhart. Miles grinned through the mouth-hole, his teeth small and pointed, but very white against the green rubber. Berger looked away at the garbage he could smell beside him. He thought of the Robert E. Lee they would quote at the Institute, walking all those Civil War battlefields with the Colonel. And now he was here, in some filthy alley in Slovakia, a gun to his head.

"Boss?"

It was ridiculous, the sort of shit you put up with just for believing in something as simple as honor.

SARA HEARD THE door open and light came through the hood, no more than pinpricks but it was like waking, a minor resurrection. She could hear now. She could smell.

They had stopped and someone was pulling her out, her left arm tucked into her side, useless, but no longer in pain.

Someone had cleaned her.

Someone had fed her another pill.

Her nose was running but her head felt better, the pressure gone.

They were speaking Russian, but beneath the hood it was hard to understand anything. Occasionally, she heard the shrill pitch of the American's voice, the one who had given her the benzo. He sounded like a scared woman, except that wasn't at all the case. She was the scared woman, and all she sounded like was slow mournful breath.

"If you say a word." A voice was beside her ear, Russian-inflected English, wet. "You go back in the focking van. You understand? Nod if you understand."

She nodded and a moment later felt the cord of the hood loosen. When it came off, she saw she was standing by a loading dock behind a building, a hotel maybe. The men—there were five of them, one missing the last link of his index finger—were dressed in chef's whites and green masks and seeing them her death felt very real and very near. But she knew that she had done her job. She had picked up where David left off. She had—how else could she say it?—she had *honored* him. Which was stupid. But it was also true.

She looked for Hugh but couldn't find him. For a long time there had been only darkness and the sound of his weeping. But the sound was gone now. Hugh was gone.

A hand turned her roughly and she went up the stairs where a man stood with a pistol against his throat. She recognized him from his picture as Chris Berger, the ill-trained bear Hugh had shown her weeks ago in Kiev.

He said nothing, and they pushed her past him through the silver-sheeted door of a meat locker. She had decided she would not think of David. Never again would she consider those nights in Greece. She pushed him from her thoughts, their moments together, their life. She had loved him. But it wasn't about him. It had taken her some time to realize that. But she realized it now.

His book was destroyed and maybe that was as it should be. Instead of David, she would focus on the Christ she had felt that night in Kiev. None of the other incarnations, the absences, the disappearances. She wanted only the one she had sensed breathe blue, that warm comfort. *That* Christ was alive, *that* Christ was always there. David was dead, but in the blue of memory she sensed a living presence.

She breathed slowly, repeated the things Christ had said.

Do not hate.

Do not fear—for fear is useless.

And what was fear against this? Against the way they had approached her in New Haven, approached her at her weakest. She couldn't get over how everyone called it a *favor*, this giving up of your life, nothing more. She saw Rachel Venclova and thought again of the way she had smelled of deodorant, the pale luster of her skin.

They led her around the empty kitchen.

She could hear people nearby, diners, cooks. The man, the Russian, tightened his grip on her arms. He was whispering in her ear, telling her not to make a *focking sound*. Then the American was whispering *it's okay, little sister, it's gonna be fine, dig* and she remembered his tattoo, *JUIF ERRANT*. The feel of his boot in her ribs.

They pushed her into the kitchen and she could smell the food—pastries, rich soups, nothing like the black bread and clear broth she'd been living on—and it came to her that the world she knew had been squandered. We wasted it. We the United States of America. We gave it away, our rights, our God. The result was already decided. And not by vote or fraud or coup. It was already decided in our hearts.

She wasn't sure what exactly she meant.

Only that it felt definitive.

The endless wars. The spying. The systemic violence while you're shaving your legs.

It wasn't right. But to hell with what was right—this wasn't Christ talking anymore. This was David. All those nights in New York, those nights in New Haven. He'd said he would bear witness. It was years before she realized *martyr* in Arabic meant "one who bears witness."

The man led her to a service elevator.

To hell with what was right.

This was David telling her *to hell with what was right* because there were things that mattered more. Like luxury, or safety, or the illusion thereof. Instead of justice you got Chinese manufacturing. In place of the most basic rule of law, drone strikes. But nobody felt it. It was all very far away and there they sit, the Bronze People, with their bullshit lives and their bullshit worries. Refinancing while families drown in the Med. Getting the kids into good schools while they rape girls in Nigeria. Snapchat. Instagram. Shooting David reminded them—or her, was it just for her?—that life was real, or had been, and now was again.

David was now a sad-eyed emoji.

David was a string of tears in a text message.

She thought of the menu in the shelled asylum, the next day's menu.

But Oh, Jesus, she prayed, don't let me go crazy.

But maybe she'd already gone crazy, and maybe it didn't matter as much as she might have thought. Maybe crazy was preferable. She thought of a line of Bonhoeffer—*The God who is with us is the God who forsakes us.*

Who forsake us—

Who forsakes—

Her mistake had been holding herself aloof, trying to alleviate human suffering as if she wasn't herself a human. Her hands weren't dirty. It was what Bonhoeffer had realized, perhaps it was what David had realized, too. Dying with a gun in his hand while she lived on, the White Savior come down to save everyone else.

She could have just killed them, the ambassador, his wife. Was that what they'd expected of her? It was what they'd expected of Bonhoeffer. Or perhaps not what they'd expected of him so much as what he'd given? His willingness not just to die—death, she knew, eventually became yet another thing. So not death. More than that, it was his willingness to give up his salvation. Not to give up his life, but the very thing his life was about.

If she lived, it would be different. She understood now. She would lose her life. It would be repetition, silence, action. She would never speak again, but my God, she would do everything else, moment by moment in the mess of it all.

She finally understood. If she lived, she'd go back to that world, rock the HIV babies in Guatemala, hand out water in Aleppo. Disappear into the work. The monsters, the cripples, the broken-boned broken-hearted. She finally knew.

She felt the elevator stop and waited for the blue light, the warm presence. She would do that, she would wait for Him, for His appearance, and if He didn't come then that would simply make Him no different than all the others who had abandoned her.

With or without Him, she finally understood.

The Russian pushed her forward toward what appeared to be a bathroom and standing on the threshold she finally understood.

They were going to have beef—the menu promised it.

But now they were all dead, weren't they?

She knew they were.

But she knew other things, too.

She knew, finally, how to lose her life.

LIAM STARTED KISSING her in the elevator, crawled two fingers between the buttons of Susan's blouse as they stepped out into a dim oak-paneled tunnel, and moved from lamp to lamp up the plush carpet and down the hall. Her blouse half-untucked, two buttons undone so that his right hand slid beneath the silk and onto the cup of her bra. His chest to her back, arms looped to grab her breasts, his face in the damp bend of her neck. She took a few staggering steps and he stopped to kiss her ear, the line of her jaw.

"This way," he said, as if there was any other direction but forward.

She stumbled on, feeling abused, this rough handling she'd not expected from hands so delicate. But she was excited, too. There was this possibility that something that might erase her apathy waited down the corridor.

She shut her eyes and sensed it.

She was a little drunk and it was easier this way, eyes closed, mind warped. They rounded a corner and Liam's palm flattened against her chest, half-undressed now, a bra strap off one shoulder.

Was Erin here?

Was Jill?

How long might she hold her breath, down in that awful tank?

"Oh, God," she said, or moaned.

"Yes," Liam whispered, "that's right."

Her eyes were almost shut, slatted like blinds so that the world appeared through the cage of her lashes, wavy and grained as she moved through the water. Because she had just realized that—Liam took a key card from his jacket—had just realized the hall was filled with warm water.

It sloshed around her ankles.

It beaded the walls.

The door opened, and he led her backward, one arm around her waist, and off came Susan's blouse, fully now. A French door led into a bedroom where a bouquet waited on the nightstand. Out the curtains were the spires of Bratislava, the steeples and stunted high rises, the square of green park with its fountains and manicured trees. The baroque slab of the State Opera House, the flags that rose from the crenellated towers.

Her skirt came off. She felt his mouth swim up her stomach to her left breast where it hovered and dipped. He was doing things to her—kissing, touching, she felt certain—but was unable to say exactly what. There was a certain numbness involved. She felt his mouth and then did not. Felt the bed give beneath her and then did not. He glided over her body—himself naked now—and she stared up at the crown molding, the ceiling fan with its gilt blades, barely turning.

When she tried to raise her head it felt strangely unresponsive.

Her legs hung off the bed, heels—she still wore them—hooked against the bedrail, and from this position she tried to make sense of things.

The water, the—

Somewhere her phone buzzed with her husband's incoming messages. Somewhere the caterers worked. Somewhere was Erin. Somewhere else, somewhere possibly far away, but also possibly very near, was her daughter.

Somewhere was Jill.

He was jerking atop her now, the strained face, the cords of his twisted neck—who was this man? She felt him shudder and buck, registered his dying fall, but nothing else. The great exhale that blew against her throat. His sweat dropping to bead against her skin. His head falling against her neck, a wrung mop, exhausted.

She unhooked her heels from the bedrail like a bicyclist unclipping from pedals.

"That was," Liam said into her armpit.

"Yes."

"That," he was panting, "my God. That was incredible," he said, and kissed her neck, pulled up from her so that she felt a sudden chill. "I've been waiting for that all day, you know."

His smirk had reappeared, that boyish entitlement she remembered hating but could no longer muster the energy to regard. He was off her now, padding to the bathroom. Susan sat up and sensed the gummy mess between and beneath her.

"Susan?" Liam called from behind the bathroom door.

"Yes?"

"You're all right, I trust. So quiet."

"I'm fine."

"You're certain?"

She found the white hotel bathrobe and stared at the bed. Atop the comforter spread a butterfly stain, damp, if already fading. She went to touch it and then did not. What was she doing here? She had to host a dinner party tonight. It was meant to be celebratory, though she couldn't recall why.

She walked to the window and stared idly down into the tiny rear parking lot where some sort of chef's truck had pulled to the dock. Men were unloading bags of something. Then she noticed they were masked and it occurred to her they weren't chefs at all. They were tiny from this height, but even from here she could tell they were photographers, masked paparazzi no doubt hunting her husband. Shameless vultures sneaking in through the kitchen. She turned away, embarrassed and infuriated.

Liam showered and came out of the bathroom wearing his pants and drinking from a champagne flute.

"I have to be upstairs in twenty minutes," he said. "Big meeting."

"With whom?"

"Why, darling, with your husband, of course."

That smile again—she would die from his smile if from nothing else—and she hurried past him, pulled shut the bathroom door and wiped herself with a bath towel. Sat down on the lip of the tub and without intending it began to cry, silently at first, and then louder. Excessively, falsely, but she couldn't stop. It went on for what seemed lifetimes, these tears. It was silly: she didn't feel it, this sorrow, she was outside it. She knew, too, that he was going to knock, to attempt some comfort, to say some conciliatory thing while silently worrying she would tell her husband and he would be sent back to Washington a broken boy.

But he didn't knock. Didn't knock because he was howling— that was his voice wasn't it? A shrill howling, loud enough to shake the mirror?

No—it wasn't his voice but an alarm of some sort, the fire alarm! The water in the hall! And now Liam was knocking, calling her name, twisting at the locked handle and asking if she was all right? could she please open the door?

"Right now, my dear. Susan?"

She opened the door just as the fire alarm stopped.

"What?"

"The fire alarm."

She turned for the hall door. "Let me just—"

"No, wait," he said, reaching for her, but she did it anyway: opened the door and there was the carpeted hall and how strange it was, how empty. How dry.

"Close the door, Susan."

"I just want to see—"

"Close the door." He pulled her back and shut the door himself. "Sit down, Susan. Something is—"

The building shook, a deep thud that rose from the floor up through the walls to rattle the windowpanes. The lights flickered, but stayed on. They looked at each other wildly for a moment, not exactly frozen, but not moving either.

What was that? she was about to say, but then it came again, the same rattling thud.

She reached for her phone as Liam turned on the TV. Another message from her husband. That were six—no—seven messages now. *Stay where you are. Lock the door and wait.* The one before that: *get in the bathtub—*

He pointed the remote at the TV screen.

"Look at this."

"Is that?"

"Yes."

"Oh God."

It was the Hotel Bratislava. The shot was live. Somewhere above them a helicopter looked down at the smoking building.

"Should we?" Susan nodded at the door. "Liam?"

"What?"

"Should we go?"

"Christ, no."

"You don't think."

"Safer to sit. Someone will come for us."

They watched as the hotel was surrounded by black military trucks, beyond that a cordon of emergency vehicles: the whipping lights of police and fire, a queue of ambulances lined down Medena Street. Then the image zoomed to the rooftop bar across the street. Two men in black, one with a large rifle, snipers. One looked up to wave away the rotorwash and the shadow of the helicopter retreated, the men growing small. A woman came onscreen and began speaking a language Susan would never understand.

"What's happening?" she asked.

"They've attacked the building."

"Attacked—who has?"

"I don't know. Separatists. Terrorists." His eyes remained on the screen. "The Energy Minister is here."

"Dear God."

"We're supposed to meet upstairs and these terrorists…Your girl, Susan."

"What?"

"Your girl."

"Erin?"

"She's doing this. Your goddamn assistant."

"But if," Susan said, and stopped. It had just occurred to her that it wasn't a misunderstanding. Her husband was right. Which meant Erin was here. "I have to call Erskine."

"You can't."

"He sent me a message. He said for me to get in the bathtub."

"Christ, he knows you're here?"

She shook her head and then her hands, shook them as if wringing out not so much a cramp as a bad dream. "I don't know what he knows. He said to get in the bathtub. He said—Liam?"

"It's happening everywhere," he said. "Look."

On the screen was a map of Eastern Ukraine and if it wasn't exactly happening everywhere it was happening: Donetsk and Luhansk were dotted with flashing red stars meant to indicate attacks. The screen cut to a wasteland gunfight of concrete and smoke indicated as a Ukrainian barracks.

"Some sort of coordinated strike," he said.

"What should we do?"

"I don't know."

"Liam, what should we do?"

His voice had risen to a high whine. "Jesus. I don't know. They're going to shoot us. Does it matter what we do?" He walked to the door and touched it. Walked to the window, touched it. They were eleven stories up. "He knows you're here—Erskine knows?"

"He said to stay put."

She could hear the sound of gunfire, knew Liam could hear it too but she said nothing, just watched him flit around the room like a caged animal, something small and vulnerable: a panicked rabbit. *Oh Christ,* he was saying, *Oh dear God.*

The firing was louder, closer. A metallic popping.

Was Erin out there?

Was Jill?

"They'll go room to room," he said. "They'll go room to room shooting people. This has happened before. This happened in Mumbai. We have to get out of here. Fuck. We have to..."

He went back to the window, spidered his fingertips against it.

"We can break this," he said.

"Liam."

"We can break this and get out. Tie the bedsheets."

"Liam."

"They are *killing people.* Going room to room. Do you understand that? Christ, do you..."

Again he stopped, but this time she understood for she too felt the need for silence: the room had just gone dark. The power was out. Only the dusty sun bled through the sheer curtain, flickering over it the passing shadow of the helicopter. Another thrum of explosion groaned from within the building's frame. A spatter of gunfire.

She walked to the door but Liam grabbed her so abruptly that she yelped. She thought he was going to hit her, but instead he put his hand over her mouth. He was crying, staring into her eyes, crying. It was nearly silent, a choked sobbing.

Slowly, she reached up and took his hand from her mouth.

"The hall," she whispered. "I want to look." She waited for a response. "Quietly," she said, and now he nodded like an obedient child. She pointed at the bathroom. "Get in the bathtub," she whispered. "You understand? Nod if you understand."

He nodded.

"Lock the door."

He was still nodding, and she realized she was holding him by his wrist, this man who just minutes ago had been inside her, on top of her, hurting her because he could.

"Lock the door," she mouthed, and still nodding he moved past her. She heard the latch click into place, the shower door open and close. She waited then. Counted to what? To nothing, just waited, put her hand to the hall door as you are taught to when there is a fire, opened it as quietly as possible.

The hall was lit with emergency lighting. A haze of red tracklights and at the far end a bright exit sign. There was no water, no smoke, but she smelled something, concrete dust, the cordite of childhood fireworks—though she knew it wasn't fireworks she was smelling. There was no sound of firing now and she eased shut the door, locked it and slid the brass bolt. The door to the bathroom was still shut.

She picked up her phone and the screen flashed to life. There were no more messages from her husband, and she scrolled back to the earliest ones, the ones that had arrived when she was in the car coming over. The first was Erskine looking for her. The second told her to stay away from the Hotel Bratislava and call him as soon as possible.

She tapped out a message but it failed to send. She tried again and realized they were probably jamming signals so whoever it was—the separatists, the Russians—couldn't communicate.

She walked to the window and leaned her forehead against the glass. The ghost of her breath. A small circle, growing, retracting. It was the vodka maybe, perhaps the sex—but she felt so disembodied. She pressed her body to the cool glass. What would they kill if they killed her? And what would it matter?

She decided to walk out. She decided to find her daughter.

She dressed, left her phone on the bed, and knocked on the bathroom door.

"Liam? Liam, can you hear me?"

There was no response and she waited until she heard the wet huff of his breathing.

"I'm leaving, Liam. I know you can hear me. You can go with me if you want. All right," she said, "I'm—" She stopped herself.

She needed to go now and she did, slowly unlatching the door and stepping calmly into the hallway. The walls were black and slick. The water came to her knees. She thought of the sensory deprivation tank in which her daughter had died.

Then it occurred to Susan that was where she was.

She was in the tank.

BERGER'S HOOD CAME off in what appeared to be a conference room. He was tied to a chair and before him stood Rick Miles and Rachel Venclova, their faces warped at the edges, curved by the red emergency lighting and whatever they'd knocked loose when they hit him in the elevator. He blinked them into something like focus, their faces tipped close, arguing, Berger thought, until Miles noticed him and came over.

"Hey, welcome back. You were out there for a bit, but look it, boss. This is what you predicted."

"Miles?"

"Right here, chief."

"Why aren't you…" Berger felt his voice falter. It had just come to him he was in his old rat year room at VMI. The block walls and wooden full-press where his uniforms hung. The bottles of Windex and Brasso, the rifle in its rack.

"What's that, boss?"

"Why aren't you in Donetsk?"

It came out as a whisper and Miles had to bend close to hear.

"Shit, chief. I told you already. The party's right here."

The other face floated into Berger's vision. Rachel Venclova appeared as no more than a bodiless head. Somewhere behind her stood Ray Shields, arms folded, pacing.

"Go find me something blunt," the head told Miles.

"Young Rachel here thinks we ought to beat you a little more." Miles bent to whisper in Berger's ear. "She says you betrayed her grandfather. But just between us, I think she's pissed you blew her off."

"Do it," it said.

"Honestly, I think you'd be better off just shooting him and being done with it." He turned to Berger. "Don't you think, chief?"

But Cadet Christopher Berger didn't think anything.

Cadet Christopher Berger was having trouble following. His old platoon sergeant had just entered the room. A lanky, violent man the color of lunchmeat, he carried a wooden dowel rod like a riding crop.

"Chief?"

"I want to make him understand first."

"Shit." Miles bent to Berger and winked. "Nobody wants understanding."

Berger watched Miles leave as the face, the head, swam back into his frayed vision.

"You never believed," it said to him. He didn't recognize her. The head he remembered as small and lovely had somehow transformed into an old cabbage of hate, not unlike the heads he'd seen in Helmand, the decapped villagers looking oh so surprised. The heads blown out of MRAPs by bombs stuffed inside dead dogs. He thought of her that cold night in D.C., hanging on his arm. But this was not the same person, not the same thing.

Cadet Berger? his platoon sergeant asked.

"You never truly believed. I trusted you and you ignored me, you betrayed me. You betrayed my grandfather who loved you. You betrayed all of us." It drifted away and smiled.

Cadet Berger? You will keep eyes forward. You will sound off like you have a pair. Is that clear, rat?

Berger's own head felt like a piece of overripe fruit, his tongue too big for his mouth. He fought it, this swollen purple muscle, pushed it toward his teeth, focused for a moment on speech.

The head spoke.

"You're in the hotel," it said. "They're all in the hotel. All the people who betrayed me. All the people who didn't believe."

Miles came back into the room with an aluminum walking stick.

His platoon sergeant showed him the dowel rod.

"Lookee what I found," he said.

"I was just reminding our friend here about the importance of belief."

"Chris."

"Chris," it said, "is not a true believer."

"I regret that," Miles said.

"I have a hundred pounds of RDX in the basement. Can you believe in that?"

Any physical contact will be understood as instructive, rat. Any physical contact will be understood as edifying in light of your aspirations to join my great institution.

Berger felt his head roll forward, and then Miles's fingers on his chin, righting it.

"Chief," Miles said. "Eyes on me."

Berger looked up just as Miles hit him with the walking stick.

Berger looked up just as his platoon sergeant hit him with the dowel rod.

Blood spurted from his mouth and when he coughed a splinter of tooth caught in a fold of his shirt.

He felt the first intimations of pain. Pain but not quite.

The second blow was worse. The second blow cuffed the side of his head and something began to leak from his left ear, a yellow film that might have been cerebrospinal fluid or might as easily have been what was left of his sense of duty. When the ringing stopped, he shut his eyes and took stock of himself. His nose was broken. His tongue was cut. His left ear seemed to be whispering some secret to the rest of him, but what it was saying he couldn't be sure.

He opened his eyes to a carpet of seafoam green, speckled with the blood that was now pumping into his mouth. A white board, a chair. But no cross on the wall, no ropes to raise him—a room for the godless.

"The second temptation," the head whispered, "was to be given dominion over all things. Hit him," she said to Miles.

Miles did, this time behind the ear, and Berger's head whipped around as if in disagreement. His neck tilted onto one shoulder, closer than felt right, like something had come irrevocably loose.

"Wow," Miles said, swinging again. "Ka-boom."

Berger caught the handle on the bridge of his nose. He made a gurgling sound, bubbles bursting around his mouth as if in speech, but when the head leaned forward and raised his chin he only coughed blood and syrupy digestive fluid.

Fix yourself, his platoon sergeant told him, ever a patient man.

The next blow was to his ribs, and the next, and the next. Horizontal strokes. Like someone felling a tree.

Fix yourself, rat.

Square yourself away.

Finally, Miles put down the walking stick, circled his arm as if stretching, and picked up a black box with a short silver antenna.

"You look like shit, chief."

Berger tried to raise himself from whatever place he occupied.

"Hey, chief?"

"Yeah?"

"I said you look like shit."

"Very likely."

Miles crouched before Berger. In one hand he held the black box that appeared to Berger as the sort of a remote control that would operate a child's toy. Rachel Venclova stood behind him.

"See this?" Miles asked.

"The RDX?" he whispered.

"It's part of our disappearing act. All of it wired to the controller. Hey, chief? Are you listening?"

He was not. He was past listening. He was past everything, and that was fine. Tucked between pain and pain he knew enough to know this was as it should be. It was the reason, after all, he had insisted on bringing Miles along. What they had started in that sand hovel with their *Allahu-Akbars* and roped crucifix, Miles would finish. Berger wanted it. He feared it, too, but hadn't his life always run in this direction? Dying for a cause means dying, after all, and here he was so narrow, so light. God had only to lift him.

"Chief?" Miles said. "Look at me, boss."

Eyes on me, rat.

The push-ups in the grass, the leg-lifts.

The scissor kicks beneath the marble glare of Stonewall Jackson.

Berger swallowed blood and realized he could no longer feel the shiver of his fingers, just the weight of nearing darkness. His shape edging closer to the statue the Colonel had shown him so many years ago, the alien form, the wild man. The holy man John the Baptist.

"Yo, chief? I need your eyes on me, boss. Ready?"

He wasn't. He needed a moment. He knew he was about to be hit, but he didn't want it to come quite yet. If he could just—

He needed to concentrate. What was coming to him was the possibility that he had finally become what he had intended to be. Everything else, every moment, every place—they had been way stations. The Institute. His time in Afghanistan. That bright afternoon on the forest road outside Donetsk. He was finally cracking open. He would finally be revealed.

"You have to destroy something," Berger started to say, but then Miles hit him in the face.

MILES DUMPED BERGER in the bathroom with the woman and Hugh Eckhart, and then sat for a moment, his back against the door. The fighting on the lower floors sounded impossibly distant though he knew it was growing closer. Five Russian commandos against how many Slovak soldiers? All of them maybe. Possibly a U.S. counter-terror unit by now. Or soon enough.

Still, there was time to shut his eyes and feel his breath attune, his pulse lower, the skin along his upper arms prickle. He breathed until he could no longer feel all the old haints jumping in and out of the holes in his head like birds in the cavities of a dying tree.

He was by a river now, the first river was home.

Bethel Baptist, a white block building, charmless but for its position on the ridge overlooking the valley and brown slug of the Tennessee River. The Wednesday service. Six years old the summer he thought the world was ending. Six years old and the day had turned to evening and the evening had turned to fire and brimstone, the horizon bleeding onto the purple ridges in a way that could signal either the return of Jesus Christ or the descent of a detached Multiple Reentry Vehicle. He knew of these, the Soviet ICBMs falling through the gloaming.

His granddaddy told them about them. The got-damn communists.

He hadn't wanted to die. Back then he hadn't yet wanted to die. Above, the sky smoldered with life-after-death.

The pastor's oldest son walked over and put his arm around Miles's thin shoulder.

Fire and brimstone, he said.

Miles felt his body heaving, but the pastor's son was calm, the pastor's son was steady.

The effect is the same as nuclear war, he told Miles. We're witnessing it right now. Are you ready?

The second river was the Tigris. Behind him, Baghdad was burning. Water lapped against the fiberglass hull of a patrol boat and the river moved before him and around him and then through him and then he was the river. He was everything.

The Humvees grinding through the narrow streets.

The far trees carrying the tang of rotting fruit crushed beneath market stalls.

He touched the sachet around his neck. He was pure. His medicine was strong.

When he resurfaced, the hall was dark, only the emergency lighting glowing ghost-like down the corridor. The fighting sounded closer. Which meant it was time.

In the conference room, he found Rachel and Ray Shields staring at a schematic of the hotel, the carpet dappled with purple gouts of Berger's blood.

"What's the word?" Miles asked. "They're inside?"

"They're on the third floor," Rachel said. "Possibly the fourth by now." She was clutching the aluminum walking stick. The remote control sat on a chair. "The streets are blocked."

"This is crazy," Shields said. He waved a cardboard tube like a wand, his eyes bloodshot. "There's still a way out."

"He keeps saying that," Rachel said.

Shields turned to Miles.

"I've been telling her. We just walk out. We were hostages."

"Not happening," Miles said.

"We just walk out," Shields said. "That's our best hope."

"No," Rachel said.

Miles shook his head.

"Man, it's just not happening."

Shields's bottom lip quivered.

"It's so simple," he said.

"Except it's really not, chief."

"We get the embassy on the line. We call Randy." Shields appeared to be staring into a blinding light. "We can be in Vienna by dinner."

"Hey," Miles said, "good for you. All that positive thinking."

"We call Randy. We walk right out."

"Right on, Ray," Miles said. "Talk that shit to anybody who'll listen."

"Please. Get Randy on the phone. Get the Ambassador."

"When I'm about to roll the stone away?" Miles grabbed Shields's shoulder. "Come on, man. You're about to see Jesus."

Shields fought the hand off him.

"We're going to die here," he said. "You understand that, don't you?"

"Come on, boss. That's not you talking."

"We stay here and we die. I'm telling you right now."

"We're in place," Rachel said. "There's no reason not to see it through. We probably couldn't get out even if we wanted to."

"I'm telling you." Shields was pleading. "Get Randy on the phone."

"And what do you think old Randy would have to say?" Miles asked. "You conspiring with the enemy and all?"

"I didn't know," Shields said. "I had no idea what you were doing. We were supposed to get Eckhart. That was all. We were supposed to get the girl."

"Come on, Ray," Miles said. "You knew that wasn't all."

"I swear to you. Hugh and the girl." He was panting. "You'll get us killed. And for what?" He picked up a pistol, rolled the schematic into its tube, and began to cry. "You're both crazy."

They watched him slink out of the room and down the dim corridor, one hand against the wall for balance, the other still clutching the cardboard tube.

"He can't get out," Rachel said.

"It doesn't matter anyway."

"What about the RDX?"

"It's set."

Miles took off his t-shirt, removed an American flag bandanna from his bag, and tied it around his head. If it was theatrical it was also necessary. He adjusted it just so and picked up the remote control he had shown Berger. It was for an RCA battery-powered car, a child's toy with its levers for FORWARD-REVERSE, LEFT-RIGHT. He opened the battery compartment and blew on the contact points.

"Behold the man," he said, and handed it to Rachel.

THE HALL WAS as empty as before, the black walls shining. The door clicked shut behind her and Susan waited, head bent close. Down the corridor, a silver room service tray sat on a cart. She walked toward it, toward the glowing exit sign beyond, her reflection warped in the tray's burnished dome.

Near the stairwell door she took off her heels and hooked them on the first two fingers of her right hand. Her toes sank into the carpet, and she stood like that until the sprinklers came on, a warm mist that sprayed the smooth black walls and dinged off the room service tray. She leaned against the door and felt the water hit her back.

When she heard something, she started walking.

It was Erin, she knew.

It was—

It was dry in the stairwell, the concrete steps and iron railing, the rain a hush behind her. She went down one flight, her damp footprints receding. There was smoke now, a ceiling of it that she ducked beneath, and as she did she saw the walls had burned in places, the wallpaper curling, bubbles of glues visible in the red emergency lighting.

It was a gun she'd heard.

She made her way up the hall, the carpet squishing between her toes. She could hear rain falling somewhere ahead of her and paused for a moment, confused.

She was inhaling smoke.

She was drunk.

She squatted beside the wainscoting.

The man with the Marin County Sheriff's Department, the deputy, the whatever he had been, and Susan sitting there with the phone in her hand, he'd said Jill was dead in California, but he was wrong. Jill was somewhere here. If Susan could find her, she could carry her out of the tank. But she had to hurry.

She walked to the fire-door and heard the gun again.

She had to hurry because all at once there were sounds everywhere. Gunfire. Voices.

The stairs turned at the landing, the smoke, the mist, thicker here and she made the turn and there—oh God. There was a body, pink and dead and flat on his back.

Not Jill. It was one of the terrorists, shot in a face that barely existed now, the body pushed into the cave of an electrical closet where he must have tried to hide.

But no—my God! was it Erskine?

It wasn't Erskine. She shut her eyes and saw someone else entirely. This man was alive again—she saw it so clearly—alive and awake and sitting in a wooden chair by a bed, something small and hard in his hand. Not a gun, something smaller. The little plastic thingy you stick in a computer—Susan forgot the word—but he was just sitting there, staring at it, and you could sense his general sort of wonder, a glow that appeared as regret as much as surprise.

His mouth dry, his stomach cramped.

Bare feet ground into the ashy carpet.

What was he supposed to do with this thing in his hand? This— thumb drive! The name came from she didn't know where. From the man perhaps, sitting there while behind him shone a yellow light, the dome bug-filled and black-flecked. There was something alive in it, buzzing, knocking against the opaque glass, but no— it was in his head, this thrumming she heard, because they were coming in for him.

He plugged the thumb drive into the computer. They came in so quickly after that, these other men. He was out of the chair and then forced back into it. Zip-tied—how her wrists hurt!—gagged and hooded while they searched the room.

They took the little thumb drive. They took the laptop. They took the note wadded on the bed. *Dear Vendela.* Then the ties come off—her fingers tingle with his—the gag and hood are removed and a trash bag goes over his head. A gun goes up inside the bag, the barrel settling on a clump of wet hair. The man is thrashing, the gun against his temple. But then he is magnificently still, so still it must be holy.

She feels the gun against his temple.

She feels the gun go off.

She jumped back, startled, eased forward and touched the body with her foot, sort of pushed it and felt it yield. She thought of the man at dinner that night, of Marco Torres. *All the world is God's own field...* She said his name aloud, whispered it. But Susan could hear nothing inside the tank but for the fire alarm which had been banging for how long she didn't know.

She left him. She went on, picked her way down the stairs and past the door until at last the sign read LOBBY and she was there, she was safe. She opened the door on a blister of fire damage and shattered windows. The drapes had burned, the upholstery of the chairs scalded yet strangely erect, wet and smoking. Everywhere were soldiers and doctors and fire fighters. Never had the lobby been so alive. And between them all came a steady stream of survivors, men and women like herself, their expensive clothes soaked and sooted, their knees and elbows scuffed like children.

A woman in surgical gloves ran up to her and took her by one elbow.

She spoke rapidly in Slovak, but Susan heard not a word.

She was searching for Erskine. She was walking barefoot across a field of broken glass, deaf but for the roaring of the tank. A stretcher burst from the restaurant door, around it men and women and a swaying plasma bag. The woman beside her ran to it, the damaged mass that once constituted a person but was now a bundle of flesh wrapped in a white tablecloth gone dark, and Susan was left alone to stumble back through the bar where she had drunk her vodka and met Liam, out onto the street not through the door, but through the great empty pane of the front window and out of the tank.

Out of the tank without Jill.

Without Jill.

Without—

She started walking.

On the street were the same fire trucks and ambulances she'd seen on TV. Black unmarked SUVs. Helicopters circled and a long plume of water leapt from an unseen truck to hit a window of pearling smoke. So much chaos and yet she walked right through it.

Someone calling to her and then not.

Someone approaching her and then not.

Reporters. Cameras. She was oblivious.

Don't die. But of course—

Her feet bled. Her daughter was gone. Someone put a foil blanket over her shoulders but that changed nothing. Someone put a bottle of water in her hand, but that did not undo the death of her child.

Susan staggered past the sawhorses and through the parting crowd. The smell of smoke in her hair. The stink of water too long corralled in pipes. Her bloody footprints someone would have to Clorox away. None of it mattered. They parted for her. They would no more touch her than she would stop. And she didn't, because she had to get home. She had fixed her mind on one single thing: her dinner party. She had to get home to check on the caterers. It occurred to her that just as Susan had walked out of the tank might her daughter have done the same?

Jill would be somewhere ahead, waiting on her.

She would be at dinner if only there was a dinner to be at.

She walked up Medena, deaf to the sirens and helicopters behind her.

Had they set the tables? She hadn't had time yet to go over the seating arrangements! She hadn't had time to do anything! She tried to walk faster and perhaps she did.

She turned off Medena and started up the winding hill road.

She had to tell Erskine their daughter was coming home.

SARA SAT ON the tiled floor, her back against the wall, her left arm cradled. Across from her sat Hugh Eckhart. He'd been in the same position since they arrived, unmoving, not even raising his head when he and Sara were locked inside. They were in a service bathroom somewhere on the upper floors of the hotel, shoved down onto the cold tiles, and, it seemed to her, forgotten.

All the while, Hugh never moved. He was no longer crying. He simply sat with his eyes grim and mouth tight. He appeared to have no desire to leave this place, as unmoving as Sara had been that night in Kiev when he had led her back to his flat.

When the door opened and Chris Berger fell into the room, half-conscious and face down in a shallow pool of his own blood, she tried to push Hugh toward Berger's tumbled shape, tried to get him to do something, anything. But Hugh only rubbed the center his face against one shoulder as if petting himself.

"You have to help me," she said.

But Hugh looked at her as if they'd never met.

"Help me," Sara said. "He'll come back for us. He isn't finished with us."

Hugh was silent.

"He'll come back. I know he will." She was talking, perhaps, about the American, about Rachel Venclova, about the Russians. Perhaps about God. *It was God who made me care*, she had told him.

But Hugh gave no response. She stared at him and eventually gave up. Berger was beginning to stir. He was disfigured and swollen, but appeared to be waking.

"Help me up," he said.

She eased him into a sitting position, but the effort seemed to exhaust him. His eyes were shut again, the lids the lightest shade of lavender, as if delicately painted. Almost lovely. It was his breath that scared her. His breath sounded wet, coming heavier now, sputtering like air trapped in a hose, and hearing it Sara knew he was bleeding into his lungs.

Berger began to cough.

"They've wired the building." He spat a long gout of blood that silvered from his lips. "Help me up."

"Sit still."

"RDX and a radio trigger. Help me."

"Sit still. You're hurt."

He looked at Hugh.

"Can he help us?"

"Hugh," she said.

But Hugh gave no sign.

Hugh wasn't listening.

Then it occurred to Sara that he was praying.

It occurred to her it had been years since she had seen someone pray.

"They wired the building," Berger said again.

"What's does that mean?"

"It means they're going to blow it up." Berger turned to her. "When he comes back get out and take the fire stairs to the kitchen." He moved beside the main door and flexed his hands.

"What about you?" Sara asked.

"I have to find her."

"Go with us."

"When he comes back stay on the floor. Don't move."

"You go with us."

Berger motioned at the brushstrokes of blood on the tiles.

"Sit in front of that mess."

"But if they've wired the building."

"When he comes back act scared."

"I am scared."

He nodded slowly. Finally, he looked at her.

"I guess you loved him," he said.

"What?"

"I was with him the day it happened."

"I—I don't want to hear this."

"We were in the forest."

Sara felt her head shaking wildly.

"What good is hearing this?"

"He was a good man."

"Please, just." She waited but had no way to explain. Except *no*, except *don't*.

"I just thought you should know." Berger fixed what was left of his eyes on the door. "It won't be long," he promised.

It wasn't. Shortly they heard a key in the lock and when the door swung open Sara barely had time to look up before Berger had the man down on the floor. One hand wrenched shut his mouth while the other pried the pistol from his hand. A cardboard tube skittered across the floor while his arms flailed as if he were trying to swim, a hopeless motion, like a man drowning in a bathtub.

Berger had one knee in his back, one arm looped around his neck, and the dying man looked once at Sara, his eyes bulging, clear, brown eyes going a murky white as they slowly began to distend. Then his leg—one leg gave a hapless little kick and she turned her head until the writhing stopped.

When she looked back, Berger was on his knees, checking the magazine in the pistol he now held. Ray Shields's arms and legs had fashioned a blurry angel and she wished in that moment very badly for an Oxy, a Klonopin, for Dilaudid, for anything that might intervene in the world, since it was clear that God would not.

Berger pointed at Hugh.

"Take him and get out of here," he told Sara, and before she could speak, slipped out the door.

Sara bent to Hugh.

"We're getting out of here. Come on. Get up."
They stepped into the dark corridor.
A favor, she thought.
That was what they all called it.

SUSAN CLIMBED THE hill, hurrying past the shops and homes and hotels that were wholly undisturbed, not a trace of disorder beyond the smell of distant smoke and the helicopters hovering overhead. The occasional siren that was like a memory barely touched.

Jill in that awful tank.

Jill in the cold ground behind the First Congregational.

She would have to tell Erskine. Her daughter was waiting for her—that was what she knew. Nothing else, as if she needed anything else. She passed the high windows, the arches and cupolas and balconies with their iron filigree. She had to get home. She had to—

And then she felt it dawn behind her, heat and light and the way it shuddered up through her feet and legs.

Don't die, she thought.

But of course—

THEY STAGGERED DOWN the hall, Hugh and Sara. There was the sound of gunshots, the sound of the fire alarm, the smell of burning wallpaper. Plaster dust floating in the air. Ahead was the faint red glow of an exit sign. But the stairwell was locked and they circled back down the hall and through another door just as a flare of light opened a fissure in the darkness. The power was back on, all white brilliance, and in its light Hugh saw two bodies in the center of what had been a banquet hall of scattered tables and chairs, an older man and woman in their Sunday best, seated and dressed for the death that had found them. Past them was a buffet. A carving station for roast beef. Vegetables steaming the underside of the glass sneeze-guard. Out the shattered windows, a helicopter hovered, banks of oily smoke pushed by the rotorwash in a black smear.

There was a service door on the far end and they made for it.

Hugh grabbed Sara's hand and pulled but she hung back.

"Listen," she said, and then the table beside her head exploded in a rain of splinters.

Hugh looked to see a man across the room, shirtless with a bandanna around his head and a shotgun in his arms.

"Jesus," Hugh said. "Get down."

Rick Miles worked the pump-action and Hugh and Sara went flat on the carpet as another table shattered. They ran then, half crouching, half falling forward, but making it through the banquet hall to the swinging service door.

Miles watched them go, crossing the room at an angle, jogging now, no longer smiling for it was no longer a game. It was thought become action. It was the end of everything easy in life.

Hugh and Sara hit the corridor, sprinting.

They were past the windows and moving away from the thickening smoke but Miles was still behind them. They crashed into another room. A wooden floor, mirrored walls. A long fitness room of yoga mats and silver balls. A sign read: WORK OUT YOUR SALVATION WITH DILIGENCE, and in front of it they stopped, dead as stones. In the smoke gathered in the room sat one of the Russians, watching them.

Then the smoke rolled by and they saw the man had no eyes, no nose, no mouth, only what was left of his turtle mask, green rubber spread around what was left of his face.

Behind him stood Hugh's Angel, eight feet tall and radiant, a thing composed wholly of light. It appeared exactly as it had that day in Baghdad, exactly as it had that day in New York with David Lazar. Sara pulled at him but he didn't move.

"Hugh."

The dead man was missing the tip of his trigger finger.

"Come on," Sara was screaming, pulling at him.

But it was the Angel who was pointing, and following the line of his hand Hugh saw it. He lifted the pistol that lay tucked beneath the man and held it as if it were something new to this world.

"Leave it," Sara said.

She took it from Hugh and Hugh let her. He said nothing. He thought the Angel might speak. If this was his surrender, he wanted at least a word. He'd waited so long.

But it only stood there, pointing down at the faceless man.

A small pink dumbbell had rolled across the room to rest by his thigh.

Sara pulled at Hugh.

"Come on," she said. "Hugh?"

He could hear Miles tearing down the hall.

The Angel stared at him.

The dumbbell read 2 kg.

"Hugh?" Sara said.

She pulled free of him and Hugh heard her leaving, the far door opening. When it did, the smoke shifted again and his eyes welled with the smell of burning plastic. He felt Miles behind him and turned to see him saunter into view, his shotgun tipped across one shoulder like an ax.

The sachet on his bare chest. The bandana a halo of stars.

Miles flipped the shotgun to port arms. In the mirrored room there was a thousand of him, receding into boxes, each holding the next.

"Too fucking easy, Hugh." Miles chambered another shell. "Where'd your woman go?"

"I don't know."

"You don't know?"

Hugh nodded, and realized he had been waiting for the sound of the door swinging shut, the sound of her leaving, and was waiting still.

Miles leveled the shotgun.

"Been a long time coming, partner."

"It is not upon you alone the dark patches fall."

Miles cocked his head. "Last words?"

"The dark threw its patches down upon me also."

"Eloquent," Miles said, and pulled the trigger.

Hugh had turned to run and felt something hit him in the back, felt the air go out of him, felt an intense heat spread outward through his body. He spun into the lap of the faceless Russian, and looked up at Miles through tunneling vision. Behind him, stood Hugh's Angel. Funny, he thought, to have run so far and so long only to arrive where he had begun. Then the Angel was gone, and Hugh had just enough clarity to lock what was left of his being on the man who stood working the gun's pump. The faceless Russian seemed to be cradling him.

"Crazy," Miles said, "this world we're living in."

He raised the shotgun.

Then his head flew apart.

Rick Miles's body took two more steps and keeled sideways, dropping the shotgun and falling in segments, knees, hips, chest and shoulders. His head was against the mirrors and in the smoke and on the floor. His head was in orbit. His head was everywhere, a billion tiny shards of brain and bone repopulating space. It took forever for the report to reach Hugh and when it did it was all he heard, this dull ringing that seemed to align everything that had otherwise veered.

Sara stepped from the door and dropped the pistol.

She bent to Hugh, her image gauzy and warped.

"Hugh?" He felt her hands framing his face. "Hugh?"

He thought there might have been a word, some utterance made in that moment of brightest light, some bit of wisdom by which he might navigate. But looking around he knew he was alone, his Angel had departed. But that didn't matter. All that mattered was that Sara was gathering him, pulling him against her body.

He felt something, though he couldn't say exactly what. It was only when he saw their single reflection in the mirror that he realized she was carrying him.

THE SKIN HAD closed over Berger's right eye, but he could see enough to stumble into the red-glow of the hallway. The fire alarms were sounding again but the sprinklers had stopped, the wallpaper splashed and speckled and just beginning to curl. Whatever was happening was taking place on the lower floors. Up here, the hotel appeared empty.

He moved down the winding halls, wiped his swollen face and turned to spot someone headed up a spiral staircase. Rattling iron. Safety tape. He climbed the stairs to find the figure gone, started down another corridor, systematically kicking open doors, the pistol before him like a lamp unto his feet and a light unto his heart. He advanced and listened, advanced and listened. His face hurt and he was having trouble breathing, but he kept moving.

He was outside a storage closet when the bullet struck the wall just above his head. He fired two blind shots into the darkness.

Eyes full of smoke.

Ears full of noise.

He knew someone had screamed but what he heard was more like the planet turning. A dull roar that hung around his busted face like a smell. He moved forward and spotted her.

Rachel leveled her pistol and fired.

Berger dropped and shot twice.

He moved forward until he reached the end of the hall and scrambled up another iron staircase, through a glass penthouse. There was a blood-trail now—he had hit her.

He followed it to a service ladder and at the top forced open the trapdoor that led to the roof. The cool air struck him and then the lights and then the noise. Helicopters jerked overhead, tails tipped up into the air as if on strings. The lower floors were burning and he watched a fan of water arch into a window. Down in the street sat emergency vehicles, police in riot gear, crowds behind distant sawhorses.

Berger moved around silver air conditioning units the size of refrigerators. Ventilation fans spinning lazily, gravel crinkling under his shoes. His hands shook—his fingers long, brittle needles—but he managed to keep the pistol in front of him.

He lost the trail, but found it again near a raised skylight.

A trickle of glossy blood led to his right and Berger took a step back to see Rachel Venclova on the roof's edge. She was no longer holding the pistol. What she held was the remote control, its silver antenna extended skyward. She lurched to her left, and Berger could see she was gut-shot, her shirt matted, her eyes wild. Hair a tangle that swirled around the still center of her face. But somehow she managed to hold the device with two hands. Somehow she managed to keep her eyes on him.

Berger took another step and she screamed for him to stop.

He paused, advanced again, and she took another step back, screamed, stepped back—a bloody minuet that took her closer to the roof's edge.

"Stop," Rachel kept screaming. "Stop, goddamn you."

Her voice was a screech and Berger saw that she was at the edge.

He inched forward and slowly lowered the gun to the ground. He knew it was true. You have to destroy something to release what it contains.

"Stop, you motherfucker," she yelled. "You won't do this to me again."

Berger was less than six feet from her now and could see the red power light on the black remote. His hands were quaking, out by his sides, palms raised, but not so much trembling as alive, two slain doves, resurrected for flight. Something was lifting them. Something had him by the wrists. He couldn't see it, but also—for just a moment—he could.

"You won't," she hissed. "Never. You will never—"

"Rachel." He kept his voice as level as possible. "Please."

"You will never."

"Come with me."

"You will never shit on my bed, do you understand me?"

He could see her body rocking unsteadily, vibrating.

"Please," he said. "Come with me."

He took a small step and she yelped as if he had stepped on her.

"Rachel," he said, and saw himself balanced perfectly in her eyes. She's brave, he thought, My God, she's brave. He felt a wave of admiration.

"Rachel," he said, as gently as possible.

He put out one hand, and a smile spread from her lips as she pushed both the controllers on the remote forward. It took Berger a half second to understand what she had done, and when he did, he felt an abiding regret. It was a terrible mistake. But it wasn't.

He felt the building shake. He felt how narrow he had become. He felt a sad wonder that seemed to bunch low and dense in his chest before spreading outward toward God and all the universe, toward everything that was lifting him up.

Exactly as he had always known it would.

CROSSINGS

August 2019

IT WAS YEARS later when he began to hear rumors about the woman.

Hugh was living in Kiev by then, working at a theater on Andreevsky Descent under an assumed name. His back had healed into a constellation of scars, waxy puckers down his arms and wrists concealed beneath his jacket. He had a new haircut and a beard, a Canadian passport purchased online. He avoided the tourist sites. He was careful. He was also hopeful. He had met a man, a playwright, and they shared a flat not far from the market where they shopped for quartered chickens and pomegranates from Azerbaijan. Lingonberries and loaves of dark bread.

It was a simple life.

A bowl of fruit in the common room.

A nightingale in the lemon trees.

He walked to work. He missed his sons, but had come to realize they were not him. The lump in his right testicle was gone. His hair had returned. There had been lesions, but like the knot, the lesions were gone. Hugh, it seemed, had been miraculously cured. Proof, he thought, not of God's love but of God's indifference. So many dying, and Hugh left to live. Hugh left to not die. It was like teaching your children math and realizing, for the first time, what you are saying. The figures, the way they corresponded to things. It was so simple it became holy, and for that he was grateful.

Meanwhile, the world went on without him.

Leviathan was pumping gas out of Slovakia.

The billionaire had been elected president, and though besieged by investigations, had announced his intention to seek a second term.

But Hugh didn't think about any of this. A war had frozen along the border with Russia. A Malaysian airliner had been blasted across a field. People were dead all along the eastern front. But he didn't think about that either. He did think about the woman.

He saw it first in the *Guardian* and later a brief online clip. There was a woman in Lesvos, little was known about her except that she had appeared almost three years ago and paid passage on one of the ferries smuggling migrants onto the island. Five hundred euros not to enter Greece but to leave it. To travel to Libya or Syria or Mali or whatever hell people were fleeing. Assad or Daesh. Droughts and failing crops. A week later, she reappeared on the island, left again. They interviewed one of the smugglers. The woman was traveling back and forth, always silent, always seated on the metal deck among the life vests and bottled water. He didn't know why. Though he suspected that so long as people were crossing, she would cross with him.

She no longer paid and the smuggler no longer cared.

She was, he said, much like a piece of his craft. When he considered her, she calmed him. Though the truth was, she seldom entered his thoughts.

The image was blurred and unsteady and shot from a great distance, but the video clip clearly showed the woman helping a child down the steel ladder onto the rocky beach. It was a gray fishing boat meant for a crew of six or seven but appeared to hold better than a hundred so that it lurched beneath an impossibly blue sky. But when they disembarked the deck seemed to rise up, to sit high in the water, if only for a moment. Just the three smugglers and the woman, whoever she was, turning back to make yet another crossing.

Mark Powell has been called the "best Appalachian novelist of his generation" by Ron Rash, and a writer "on the verge of greatness" by Pat Conroy. The author of six novels, Powell has received fellowships from the National Endowment for the Arts, the Breadloaf and Sewanee Writers' Conferences, and in 2014 was a Fulbright Fellow to Slovakia. In 2009 he received the Chaffin Award for contributions to Appalachian literature. He holds degrees from Yale Divinity School, the University of South Carolina, and the Citadel. He lives in the mountains of North Carolina where he teaches at Appalachian State University.